T0063391

WHAT A PARADISE!

WHAT A PARADISE!

SMITA KALE

PARTRIDGE
A Penguin Random House Company

Copyright © 2014 by Smita Kale.
Cover design Smita Kale
Cover art Devika Kumaran

ISBN: Hardcover   978-1-4828-3679-0
             Softcover   978-1-4828-3678-3
             eBook   978-1-4828-3677-6

All rights reserved. No part of this book may be used or reproduced by any means, graphic, electronic, or mechanical, including photocopying, recording, taping or by any information storage retrieval system without the written permission of the publisher except in the case of brief quotations embodied in critical articles and reviews.

Because of the dynamic nature of the Internet, any web addresses or links contained in this book may have changed since publication and may no longer be valid. The views expressed in this work are solely those of the author and do not necessarily reflect the views of the publisher, and the publisher hereby disclaims any responsibility for them.

To order additional copies of this book, contact
Partridge India
000 800 10062 62
orders.india@partridgepublishing.com

www.partridgepublishing.com/india

PROLOGUE

They sat somberly in the high ceilinged antechamber of the historic Town Hall gazing nervously at the imposing rostrum and elaborate, velvet covered chairs on the wooden dais. The hall was full to capacity with eager immigrant families, an aura of triumphant pride lighting up their faces.

Unconsciously, she rubbed her hands nervously looking uncertainly about her at the motley crowd. Some were dressed in their Sunday best, others in traditional ethnic attire reminiscent of a costume parade. Strains of music floated up from the atrium of the Great Hall to the rafters of its massive cathedral ceilings.

The strident voice of the man at the podium echoed off the walls, "This country does not expect you to forget your origins. We invite you to enrich the tapestry of this rainbow land with your own special colours…"

She shifted in her seat doubtfully. Her ancestors had, in all probability, labored to evict the forefathers of these people out of their homeland. Could she honestly swear allegiance to an alien land?

The voice on the stage droned on, "Responsibilities and rights; rights to political freedom; rights to education…"

Every person in the audience listened with rapt attention, the air heavy with a thrill of anticipation. She glanced at the familiar profile of the man next to her intensely following the solemn proceedings on stage. On the other side sat a serious faced little boy absorbed in the man's speech. The voice boomed out,

"A nation whose rights and liberties…"

It was white noise to her.

Everyone soaked in his words, "make it a better place in which to work, live and play…"

She leaned back in her seat and scanned the doors. They were wide open - unguarded.

"Uphold its democratic values…"

The doors were no more than two, maybe three steps away. They could be out of here in a flash.

"Please stand for the pledge."

With a shuffling of feet and a screech of chairs the congregation rose to its feet.

She stood up, her mouth gravelly and parched as she tried to calm the knot in her chest. She swallowed to ease the dry pain in her throat. It was now or never. With trembling fingers she reached out for her son's hand. He took it in his soft fingers and squeezed it turning a chubby smiling face to her, his eyes aglow with excitement.

ONE

Trolley wielding passengers crisscrossed paths, their eyes scanning display boards, ears tuned in to departure information echoing off the airport's lofty walls. They resembled worker bees buzzing about in a largish hive. In a quiet nook surrounded by luminescent screens Arti typed amateurishly on the airport computer, fingers hovering uncertainly as she deliberating each word.

My Dear Diya,

Thanks for making it such a memorable holiday for me. I promised I would call as soon as I was checked in but couldn't locate a pay phone, so here I am using the airport's free 15 minutes on the Net. The taxi ride and my check in were eventless. I am at the gates already. Your gifts, the novels, the snacks and Sudoku puzzles should keep me occupied.

I may as well keep typing till my remaining nine minutes are over! The airport is buzzing around me as the mind keeps flashing back to all the exciting moments we shared in spite of your packed schedule.

I just saw a lady travelling with three kids! They're pulling her in different directions all at once and yet, I never in my life saw such a calm mother. She is either immune or petrified. They are probably on our flight. A long flight, a miscellaneous crowd. I see pensioners on vacation to warmer climes, a self conscious cosmetic advertisement surreptitiously peeping into a small mirror every now and then, young chaps, possibly students striking up a conversation with a sweet young thing. It really takes all kinds!

Arti jerked her head up and looked around. It was like a brief flash and then it was gone. She gazed around at a mob of strangers. Probably, nothing. She returned to her typing.

For a minute there I felt as if someone familiar came close. How strange! This girl at the next computer just smiled at me. An all black outfit and Gothic make up. Black lipstick, lots of kohl and a profusion of piercings... I don't quite get it. Either the jeans are too low slung or the top too short. They don't appear to meet anywhere. Hmm. you can rest assured I shan't be bored and neither will I open any of the books till I'm on the plane!

Loved my holiday and look forward to seeing you again whenever possible. So terribly proud of you!

Hugs,

Mummy

Arti smiled sweetly as she slid out from the console and moved briskly to a seat in the far corner. She looked down at the two books in her lap. Her daughter had watched with a smile as she carefully covered them in gift wrap.

"Why do you do that?"

"Cover books? To keep them clean." Arti had replied as she folded the corners neatly into points and secured them with tape.

"Why with gift wrap? I remember it ever since I was so high!"

Arti held up her handiwork with approval and turned to the next book. She examined the array of gift wrap spread out on the table and picked one. Speaking through clenched lips as she held bits of cello tape in her mouth she replied, "Because it looks pretty. Newspaper is never strong enough and it stains your hands and brown paper is plain boring."

Her daughter had laughed as her mother hummed happily covering her new acquisitions in gaily printed paper.

Arti lifted the books in her lap and slid them into her carryon bag. It was to be a long flight. She would read later. She gazed out at the sun soaked runway as planes took off and landed, their streamlined sleek bodies glistening in the bright sun. She glanced about her at the spacious waiting hall thronging with holiday crowds being carried up and down energetic escalators soaring up to the high ceilings past gigantic murals on the lofty walls. Arti found she was seated at a particularly suitable spot to surreptitiously observe the assortment of humankind hurrying about. Almost everyone appeared to be in a rush. She was, as always, in very good time.

Finally their flight was called. Arti rose, brushed muffin crumbs off her clothes and tamely joined the queue of straight-faced passengers. They always overbook during the holidays and what with the wicked and abruptly active volcano it was just another excuse for more than the usual hysterics. It had been tricky coordinating their connections and she thought herself lucky that the hurriedly planned visit with her daughter had been smooth sailing. Finally the queue came alive as the big gaping hole began swallowing up passenger after passenger.

Arti hauled her plain black laptop trolley circumventing it hastily down the crowded aircraft aisle. An abrupt tug broke her momentum. She swung around and saw an outlandish hot pink cabin bag entangled with hers. The owner bent over with an enthusiastic shriek of apology to free the bags. Most passengers stopped and stared at the startling interruption in their otherwise lackluster passage. Arti saw a mass of multi hued hair atop a bright orange sweater struggling over the seemingly inextricable bags. She hesitated, not sure of what to do, but quite certain the woman was making things worse. Arti lifted her bag with a determined tug and unexpectedly released it. She promptly turned to proceed towards her seat relieved to escape the little sideshow she had become an unintentional part of.

"Arti?" She wasn't sure she had heard correctly. A much too familiar tap on her shoulder halted her for the second time.

Awkwardly glancing back she looked into the glowing face of the owner of the errant kitschy bag.

"Is there a problem?"

"It's Arti isn't it? I'm Jane…do you remember me? From college?"

She gazed uncertainly into the vibrant, cheery face and shook her head uncertainly, "I'm sorry..?"

The line behind them was becoming a throng. Most uncomfortable, Arti felt impelled to move on. Pointing towards the rear of the plane, she murmured incomprehensibly and turned to move on purposefully.

"Yeah! Let's get a move on!" the shrill voice added encouragingly.

For the second time in five minute Arti felt waves of relief as she slouched into her corner seat and disappeared behind the airline's duty free magazine. She seemed to have shaken off her mystery 'friend'. She ran college friends' names through her head pretty certain there had never been a Jane. She frowned, narrowing her eyes. Though the face didn't look altogether unfamiliar! She pulled out a magazine from the pocket and leafed through it glancing at overpriced doodads while other passengers filed past.

"Hi! Here I am! I'll just stay and chat till this passenger shows up!" Jane gestured at the vacant seat beside Arti's. Peering warily from behind the magazine, Arti searched for the right words, baffled at such familiarity from a stranger.

"I don't believe you still can't place me - Janvi from college!"

Arti stared, her eyes lighting up. Of course she remembered Janvi! She took her in from top to toe. "Gosh Janvi, is it really you? How long has it been?"

"Ages, but who's counting? There's so much to live for in the here and now!"

"How are you? You look amazingly fit...I mean..." Arti broke off embarrassed.

"Whole you mean whole and in one piece. Sure, I get it. You can't help it. You're remembering that streak of bad luck back then with all those crashes and bash ups."

"That's hugely understating it!"

Jane neatly hauled her swanky florescent bag into the overhead compartment and slipped out of her jacket.

"Yeah it was a taxing phase. Major health scares!" She looked through heavily made up eyes at Arti as she stuffed the overhead space and slid into the adjacent vacant seat.

"We had very cruelly stuck you with weird nick names like 'Typhoid Mary' and 'Calamity Jane'!"

"I know and I hated the names which were not just cruel but grossly incorrect! Neither describes what happened to me. I'll tell you more about my supposed misfortune in a moment." Jane was fussing with the airline blanket, the seat belts and her shoes all at once.

"Don't you want to find your seat now?" Arti eyed her over the large designer handbag Jane had deposited in her lap before shinnying up to set right the valise in the overhead compartment.

"All in good time!" Jane beamed, carefully lifting her bag off Arti's lap. She turned excited eyes made up in shiny turquoise toward Arti and exclaimed, "It's so good to see you! Such coincidences only belong in story books or movies!" She patted Arti's hand warmly, carrying on like an animated sixteen-year old. "So you're surprised to see me looking alive and well!"

Arti nodded smiling awkwardly, "I am sorry it came out like that. I remember it so well! That freaky streak! You were majorly accident prone as if there was some crazy, ominous jinx on you." Arti looked at her, "Remember?"

"Yes of course I remember! Would anyone forget nearly dying not once but twice?"

"Did you know that most of our parents never believed us? They thought we had been making it all up." Arti looked at her friend, "You must be some kind of medical marvel! I can't forget how everyone was talking about you those days." Something came to her mind unexpectedly, "They even had a feature on you in the Times!"

"Yup that was me." Jane cheerfully replied, "I went in to hospital with typhoid and contacted malaria during the convalescence. There were mosquitoes in the water coolers. The entire ward got Malaria and I think some of the nurses too." She moved her index fingers around as if indicating the surrounds. Some form of hospital cross infection they called it."

Arti gazed unblinking at her new found companion, awestruck at the uncanny regularity with which calamity had struck her friend, and even more by the nonchalance in her telling of it.

Jane sprang up abruptly, "Just a minute." She wove her way deftly through the crowd. Arti watched as the wild haired woman was swallowed by a host of incoming travelers. Clueless on what might have possessed her, Arti tore open the plastic and draped the blanket shawl-like about her shoulders. Jane had ambushed a stewardess and was delivering an exhaustive explanation.

The stewardess turned in the direction that Jane helpfully pointed to. Her wandering eyes came and rested on Arti who blushed prettily and lowered her eyes feeling unreasonably guilty. The woman smiled widely and turned to Jane who let off another animated torrent. The stewardess's calm reply appeared to delight Jane. Arti watched a content and beaming Jane beginning to sashay her way back.

A couple with three young children in a bit of a fuss plodded along, scrutinizing seat numbers and trying to calm a little bald baby sporting a pink lacy hair band.

"Why do they do that? It's obvious she's a girl and a very pretty one too" thought Arti to herself.

The eldest boy slumped into the seat next to hers and grinned up at his dad who, peering at the sheaf of boarding cards in his hand, shook his head and motioned to the little fellow to move on.

Jane, waiting behind them, slid back into the seat. "We can swap seats with this passenger." She announced breathlessly, eyes shining with a sense of triumph as shapely fingers pointed downwards. "Hope he is an accommodating sort." she added moodily.

Arti too hoped so. It is rare to be blessed with good company while flying and she usually had to resign herself to watching in flight entertainment or reading. She gazed at her new found acquaintance from the distant past, her eyes taking Jane in. "It seems to have all worked out for you ultimately. It's strange how one's memory retains just the horrid bits!"

"Not that there was much else. It was one disaster after another." Jane spoke in a blasé, detached sort of manner about all her past miseries. She began mostly mid sentence. "Then, back at college, I optimistically signed up with the hiking society and guess what, a rockslide ended that ambition! Strangely, I was the only one that got buried under it." Her hands formed an imaginary pile. She punctuated every statement with a characteristic pointing of her index finger as if presenting something on a spreadsheet.

"People thought I'd lagged behind and called me a straggler. Weakness perhaps, with all those illnesses, they thought, but in reality, I had stopped to tie a shoelace when unexpectedly I was drowned in all that rock and mud! Luckily the back didn't break but I had a few bumps on my head and lots of bruises and scratches." She blinked at Arti affably.

Arti couldn't help giving a small laugh, "It's as if you're describing someone else's mishap. It must have been awfully painful!"

"C'est la vie!"

Arti recalled that familiar sight on campus hobbling about on crutches usually scrounging for notes and reference books. Nobody had had the heart to say no. Some went out of their way to help, others just looked at her pityingly but nobody brushed her away with the archetypical indifference of college kids.

The following year, just as things started looking up, she got hit by a bus. News strayed in that Jane had a few broken ribs and a fractured femur. Everybody commiserated with the weirdo. Someone brought a gigantic card and passed it around the canteen for signatures and messages. Arti remembered signing it. Professors at college began to doubt she'd ever graduate and it became the least well kept secret that the Sanskrit professor wanted to take a peek into Janvi's horoscope. But in time that chaotic campus, abounding in frenetic action, swiftly forgot Jane and her tragic and repetitive misfortune.

Until one day, the plucky Jane was back on campus yet again; this time assisted by her father's driver who carried her stuff to class.

Back in the land of the living, Janvi had a knack for socializing without commitment, so everyone knew of her but no one really knew her.

"I had more medical leave than attendance." Jane laughed. "There was that movie, One Flew over The Cuckoo's Nest and I just relate to that sentence by McMurphy "I'm a goddamn marvel of modern science." Jane grinned at her.

Arti looked at her, "You look so different! I wouldn't have recognised you at all!"

"You didn't! I had to shake it out of you!"

"How did you recognise me? It's been ages!"

Jane laughed. "You're kidding? Never before was the phrase "you haven't changed a bit!" been truer. The same hairstyle, the same walk, I don't think you have even changed the frame on your glasses! It was like walking into class thirty years back! I recognised you from behind."

More passengers trouped in. Some faces bore that blank zombie-like look that usually graces a face doomed to protracted hours of air borne captivity, others scanned the vestibule as if anticipating some theatrical performance and the rest just checked out the attractive stewardesses melted into their snug cheongsams.

Jane nudged her and spoke from the corner of her mouth, "Which one is he?"

Arti glanced up and immediately looked down. It was as if all eyes were on her. "How do you know it's not a "she"?"

Passengers filed past and the cabin assumed that urgent busyness when stewardesses glide through the aisles hurrying people along, expertly clicking shut overheads lockers.

Jane abruptly sprang up and addressed a man advancing down the aisle, "Hi! 44 B?" She smiled at him as if to say 'We've been waiting for you!"

The startled fellow stammered, "No 51C."

"Okay that's further down I guess" Jane swept him down the alleyway flinging her arm back. She knocked the glasses and earphones off of a fellow passenger and immediately followed up with a profuse and unnecessarily long apology.

"He looked like he may be our guy."

Arti smiled at her use of 'our', "How can you tell?"

Stewardesses bustled about busily and the aircraft gave a jerky joggle.

Jane raised herself and peered out, "They're shutting the doors, where's He? She craned her neck to peer across the cabin, "The plane's full and it's just my seat that is empty. I'll ask the stewardess."

"Let it go Jane. People miss flights all the time."

"Now where's she disappeared?" Jane looked around scanning the faces of the stewardesses, "She looks like Rose from The Joy Luck Club. Rosalind Chao I think her name is."

Arti burst into laughter, "you still do that!" She recalled how Jane used to describe people by comparing them to some well known character. "You haven't changed a bit!"

"Except," Jane raised her hand warningly, "except I have become luckier!" She looked triumphantly at Arti, "like the guy in Night Shyamalan's movie, I too am unbreakable now!"

"You've had your share, paid your dues so to speak!"

"I wonder what he would be if he were knighted? Sir Knight Shyamalan?"

"Stop it." Arti giggled like a girl.

The aircraft gave a lurch and reversed. Jane leaned across Arti and gazed out of the porthole as if the missing passenger might be chasing the aircraft on the tarmac.

"What happened to him? Maybe his kid fell sick or he got hit by a bus."

"Not as common as you think. Well I guess you can sit here now! What a relief. I just hate travelling alone."

"Why? Don't you make new friends?"

"Never. I don't usually talk to strangers."

Smiling, Jane took her friend in, "Still the same timid Arti!"

Arti glanced at her companion's profile. She had the slightest hint of an insignificant twitch in one eye and her mouth drooped to one side ever so faintly. Arti decided that only one who knew Jane's history could detect such imperceptible defects. She asked her with a laugh, "And you? You make one new friend each flight?"

"I never pass up the chance to create a friendship. Don't keep interrupting me. We have years and years to catch up on and this is what, a fourteen hour flight? It'll pass in no time. So, as I was saying…" Arti settled back comfortably enveloped in the rare warmth of friendship. She hugged herself in contentment barely listening to Jane rattle on.

"And then, one day, I went in to use the loo near the common room and left my bag on the basin counter. I must have been gone two minutes and what do you know, my wallet got picked!" She looked at Arti expectantly.

Arti wasn't sure how that was half as important as near death by burial in a rock slide or the prospect of virtually losing both legs under a bus. She looked at Jane uncertainly.

"So I guess what I was trying to tell you is that the day my wallet got pinched was the day my life started to change."

"How well you remember it all!"

Jane's face was aglow, "Don't you remember? I went with you guys to the cafeteria, reached in to my bag to pay for my samosas and boom, my wallet's not there! Vanished! All my stuff was in it. Library cards, student ID bus pass, pictures of my parents, my nephew, my dog, some receipts, about a hundred Rupees, all gone."

Arti was troubled at how she was itemizing. There's a limit to one's memory. She could barely recall her last meal.

"I had to go report my stolen library cards. You guys went along with me to the British Council Library."

"Gosh I think I do remember!"

"It was sweet of you guys to take me though I never understood why the four of you had to come along."

"Are you kidding? We did everything together and anyway you were distressed. I think we were probably anxious to see that you don't fall off a bus, collide with a cow…"

"Even when the doctors had started writing my obituaries, I remained positive." She grinned and then became grave. "Maybe it was all that optimism that pulled me through! You know when I see all the emphasis on positive thinking these days I guess that might have been it. Frankly, never once did I fear that I would die or remain handicapped!"

"And where did that strength come from? Weren't you put off by the pain and discomfort of being in and out of the OT?"

Jane looked solemnly ahead at the map on the screen charting their flight path but not really looking at anything, "You know there used to be this girl in our batch who was battling cancer? In fact she passed away before we finished college. I used to look at my disabilities and gave thanks that they were temporary."

They both fell silent. It was years since Arti remembered that girl. "Dear lord! God Bless her!"

Jane pondered, "If she were reborn as soon as she went, she would be nearly thirty today! She might know us but we wouldn't know her. She could be anywhere, even on this plane!"

She used all her fingers to point at the surrounds. "She could be our missing guy! Spirits have no gender."

Arti was lost in the recollection of their lost classmate. She was so beautiful! She felt sadness coupled with curious guilt.

Jane unraveled her blanket and fussily bunched up her hair in a scrunchie. Arti broke the silence. "You've obviously come a long way! Have you been in the U.S. long? Did you come as a student?"

"Yes, decades back. Struggled in unimaginable ways but survived the disenchantment of immigration!"

"Yes, I hear that sometimes you get overwhelmed by the sheer abundance!"

Jane shook her head. Her eyes darted about unsurely, "Abundance my eye! I had to work for every morsel."

Arti giggled uneasily at the exaggerated declaration and Jane looked deeply at her. "You'd better believe it! It was a crazed chapter of my life. Looking back I can't even imagine how I lived through such an insane routine for three long years! But at least I didn't have to live with uncertainty about part time work."

Arti tried to get her friend to lighten up. "Remember Dr. Varma used to say "hard work never killed anybody!" in her squeaky voice?"

Jane smiled, "Yeah she would have freaked if she knew how I lived during my first foray into the outside world. After weeks of chasing the few odd-jobs advertised on the college notice boards, I was introduced to the owners of this little café by a senior of ours. They were an elderly couple that she had worked for, the Blums." Jane fixed large eyes at Arti, "It was fate that we met at all. I remember that day, I had just scanned the notice boards for part time work and turned away disappointed when I bumped into her. I barely knew her but she was one of the girls I had always smiled at in the cafeteria.

She was in a huge hurry, "Do you need a job? This one's not a temp position. Fixed timings, fixed pay, food and lodge thrown in. Interested? She threw all these questions at me in a rush."

"Sure," I said, "but what sort of job?"

"I'll fill you in" she said shoving me on to the bus. She explained the deal. She was moving out and had to get them a replacement pronto. I realized later that her need had probably been greater than mine but it certainly opened a door for me. It was kismet we met!"

"So you waited tables and they even let you stay there?"

"Uh huh. I moved in my only worldly possessions contained in a shabby suitcase and started my new life. Just think of the saving on campus accommodation and food! It was a tiny room. Fortunately this girl, Tina, left me all her furniture, including a rundown TV. In fact the first bit of news I watched on that TV was about Indira Gandhi's assassination!

It was the kind of lucky break you read about, dream of. Nevertheless let me de-glamorize it for you. It was back breaking work. I woke at five am to open the cafe at six, put on fresh coffee, baked bagels and muffins, dusted the shelves, lifted down stacked furniture and got the place spick and span in an hour. Some of our regulars would stroll in that early! They sat around for a chat over coffee and left with the papers tucked under their arms. Normally the owners came in and relieved me by about half past eight so I could make the bus to classes. I usually returned to work by late afternoon and worked till closing time."

"What about weekends?"

Jane dismissed the query with a shake, "This was the routine seven days a week for three years nonstop. That's the magic of perseverance!" She added comically! "But I did get all those breaks from school when I could catch up on research and studies. I lived in a one-room loft above the store and shared a bathroom and toilet with some other lodgers."

Arti said admiringly "That sounds like a tough deal! Can't have been easy to work such long hours and also attend classes."

"Of course it wasn't! And an utterly soulless job but I decided to make a go of it and ended up making many friends. The average age of our customers was eighty!" Jane smiled, "But it was clean honest work. Thankfully, I didn't have to resort to anything illegal so I kept my conscience clear. In college the temptation to make a quick buck is huge and I came across all kinds, some opting for desperate measures.

I remember this one girl who had a pretty organized modus operandi. She would go all dressed up to parties mainly to the really rich kids' houses. Typically at parties they would pile the guests' coats on a bed inside. All she did was to pretend to use the bathroom, lock the bedroom and rifle through the coats skimming just so little that it wouldn't be missed. Amazing thing is she was popular at parties! Incredible legerdemain. Of course she was miffed when at times she found only credit cards. She didn't want to walk away with credit cards. Cash is different; people don't usually miss a few dollars. It helped tide her through some tough times she says, but I don't think I would have been able to live with that kind of guilt. I mean, some of those kids were strugglers like the rest of us and that cash might have been all they had!"

Arti muttered, "It must have been hard for her to live with herself!"

"One wonders. Also, the visa is a huge concern. One wrong step and you're history! I for one simply couldn't afford to blow it."

Arti nodded briskly, "I think it was ingrained in our sensibility from birth, this sense of right and wrong. Perhaps a bit exactingly. All our parents were strong, self made people who drilled those principles into us, as if the heavens would open up and swallow us if we put on toe out of line. I so hated that!"

Jane was a little taken aback at this fierce declaration from timid Arti. "Yeah true," she murmured uncertainly, "but those values have made us the individuals that we are."

"What's the use? We may encounter the most unprincipled losers but we have to stick to our principles as if a thunderbolt would strike us down at one wrong move!" Arti looked momentarily agitated but subsided in a jiffy. "Sorry, you were saying?"

"No nothing. It was about that kid I knew. Oddly enough, this kid knew the meaning of roughing it out! After all you can't crash every party. I wouldn't like to imagine what other means she used when she was strapped for cash. But she retained her student visa alright. So whenever I felt low, I'd match up my situation to hers and immediately feel better. There were days she'd spend time on the streets, living at the "Y" or at other times sleeping on park benches and I thought only guys did that!"

"Once you get used to easy money, anything you earn through hard work will not suffice."

"Oh I don't know. This was just to get by I think. But yeah, many people who come into a fortune by some stroke of luck or just inherit wealth usually lose their motivation."

The stewardesses dragged a squeaky drinks laden trolley between them and Jane asked for a cocktail chatting with the lady as if she were an old friend. She handed Arti her tomato juice and continued chattering.

She asked if they had any more snacks and soon had the stewardess rummaging through her stock. Arti gaped at Jane but didn't interrupt. Within minutes Jane was tearing open packets of nuts.

Arti watched as Jane placed a paper napkin on her tray table and emptied some nuts on it.

She asked, "Didn't you get confused? I mean everything is so different in the 'States."

Jane scooped up a handful of nuts and shoveled them into her mouth nodding, "It was tricky at first to figure out what was expected in the assignments and really we girls from India had no idea! The libraries helped as did the teachers and in a matter of weeks, everyone wanted to be a part of my group!"

"Because of your brilliance!"

"I guess. I couldn't be bothered with those puerile wusses. I was set to make the most of the opportunity not hang out with those girls who planned shopping afternoons. Their route was charted out quite well, fool around, somehow complete the course, return to India, play the vestal virgin and hook some unsuspecting industrialist's son. What a waste! That seat could've been put to good use by some bright but poor kid."

"So your employers, were they decent people?"

Jane's eyes lit up as she crunched nuts and gushed, "The Best! Mr. Blum was absolutely the kindest man ever. He and his wife of get this, 45 years, were a really special couple. I resolved I would only marry if I could find a love as pure. They made good their escape from Europe during its most troubled period in history and started this little eatery and boarding house. They kept it neat as a pin. The old man would climb a ladder in his overalls to clean his café' sign or change a bulb, sprightly as a 20 year old, while she sat polishing the candelabra or the glasses keeping everything in immaculate order. Like they say, you could eat off the floor and fix your make up in the toaster. Naturally I had to learn a lot about spit and polish but they were kind and patient."

"My gosh, It sounds scary!"

"Yep, I was daunted to begin with but once I got on track, it was as if I was on a roller coaster that I couldn't get off from. Save for an eight hour night, every minute of my day belonged to somebody. I was an automaton. But I gave thanks every single day for the opportunity! Nobody would have given a disfigured, personality less girl like me a second glance let alone allow her to wait tables and run a people friendly place!"

"Shut up. You don't need cosmetics, you're a natural beauty."

"Arti, my cheeks were sunk; I had lost about 20 pounds and had neglected myself completely. Can you believe I hadn't had a haircut in 2 years, hadn't done my nails or bought anything new to wear except maybe snow boots and a warm coat. One day, I came face to face with a junior of ours from college, Shireen something or other. She was one of those girls who had it all, looks, brains and a rich pop."

Arti nodded slowly, "Shireen Contractor, sweet girl, porcelain skin?"

"Right, Cover girl beauty. It's the community I think. All those beauty queens and Hollywood type stars, and I know Shireen was a congenial, lovable kid!"

Arti nodded, "Hmm. Really sweet."

Jane replied, "And she looked through me totally. Now I know she wasn't a snob and it wasn't deliberate. It came to me with a shock that she really did not recognize me! I had become invisible."

Jane sat back, her face darkening, "And the strange thing is that I wanted to be invisible. I had my reasons I think."

"You wanted to be ignored. You?"

Jane nodded, "Because of my complicated situation! See it wasn't the easiest thing to explain. Not everyone from home would have understood it and honestly I was in no mood to be judged. It wasn't that I was ashamed but I guess back then, maybe a little embarrassed. I still carried a legacy of the lifestyle we had enjoyed back home and earning one's keep through menial work didn't quite cut it! I mean I did clean the toilets, wash dishes and oh I don't know!" She turned an anguished face to Arti.

"I know exactly what you mean but you don't think like that today do you?"

"Of course not. Quite the opposite! It was what they call "character building". I'm proud now of it all, but back then I guess I didn't want people judging me. I mean when you're young such things matter. And also there was the subconscious fear of being found out. I haven't told you how I came to America!" Jane smirked mysteriously, "Quite a tale! I ran away!"

Arti raised her eyebrows.

"So inevitably, there would have been some sort of scandal back home after my sudden departure and I'm sure a majority of the rumors claimed I had eloped. And yet, I was wary of being judged for choosing higher education over marriage."

"As if you were dabbling in criminal activity!"

Jane's face momentarily betrayed an inner wretchedness. It was evident that the struggle to shape her future had been gut-wrenching. She looked doggedly at the screen not really following the glowing flight path, "Arti, you wouldn't believe my discomfiture at my brother and sister in law's ridiculing the idea of my making a stab at overseas studies. They scoffed at my ambition and feigned surprise that some university was actually considering my application.

"It is a polite way of saying sorry!" my brother informed me. "Don't these applications call for a photograph?" and then he collapsed in a paroxysm of laughter. He really believed that one look at my misshapen face and the application would be trashed. How warped was their assessment! In their eyes a quick marriage was the easiest option."

"Did they get you engaged or something?" Arti gulped down her drink staring wide-eyed at Jane.

Jane shook her head slowly "Imagine my absolute horror! One day I hop off the University special and limber home and to find it all transformed! Sweets had been brought in from the more costly mithai (sweets) shop...we usually used the cheaper guy, and every table cloth was changed in the living room. Even the slip covers were removed from our sofas to expose the brocade underneath; a rusty orange shade that I had forgotten was under there. This proposed groom was on his way and the house was being dressed up like we would be married that very evening." Jane's fingers were working extra briskly to punctuate her words and shovel peanuts into her mouth. She thrust the packet towards Arti who vaguely abstracted a few nuts, staring at Jane.

"Did you get to know him at all?" Arti chewed slowly.

"Don't be silly. You're expected to sit with your head bowed, hold your tongue and watch them seal your fate. It wasn't one person; it was a troupe that pulled in. At first glance he looked pretty weird and sort of creepy. He came accompanied by a few overdressed, large women who really appeared to be dressed for a wedding. They walked about the room, taking in everything with a critical eye and even fingering the curtains to check for quality. The lady's painted mouth had a permanent downturn and she inspected our place with her heavily done-up eyes as if she would have plenty to say about it later.

I didn't even know that my brother had doled out copies of my pictures to marriage brokers, aunts and uncles and even our neighbours! It was mortifying to think that everywhere I went there was someone holding a picture of me taken at some cousin's wedding!

Arti nodded as if she understood and knew quite well the procedure.

Jane rattled on, "Nothing will ever upstage this as the most awkward, uncomfortable and embarrassing evening of my entire life! Nobody could see the plight I was in. I felt like a caged animal! The whole "meeting" was a disaster. After they left, everyone quietly went to their rooms as I naively assumed there would be no further mention of the whole episode, until that fateful night about a week later.

It was a late night trunk call. I lay in bed reading and involuntarily listening in on my brother's side of the dialogue. I had the radio softly playing "Binaca Geet Mala". It was a very hot night. I lay there watching the blades of the fan cast swirls on the walls. The family in Sonipat had called back confirming auspicious dates for my marriage to their dropout son. They had even lined me up with a lecturer's job at some MSB College for Ladies! All they wanted was a "decent" wedding and no dowry. My brother had sort of placed my education as collateral and in so doing knocked off any question of dowry from the negotiations. I heard relief in my brother's voice. After the call I heard my brother's footsteps stop near my bedroom but he didn't enter. He walked to his room and shut the door. Long after the phone call, the blades kept spinning and I lay there numb and speechless.

Sleep eluded me that night. I sat up weighing the situation, almost paralyzed by terror. Was this my worst nightmare coming true? They were considering dates barely a month away! Was I so unwanted? So ugly, so unattractive that I was being forced to marry that creep? Marrying him, in my mind translated to having teeth pulled without anesthesia. That didn't sound so romantic. Never a huge fan of romance novels, I nonetheless had some hazy concept of a marriage in my head. This wasn't what marriages were meant to be about. This was to be my husband. Then how come I felt loathing and the flesh creepy feeling at the sight of this guy?"

"Didn't you have a chat or anything?"

"Arti I loathed the very sight of the creep. Why would I even talk to him? He had a thick gold chain shining on his hairy chest and I saw it because he hadn't done up his shirt buttons." The mere memory of that incident troubled Jane acutely. She turned to face Arti squarely, "Okay, to give you an idea, he was like one of those roadside loafers who whistle or pass lewd remarks on the streets."

Arti drew in her breath and hissed, "Shut up!" and then added quietly, "Yeah I know how it is. The girl has no right to any opinion in such matters."

Jane continued grimly, "Destiny, Karma who knows what it was but certainly my good angels were outshouted by the devil hell bent on stuffing up my life."

She turned to glance at Arti a bit and clenched her fists tightly, "It was now or never. I was in no mood to hear, "Do you want to stay unmarried all your life?"

I was in a dilemma. I did not want to hurt my brother but also couldn't bear to be married to that guy! I truly felt for my brother. He would have made an excellent bureaucrat like my dad. When they gave him a clerk's job," She paused and glanced at Arti, "it was standard government practice to give the son of the deceased a job, and in our case, it came as a relief I suppose. But my poor brother's dreams came crashing down and he started looking all worn out and grim. I knew he had an awful time at work. He was obviously a cut above the rest but then, nobody passes up an opportunity. Sometimes the bad guys prevail. He was assigned tediously mundane jobs and made to sit amidst these lazy, middle aged clerks cracking bawdy jokes and riding roughshod over him.

I really didn't blame him for trying to rid himself of me, then again, I wasn't going down without a fight either!

The next morning I left the house determined to give it my best shot. If I failed, I would have to bite the bullet and knuckle under but it was well worth a try. Since I already had been accepted at more than one college in the U.S., all I needed was a loan." Jane's eyes widened, "A substantial loan!

Anyway, here I was standing in front of the gigantic Nehru Place not knowing what to do next. I had arrived there fully aware there was no way I could find an office without its address. How I wished I had paid attention when everybody was making out those applications to the Tulis for grants.

I just had the name "Tuli Saab" or Mr. Tuli and I knew that he operated out of some office near Nehru Place. I racked my brains to recall that day in college when I had overheard this girl giving directions for Tuli's office. The only detail that came to mind was that it was "just a five minute walk from the bus stop".

Hot July winds swept up grit into my eyes as I stood uncertainly at the bus stop hanging on to my credentials. Five minutes from here, but in which direction?"

Jane shifted in her seat and turned to Arti. She shook her head slowly, her thoughts taking her far back.

"It's amazing how one can get around in India without a GPS or even street maps! I got precise directions to Tuli's office from the photocopy guy! He took one look at my paperwork and figured out where I was headed, adding rather expertly that all college kids with chubby files usually thronged to that office.

I found it in a jiffy, a palatial mansion. It beats any of the luxury homes on "Lifestyles of the Rich and Famous"!"

Arti snuggled under her blanket listening in captivated wonder of her friend's phenomenal experiences.

"I entered clutching the file with all my admission paper work and looking rather disheveled and unimpressive after a ride on a rickety DTC bus and a mile long trudge in forty degree heat. I saw a hall full of smart and cool applicants accompanied by parents and sponsors. Flinching under their searching gazes I sat there fixing my hair and trying to look presentable. Arti, honestly, in my eyes I was the least bankable candidate. On really wobbly legs I entered the interview cabin sporting a hideous smile trying to cover up all my drawbacks.

After I started talking to them about my ambition and dreams, I think something impressed them. Perhaps the fact that I had come to the interview all alone, but then, I had been used to doing things independently. They were genuine philanthropists. All round decent people with a social conscience and I just didn't see any point in bluffing my way through. Maybe the upfront and direct approach works best. I told them clearly that they were my sole hope and that I needed help with first year fees, airline tickets and visa fees! Most others had brought along a sponsor willing to fund the air fares and some candidates already had their paperwork in place. It was God's goodwill that they picked me even though they were required to pay out much more for my candidature."

Arti beamed, "Good show! You must have been ecstatic!"

Jane's face glowed as she relived the moment her life changed, "I floated on invisible clouds at the sheer serendipity of this fateful turn of events." Jane turned to glance at her friend, an intense somber look coloring her face, "We get such a break once in a lifetime. If we don't seize the opportunity, it may never come again! It's as if we did not value it in the first place; it feels rebuffed and goes away, forever! If I had not lapped it up, it would have faded into oblivion and I would have been the fat wife of a flour mill owner in Sonipat. That was the one moment when the stars conjoined for me, a new door opened and I stepped through."

Arti fixed her eyes on Jane. "Yes I know the exact feeling." She whispered, "this, the scholarship must have come with a proviso."

"Their only stipulation was that I should send back to their foundation an amount proportionate to what I had received once I was able to. Can't understand how there can be such good hearted, generous people and I remain puzzled how no one has hoodwinked them given the scenario back home! I got lucky that's all! Once the jinx wore off, it was all smooth sailing! All my good karma paid off that day. Maybe my guardian angel whispered in their ears. I still can't figure out what made them pick me."

"I think they were smart. They backed the brightest candidate. Did you repay?"

"Oh yeah I did. And I send a small donation each year on my birthday. I have a huge emotional investment in that foundation. It is run by the son and daughter in law now as old man Tuli is semi retired." She pointed to her heart and added solemnly, "He had a multiple by pass. This one action of theirs changed my thinking forever. Inspired by their largesse I vowed to contribute

21

as much as I could spare to support deserving charities. And I began doing it as soon as I was self-reliant. That's what brings me to India a few times each year."

"That's wonderful Jane. I'd love to know more. Maybe I too could use my spare time fruitfully. But yeah you were telling me about the funding and how you managed to squirm out of that appalling marriage."

Jane spoke in a trance. "It was a crazy time! Even to think back on it creeps me out." She waggled her hands about, "I was really excited about receiving the grant and I was bursting with the great news but the household was organizing a wedding! I couldn't bear to face my brother. I knew in my heart he would not see it from my point of view. I finally left without saying anything to anyone. It was surreal. At the airport I thought a million times of calling them." She let out a long sigh, looked briefly at Arti and then beyond her into the cobalt skies outside the porthole, "I can only imagine the mayhem I left in my wake!" she murmured uneasily.

Both ladies fell silent. There was not much to say. Arti sighed and gazed out of the porthole giving Jane space. The warm rays of the sun cast an oneiric haze as their aircraft soared across sapphire afternoon skies.

The drinks trolley made its second round. They sipped their drinks and chatted happily, pleased at the opportunity to catch each other up. Jane, it appeared, had a need to share. She began, typically in the middle of a thought, "I had made good my escape, now I had to capitalize on this one-shot opportunity.

I am not sure if the lure of studying abroad was greater than the urgency to escape that awful marriage, or perhaps both factors prevailed in equal intensity. Also, there had always been an underlying aspiration to visit this fairy-tale land of opportunity. All those days laid up in hospital beds, my leg stretched in traction, I was an indulgent woolgatherer escaping to more pleasant and intriguing visual passages. There was an image in my mind of a utopia. I had these cousins who would visit us each summer from the U.S. and I got a glimpse into their "Life, liberty and the pursuit of happiness" way of life. Today I have come to venerate those unalienable rights Arti!"

Arti gaped at Jane "I notice it happens to people who settle in America. The shiny American Dream!" she whispered.

"It's getting a touch murky these days but yeah that was what drew me to the States. Even as a small girl when I went up on tippy toe to get a glimpse of the Moon Rock, I've got to say, I hardly understood what the fuss was all about, but I knew it was a big deal."

Arti nodded vigorously, "I too remember waiting in those long queues to take a look at it and at the end, and it looked just like a bit of mud from the back yard! Didn't we get a badge of some kind?"

Jane nodded, "Yeah the "I saw the moon rock" button. As I was saying, those cousins of mine did me a good turn I'd say! They usually came laden with American emblems, like Planters' peanuts, Lay's chips and huge jars of Tang. I remember once my aunt presented my mother with this perfume called Chloe by Karl Lagerfeld I think and we all held it and admired it and sniffed it in awe, but nobody knew how to pronounce it! That bottle went straight into my mum's locker never to be used. She decided to stash it away for my marriage! Wonder what became of it! Scavengers creep out of the woodwork when a person passes away!

Anyhow, back to the pronunciation drama, there was this family friend's daughter who was learning to speak French and she came along and declared that we had to pronounce it 'shlow'! I mean, it had the accent at the end and all, but this was what she told us. Can't say she learned much at that foreign language place!" They both laughed easily.

Arti giggled, "Why blame them? I didn't know the correct pronunciation of "extempore", "ensemble" or "penchant" when I was at school and only lately learned that you have to pronounce the last vowel in "epitome"!"

Jane glanced at her and said gently, "But you didn't go to French speaking classes! So anyway, these kids, my cousins, would bring their pictures and videos along and it looked incredibly smart. Well equipped schools, clean Toyland like streets, plush comfortable homes. I just wanted to go and see for myself if this place was for real! In fact after my injuries, the ones I got in the landslide you know, there was not much progress with the physiotherapy so my uncle had invited me to go live with them for physiotherapy and I was beside myself with excitement! That was the time that I lost my parents one after the other in less than a year!"

"I am so sorry! I honestly had no idea! Jane you did not deserve it."

"No one does but bad things happen. When I think of all the hard knocks I have endured I can say bravery is not inherent. It is produced with every blow."

Arti clumsily changed the subject, "So there you were, just a simple straightforward Indian girl in an Anglo Saxon majority. How long did it take to adapt?"

"I felt absolutely at home instantly! And anyway it was far from an "Anglo Saxon" majority but that's beside the point. They were all foreigners.

The local's opinions vacillated between hackneyed notions of India as the land of snake charmers and the contemporary perception of India as an audacious contender in the arms race since we had just conducted nuclear tests under a female leader. Very few knew this and most people were unclear of what to expect from an Indian. This was the eighties and most of American society was teetering between the modern and the traditional. They were getting spooked by the new AIDS virus, Exxon Valdez had spit up on their beaches and most youngsters were redefining themselves. I came across as well read, pretty smart and friendly." Jane paused and looked meditatively at Arti, "Do you remember those guys who sold posters on footpaths? The one thing I took with me was a poster off my wall that I had picked up from them years ago! It was a beautiful quote: "It is not the strongest of the species that survive, or the most intelligent, but the one most responsive to change." Charles Darwin."

Arti nodded wide-eyed, "I remember those shops. They also sold second hand books. So you had this poster up on your wall and adhered to it in your heart!"

Jane smiled, "Adaptability is the key. But on the whole, it was a massive contrast to where we came from! It's not now of course! When I visit India now I am astonished at the phenomenal transformation! Everyone I know is rich beyond belief! The whole attitude has changed with the outsourcing business. I think overseas clients are finally coming to terms with sharing their credit card details with some Nancy and John who're actually Neha or Jaspreet."

Arti shook her head. "A lady friend of mine conducts these classes in Delhi."

"Ask her to stop the pseudo accents and start on better language. It's weird. They start off with a faux American accent, lose it half way and then get a twang as they bid you goodbye. It's appalling when someone wishes you Happy Memorial Day!"

"They had a change of tack lately. The focus is on a neutral accent now. They still need a bit of cultural background to go by, but all they do now is address the issues and move on. In fact I think overseas operators are far chattier. I dictated a recipe for chicken tikka masala while placing a seat request just last week."

Jane laughed, "And yes, it is nice to be able to look at an elegantly designed outfit in chic boutiques here and find the Made in India label. I feel very proud. My charity, the one for battered women, churns out such fabulous pieces Arti! The women do much of the bead work detailing for overseas designers. Exporters bring their stuff to these girls and of course we make sure they are paid a decent wage."

"That's good. Far too many such people are exploited."

Jane shook her head slowly "You wouldn't believe how dishonest employers can be!"

"Cheap third world labour."

Jane continued thoughtfully sipping her cocktail, "And yet," she lapsed into her academic persona, "yet every Indian today is struggling with issues of identity. I heard recently that there are nearly 600 million people in India under the age of 25. Suddenly our greatest liability, the population, is turning into our biggest asset! What were we talking about? Oh yes! Okay. So to answer your question, no there was absolutely no discrimination of any kind. Everyone minds their own business. Nobody even appeared to notice or care about my limp, my slur, my distorted features or my squint! I was a very good waitress because I had become a people pleaser very early in life."

"You, a people pleaser?"

"Totally. Even in primary school, I used to yearn to be liked by the teacher. I did everything to make her like me. I would hang on to her every word. If she said, "I like smiling children", I pasted a smile on my face even though a pesky hang nail hurt like crazy. If she complimented a kid on how straight she walked, I would walk ramrod straight and stiff but all I got from the hard hearted teacher was a royal ignore. Finally it was time for the annual day performances and I absolutely knew my acting would please her. I memorized my lines perfectly. Then I'd go around asking anyone at home to watch me act. I even rehearsed my part in front of the mirror. We were to go attend this family wedding in Lucknow, and I had got this new satin "sharara" stitched for the wedding. But as the date for our departure approached, I saw that going to the wedding meant missing a day of school and I was afraid that Mrs. D'Sa would arrange for our auditions on that very day so I gave the wedding a miss.

I kept at my practicing. I was trying out for two parts and I knew I would certainly get one. I spent every morning on the bus repeating my lines hoping that the auditions would be that day. Do you know what happened?"

"What?"

"No Auditions. Mrs. D'Sa called out some names from a list and arbitrarily assigned the roles. My name was nowhere. I wasn't even the understudy or curtain puller. I was heartbroken and wept continuously for two nights. It was much later that I realized what a fake that sorry apology of a teacher was, a poorly qualified, mean minded, malicious, hurtful woman. That was one teacher I cold shouldered when I became the head girl five years later."

Arti sighed at the recollection of her old school with its Spartan classrooms and simplistic resources. She had often wondered what it must have been like to attend a posh school.

Jane continued, "The only other time I felt repulsed by my appearance was when I went looking for work at a nearby Indian Store right after I landed in the U.S. The look with which he took me in from top to toe was a combination of disgust and naked revulsion. I never returned to that shop. I did quite a few odd jobs in my early days before I got the one at the diner and I just have to say, I had completely forgotten there was anything the matter with my appearance. But that day I realized what huge hypocrites we Indians can be wherever on this planet we live! Even as a child..."

Food smells floated about and the cabin crew began their dinner service. "Another drawback of these seats, we get our food late!" Arti complained.

"What's the other drawback?"

"All those people queuing up for the washrooms, doesn't it bother you?"

"Nope, I didn't even notice. What I like is that we can recline our seats all the time and that it's just the two of us so we can yak to our hearts content."

Arti laughed, "Yes that's nice. So anyway, what's this about hypocrisy?"

Jane continued, "Yes I was saying that even as a child I had witnessed but not wholly comprehended prejudice and intolerance in our own family. Mum had taken me to her aunt's place in our native village a little sea shore hamlet, for the summer and that innocuous incident is etched in memory.

It was a long, low building with a sloping tiled roof. Rooms were arranged in a straight row with no particular plan. You entered in the middle into a spacious drawing room with ornate period furniture and went straight through to the dining room. I remember it especially because of its black and white checkered floors. Doors led off the bedrooms to attached toilets which opened on to the muddy courtyard. The cleaners usually came in from the courtyard and did the cleaning.

I remember one summer morning the sweeper woman had finished washing out the toilets and stood outside all sweaty and red faced. She asked for some water so I poured out a glass of cold water and handed it to her. Almost immediately there was an echoing shriek from across the living room. Great aunt had spotted me from her vintage armchair and started screeching hysterically. My mother rushed to me shouting apologies to mollify her aunt and shooed away the cleaning woman. It was a good while before my mother could get me to understand that great aunt wouldn't permit low caste people to use her eating and drinking utensils. They could not even cross the threshold! That was my first encounter with castes and possibly my last except for the civics lessons at school."

Jane's narration was done comically and Arti couldn't stop herself from laughing out loud. She looked at her wide eyed, "That's ridiculous! I mean I come from a fairly conservative home but I've never heard of such a thing!"

Jane added, gesturing with her fingers, "Oh and incidentally the glass wasn't allowed back into the house. My poor mum copped it for not suitably educating me in the ways of our high class families! Gosh, I remember that holiday vividly. Those few weeks were idyllic in every way and a bit sneaky too. Every afternoon I would go play with the servants' kids. We would shinny up a tree, pluck and eat raw mangoes dipped in rock salt and watch the peacocks and buffaloes in the pond. As soon as we spotted their mum entering the house at tea time, I would scramble down and scuttle back to the bungalow. So when great aunt was wheeled out to afternoon tea, she found me sitting demurely in a starched frock, reading calmly."

Arti stared spellbound, "Thank Goodness your parents didn't observe such prejudices!"

"And yet," said Jane thoughtfully," my mother's aunt wasn't a petty, old fashioned, small minded woman as it would appear! She had virtually adopted all the families that tended her fields. She made sure each one living on her large estate was cared for. Their kids were well fed, educated and trained for a skill. She even helped arrange their marriages. No one living on her farm ever wanted for anything. It was just this age-old practice that she adhered to rigidly."

"Noblesse oblige."

Jane nodded, "I used to go and sit in the large kitchen chatting with the cooks. It was such an interesting place. I had tasty treats handed to me from shiny steel goodie boxes or roasted potatoes pulled out of an earthen kiln in the ground. It burned all day with these gleaming copper pots placed on top. How they labored to cook those elaborate meals! I watched them toil away at the mortar and pestle and the thick grinding stone as I chatted to them about my friends back home. They told me village tales of when a leopard strayed on to the plantation or when they found an injured hyena, nursed it back to health and set it loose in the wild again.

I remember that holiday in great detail. Some things just stick in one's mind. The images of their cracked heels, knotty, gnarled fingers and dirty black toenails are fixed in the mind's eye! There is nobody I know, as proud as I am of our heritage but there are exceptions." She glanced at Arti, "so that part of our culture is certainly not something to be proud of."

"Sins of the fathers! Governments to come will strive to make newer laws to erase that blot."

"My dad used to be scornful of rituals and practices but my mother's side was big on all that."

"Your father, wasn't he with the Intelligence Department?"

Jane nodded, "I.B. Yeah, India's FBI. He was real smart and knew stuff - Top secret stuff. When he passed away the Intelligence guys came and combed his room taking all the sensitive information that might have been in his charge." She paused a bit, then looked at Arti, "Like I was saying, the repulsed look that the Indian Shop owner had on his face, reminded me of this incident in the village. That day I experienced firsthand how these marginalized people must feel every day. It took me back to the stinging barbs my brother lobbed at me. Perhaps not as malicious and maybe a little more pitying but it was the look that said to me "you're a weirdo". No complaints though as I got sincere affection from my employers, Tikvah and Adam, you know, the Blums! They even left me the little tea shop! Can you believe it, I an heiress?"

"Really? Didn't they have any kids of their own?"

"No. No kids. They were the closest thing to family for me. The Blums were the new parents I found in a far off land and I have no qualms in saying they meant more to me than family. Funny coincidence, Tikvah means 'Hope', the same as my mother's name, Manasvita! I continued to work part time for them even after I got a steady income. Slowly, they grew too feeble to run the place and my visits tapered off."

"Why?"

"The doctoral thesis was demanding."

Arti's look was reproachful. "They sound adorable."

"They were the best. I did look them up off and on."

"Bet you did your best. Or why would they have remembered you in their wills?"

"They had made quite an unambiguous will leaving a huge amount to a charity they had long supported." Jane's eyes widened. "More money than you could shake a stick at." Then she looked a little muddled, "Strangely enough, there was no mention of any family in the will. But then within days, a bunch of relations staked a claim on the place! That scared me. I didn't want to take on so many powerful people and really I had no use for the café. I was comfortably off by then so I told their lawyer all I wanted was the lovely pieces in the curio cabinets. They had held special memories for me."

She looked at Arti and using her expressive hands created an image of upright columns. "The salon had these fine cabinets with painted tiles down the sides and glass doors with crystal knobs. While I worked I would amuse myself by looking at the beautiful curios inside. It was a cabinet of curiosities for me to daydream with. I used to stare at the little china figurines and coloured glass ornaments shining brightly under those halogen lamp around the café."

An absorbed Arti nestling her head in her locked hands asked indolently, "You mean like old porcelain and crystal?"

"Yeah," Jane said absently as she saw the meal service trolley approaching. She pulled out the menu from the seat pouch and examined it.

"Are you having the smoked salmon Tuscany or the crispy Duck?" She inquired as if she were a maitre de at some highfalutin place.

"What?" Arti looked at the menu in Jane's hands. "Oh the meal option; is the trolley here finally?" She lifted herself out of her slouched position, straightening out her blanket and pulled her tray table out.

"Hey, aren't you vegetarian?"

"My, you remember a lot I must say! My special meal will arrive shortly. Oh Jane, you have had quite a life!" Arti giggled, "You said "cripsy". So cute!"

"Great! So now you make fun of my lisp. After hearing the saga of "Jane the invincible", all you can comment on is the lisp! Ah! Here comes your vegetarian meal."

Jane conversed with the steward while he fixed her drink. They chatted like old friends and Arti stared, quite amazed.

"Do you know him like from another flight?"

Jane shook her head and took a long gulp. "No, just chatting. Nice fellow."

The two ladies dined happily basking in the warmth of old friendship.

"So, tell me, did they give you some mementos at least?" Arti asked.

Jane regarded her with a beguiling smile. "Sure! They let me have the curio cabinets too. Relieved, I think that I wasn't going to contest the will. I later learned the value of those cedar cabinets from a wood polisher. Priceless! I also took away some invaluable bone china tea sets they said they had no use for. Turns out I benefitted more than the so called extended family! The Blums had not obtained a clear title to the place and by some fortuitous oversight, had lived rent free, imagining they owned it."

Arti gulped, "And those dubious relatives?"

"Not a dime! To think that an old couple, who had enough capital to buy up a few buildings, occupied a place for decades oblivious that it wasn't theirs!"

"How weird! Those other people must have been furious."

"Oh they were mad! But I seriously doubted their legitimacy. I don't think they would have won in a court. I just ceded to their demands as I didn't want any trouble. Anyhow, long story short, what I thought were pretty glass ornaments also turned out to be valuable collectors' items! They mean the world to me but I never imagined how much they were worth in monetary terms." Jane brushed off tears and there was the hint of a tremor in her voice." She shrugged her shoulders giving a short laugh.

"I was a mere factotum, a student from a poor country. What did I know about Lalique or expensive Dresden China?"

"It has to have a crown somewhere in the pattern." Arti quipped quite unexpectedly.

Jane turned in surprise. "Yeah, that's right! You're well informed!"

"I educated myself. I like beautiful things and I like reading! Every time I have a little money I buy a book or a nice collectors' magazine."

Jane processed the statement briefly. Arti's plain, conservative appearance could have fooled anybody! "Really? Have you...I mean do you collect things?"

"Blue pottery, I have a weakness for it. And some other beautiful things like old silver and old furniture too." Arti didn't appear to have noticed Jane's stares, "But we're digressing. You were saying?"

Jane's eyes were fixed on Arti and she spoke slowly, "I was just wondering where you live in the US."

Arti shook her head, covering her mouth as she chomped. "I am flying back home to India. I was visiting with my daughter. She brought me here for a holiday."

"I see and what does she do?"

"She's a doctor doing post graduate work in London.

Jane gave a little whistle, "Whoa! Your little girl a doctor! Specialty?"

"She hopes to be accepted for Oncology."

"That's huge!"

"Noblest profession!"

"Totally! You must be terribly proud of her! It isn't easy making it into a medical college in India Look where she's at now, Oncology! Speaking of which," Jane's eyes were large saucers, "did you read," Jane straightened out, undid her seatbelt and leaned across to the magazine holder on the bulkhead behind them, "this?" She pointed to the pictures of a doctor duo that had graced the front page of most newspapers and magazines that week.

"What about them?"

"This is Doctor Anil Suri!" She declared slapping the magazine with the back of her hand with a dramatic flourish that was clearly second nature to her.

Arti frowned, "Who?"

"Don't you remember? Rukmini from college is married to him! One of the world's finest Oncologists!"

"Oh wow! I really can't place him," Arti said examining the grainy picture closely. They didn't visit India much you know. She peered closely, "He appears to have lost some hair."

"Weren't you at their wedding or something?"

Arti screwed up her face in deep thought. "It was a lifetime ago. I can't say I remember it at all." Then it came to her slowly. She smiled. "Yeah, our grandparents were friends. It was one of those instant weddings. Quite rushed. Wonder what it is like to be married to such a phenomenal genius!"

TWO

The car navigated at snail's pace through Delhi's colourful, teeming streets. Openmouthed, her children peered out at the pulsating activity as office goers, students and haggling buyers at the fruit and vegetable handcarts jostled for space on crammed pavements often spilling out on to the roads in the path of a hulking bus or rickety auto rickshaw. The heat and humidity failed to dampen their vigour as they went about their routine with enthusiastic gusto and much passionate chatter.

The children were full of questions for Rukmini, their mother.

"What is the gross looking green stuff those people are drinking?"

"That's sugarcane juice. See that thresher? That's where he is extracting it. It's very refreshing!"

"Mum, are those kites?"

Rukmini turned to follow her son's gaze, "Yes! They are making kites over there see!" she pointed to an open air assembly line with chaps unfurling reams of coloured paper and rolls of string. Her son gaped in wonder at the palette of multicolored hues and her wide-eyed daughter whispered, "Is it some sort of a fun-fair?"

"No these are the street side markets. They get busy in the evening."

"They're like this almost all day." Asha, her friend glanced back with a smile, "you'll get used to it."

Asha was almost continually on her mobile phone following up on the hurried arrangements for Rukmini's father in law's funeral.

Rukmini looked at her childhood friend, "Thanks so much Asha, for all your help. Anil would have been completely lost trying to organize a funeral here."

Asha waved away her thanks, "Not a big deal. People rally round. Friends and neighbours, you know, who were close to your in laws. I just feel terrible about the way he went, all alone with no one to hold on to or connect with in his last hours. I keep thinking about it. No one should have to die like that."

Anil took off straight after the funeral leaving Rukmini to clear up, donate all his parents' things, and sell the house.

"I can't believe it! These people know which Bhajans your granddad liked and his favourite piece from the scriptures!" Rukmini tearfully murmured to her children as they sat solemnly, strangers at their grandfather's funeral service. Rukmini participated in the melodious strains of Vedic chanting by mourners of a dead man she barely identified with.

Condolences poured in and over the next few days Rukmini met with people she did not know at all. The children took it all in wide-eyed and curious.

"You should take your meals with us for as long as you are here" offered a lady she faintly recalled meeting.

"It's very kind of you but I can manage." Rukmini replied gratefully. Nonetheless, meals arrived with precise regularity accompanied by a steady stream of mourners. It was a few days before she and the kids were allowed to be by themselves.

The grandparents' house was a standalone bungalow with a pretty garden, complete with a sit out and a two seater swing. Death had not marred its beauty. Bright magenta bougainvillea bordered the gleaming white fence and birds hopped in and out of the stone bird bath under the gulmohar tree. It looked so lived in that at any minute one expected somebody to come out from the kitchen, clear away the tea tray, replace the faded flowers and maybe run a mop on the shiny marbled floor.

Their grandfather's spectacles sat on an open newspaper in the study. Ants had laid siege to the snacks on a plate and rank mustiness enveloped the stuffy room. Books had been pulled out from the wall-to-wall bookcases and lay opened on or around the cozy armchair.

In the next few days his grandfather's books drew Sameer in while Natasha began helping her mother sort through the sprawling house. It was no mean task. The wardrobes spilled over with packages, shopping bags and bundles of clothes. The storage spaces were piled high from floor to ceiling with suitcases, airbags and cartons. Taking a virtual inventory of the overflowing storeroom, Natasha whispered aghast. "Where do we start?" She had never seen such clutter and felt certain her clean freak mum would collapse of shock.

"I'll work with you." she suggested encouragingly to her horror-struck mother.

Slowly they worked their way through bag after bag, hauling them to some cleared out space in the living room. Between them they unpacked the DVD player sent to the grandparents as a gift years ago still in its original packing and handed over a camcorder to an astonished Sameer. "Do what you like with it, if it works." His frazzled mother muttered.

"They were hoarders!" Natasha stood back and stared in amazement at the contents spilling out of a suitcase.

"Duh!" Sameer snapped

"Like most Indians." Her mother replied.

Over the next weeks mother and daughter concentrated their efforts on sorting through the insurmountable stashes. Natasha was staggered at the things they unearthed from the capacious wooden wardrobes and the lofts above. Lotions and creams, sweaters and scarves, colognes and perfumes, cameras, binoculars, pen sets and handbags galore!

"Isn't this some of the stuff you sent them Mom?" Natasha asked holding up a Christmas gift pack.

Rukmini nodded, "Basically every gift that was ever sent to them in original packing, almost in chronological order, all kept preserved, never used." Rukmini replied grimly. Guilt and remorse overpowered her as she gazed in amazement at the swelling mass of white elephant pieces she had habitually inflicted upon the old people.

There was a stack of about a hundred or so carry bags bearing the names of famous British retailers, neatly folded and fastened with a rubber band, labels written in her hand still intact on them. She looked at a Harrods's bag with the large paper pasted on with cello tape. She could even recall some of the occasions when she bought the gifts. Each time she heard someone was going to India, she'd take off during her lunch break, pick out something nice and deliver it to the traveling family with the handwritten address pasted on the parcel:

Mr. and Mrs. Suri,
D –1060/1062,
Greater Kailash,
New Delhi. 110019.
Ph: 6023187

There were no signs of the Marks and Spencer's biscuit tins, Walkers' snacks or Kraft cheese tins. "Maybe gifted away" she assumed, "Or eaten", she hoped.

She had been struggling to recover from the first shock of stock-taking in the kitchen. Kitchen containers made from recycled Bournvita tins, neatly labeled in Hindi alongside old jam and pickle jars filled with spices were lined up on the shelves. Hundreds of milk pouches rained on her when she opened a cupboard. Her in laws adhered to the adage of "repair not replace". The fridge was over twenty years old and still functioning and the TV was certainly the same one they'd had when she was married. It enjoyed pride of place in the sitting room, covered in a white crocheted tablecloth.

Kamala the maid would come in daily to do the cleaning and usually planted herself on her haunches in whichever room she saw them working. Aware that the woman was looking forward to getting some of her late employers' things, Rukmini, made out generous bundles for her.

She started taking an interest in the simple woman's nonstop chatter. It gave her a chance to acquaint herself with her late in laws.

She learned that her father in law went for a long walk each morning and liked his tea piping hot served on a tray. In the summer they had morning tea and breakfast outdoors and in the winter they ate their lunch on the glass verandah at the back. Her mother in law made large jars of pickle seasonally and gifted them to friends. "All said and done bibiji," sniffed Kamala drawing in her breath for a long chat, "They really wanted you people here. Whenever you sent your children's photographs, I got 'inaam' (a reward) but all your mother in law did was to sit there", she pointed to the wooden rocking chair, "with the photos in her hands weeping her eyes out. She never spoke out fearing your father in law's temper but there were times she talked to me. She did miss you all a lot. That was why she involved herself in all the charities and activities, just so her mind would be occupied."

Kamala decided to work extra hours each day to help Rukmini with the mammoth clean up. Sameer often sat listening to the woman's tales though he struggled a bit with her dialect. He asked her if she could make "Alu ka paratha" and she laughed and said, "Once you eat "Alu Ka paratha" made by me, you'll forget all other parathas, Sameer baba". She was right. The children polished off her cooking sooner than it could reach the table.

Rukmini believed she would never have managed to clear out the clutter without Kamala's unstinting help. Within days she could see the end of the mammoth clean-up project approaching.

She informed Asha that she believed she would be ready to open negotiations for the sale of the house by the following week.

One afternoon, a puzzled Sameer asked his mother to translate the word "Filote" to him. Ever since he developed the kinship with Kamala, Rukmini was frequently touched upon for a translation.

"Filote? What's that?"

Sameer frowned impatiently, "It's something she needs. What is "Nilam"?"

"Nilam means auction. What is she going to auction?" Rukmini asked absently peering into a suitcase with distrust. Earlier that day a couple of mice had jumped out from behind the stacks in the store and she chose to be wary.

"Auction!" Sameer's eyes lit up at the prospect of some commercial dealings in the life of one he had come to regard as his charge. He sat down again, "So what's "Filote"?"

Rukmini abandoned her interest in the suitcase and relegating it to the growing pile of discards she turned her attention briefly to her son.

"Sameer, I have never heard of such a word. Now get away from here. It's too dusty."

She called out to the rag picker waiting outside and instructed him to clear out all the junk from the store-room. Shedding her dusty apron she glanced around hoping to touch Kamala for a hot cup of tea.

Sameer returned with the maid in tow. "Explain it to my mother." he urged the timid thing.

Rukmini asked her what she meant by "Filote" and the poor woman laughed nervously, "Sameer baba was asking me why I was leaving early today. I told him that I had to go and line up for the 'filote' and he came and told you. I didn't mean to trouble you I just mentioned it…"

"Yes but what is it? What does "Filote" mean?" Rukmini asked gently.

"Zameen. They are going to cut up "filotes" and auction them." The simple woman looked surprised that nobody understood her, "From the government. Elections are coming so they will start handing them out. I want to be ahead in the queue."

"Oh gosh, she means a plot! She's going to try and get a plot of land." Rukmini exclaimed.

Sameer looked ecstatic and most encouragingly told the poor woman to go right away and get her filote.

Kamala smiled warmly at his compassion, "he takes after his grandparents, your son! They were Godly people. I will just finish cleaning up and go Sameer Baba."

Sameer murmured to his mother to extend a little cash her way. "Stop it Sameer," Rukmini angrily pulled him away, "I am paying her more than enough. I could help her with buying the plot in case they need to pay anything, but I suspect it will be practically free. It is more a matter of reaching there soon, sort of being in the right place…"

Sameer promptly walked up to Kamala and took away the broom and pail. "Go, Hurry!" He waved the broom towards the door, "Or they will give the filote away."

Kamala allowed herself to be steered out bidding a hasty farewell to Rukmini, "Namaste I'll see you tomorrow."

His mother sighed, "I presume I must make my own tea then!"

Sameer followed her into the kitchen and declared that Kamala reminded him of Anakin Skywalker's mother, Shmie. He gave her a very moving speech about exploiting cheap labour. He had been astounded to hear that her meager salary, equating to about 600 British Pounds a year, fed and kept her family of five.

He brought to his mother an accounts book maintained by his grandparents, which indicated that the couple regularly provided for Kamala's family. His heart swelled to read some of the entries

> Quilts for Kamala Rs. 500
> Kamala's son's shoes Rs.300.
> Kamala's family ration Rs 850
> School books and stationery Rs. 1350

Rukmini took the account book and sat down to examine it. She realised her in laws had provided substantial support to Kamala's family. She felt a special deference for the elders and recognised with disquiet that Kamala had been aware that she would be deprived of a considerable cash supplement in future but never thought to mention it to her.

In the coming days while Sameer warmed to the helpers and visitors, Natasha maintained a distance. She couldn't understand why her mother encouraged Kamala to talk so much and found the incessant stream of callers annoying. "Why does every old lady have to hug and kiss and touch me? It's icky. How long before the computer chappie fixes the Internet thingy? I feel so cut off in this dump. Can the driver take me to the Internet café' now?"

Rukmini sighed, putting down a pile of pashmina shawls, "How many times do I need to remind you that you can't go out alone."

"What can possibly happen? Many young girls roam around dressed just like me."

"They know their way about. Please don't start with me again Natasha. Mrs. Chandra rang this morning to say that you're welcome to go use their computer. It's the red roofed house two doors down, just by the park. I'll remind the computer technician again".

"For the hundredth time, why is everyone so slow and stupid here?" Natasha looked into the mirror fixing her hair and dusting off her jeans.

"Mum I cannot go by myself. There are cows outside their house feeding on the rubbish heap. Can Sam go with me?"

"Sure I'll go but what's so scary about those cows? I like to observe their mouths when they are masticating."

"What!"

"It means chewing." Sameer pulled on his sneakers and moved to the door. "I think you should also know that a huge percentage of Silicon Valley comprises of Indians, hence…" Their voices trailed off and Rukmini was thankful for some peace and quiet. Natasha would get a complete account on smart, enterprising Indian techies working hard under adverse conditions. It was, she considered, to her daughter's credit that she rarely argued with her younger brother when he expounded his ideas or provided in-depth information on topics varying from biological terms and the contribution of India to Silicon Valley's cumulative intelligence quotient to the origins of their favorite game of chess in India.

Rukmini settled down to sort through large piles of clothes for donation. Kamala picked up yet another bundle of clothes to take home. Rukmini handed her some money and instructed her to buy vegetables for the night.

"Not from here. My husband will bring them from the defence farms tomorrow."

"Why not from here?"

"These fellows bring poisonous vegetables." Kamala declared warily.

"What rubbish. How can vegetables be poisoned? They are the safest things to eat in this weather."

Kamala argued mulishly, "No bibiji, that's not true. Don't you know? It is in the papers too. These farmers are such cheats they inject some chemicals in water melons and vegetables to make them look attractive and juicy but that is not good for our health!" Kamala's eyes were as large as saucers. "We are also farmers but I never heard of such a thing before!"

"The guy who brings his handcart on our street was arrested by the police but he is back. The people living in the yellow house had reported him to the police because they all got food poisoning after eating his watermelon and they had to go to hospital to have their stomachs flushed clean." This was all said in a fearful rush.

Rukmini gaped at this new revelation. "What are you saying?"

Kamala looked pleadingly at her, "Go bibiji ask them. They will tell you. Everyone knows, it was in the papers and they showed it on TV as well! I will bring you fresh vegetables from the Defence farms. Please don't eat these fruits and vegetables."

Rukmini was promptly on the phone asking all her friends if they had heard about the fruit and vegetable contamination.

As always Asha enlightened her. "Yes, they use banned pesticides and something called oxy toxin that changes their appearance. Can you imagine! What are we to eat now?"

Rukmini was aghast at her casualness. "What are the authorities doing about it?"

"I guess they'll slap them with a fine but it would take a pretty huge machinery to catch all these crooks!"

"Asha, where do you get your vegetables from?"

"Roy's friend's farm."

"Kamala says she will bring me vegetables and fruit from some Defence farms."

"Sounds perfect," said Asha encouragingly. "Relax Rukmini not every piece of fruit or vegetable is poisoned. These are stray cases and most of them were caught outside Delhi. I'm sure checks are made in the fresh markets here."

"Why would anyone be allowed to poison vegetables?"

"They rationalize that to keep vegetables pest-free, some amount of pesticide will have to be permitted because the nutrition we get in return outweighs the harm done by the little bit of pesticide. I say, if you need a change, we could take the kids out one day. I'm always happy to get out and about. But listen, don't panic. And maybe avoid watermelons and brinjals. Also, let me know if you need meat or fish. I'll get it for you. Not all places are totally hygienic."

Rukmini shook her head in disbelief. Her head in a whirl, she returned to the piles of illogical jumble that had formed in each room.

One morning as she lay awake, Rukmini remembered waking up the morning after their marriage to the chatter of wedding guests, the smell of tea brewing and the rattle of cups and saucers. No one allowed her to do any work. Anil's aunt said, "It's tradition that you don't make a new daughter in law work till the henna fades from her hands."

Another aunt had implored, pressing a bio-data and photographs into her hands "You can look up some good grooms for my Babli? She is fluent in housework and has just completed course in Continental and Chinese "cookry" and decoupage". All of it was said in a hushed whisper. "Pushpa Bhabhiji (sister in law) is also thinking the same thing for Sweetie, I know but you must think of us first haan! Sweetie is still young. For Babli right time is now. Okay darling? Don't forget. I had asked many times Anil also but he's a man." She smiled conspiratorially, "This is a lady's work."

A little taken aback, Rukmini had promised politely, "Yes, of course Buaji, I will do my best."

Her father in law had promptly instructed her to do absolutely nothing about it. "That silly Babli will never cope with life abroad. She needs her kitty parties and fleet of servants. Her parents should get her married to an army man like her father."

Rukmini smiled recalling her early days in the Suri household. She turned on her side and caught sight of herself in the long wall mirror. It evoked the memory of herself as a young bride studying her decked up reflection. Inundated with gifts of jewels and expensive clothing she had felt as if it was a dream. "My cup runneth over." she had thought. A thrill ran through her as she remembered her euphoric exhilaration vividly. "What more can a girl dream of, a loving family, a highly qualified, husband and the prospect of a new life overseas?"

Rukmini glanced up at the ceiling. Damp patches and cracking plaster evidence a lack of maintenance. Her father in law used to be particular about such things but appeared to have lost interest after his wife's passing. She lay in bed watching the tall trees rustle against a pink and golden morning sky. Sunlight streamed through the French windows. She tiptoed to the kitchen to make tea. Morning showers had left little droplets on the lawns glimmering under the rising sun.

Sitting out under the trees in the garden, sipping tea just as her in laws must have done, she peered into a large plastic packet that had emerged the previous day.

She flicked through the pictures of Anil's boyhood usually with some medal, trophy or certificate for proficiency. A consistent National Science Talent champion, he had been interviewed by the newspapers on acing his school leaving exam and his parents had fondly placed the cutting in his album.

She put away her teacup and looked around trying to chalk out her day. She was loath to looking through another grotty box or lizard infested cupboard. Curtains flapped out of the window as cool breeze wafted in. It was a day that only Delhi's monsoon could turn out with damp breeze shaking crystal droplets down from the just washed leaves as the sun peeked out of a partly cloudy sky.

She placed a call to Asha's. "I am willing to take you up on your offer. Can we go out today? I'm sick of this unending spring clean!"

A day's jaunt around the markets, sampling local cuisine and relaxing with a leisurely lunch at the cozy Nirula's "Potpourri" restaurant worked wonders. Jan path's low cost clothes and footwear had Natasha ecstatic and very soon she was squatting in the middle of the market studying the intricate swirls of cool henna tickling her palms. Sameer bought books, P-C games and a poster of Yoda.

"Why you want that silly old man's poster I can't imagine" said Natasha.

"Yoda represents the wisdom of the ages and is not a silly old man. Mum, make her say she's sorry."

"I rather think he bears a resemblance to The Buddha, and Natasha I wouldn't insult the Star Wars family, if I were you. Apologize to your brother."

"Sorry".

Sipping "DePaul's" cold coffee sent the ladies harking back to their college days when they would flock to the celebrated store for branded cosmetics. Amidst vendors hawking colorful wares and shoppers bargaining uncompromisingly in the frenzied market place, Sameer observed a man inventively twisting metal wire into different shapes and displaying them on a grubby cloth on the pavement. The children were captivated as his deft fingers moved effortlessly to produce those masterly creations.

Sameer bought a bicycle and a car and Natasha got herself a pencil holder and a few other things as gifts. "Our school took us to the Science museum and there were displays just like this in multicolored wire." She remarked holding up her purchase admiringly.

"Yeah I bet they'd give this guy a Ph.D." Rukmini remarked paying the man the paltry sum he asked.

The children took pictures of the vibrant markets, juice stands, pavement book stalls and misspelled posters, their favorite being, a brightly coloured banner boasting "quick success" through their tuitions with the caption "Looking English Tutor For Your Child?"

The white "Toyota Altis" pulled over at the Suri's house and Ram Singh yanked the bulging shopping bags out of the boot.

"Asha aunty thanks so much for a really great day!"

"No problems kids. I enjoyed it too! Hope the clothes fit. I better rush home. Roy will be back in a few hours. Rukmini, don't forget tonight's the music evening at ours. Many of the old girls are also coming. I'll send the car at eight."

The stewardesses completed act one and wheeled away their trolleys, dimming their lights to signal bedtime. In the luminescence of the silent vestibule, thousands of feet above land the two friends swapped stories of challenge and defeat, struggle and survival.

"So tell me about your last twenty-five years!" Burrowed in the blanket's fleecy softness, Jane resembled an orange headed polar bear. She asked in a hoarse whisper, "What's Mr. Arti like?"

Arti lifted her head and sighed, "You didn't marry the chap selected by your folks," She turned and looked at Jane, "but I did!" Arti struggled with herself. To narrate a story she had willfully erased from her mind would be painful. Maybe because of Jane's willingness to share her own story or because they were old friends, Arti felt she was ready to recall the most painful period of her life. As most passengers drifted off to sleep in the aircraft's calm thousands of feet above the earth, she softly narrated that chapter of her life that she had blocked out for a very long time.

"You know how those people traipsed in to "see'" you? Well, it was almost exactly the same scenario except that I had consented to meeting the boy. I wanted a marriage, in laws to look after, a place where I could nurture a family, so I was ready to meet him. We were introduced by a distant relative."

She observed uncomfortably, "It's a weird system but works well in our society. Girls are expected to marry by a certain age and the actual observance of the ritual assumes more importance than whom she marries!"

Jane added, "And love features nowhere"

Arti smiled and looked at her shaking her head, "Forget it. It has to surface instantly! So the parents' job is to get her married. Then she disappears and nothing more of her life thereafter is of any consequence. How she copes, what she has to tolerate is never taken into account. And yet the parents are put in the dock if she is not married. But I don't need to tell you all this Jane you have experienced it."

Jane looked curiously at Arti, "Yes, but I escaped. How about you?"

Arti sighed, "Okay! Listen to Arti's story and don't ask too many questions. It isn't easy. This is absolutely the very first time I am sharing my tale with anyone. Arti is narrating Arti's story, so, no interruption, okay?"

Jane nodded vigorously and cupped her chin in one fist as she fixed a contemplative stare upon her friend. "Arti's story hmm? Okay."

"Also, don't stare at me." Arti gently turned her friend's face, "look there."

"So who did you marry?"

THREE

Arti fixed her gaze at the blank TV screen considering the question. Whom had she married? She thought of her relations with her husband. She often wondered what he had really felt about her. He had looked utterly uninterested when they first met at Delhi's Asoka Hotel. He had refused to make conversation, declined all food and drink, looking ill at ease as if he would rather be anywhere else on the planet. He was all but pointedly rude to her parents as he answered their questions brusquely looking away when they tried to address him. Arti had spent most of the time talking to his kid sister and a little to his mother. She felt uneasy just looking at him. He seemed standoffish and cold.

He, on the other hand, had found the entire exercise quite futile as he was just not interested in marrying. This particular girl looked glum and studious, quite unlike the sociable, gregarious crowd he was accustomed to. Yet within months they were "fixed up" and expected to make a go of it. Arti thought that, in a sense he was as much a victim as her in their charade of a marriage.

She winced at the recollection of the scant moments they had spent together. One day early in their marriage when she was about six months pregnant, dressed in a gorgeous kanjivaram sari she laid out a set of clothes for him.

"The wedding reception is at eight."

He looked puzzled.

"So?"

"Aren't you going?"

"Yeah, but no one said that you were going. We never leave the house completely empty, so you'd better stay back."

She gaped at him stung by his malicious tone. Couldn't he see how carefully she had dressed up? How cruel was he! There were times she wanted to scream out in anguish, lunge at him or claw his eyes out just to give him a sensation of the pain he was causing.

44

Arti secretly admitted to herself that she was, overall, pretty mediocre in every way. She had never been good looking, witty or talented and while she had performed fairly well at school and college, it didn't add up to much when a man sized you up as a woman. She shrugged dejectedly and said to herself over and over again, "No man wants a grumpy wife" Across a few years, the tediousness of a dull marriage had left her mousy and vapid. Her personality shone when no one was watching, in the company of her child. Arti experienced pure joy when her baby girl gazed into her face! That was when her face lit up and her eyes twinkled glowingly.

If her in laws felt sorry for her, they never showed it. In their early days she used to ask him questions, protest about his long absences and sulk and shout a bit but mostly to no avail. He simply didn't care.

When he didn't take any interest even after the birth of their daughter, she had come to accept that her marriage was a farce and there was no running away from the truth. In a sense she felt a strange relief at his indifference and apathy as she had come to loathe him and the notion of any form of intimacy with him was repugnant to her.

One day while returning from the pediatrician's she tried to make conversation, "Thank God all her shots are done. I hate to take her to the doctor by auto rickshaw or bus!"

"Learn to drive." He snapped.

"I can drive! But your parents don't let me take the car. I never go anywhere when you are not here. "In fact," she added teasingly, "I never go anywhere with you either!"

He kept his eyes on the road, a dour grimace contorting his face.

"So, how long will you be gone this time?" She asked, "I heard it from the cleaning woman. Even the maid knows more about you."

He did not reply, but swerved to the side and stopped the car.

"Get out or shut up. I've had enough of your cross questioning."

"What's wrong Manoj, can't a woman talk to her husband? You are a father now. At least take some interest in your daughter. How can you resist such a sweet baby? I know you hold a grudge against me or whatever I...I don't know what it is and you know how malicious your family can be at times, but this is your own child!"

"How dare you! My parents are not malicious. You haven't been able to endear yourself to them, to any of us, so stop flinging blame around." He roared.

"Manoj, I was just saying…"

"Get out!"

"What are you saying? How will I get home?"

"Go!" His shout so startled the baby, she bawled out loudly.

"Manoj, please, I'm sorry. Just drive, come on, and let's go home. I won't say anything, I promise. Let's just get back."

He got out of the driver's seat his face aflame, walked around to her door and opened it. "Leave quietly. He snarled, "Remember, no one insults my family."

The baby was crying inconsolably and Arti rocked her helplessly, "what are you doing Manoj, people are staring." It was a remote and desolate part of the city but there were passersby who turned around to look at them.

His enraged face was dark as thunder and he looked as if he was about to strike her. Earlier in their marriage he had hit her once and Arti had learned to recognize the fury of his temper, even to dread it. So in a sense his indifference in recent months had been quite welcome.

She got out carefully cradling the tiny child, an awkward, self-conscious hint of a smile on her face. She wished the onlookers would just disappear. "Manoj, I have no money." Within a few seconds he had driven off leaving her staring after him.

The bystanders gawked brazenly and one of two cyclists who had got down to watch, muttered, "Come with us; we'll take you wherever you want."

Arti scanned the road on either side for auto rickshaws but this was a quieter part of town and nothing ever came that way. She had no choice but to walk. Covering her sleeping child with her sari, she started to walk on the hot and dusty road, tears of humiliation stinging her eyes as she shrank from the swerving cyclists brushing close to her murmuring obscene suggestions.

She hadn't paid attention to where he was driving and had no clue where he had dropped her. She didn't even know if she was walking in the right direction but keeping the hills ahead as a point of focus she trudged along.

All she wanted was to get on to a familiar road before dark. The lonely stretch led to a tiny village which was no more than a bunch of ramshackle huts amid piles of garbage. Several dilapidated cars were being stripped by some chaps. They all stopped yanking car parts and stared as the well dressed lady with a baby plodded through.

Fetid smells of petrol fumes mingled with outpourings from wood fires and putrid vapours from open drains. A whole bunch of naked, runny-nosed kids badly in need of washing followed her in a train fascinated to see such a specimen in their midst. She got a glimpse into their sparse and pitiable "homes" as she ploughed through the over flowing gutters of waste, grime and effluence washing away from the motor car "workshop". The string of cinnamon coloured sinewy urchins turned back once the novelty of her walking single mindedly through their world wore away.

She glanced back relieved but felt afraid again. The landscape looked completely unfamiliar. All she could see were twisting lanes and a weed covered canal flowing along at a distance. She was approaching what appeared to be a respectable neighborhood. There were a few large houses, almost like mansions with big sprawling grounds, and a dog or two at the imposing wrought iron gates.

She debated whether to go in and ask for help but felt intimidated by the growling canine that each mansion boasted. Fortunately her baby seemed to enjoy the rocking and slept on peacefully. The large road narrowed into a lane lined with trees on one side and neat little houses on the other. She walked past a house with a pretty garden and portico. The living room door was open and she heard a radio or TV playing loudly. She stopped and peeped in. Would they be able to help her? She was looking in at a beautifully manicured garden with a red brick wall and bushes of multi coloured flowers thriving bravely in the heat of summer. The porch had pretty white and red wicker chairs and hanging flower baskets. Through the arched door she could see a wood paneled wall with books, bric-a-brac and china ornaments. It looked a happy place. Would they have a phone? Could she have some water? May she sit in those lovely chairs for a bit? She looked longingly into some nameless stranger's little world. What would she say? How would she explain what she was doing there? How would she pay for a taxi?

Arti wiped her brow with her sari pallu and checked on her baby, still sleeping soundly. She decided to walk on. A young couple was walking towards her. The man was carrying a small child and the lady had a bunch of wild flowers in her hands. They were the picture of blissful contentment. They looked curiously at her but she just plodded on with downcast eyes. She glanced back as they undid the gate and entered the house she had been admiring.

It was a lonely trudge and when she returned a couple of hours later, sweaty and tired with a wailing hungry baby, there was no sign of her husband or his family. It was probably tambola night at the club.

After that day she lost whatever little respect she had had for him and was certain that there never had been any feelings of love between them. After the birth, he had moved to the spare bedroom as the baby's crying disturbed him. It suited Arti fine. She felt the happiest in the company of her little girl and delighted in her every action. The baby had brought with her a new hope, immeasurable joy and new dreams.

Human nature can be incorrigibly optimistic even in the face of hopeless adversity. She used to get agitated by gossip about her husband's straying but now she just didn't care. She pretended she didn't have a husband and went about her daily chores efficiently so she could spend more time with her pretty little child. It wasn't easy to run away from her situation and though she was constantly troubled by it she foolishly waited for some unknown miracle.

Divorce was not an option she dared consider for the stigma attached to it. Knowing that she could expect issues with alimony, she was acutely aware that her parents would not be able to support her and her daughter for long. Arti was not talented, smart or beautiful and these people made her think even less of herself. She never wanted to bring disgrace to her parents and was conscious of how they had struggled to get her married and lavish her husband with gifts that they could ill afford. She often thought of how they would feel to see her treated in this sub human way." Arti stopped to clear her throat and gave Jane a fleeting look.

Jane took a deep breath, "What did your in laws expect from you?"

"I think it was all about money. At least the rest of the family would have treated me with some respect if I had come with a dowry. I am not so sure about the guy."

Jane could not help noticing she referred to him as a stranger, someone you hardly knew.

"However qualified a girl may be, her worth is still measured in monetary terms. Even respectable people need a dowry. They just don't lay it out in black and white…"

"Want to keep it legitimate?"

"Exactly."

"Why wasn't it made clear?"

"That is a bit of a mystery. I think the go-between had made us look wealthier than we were a middle class bureaucratic family of five subsisting on one man's income. Maybe the large residence and servants painted an incorrect picture. They expected a substantial dowry, large wedding and some way by which his dad could be let off for tax fraud."

"Oh gosh, because your dad was an Income Tax Commissioner!"

Arti looked circumspectly at Jane, "That would be the logical conclusion, yeah. I was what you might call, speciously attractive as a package deal. It didn't even cross their minds that they would come across an honest Income Tax commissioner who lives solely on his salary, someone as upright as my father!"

"Good God! The whole middle class affair must have come as a rude shock."

Arti glanced sidelong at Jane "A total let down. It was this huge misinterpretation. At the end they decided to vent all their anger and frustrations on me. All my flaws were highlighted and I was suddenly the unwanted commodity - the dud deal."

"They sound like a sick lot!"

"Totally! Their attitudes were crass and vulgar. I felt their disgust and revulsion seep into all our conversations and soon got tired of trying to please anybody. Nobody ever complimented my cooking, though they ate heartily. I was mostly invisible. My brother in law had a habit of sniffing the air whenever I was near and derisively enquire, "What's that stink?" And then everyone would chuckle. He was so insolent it made me long to slap him hard."

"What a loser!" Jane spat out.

Arti nodded in agreement. "It was my duty to hang around during meals leaping to hand out hot chapattis when anybody finished. My brother in law routinely rejected chapattis offered by me and somebody had to take them from me and pass them to him. I remember one day he angrily walked away from breakfast because I'd forgotten to put green chilies in his omelets." She looked at Jane wide eyed, "And no one said a word to him. Can you beat that?"

A seething Jane queried angrily, "Arti at what point did you begin to assert yourself? Please tell me this ends well."

"Quite well, actually you might be surprised how like you I acted!"

Jane looked up at her with glowering eyes brimming with angry tears. "Boy what a sucker! I would have credited you with more gumption. So the Master's in psychology had taught you zilch"

"They were terrible circumstances Jane. I was scared they'd send me packing. In fact I think that was the plan."

"To make life hell for you and force to you to run away?"

"Something like that. Thing is, I had nowhere to go! If I returned home my parents would be the butt of social ostracism and they believed back then that they couldn't possibly have got my sisters married." As a clearly infuriated Jane clicked her tongue impatiently, Arti continued, "Besides they just didn't have the resources to help raise my child. Government employees have all those frills but live hand to mouth."

"What" Jane's indignation was palpable as she spoke through clenched teeth, "about your own capability?"

"I'm coming to that Jane, don't get so angry. I was always, as you know a nervous sort of person, not very confident or smart and certainly not good looking. You know unlike you girls with the unique personalities. Well I had started wondering not so much about my own but about little Diya's future. I couldn't bear raise my child in such a suppressed, unstimulating environment. I wanted to give her a well rounded upbringing.

As my little one grew, I began making enquiries about a nursery school close by because I felt a little social contact was necessary for my child. It being a cantonment, the only good schools were those for children of defence personnel.

"You can still fill out an application, but we don't guarantee admission" the lady told me.

I went home and told my mother in law, "It's either the army school or the local municipal school,"

"There are two more years to worry about all that. Anyway how much education do girls need?" The woman had replied casually but I recognised the slight was a hit at my own post grad education. I had to resignedly accept the woman wasn't entirely incorrect. After all, at that point my qualification was worthless.

Mind numbingly humdrum housework and taking care of my child occupied much of my day, but it didn't stop me from fantasising about my child's future. In my daydreams my baby was always the smartest kid in class, a high achiever, an all rounder with a flair for writing, painting or swimming. In the future I saw her growing up into a gorgeous young lady with a magnetic personality and a phenomenal career. I think we always want more for our kids than we have had!"

Arti sighed, "Anyway, to continue Arti's story," she turned to Jane, "I barely recognise that Arti anymore! Is it weird that I'm telling you her story like she's somebody else?"

Jane considered. She cocked her head to one side and shook it, "No. It's your story; tell it the way you like!"

Arti smiled. "Okay, here goes. It was pretty much her little girl and Arti who lived in a small private world by themselves. The guy had practically no contact with them. He had an escape route. He went off every few months on contacted work to the Middle East. But when he returned there she was like a constant thorn in his side with her gloomy face and lackluster style of dressing.

She bored him. He was long gone emotionally and physically and what was left of her was a dull unimaginative killjoy. More of an albatross around his neck inducing him into an unfamiliar state of depression He had been accustomed to the vivacious crowd at the club. This one had no personality. Nobody gave her a second look unlike some of the glamorous girls he had usually dated. This woman didn't enjoy dancing, shrank from having a drink, dressed about ten years older than her age and was constantly scowling or looking sad. Maybe they were not compatible; maybe there were issues with his parents but he really couldn't be bothered. He just didn't like being married, period. It was claustrophobic and restricting and he decided that he wanted out. The child was a complication and in his mind, his greatest regret.

Jane narrowed her eyes and screwed her face up.

"Another old habit" Arti smiled.

"What?" Jane untwisted her face.

"That scowling thing you do when you're sorting things out ...you know!"

Jane stared at her companion's flushed face and shining eyes. "Concentrating?"

"Yes!"

"That's an old habit. It's a subconscious sort of tic. My face gets all contorted when I'm thinking hard and I never even realized it till I happened to catch a glimpse in a mirror! I must look horrible!"

"Uh huh, not really and it's not a tic! Anyway it's cute."

"So continue and don't keep getting distracted."

"Arti had started looking for ways to make a good life for her child. One particular day an opportunity presented itself and really, if she hadn't taken it, she'd have been pretty much stuck where she was in that awful hole of a place.

That afternoon as she served lunch to her father in law, her husband strode in and pulled up a chair. She offered to get him a plate but he waved away the suggestion with "I ate already." She had observed he had been in an exceptionally rotten frame of mind for a few days.

He addressed his father brusquely, "Where is the cash that I had given you to keep?"

"What?" His father looked puzzled.

"Don't you remember the money I had given you? It was in dollars. How could you forget?"

Arti ate quietly anticipating yet another showdown between father and son. They had become quite frequent lately. She examined her food moodily. There would be yelling and shouting, one would win and the other would storm out. Either way, they'd look at her as if she were a sewer rat. It was of no consequence to her personally but she couldn't help overhearing.

"The money that you had brought years and years back?" Her father in law looked surprised that anyone could be asking for something from so long ago.

Her husband looked as if he were about to burst. He took a deep breath, "I gave it to you last year. I want it. You couldn't have spent it. It was all foreign currency. Where did you put it?" He yelled desperately.

"Oh, yes. There were dollars weren't they? I remember now. You have put it all in the sweet tin. You know the turquoise blue tin with gold etching and a round knob at the top?" The old man gestured a screw top looking up at his son hopefully.

"Dad I do not think I would have put cash in some rusty old sweet tin. It was in packets fixed with rubber band and I had written the amounts on each packet. Please try and remember, it was a lot of money!" At the end of his tether he grabbed the elderly man's shoulder and pressed it unkindly.

"Not thousands?" The old man peered up at his son chomping with his clicking dentures.

Arti made a swift sidelong glance to see if anyone was watching her, but both the men were fully occupied in the seemingly fruitless dialogue. She debated whether or not to say something. Her eyes narrowed ponderingly.

Steadily crunching a mouthful of roasted papads she decided that it might be worth her while to pay a little attention.

"Yes, Yes!" her husband talked to the old man as if he were trying to talk to a very small child or a demented person, "yes it was in the thousands and at today's rate, it would be in the lakhs, I need you to find it now."

The old man looked about the table and paused to stare as if the chutney was particularly interesting. He chuckled wickedly and sized up his son. "You in financial trouble?" Then he sobered up and asked his son severely, "Where is that blue and gold toffee tin?"

"Dad we store some locks and keys not cash in that old blue tin."

The old man shook his head and stared dreamily ahead of him, "No not that one. That was the old tea tin. Don't you remember that other one, it had gold etching and it was blue. Yes, I'm sure it was blue. Prabha had brought it for us in 1959 as a present. He focused on the rice plate and smiled benignly, "How sweet of her."

Her husband gave up. He rose looking disgustedly at his father, "Let me know if anything comes to you." He did not even glance at her as he strode out.

She sat watching her father in law through lowered eyes, her mind in a whirr. She saw that the old man made perfect sense to himself. He rose muttering "1959 or was it earlier?" He walked away temporarily displaced somewhere in time and space.

She looked at the checkered tablecloth and chomped on her food reflecting on the latest father-son exchange.

The entire family was going to Mumbai for chacha's daughter's wedding. As usual, she was to stay back as they never left the house empty. She was accustomed to that and quite welcomed the prospect of a bit of peace.

"Don't worry, you won't be alone. Bai's brother Kashiram will arrive by dinner and remain here till our return" Her mother in law assured her. That wasn't welcome news. Arti hated the chap. She thought him lecherous, gross and altogether repulsive. He leered at her in a most obnoxious manner and Arti had come to despise his regular visits. She often tried to tell her in laws that she would be just fine with the maid but they believed it was important to have a male presence in the rambling house.

As she watched the wedding party prepare to leave, Arti moved restlessly from room to room trying to help with the packing and organizing meals for them to carry. Her in laws never liked to buy food on a train and she handed them a picnic basket large enough to feed an army. She kept an impatient lookout for the taxi and could hardly wait for them to go.

She knew where the blue sweet tin with gold etching was.

As soon as their car was out of sight she locked up and gently encouraged Bai to take a nap. She sat in the living room reading a 12-year-old edition of Reader's Digest till the old hag's snores rang out and then moved swiftly to her bedroom locking the door.

She dropped to the ground by her bed. There were about five or six ancient steel trunks under the bed. Each held stuff from her husband's childhood including old woolen clothes, albums, toys and books. She stretched her arm out as far as it would go reaching for the green painted one, but it was just a little out of reach. She pulled herself out and looked around for a stick. She reached out for an old umbrella with an extra long curved handle. This would do the trick. She lay flat on the cool floor and pushed. The umbrella handle hooked into the trunk and it moved grudgingly sending a fat lizard scuttling across the floor. She winced as the hideous creature sought refuge under the other trunks. She gave the heavy box a quick strong tug. Out it came screeching against the marble mosaic. She looked up to the bed to see if she had woken the baby, but the tiny figure slept soundly in the heat of the summer afternoon. The rusty lid lifted grudgingly with a loud crack as the metal top opened to reveal treasures from a young boy's childhood. She pulled away the cloth covering to expose piles of comics, Biggles and Billy Bunter books and stamp albums. Under an Ovaltine tin filled with a coin collection, she saw the toffee canister.

It was scratched and dented and may have been turquoise once with gold etching around the borders. It looked tarnished and discoloured, much like everything else in the trunk. She gingerly lifted the rusty tin pushing much of the other stuff out higgledy piggledy. It felt heavy.

The tin stood on the mosaic tiled floor with its cover firmly pushed down. The lid took a mound-like shape and was topped by a white ball for a knob. Once it had boasted a gorgeous pattern depicting sea routes of explorers, the outlines of the continents marked in gold. Once it had held an assortment of delectable confection in shiny, jewel coloured wrappers. What did it have to offer today? Arti's heart was racing. It definitely fit the description that the old man had been talking about, but was it the right one? The lid was jammed and unyielding. She yanked firmly at the knob and it broke away from a corroded puncture.

Arti sighed. She looked around for something to prise it open with. She went to her dresser drawer and rummaged about. She found a nail clipper and pulled open its file. It fit right into the groove and she pried the rusty lid off. She peered into the dark cavity. It was stuffed with bundles of bank notes. With trembling hands she lifted out a wad of notes held by a dry, old rubber band. She tried to ease it off but it crumbled in her hands. She gazed at the cash inside the toffee tin. How much would it be worth? Arti had never seen, let alone held such a colossal amount of money! She pulled out the bundles awestruck. This would take some examining. She placed the tin on the bed and meticulously packing away the contents of the trunk thrust it back under the cot. On the bed, she drew her legs up, her arms cradling her chin as she stared intently at the blue and gold tin holding the elusive treasure.

Her mind flashed back to the three years she had lived in the mansion. From the day she arrived as a bride to this day she had been placed on a regular "allowance" of Rs. 15 per month. It became obvious to her that except for the shell of a house, they had nothing. Her in laws depended entirely on their sons' earnings and were therefore clearly disappointed at her arrival with absolutely no dowry. She had wondered what became of the money she had brought with her in a banker's draft from her salary account, but never got any proper answers and finally tired of asking.

All her attempts to ingratiate herself had met with such unreceptive hostility that after a few months she just gave up. She knew she would have to live with the taunts and abuses as there was no turning back. Three months pregnant, she had watched helplessly as her husband's sister was married in her gold ornaments. As she bade her farewell, she cried softly wishing her better luck with them.

Things only got worse as her husband seemed to be spending more than he earned. He was also spending much more time away from home and she dared not speculate on the "where" and "who with" questions. Deep down she had the answers. She had hoped that with the arrival of the baby, things would improve between them. Luck was definitely not with her. They still looked at her as if she were a smelly slug. The adorable little bundle that made her heart sing with joy was given an icy welcome.

"I knew it would be a girl. She has three sisters, what else can we expect?"

For the first time Arti felt a gnawing loathing for her husband's parents. It was no longer about how they behaved with her. She couldn't bear the idea of anyone being cruel to her baby. For her it was hard to believe such unfeeling people existed. Given her husband's aloofness, she used to feel a sense of immense relief when he went away for months on end to his job in the Middle East.

Here in this bedroom with her little princess, she found bliss.

She lay down staring at the tin as she fondled her sleeping baby's soft curls. In her empty life there had always been a hope that someday, by an extraordinary stroke of luck, things would change her little girl's destiny. She would spend hours ruminating about the future of her baby girl. Would she also live this meaningless existence and be married off some day into a loveless sham of a marriage? Not if Arti could help it. She was determined to get her daughter every possible opportunity. But the sad truth was that Arti completely lacked in drive.

Her little one awoke and turned to look into her mother's eyes. She smiled. "Hi sweetie! Slept well?"

"Lolly?" The child had started forming small sentences and Arti loved to hear her talk.

She pointed to the pillow. "There's your dolly!"

The little girl smiled and gently lifted her doll into her arms. Arti loved the child's quiet and tender ways.

She packed away the cash pushing it to the deep recesses of her wardrobe. She smiled at her little one combing out her doll's golden hair. Her endearing and gentle presence brought a sweet calmness to Arti's troubled mind

The next three days would be easy. The maid usually cooked for herself and Arti just ate soft rice and dhal with her baby. She thought she would let the little one play extra long in the park for the next three evenings as no one would be waiting for their meals, hot water foot soaks, or their oil massages! She settled back with a smile. Three days of freedom!

There was a rattling at her bedroom window. She turned around to see a brown face with a hideous grin leering at her.

"Open the door, I am here!"

FOUR

Kashiram! She had forgotten about him. How long had he been staring at her? She rushed to open the door.

Luckily Bai had also awoken by the noise. She took him into her room at the back of the house. Kashiram looked rather pleased with himself and asked how long everybody was going to be away.

"They will return on Tuesday, but you don't have to stay beyond the weekend." Arti said to the disgusting little gnome of a chap.

"No, no, I'll stay as long as you need," he drawled, "I like being here."

A familiar shudder crawled up her spine and as always, Arti felt utterly repulsed by the disgusting fellow. She turned to her room planning to dress her baby and take her for a longish outing when Bai called out to her retreating back, "Please cook for my brother when you do for yourself. I have a sore hand."

Bai and her mysterious sore hands that always surfaced when there was work to be done!

"Let him eat this morning's leftovers." Arti replied rudely and slammed her door shut. She could just imagine the look on Bai's face and the dramatic recount that her mother in law would be served up, but somehow, right then, she just didn't care.

It looked to be a warm evening. She dressed her baby in a frilly summer frock and tied her hair in curly pigtails. Just as she was about to call out to the maid to come lockup, she noticed some activity in her in-laws' room across the spacious living room. From where she stood she could see indistinctly through the partially drawn curtains. Kashiram was turning up the mattresses and feeling under each one. She stepped back, afraid that he might see her but he was too engrossed in pulling out something from under the mattresses and stuffing his pockets. Arti stood rooted to the ground. What was he doing! She debated whether to watch quietly or just walk in and surprise him. Suddenly the silence was shattered by Bai's shouts summoning her brother to the outhouse.

Arti briskly stepped backwards and came walking out as if she had just left her room.

Peering into her handbag she addressed the rascal, "Kashiram, please tell Bai I have taken the baby out."

"Sure" He helpfully reached out to get the front door, roughly rubbing the back of his hand against her bosom as she bent to clutch her daughter's hand. She recoiled and turned to glare at him, but he smoothly placed his hand on her back and pressed ever so slightly. With a hideous leer through ugly paan-stained teeth he waved cheerily to the little girl. Arti rushed out, her face flushed hot and red at the deliberate hint of molestation.

The scheming swindler! He was not above taking brazen liberties, either with her or the family funds. She wondered if he would have felt any shame if she had walked in on him rifling through her father in law's things! She knew the family trusted him implicitly and it annoyed her how the revolting guy strode about with a nonchalantly powerful air about him.

She shivered involuntarily on that warm summer's evening at the memory of his loathsome caress. As she walked away, she sensed his eyes boring into her. She thought it best to keep walking, thanking her lucky stars she had locked away the toffee tin in her "Godrej" almirah. It was most unlikely that he would go exploring her room. He knew she had no money or jewels.

Seated on the park bench, she watched her little angel playing in the sand with the other kids. Arti's mind was abuzz. What she had accidentally witnessed was unimaginable. The family trusted this guy enough to leave the place in his care! In fact they trusted him more than they did her and he was nothing but a lecherous lowlife, a fraudster, and a thief!

She imagined how she would enjoy exposing him to everyone. Finally, a way to avoid having the scoundrel landing on their doorstep every now and then! But, what would she say? Would they believe her? What if they didn't? He would come on to her ten times worse after that. He didn't just creep her out, he actually scared her little and she always locked her door whenever he blew in as acting caretaker. And now she could expose him for what he really was! The idea thrilled her but she quickly sobered up. "He is no pushover." She said to herself. This required careful deliberation.

That night she hurried with dinner and took the baby away to their bedroom. There was no sign of Kashiram. She bathed the little girl, dressed her in her night dress and tucked her in carefully positioning the mosquito netting over the bed. She dimmed the lights and settled down in the armchair for her nightly read. Baby had had a tiring evening and fell asleep almost instantly. Arti firmly shut the windows and drew the blinds.

She usually brought the newspapers in to read after everyone else had finished. They lay unopened on her lap. The blue and gold box surfaced again in her thoughts. She opened her "Godrej" and extricated the hidden treasure from under stacks of clothes. She sat staring at the wealth, mere pieces of paper but cashable, like a blank cheque. A quick glance through the day's newspapers confirmed her belief that she was holding a small fortune. After all, the most money she had handled in that place was the Rs. 15 monthly allowance. This was perhaps a few thousand times as much! She shivered involuntarily.

It was surreal! She could hardly believe the bountiful cache lying before her! This could solve all her in laws' cash problems! No wonder her husband was going ballistic looking for it! Would this bail him out? She arranged and rearranged the bundles of currency piling them into different shapes. She stacked them into a little hut with a sloping roof. She had had so little in life that she had hardly any awareness of the real value of the money she held. Would it make her husband debt free? Would they be able to fix the leaks in the house? Would he be happy that she found the money for him? It may not elevate her status but perhaps, a little gratitude? She screwed up her nose and scowled. She seriously doubted that. After all it was his money. She only found it.

Arti let herself drop into her favourite pastime - daydreaming.

What could this stash buy? A good education for her child? A place to stay? Would it buy her freedom from this hole of a house, and from its whacko occupants? She toyed with the prospect of never having to see any of them again. That sounded too good to be true. Arti knew she didn't have that kind of courage.

Years of disciplined upbringing had taught her one thing, never covet what is not yours. Obviously she must keep the box safely away and hand it over when they returned.

A voice inside of her repeated, "Finders keepers!!" and another yelled, "It's not yours. This guy is in some financial trouble. He needs it. It is his hard earned money."

She settled in the armchair to read but couldn't concentrate. Her thoughts came racing back to the recent unearthing. Not daring to allow her mind to wander in forbidden territory Arti opened the magazine's well-liked "Laughter Is the Best Medicine' section.

There was a soft knock on her door. She hurriedly packed away the toffee tin and came to the door. "Who is it?"

"Arti bai, it's me."

Kashiram, so late at night?

"What is it?" She asked wrapping her robe around her tightly, "Baby is sleeping".

"Bai is unwell. She needs… can you open the door?"

"What happened to her?"

"Open the door!" His voice changed from a whisper to a command. "I said open the door!" His fists banged against the rickety door.

She stood rooted to the ground. She could tell that his face was pressed against the door and he was inches from her. She looked up at the rattling bolt that latched the bedroom door. If he shook the door vigorously, it would slide down. She was terrified.

She heard the shuffle of feet. "Come on Arti" His voice was slurred. The bastard was drunk.

Arti pressed her body against the door and swiftly shot the other two bolts that fell into holes in the ground. That should hold it in place.

"I just want to tell you something."

Shaking like a leaf she held her breath and stood watching the door as he shoved against it. He can't come in, he just can't.

She heard Bai's sliding, shuffling walk in the hallway. There was a muffled exchange. She heard the woman's voice telling him to go to bed. He muttered something incomprehensible and Arti heard the two voices argue, his adamant and sputtering, hers cajoling. A few harrowing minutes later she heard them walk away.

Arti crashed to the ground bathed in sweat. Just the notion that this lecher believed he could enter her bedroom left her shaking. Her legs barely held her up. Suppressing her sobs she returned to the bed and checked on her little one. She was stirring uneasily and raised her curly head squinting in the lamplight. Arti softly patted her as she fell back to sleep. She lay there watching the baby's steady breathing, drawing solace from the serenity.

Kashiram's loathsome face haunted her. A part of her howled, "I am going out of my mind. What am I doing in a place where I am so unwanted?"

Why would her in laws defend her against a servant when they didn't even chide their adult son for his repeated misdemeanor? Kashiram's duplicity ran deep. She knew everyone trusted him and held him in high esteem and why not? He was the picture of humility and decency before them.

His eyes would obscenely follow her around wherever she went. Trembling she recalled an ugly encounter earlier that summer which hauntingly replayed itself in her mind.

One afternoon when the household was asleep, Arti heard loud winds and the rumble of thunder. She smelt the dust that usually preceded a thunderstorm and ran up to the terrace to collect the washing. Strong winds blew dust into her eyes as she unpegged the clothes briskly. Ominous black clouds came rolling across the skies and big blobs of rain fell on her. As she hurriedly forced shut the terrace door against strong tearing winds, partially blinded by the huge pile of starched saris and bulky towels, she felt strong arms engulf her feeling around her bosom while a finger pushed its way where she never dreamed anyone would touch her. She gave a muffled shriek and leapt away.

She had a hazy recollection of how she pushed him aside and stumbled down the ancient spiral staircase. Shaking and sobbing she had fallen on her bed distressed, sullied and defenseless."

Arti turned tearful eyes to Jane, "How stupid was I! I thought he was trying to help me with the washing!"

Overcome by powerful emotions, Arti buried her face in her blanket sobbing. Jane put an arm around her. "Why did you keep it to yourself? Are you insane? Somebody would have done something! They couldn't be that unfeeling and merciless."

Arti nodded. "They were odious. Besides, remember they wanted me out anyway. This would have been the perfect pretext."

"But that's preposterous!" Jane retorted in a loud angry whisper. She looked into her friend's face and asked her kindly, "are you alright? Do you want to stop? Is it too painful? Just a minute." Jane got up and made her way down to the galley. Arti wiped her eyes and looked out at the night sky thankful that everyone was either asleep or focused on watching TV in the dim cabin.

Jane teetered back with two cups of coffee. "Here," she placed the cups on Arti's tray table, "and I have some more treats. Just a minute." She turned around and picked up a blanket that had slipped off a sleeping child across the aisle. Gently tucking it in, she slipped back into her seat. She cast a quick glance across. The tired mother was sound asleep and the child now quite cosy. She yanked bars of chocolate from her pocket. "Candy! Guaranteed to make the boohoos vanish." She said as if addressing a small child.

Arti composed herself. "I'm fine. This should be therapeutic since I never did get a chance to share it with anyone. Not in such detail. Never. Anyway, back to my blue and gold sweet tin!" She sipped the warm beverage and stripped the shiny wrapper off a chocolate.

"Arti's mind was in turmoil ever since she had found the tin and she barely got any sleep that night. When she awoke the next morning she lay in bed absently ruffling her little girl's curls and pressing up close to her warm soft body. She turned over the events of the previous day in her mind. She debated whether to get up and go to the kitchen or wait to hear Bai's movements around and about the huge mansion before emerging from her room. On no account did she want to run into the rogue.

A rustling crackle made her sit up. Some feathers floated down with a bit of hay and landed softly on the canopy of their mosquito netting. She looked up. High up at the top of the lofty tapering ceiling a trapped bird was fluttering frantically. It flew in a chaotic orbit repeatedly crashing into the glass ventilator. If it flew a little lower it got buffeted by the blades of the fan. Arti sat up watching the desperate, frenzied struggle. When did the little creature come in? She wondered. It had probably slipped in the previous evening. She winced each time the bird flew around the room and smashed against the little ventilator getting more and more desperate. There was no way of releasing the catch on those high ventilators so far up. The little bird flung itself again against the murky glass.

With her eyes following the little creature, Arti slid out of bed, briskly turned the fan off and opened the large bay window. She peered out onto the large veranda and the expanse of green lawn as if expecting Kashiram to pop up from behind a bush. Picking up a towel, she started swinging it around so the bird might sense the open window below and get out. It was perched on a beam gauging the situation. Arti sat down very still so as to not scare it and watched cautiously. The little creature cocked its tiny head to one side and fluffed out its wings as Arti peered anxiously at it.

A rattling at her door startled her. She rushed to crack open it. Bai was waiting with a tray of tea! She could hardly believe her eyes. Bai, who had always treated her like a pariah dog was bringing her morning tea! She opened the door carefully checking over the woman's shoulder.

"Sorry I overslept" she apologized taking the tea tray from the maid.

The open door provided an escape for her hostage and it whizzed out over their heads dropping a few bits of grass on Arti.

She sat down and started mixing sugar in her tea. The maid came in hesitantly.

"Yes?"

"Please don't tell anyone about Kashiram last night. Those fellows from the village came and took him with them last evening and then they made him drink. Otherwise my brother is not like that."

Barely acknowledging the cover up, Arti said, "I have some letters to post today, so I will probably go out after breakfast."

"What time?"

"Why?" Arti looked up over her cup.

"No it's nothing. Kashiram was going to take me to the shops this morning. I was planning to tell you last night."

"It's okay, you can go."

"And your letters?"

"They can go later, there's no hurry. You go."

"Shall I make some lunch for you?"

Arti nearly choked on her swallow of tea.

"You? No thanks I will make something for baby and me."

The old maid had long enjoyed lording it over Arti. In that entrenched hierarchy the lowest rung had been reserved exclusively for the maid but with Arti's arrival she got an opportunity elevate herself quite sure that Arti had nobody to take up cudgels for her.

She hesitated. "I think we may be gone the whole day. We wanted to go and visit my uncle in the next village."

"No problem. Take your time." Arti said calmly.

The woman stood looking around uncertainly.

Arti looked at her quizzically. Surely she didn't expect her to have any cash to spare.

"You won't tell anyone about last night?"

Arti placed her teacup on the tray and looked squarely into the woman's face. "If you want to go, you should start getting ready."

With Bai and Kashiram gone, she felt free to mull over the strange events of the previous day. She sat on the verandah outside watching her baby blow soap bubbles and chase them, her tinkling laughter ringing true in the soft morning sunlight. Arti couldn't help giggling with her little girl and she decided to stay there and enjoy the quiet while the nasty duo was out. It was a slightly overcast day with a lovely cool breeze. The sun peeped out now and then from behind feathery clouds. Sweet air from the rajnigandha wafted over the mother and daughter. The amazing and a little scary turn of events flashed through her mind. She sat in disbelief thinking about the stash uncovered the previous day. She wondered about the reaction, if any, she might get from her husband. At least it would help ease some of his financial burden. Would it herald any changes at all for her or her baby? She doubted it.

She thought she was subconsciously putting something out of her mind; something troubling. Her mind returned to the rogue stealing from the mattress in her in law's room. Her eyes narrowed. Was there really something in the bed? In a flash she was in the old people's room feeling around under the bedding.

The cotton wool filled mattresses had seen better days. They were flat and lumpy.

She remembered how in their childhood, the man would come to their house at the start of winter and spin the cotton wool to make it all fluffy. He filled each quilt and stitched it up again. As small girls she and her sisters used to love to fling themselves into the mounds of cotton wool. Her mind generated patchy images from the past. They were happy. Not rich or poor, just happy, it was the kind of happiness that had little to do with riches or status, just simple contentment.

For the thousandth time she asked herself why her parents had acted so rashly on the most important decision of her life.

She brushed away tears and peered beneath the mattress she had lifted. There were a number of mattresses on the beds and there was money under each one! Thousands of Rupees! She stared at the bundles of notes. Amazing! Wealth was creeping out of the woodwork today! She chuckled, barely comprehending the surreal turn of events. For years she had hardly touched any money and in the passage of barely a day, she was holding tens of thousands and yet, none of it hers to use. She let drop the heavy mattress and straightened out the bedspread. Leaving everything exactly as it was, she slipped out of the bedroom. So, the old man had plenty of money!

On the verandah, rainbows were dropping on her beautiful child. Those bubbles were strong and light! She sat watching the cherub prance about amid tinkling laughter, cooing and gurgling in perfect happiness! Again her thoughts went rushing back to her girlhood back when walking in the rain, splashing in muddy puddles and gazing at rainbows in oil slicks were life's true pleasures!

Arti sat staring at the pretty picture. Her mind had been inundated with a flood of ideas, some quite outlandish. Could this be an escape route? Maybe this was what destiny wanted for her.

Sometimes, you have to grab with both hands whatever opportunity comes your way or the moment is lost forever. She thought back to the day her parents were finalizing her marriage. She had gone into her room and looked out of the window, watching her would-be in-laws leave. She didn't see herself belong to that lot. There was an uneasy aching inside of her and her hands and feet trembled at the idea of going to live with them. When her mother came in to congratulate her, her throat went dry with fear. She said, "That guy didn't say a word to me", she swallowed, "I don't know him at all!"

"In arranged marriages, no one knows their husband before marriage. Once you are married, everything will be alright." Her mother brushed away all her protestations with the same standard phrase.

"If only I had put my foot down and said a firm no." She had repeated the sentence over and over again thousands of times after that.

Never a strong person, Arti recognized that motherhood had further weakened her and made her ineffective. But for the little one, she would have walked out of the tyrannical household long ago. In fact, she suspected that it was probably what they expected her to do anyway, but she had stuck it out. She had learned to accept that nothing would change.

Arti sighed as stirred together dhal and rice for herself and her daughter. She sat on the swing in the cool breeze and fed her baby. It started drizzling, the rain making dark brown pools in the dry earth. The smell of rain on dry soil lifted her spirits. The garden looked fresh and clean. It was like looking at the landscape after wiping the dust off your glasses. She smiled lazily. No Bai, no demanding family. The smile soon vanished from her face. They would be back tomorrow. Arti scowled. She was tired of being looked at as if she were a worm. Her worthlessness and inadequacy frustrated her, but what could she do? Not doing anything would probably mean living on in this meaningless existence trapped like the bird she had released that morning.

She looked around uneasily. The cloudburst gave over and blue skies peeped out from above the floating grey masses. Bright sunrays pierced the firmament casting a golden veil all about her. Arti took a deep breath.

She could see clearly. It all became obvious. Everything looked clear. In an insane world it was the sanest option. She made the decision that would mark the rest of Diya's life. She could give her child the life that she had promised herself she would.

Would anyone find her? Never! Because they wouldn't even bother looking, because they wouldn't want to answer to her parents, because the chap she was married to couldn't give a fig, because she could easily be replaced by a couple of maids...

Most importantly because nobody knew that she had found the toffee tin.

Arti had never moved faster. She was like a woman possessed. With her heart rattling in her chest, she put through a call to her dear friend Asha in Delhi asking to shack up with her for a few days. She rang the station for tickets and threw their things into a suitcase. She deliberated whether she should leave a note. Should she leave the empty tin?

No. Take it all!

She opened the wrought iron gates and crossed the lane. Carrying the baby, she dragged her suitcases with one hand across the small road. On shaky legs she stood hoping for an auto rickshaw to come by on that sleepy afternoon. That could be the only spoke in the wheel to making good her escape. It wasn't a long way to the station but quite impossible to walk in the summer heat with a baby and bags.

Clutching the child's tiny hand, she stood under a canopy of hanging bougainvillea, her two suitcases at her feet. Arti licked her dry lips and looked down the dusty, lonely street mirages rising from it in the intense summer heat. She glanced at her watch impatiently. The station master was going to hold her tickets for just fifteen more minutes.

Her heart beat quickened. From the opposite side, an auto rickshaw seemed to be coming their way kicking up clouds of dust and smoke. Arti swallowed. Could it be Bai and her brother? Her eyes squinted as she peered out on the sun flecked street. It appeared as if there was just one passenger. How far were they going? Would he turn around in time? As it approached, she saw the driver peering out. He was an outsider who had driven up from the next village to drop old Mrs. Daruwallah's sister. She shouted to him to come right back and he nodded in assent. He looked pleased at the prospect of a passenger with baggage.

The railway station seemed to move further as the rickshaw lumbered along, hissing and spitting on the dusty track. She had to make it! "Can it go any faster?" Her voice trembled.

"It was fine and now I don't know what has happened."

The driver turned to look at her and loosened his grip. The vehicle slowed down even more.

"Ok! Ok! Just keep driving."

A quick check of the watch told her she had less than 5 minutes. The station was right up ahead. She could see it. If only he would move a little faster and if she could only get a coolie to run with her bag to the platform across!

The auto rickshaw spluttered with a gush of gassy fumes and came to a rickety halt. The driver stepped out looking puzzled.

"Please do something. I'll miss my train."

With a screaming whistle a train came chugging in to the station. The young man looked towards it and then at his passenger's terrified face. In one swoop he picked her bags and made a dash towards the station.

"Chalo!" (come on) I will reach you there in a minute."

Arti swung the baby on her shoulders and scuttled clumsily behind the sprightly man. He shouted to another coolie asking about her train. The man slapped his hand to his forehead and barked out pointed in the direction of the receding train. The driver put her bags down and thumped his fist into an open palm. Arti loped up breathlessly, "What?"

"Gone." He saw despair writ large. The woman looked as if she was about to cry.

"What shall I do now? What can I do now?" her hysterical raspy shouts disturbed him. He felt it was somehow his fault. He looked about him. The fat station master strolled up with the content air of a man who had satisfactorily concluded the major event of the day.

"Let us talk to him."

"What's the use?" Arti yelled in a panicky cry. "There was just one train."

The driver had accosted the station master who took in the situation contentedly chewing paan. He longed to get back to his cool office, slouch in his chair and daydream. Hadn't he done his duty for the day? His job obviously agreed with him. The buttons on his uniform were bursting and his tie in a cheeky defiance of gravity fell from the knot at his neck, travelled over the curvature of his rotund stomach and stuck out at the widest part. He sized up the woman and child and sticking his lower jaw out asked, "Dilli?"

"Delhi, yes." Arti looked hopefully at him. Was there any way she could catch up with the train? Was there anything he could do for her? She swallowed her dry itchy throat as she looked nervously at the portly figure. The rickshaw driver looked at the two faces without much hope.

This whole episode had lost its excitement. He was beginning to get edgy. He had to resuscitate his lifeless engine head back into town and snare some evening passengers.

"You are very lucky. The station master announced impassively through "paan" (beetle leaf) drenched lips. This morning's Frontier Mail is running late. It should be here soon. He sprayed a red torrent of betel nut juice into a corner patterned in all shades of red from years of spit. Wiping his lips with a large kerchief he rolled to his office. He looked down at the tickets in her trembling fingers and declared sadly, "These tickets are gone. You have to buy new tickets."

"It's okay!" Arti's eyes shone as she reached into her bag and spied a long navy coloured train snaking its way towards the station. She chivied him about like a clucking hen while he proceeded to fill out laborious paperwork to procure the tickets all along promising that the train would not leave till she was on board.

"It is already twelve hours late," he lamented. Arti saw that moroseness was an embedded facet in his persona as was sluggishness. He rummaged around for a rubber stamp that was clearly visible on his cluttered desk. She wanted to scream in aggravation but calmly reached out and handed it to him. He finished the process of issuing her the tickets and drummed his podgy fingers on the table as he regarded them with satisfaction. The only hint of a smile she saw was when she handed him a generous tip with her payment.

She sat waiting for the train to start, chilling thoughts plaguing her mind. What if Bai came home early and found her gone? What if she sent out Kashiram to the station? What if someone recognised her and called at the house?

She prayed for the train to start soon. On the platform there were a few familiar faces. Faces she knew, but to whom she was a non-entity. Most of them were army wives and families. She recognised the kids from the park. There was a slim chance that any of them would know her, if they did, they would probably mistake her for little Diya's ayah. Arti glanced nervously at her watch, a few more minutes. She kept her head bowed as she sat by the window playing with her child. Diya too gazed around curiously, never having been on a train or even to the station. She looked up at her mother and smiled, pointing to a puppy on a leash that some people seeing off their family had brought along. Arti gave a little laugh and cuddled her, an unfamiliar thrill shooting through.

Vendors selling nuts in paper cones sauntered through the vestibule chanting crude jingles. Beggars walked past peering in through the darkened glass of the air conditioned coaches hoping for alms. A transistor droned cricket commentary while another belted out popular Bollywood music. Arti felt as if she were about to burst. She rubbed her hands together apprehensively and placing the little one on the berth, carefully latched the coupe door as if that would have prevented anyone from finding her if there ever were any intention.

After what seemed like eternity, the train lazily awoke to life and gradually chugged out of the station. Her heart sang out as she prepared to settle in for the long journey, escaping from her worse than death captivity!"

Arti took a deep breath and turned to look into her friend's face.

Jane listening in rapt wonderment took a moment to realize Arti had stopped speaking.

Arti brushed away tears and turned to the porthole. Recounting the details of her escape disturbed her even so many years later.

"Bravo! Good Job!" Jane patted the shaking Arti.

"It was the hugest thing I ever did in my entire life!" Arti accepted tissues from Jane and dabbed her eyes looking fervently at Jane, "Also the worst!"

"I disagree but first get a hold of yourself. It might help if you could remember the incident without reliving it."

Arti smiled through her tears, "I raised my little girl well. I exposed her to a myriad of interesting activities. I wanted to give it all to her and I did! She seized every possible opportunity I could afford. She read voraciously, travelled, went to shows, dabbled in theater understood and learned music, appreciated the cinema and studied well!"

Jane drained her cup and turned to look at Arti staring at a metamorphosis so complete it appeared contrived. "And look at how well she's turned out! You make me so proud Arti! It couldn't have been easy on that small income of a nursery school teacher I am sure. You could be a beacon for other hapless victims. I should have you address the battered women in my charity! You're quite an inspiration."

"But didn't I do the wrong thing? I paid them back of course."

"Why?" Jane asked in a loud, hoarse whisper, "Why on earth? I wouldn't have given them a cent! Heck they took away all your earnings, your gold, not to mention your own self respect and dignity. Who puts a daughter in law on a fifteen Rupee allowance for heaven's sakes?" She turned to Arti, fuming. "That was a real bad lot and you should have sued them for their abusive behaviour and harassment. Thank heavens you escaped! It was either that or a gradual descent into insanity. These damn arranged marriages are made in hell."

Arti managed a weak smile, "Let's just say, not every arranged marriage is made in heaven! I cut them out completely from my life and even the memories have faded. There is nothing to remind me but for a robust Tulsi (Basil) plant in my garden. It has a most unusual pot! An old sweet tin that was once blue and gold."

Jane looked delighted. They laughed easily and Arti accepted another piece of chocolate from Jane's outstretched hand.

Jane asked Arti softly, "So are you settled in Delhi?"

Arti nodded as she chomped.

"Where?"

"It is a DDA flat. Safety is of prime concern in Delhi."

"Always has been. We girls used to have a seven pm curfew remember?"

"I live in a DDA flat and ran my nursery school out of one too. They are cosy, compact and safe apartments and if you're lucky, you can land yourself great neighbours. I'm being received by mine. They're lovely. The keys of my house are with them and they will make sure it is cleaned regularly. I'm sure there will be fresh flowers on my table along with all my mail and I am assured a warm meal on arrival!" Arti's eyes shone as she grinned at Jane. "Do you know this sweet lady even sent home made sweets for Diya? They have been my major support all along and love Diya as their own. I don't know how I would have managed without them! They are such an important part of my life." She turned to Jane, "Where will you be staying?"

"Some guest house Asha has booked me in. "I'm in town just for the wedding. Mamta's daughter, you know. Namita's also coming."

"Where's Namita coming from? She lived up the street from me. Her son attended my nursery."

Jane wrinkled her forehead and murmured uncertainly, "Australia? I seem to remember someone mention Sydney I think? I know she's been living there for many years."

"You can come and stay with me. I have a few spare bedrooms and you can show me around these charities of yours. I have time on my hands and perhaps I could, you know, make myself useful? I'm attending the wedding too! The celebrations start the day we arrive."

"Honestly how long do these marriages take? There are some five ceremonies and a trip to Rajasthan to boot!" Jane looked a bit put off.

"That's the way they use all that spare money I suppose." Arti laughed.

"If Asha hadn't insisted I come for all of it, I would have only arrived later this month. But I can't turn Asha down, she's such a sweetheart!"

"Oh absolutely, Asha has been a lifesaver for Diya and me. I'll never be able to repay her for as long as I live. I bunked with her after my getaway. She harbored me till I picked up the, you know..."

"Nerve?"

"Exactly. And when Diya went to New York, Asha's son showed her around. It was her very first time abroad and we couldn't afford two tickets so she had to go alone. And Roy! Oh my! His business acumen is astute! He guided me with investing in property."

"Yeah, Asha's family is just terrific. So, little kids eh!"

Arti nodded, "Pre nursery and nursery! I surprised myself there actually. I got results. The kids made it to some really great schools and I slowly built up a reputation. I ensured the kids were up to scratch so they would make the cut."

"You have investment property in Delhi?"

Arti tilted her head, "Gurgaon actually. There was a massive expansion over a colossal stretch outside Delhi. The properties far off were cheaper and Roy said it was just a matter of time before they became satellite cities of Delhi. Plus I could pay for it over small installments."

"Fantastic! It must all have appreciated many times over!" Jane rolled her hands.

Arti gave a small laugh, "That should answer your question about Diya's education funding!" She fished out her ipad and showed her pictures of Diya and herself.

"She's stunning Arti! The guys must be lining up at her door! Does she have any significant other in her life?"

"I don't think she's seeing anyone. I just don't want her to go through any heartbreak or suffer in an abusive relationship. For now I am glad she is such a gorgeous young woman and a successful doctor. I'd like her to meet someone who cares for her, respects her and whom she can look up to. Aren't those the pillars of real love?"

"Absolutely!"

"If it is meant to be, it will happen."

"I'm sure it will. She's smart and she's fabulous!" Jane offered her some more miniature candy bars.

"No thanks."

"Come on they are bite sized. I'll go bring more in a while." Arti took one smiling, "No need. I can't eat so much when there is no activity." She suppressed a yawn. "I would love to sign up to volunteer with any of your charities."

Jane leaned her head back and murmured, "What I am honestly looking forward to is this project I am visiting in inner Maharashtra." She murmured, a little lost in her thoughts.

Arti fixed her a querying look wondering if she had fallen asleep.

Jane continued ponderingly "It seems like the real deal. I told you how I keep looking for some meaningful venture to sink my teeth into. Well this, I feel, is it. I despise stagnation and that's what happens to many projects that take off enthusiastically in India."

Arti was genuinely interested. "Jane, tell me more. You're nodding off!"

"I'm not. Just resting my neck. It's tired of craning in your direction. It was on one such long haul flight that I found the story of this inspirational woman. You might want to read it." Jane abstracted some more candy bars from the seat pocket.

Arti declined wondering if there was a limit to Jane's insatiable appetite. "That's nice. What with all the scams you begin to wonder what is genuine anymore. Does she represent some organization?"

Jane shook her head as she chomped on the chocolate. She turned her large expressive eyes at Arti unable to say anything with an overfull mouth.

"Is she a friend of yours?"

Another violent shaking and then a nod and a shrug followed. Jane held out her palms as if to say "I don't know."

"So who is she? And for heaven's sake empty your mouth before you answer you twit."

Jane giggled and gulped down a mouthful choking violently in her tissue. She looked up at Arti flushed, tears streaming down her face. "I don't know how to answer that in one sentence. She is the parent of someone I worked with, but I would have to say that now I feel close to her. She is dedicated to involving herself in charity work in India, albeit the red tape and corruption having quadrupled! This cause is dear to her heart and I admire her hugely. She's had an incredible life! Do you know she was born in a village that had no running water or schools?"

"Not another rags to riches story!" Arti protested

"Not at all! Her family owned the village and half the district or something. This was ages back during Colonial India."

"She must be ancient!" Arti slurred as she nodded lazily.

"As is her story but once I read it, I was captivated. I knew I simply had to get acquainted with her. Arti she's such an elegant woman!" Jane took a deep breath and her eyes looked heavenwards. "She looks like Helen Mirren's sister!"

Arti slumped in her seat and drew the blanket up to her chin. She asked quizzically, "Does Helen Mirren have a sister?"

Jane looked perplexed, "I don't know!"

"So you mean she looks like Helen Mirren."

"Yeah whatever, But I say, go to sleep now.

Arti yawned and covered her mouth embarrassed. "Sorry!"

"It's a long story. I'll tell you when you wake up. You're wilting."

Arti's head slumped. "Jane isho nish to shee you again."

"Yeah nish to shee you too."

After all the late nights and touring about New York's top spots, Arti was dead beat. She fell asleep almost instantly.

FIVE

Jane peered out at the night sky beyond Arti's resting head. A few stars sparkled on the inky blue expanse as the aircraft ploughed through fluffy grey clouds. Inside, the cabin was bathed in a serene, neon glow and almost everyone slept. Jane absently nibbled on another chocolate.

She turned on her TV screen and was soon absorbed in a film starring Russell Crowe. It was an odd title, something about three days but Jane was quite riveted as the thriller unfolded.

Liam Neeson drawled "No prison in the world is airtight. Each one has a key. You just have to find it." Jane put the film on pause.

She studied her friend's calm sleeping face recalling the story of her valiant escape. "Indian girls" she thought to herself, "Indian girls are survivors! Each of us a fighter, even the most timid and unassuming one! Jane smiled to herself, her thoughts still on the story of Arti's escape. How had she picked up the pieces and started off again? No woman is more vulnerable than when she has a baby. It couldn't have been easy! She glanced again at the resting figure. She recalled Arti's face bursting with pride as she talked about her daughter. She toyed with the idea of staying at Arti's instead of the guest house.

She stared out of the porthole. The plane hurtled across an endless ocean of azure clouds. Thoughts zigzagged in Jane's mind at top speed recalling the bizarre ordeal of yet another surgery on her legs. Survival, what was it? Luck? Destiny? What had really happened that day decades ago in the Operating Theater?

She was floating near the pelmet, looking down at her own body as doctors and nurses feverishly struggled to find a pulse. She felt as if she was being sucked upwards into a tunnel taking her far from the hospital. Disjointed memories clashed in her consciousness.

Her knee hurt and her brother had tied a handkerchief on it. Her frock with the pink embroidered roses had ripped and soaked in her blood. But wasn't that a long time ago? Jane was confused. She was flooded with a tranquil sensation as she soared towards a most wondrous kaleidoscopic light. It swirled making colourful spirals about her as she felt her body weightlessly glide toward a distant bright light.

A smiling face with outstretched arms floated before her. That face! It was unmistakably the most beautiful face she knew. She longingly leaned towards those arms. Her mother laughed blissfully overjoyed to see her lovely child. Her face glowed with pure joy. She appeared to send out blessings towards her, assurances of happiness and triumphs. Jane stared at the face radiant with spotless purity. Then slowly the smiling visage morphed and the gorgeous face looked troubled. Many hazy images floated past. Jane lost the face. She squinted, focusing on the spot where her mother's laughing face had been. Where was she? Jane strained to peer through the vaporous haze. The face appeared again. A little blurry at first, coming into focus slowly. It was not smiling. The lovely face looked worried. As Jane drew closer her mother looked alarmed and panicky. She put out her hands as if to try and ward her little girl away.

She didn't want her daughter to come any further. Jane stopped. Her heart sank. She stared helplessly across the chasm at her beautiful mother's uneasy expression. Dismally, she looked down at her scraped knee. The hem of her pretty frock was bloody. She had been in the muddy, scraggy field behind their house, chasing butterflies. She had tripped and hurt her knee on a jagged rock. She bawled loudly. Her mother had run to her and scooped her up in her arms. It was a warm soothing feeling.

But her knee still hurt. Jane felt as if someone was jabbing a needle into her flesh. She murmured incoherently. The pain was more than she could bear. Why did she not feel her mother's arms around her? She groaned again and moved her head from side to side. She opened her eyes and looked into a large bright light and masked faces. Feebly she recognised the pale green walls and shiny apparatus before everything went dark again.

Looking out at inky blackness outside the plane, Jane touched her dank eyes. She allowed the tears to flow freely down her cheeks. The cathartic flood washed away years of hurting. She thought of the canvas adorning her mantelpiece at home - a replica of Hieronymus Bosch's painting "Ascent to Empyrean" depicting the tunnel leading to a mysterious light.

Beside her Arti dozed soundly, oblivious of the ache her companion carried in her heart. Jane had never spoken of it to anyone. What would she have said? "I saw my mother. She assured me everything was going to be alright."

Over the years she understood. Her mother had sent her back to live her life abundantly, enjoying every moment to the fullest and that was exactly the way she lived. They would meet again. Jane had often thought of her mother's painful death and had wondered if she still felt the pain but after seeing that wondrously peaceful face she was able to calm herself.

Her thoughts shifted to Delhi and her dear friends. Asha, dear Asha, so generous and welcoming! Jane felt twice blessed that her friend had married an equally caring man. She recalled Asha's last email and glanced at her watch. They must be gathering at her party now!

Asha's South Delhi house shone with miniscule fairy lights as if dressed for a wedding. Shiny chauffeured cars lined up at the gates to deposit guests from Asha and Roy's select circle of friends. Rukmini could hardly believe how stylishly the place had been transformed.

The glass fronted lounge opened on to a massive marbled terrace bedecked with aromatic candles and hurricane lanterns. Instrumental music tinkled in the background. Lace swathed circular tables sported crystal centerpieces with floating rose petals. Liveried waiters attended behind canopied food stalls, a tandoor and a bar. Musical instruments and mikes decorated a low, spotless white dais. It was a magical summer evening tickled by a light breeze.

"You pulled this off in just one afternoon?" Rukmini looked Asha up and down admiringly. The rhinestone embellished onion coloured net designer sari drifted around her floating in the gentle breeze. Asha appeared to have stepped down from the glossy pages of some chic magazine.

"I would have never asked you to take us shopping if I knew you were preparing for such a big bash!"

"No problem," Asha patted her hair and gave the place a cursory once over. "Everything's outsourced. All I did was to dress up. Have a drink." She directed a tray-bearing swain towards Rukmini and turned a radiant face to greet her new arrivals, "Here they are! Hey lovely ladies!"

A bunch of chic couples breezed in. With open mouthed elation Rukmini looked into the faces of old friends. They looked changed after so many years, but she could place them with little effort. Asha ushered them to the tastefully decorated tables and made swift introductions.

Rukmini, happy to meet people from a bygone era, was somewhat at a loss after the initial introductions. She turned to Asha who steered her to a corner, "Oh by the way, Lekha is here and she and Avatar are not together, but they are. Just remember that and don't ask any silly questions."

"What?"

Before Asha could reply, a smooth voice hailed her.

"Rukmini!"

She saw a graceful vision gliding towards her in a ravishing turquoise sari. She could never mistake Lekha's distinguishing good looks and striking personality. Rukmini smiled, genuinely happy to meet a dear friend from the past.

"Hi Lekha! How's everything?"

"Great!"

"Still single?"

"U huh, blissfully!"

"How is your mother?"

"Not with us anymore."

"I'm so sorry!" Rukmini hesitated, "Any contact with Avatar?"

Lekha turned her radiant face to Rukmini and smiled brightly, "Hmm." Her eyes sparkled in the candlelight as she nodded demurely, "We are in close contact." She grinned impishly.

"Is he… are you two?"

Lekha shook her head firmly, "No not really. He's married. He lives in California.

In the U.S." she added, trying to answer the question mark on Rukmini's face.

"Yes. I remember he was in the computer business." Rukmini muttered rather unnecessarily adding, "wasn't he?"

Lekha nodded in exaggerated agreement, "Yeah! That's what he does." Then she turned and took a few steps away. The cynosure of all eyes, Lekha strolled gracefully around the periphery of the terrace stroking the flowers in burnished brass planters on the marble topped wall. Rukmini walked along.

"So what the hell you doing getting involved with a married man?" She wanted to shout out but said nothing.

She glanced around, conscious that Lekha still attracted more attention than anyone she knew. She wasn't sure Lekha had any awareness of her own charisma.

She tilted her head to one side squinting admiringly and blurted out, "I mean look at you! You're lovely! Any man could go for you."

"He's the only one for me."

"But he dumped you how can you forget!"

Lekha walked on as if she hadn't heard her, stopped, turned around, surveyed the gathering and settled down at a corner table the cool evening breeze caressing her gorgeous chiffon sari. She turned her face up to the skies. A glorious bronze dusk descended unhurriedly as the sky glowed smoky blue with azure streaks, and an early star peeked out of ruby clouds.

Asha walked busily towards Rukmini and rattled off breathlessly, "He is about to start. You need something to drink? Hope you're enjoying the evening." She spotted someone at the door and patting Rukmini absently added, "Don't get preachy with Lekha, not now". She hurried over to the new arrivals.

Rukmini turned to her friend and started whispering, "Lekha, honey, why are you messing up your whole life?"

"Shut up I'm happy"

Mikes were starting up shrieking a rusty, metallic cacophony. Rukmini was about to whisper back.

"Shh the music's starting up." Lekha looked at her, finger pressed against her lips. Giggling at Rukmini's befuddled face; she turned her head triumphantly towards the party smiling at no one in particular.

The terrace had filled up quite a bit. Forgetting all about Lekha's little imbroglio, Rukmini lost herself to the magical evening as people wandered around nursing exotic cocktails and the ghazal singer belted out verse after tuneful verse. How long was it since she had heard any of those numbers! Her husband did not listen to ghazals and she had a faint recollection of listening to the maestro, Jagjit Singh over and over again on the primitive tape recorder with piano switches during her younger days.

Lekha looked up at spectacular sapphire skies streaked with brilliant orange. The fresh, just - washed look sent a thrill through her. The young singer, handpicked by Asha and Roy, carried a mellow tune displaying that rare ability to evoke a distinct response in each listener. Lekha was soon lost in his evocative music. Her very first gift from Avatar had been an audio cassette with this piece. He had sandwiched it between two slabs of her favourite chocolate, Bourneville dark. She smiled to herself as memories of early days in their courtship floated on waves of nostalgic music.

It was her first day at Sarkar's computer class. Even in her ordinary cotton salwar kameez she was striking. For some reason he couldn't keep his eyes off her and fumbled clumsily with the roll call in an effort to catch her name. Quite unaware of his nervousness, Lekha struggled to keep pace trying to take notes while following the lesson on the monitor. "Please note this is a hands-on class and you should not require notes if you pay attention." Her instructor had announced smiling benevolently at her but addressing the class as a whole. Lekha put her pen away and tried to commit every command to memory. It was imperative she mastered this programme. A lot was hanging on it. After class she had rushed out to catch the bus home. Her instructor stared after her and then turned to look at the place she sat at imagining she was still sitting there but this time she was smiling at him. Then he saw the notebook. He snatched it up and dashed out frantically, just in time to see her getting on to a bus. He knew all the bus routes quite well. If he was quick he would catch up on his scooter. He gave chase swerving maniacally as he tailed the bus keeping a lookout for alighting commuters. He arrived at the bus stop just as she alighted. She walked briskly along the crowded street. His brakes screeched but she didn't even glance back. Flinging his scooter to one side he charged after her as she crossed the road. Wheezing and panting he loped across the street and called out desperately, "Excuse me!"

Turning to see her "sir" with tousled hair and disheveled clothes Lekha couldn't hide her astonishment. She noticed the notebook in his outstretched hand. "Your book!" He hissed, clearly out of breath.

She shook her head and pulled her notebook out from her bag.

Resounding applause brought her back to Asha's terrace. People were calling out requests and the young artiste was happy to comply. Roy strolled across the patio and stood behind his wife's chair. Asha looked back at him and smiled. He motioned with his head towards the singer and pointed to her. From the very first strains Asha recognised he had requested for their special song. How young they were then! She glanced to her side and felt his presence.

She considered herself the luckiest woman alive that her husband still courted her just as he had done for most of his life.

Lekha's thoughts remained in the past as reminiscent music carried her away into a time when life was perfect. Life, in her opinion was perfect today as well. She played a vital role in the life of her beloved and knew in her heart that he adored her. That was all that mattered.

When the musicians took a break, Rukmini challenged Lekha. "It's not going to end well."

"Who cares? He sees me a few weeks each year; we communicate all day and chat online for hours. That's more than most wives get in a lifetime. He's here now!" She added with wide eyed innocence.

"Where?" Rukmini looked about.

"I meant he is in town." Not wanting to discuss the matter anymore Lekha walked away.

Asha materialized next to Rukmini, "Leave her be. They are serious about each other! You have to see them together to believe it. It's like you are watching a beautiful serenade by cool moonlight. There is that rare harmony of the souls."

"Harmony my foot. He's a married man." Rukmini was vehement. "There's no way Avatar will ever give up on his marriage. In the state of California he will have to part with most of his assets in the divorce settlement or the alimony will kill him!"

Asha looked at her in surprise and Rukmini was herself quite taken aback at how strongly it came out.

She sighed. "I'm sorry. I know you have to take care of your guests and ..."

Asha said, "How long is it since you met Namita?"

Rukmini beamed. "Namita, is she here, really?"

Asha nodded, "Just arrived. Come." She ushered a smartly turned out lady towards Rukmini who immediately declared she would have spotted Namita in a hundred people.

Namita filled her in sketchily on her life in sunny Sydney and inevitably the subject turned to Lekha.

Asha looked quite appalled, "Really Rukmini, I'd imagine you would be more accepting that any of us!" she murmured.

"Why, just because I live in the U.K.? That's ridiculous! Adultery is adultery on any continent." Rukmini hissed back.

Namita nodded silently. From across the terrace Lekha watched her friends, a curious look on her face. She lifted another cocktail from a passing waiter's tray.

Asha realised that Lekha was looking at them from across the wide terrace. She murmured self consciously, "But she's devoted to him and all she needs from us is support. Get it? I should go. Come and sit down with the rest of them." She shepherded them to the table where all their friends sat.

Mamta, whom Rukmini recalled to be a rich businessman's daughter, struck a fork against her glass, "Ahem! Just a small but important announcement! As most of you already know, my daughter's getting married soon!"

This was followed by cheerful shrieks and congratulations.

"We are expecting all of you at the Mehendi tomorrow and you have to all accompany us to Rajasthan for the wedding!"

"Of course!"

"Goes without saying."

"Anything we can do?"

"No I have a wedding planner so my worry is cut by half."

"It should be cut altogether."

She turned to ask Rukmini her address with a promise to have the wedding invitation delivered.

"Just mail it!"

Mamta didn't hear her but Asha rejoined, "No. It can't be mailed. You'll see why when you receive it." Adding in a whisper, "it will be delivered in a silver box with mithai!"

"Really?"

"Hmm. tied in gold ribbon."

Immediately as dinner got over, and the guests had left, a team of the event management agency briskly moved in to dismantle and pack away the furniture and equipment while close friends and family moved inside to Asha's elegant drawing room. Roy made introductions for his niece and nephew, both aspirants for overseas higher studies.

When they heard that Namita had come from Australia, the youngsters came down on her like a ton of bricks. The young girl declared loftily "I will join any course in any university anywhere in the world but I will never go to Australia!"

Taken aback, Namita enquired, "Why not?"

"It's the most racist country on the planet!" She might as well have added "Duh!"

Namita smiled, "obviously, you are grossly misinformed!"

"I don't think so. I have been reading about it in the newspapers and on the Internet. Can they all be wrong?"

"Perhaps they are not entirely wrong but they are certainly not totally accurate..."

The girl's brother joined in as the rest of the company fell silent. "Okay so Indians get murdered but it's no one's fault in Australia?"

"What's the use of avoiding the question?" The girl smirked smugly.

This kid was beginning to annoy Namita with her supercilious, judgmental air. "Yes there were deaths and no, they were not race based crimes. Look, obviously I am not going to advocate any sort of discrimination against migrant students nor am I endorsing the violence. What happened was tragic and everybody mourned for those students and that includes Australians."

"Oh Yeah?"

"If you are willing to hear me out without interrupting I would love for an opportunity to set the record straight. That Indian student's death was an absolutely inexcusable, painful tragedy, one that haunts many of us even now. I feel inadequate to express how moved and shocked everyone was at the senseless crime. Sadly, his death was immediately described as a "race attack" by Indian media, and it sparked a particularly strong reaction in an excitable people! You may not recall it, but I seem to remember how an Australian missionary was killed in India and a teenager abused and killed on one of our beaches. It was reported responsibly in the Australian media. But in India, it was as if each news hound was trying to outdo the other with more poignant sensationalism. But..."

"So you are saying there is no problem for Indians?" The girl interjected again. The kid was on the warpath!

She took a deep breath and addressed the young woman in her coldest professorial voice, "You interrupted me again. If you ask a question, it is only polite to wait for the responder to finish. Australia is one of the most multicultural nations in the world. It is without a doubt the loveliest place to live in. Can't deny there are problems. All I am saying that we Indians are a part of the problem. This was never such a serious issue in the past and Indians have been immigrating in fairly steady numbers for decades." She looked into cold hostile eyes. She smiled nervously at her friends and added as an aside, "I can't believe I am having this discussion! To think that on the one hand Tendulkar is named a member of the Order Of Australia and on ..."

"Just a shoddy peace offering!" The girl interjected. Her mother glared at her and murmured something fiercely.

Sitting in Asha's elegant living room, Namita felt prickly hostility from a Kangaroo court. She cleared her throat and continued, "The Diaspora of immigrants has changed as has their motivation to immigrate." She glanced about the room hoping to garner a modicum of sympathy, "I mean, it seems a bit irrational for these kids to go all the way to Australia to study Cooking or Physical Therapy paying princely fees when they could easily be trained for the same right here for a pittance! Naturally, they are after the Permanent Residency that comes with it. These children opt to live in poorer neighborhoods with a high crime rate. They pick up part time jobs and return late from work so they become easy targets. It could take long to explain and this is not the time or place for it. But everyone should think long and hard before applying to move there." Namita paused satisfied that she had a rapt audience.

"Why?"

Namita answered not missing a beat, "In your case, it most certainly would be the dumbest thing to do."

The girl stared at her, "but weren't you just blowing Australia up as a dream destination?"

"I was but I wasn't trying to sell it to you. I'd still maintain that in your case it would be most unwise."

"Why?"

"You have formed an indelible picture in your mind of Australia's racist bend. Any and all experiences will be viewed through those lenses. I suggest, stay away."

"So it's ok for others to go?"

"Someone with an open mind? Yeah. Let me put it this way, a visitor here would be bothered by what are for most of us, set patterns! You walk down the street here, or just step out of your house, there is a band of hooligans sitting across at a road side tea stall and they whistle."

"It goes way beyond whistling these days!" Rukmini added with a small laugh.

"Right. So they make lewd suggestions, remarks, you are in a hurry and you get into your car, stepping over a pile of cow manure without cringing, and you'd be lucky if it is animal excreta and your driver drives you away. You are oblivious to it, totally desensitized. In places like the U.S. or Australia, you don't run the risk of being pawed by perverted men, but when you move there, and a checkout girl is short with you, you would react belligerently."

The girl retorted in a raised voice, "Naturally if people are rude…tell me…"

"I am not finished, young lady", Namita said firmly, "I could continue defending Australia and you could go on debating issues based on hearsay." She shrugged her shoulders dismissingly. "It's a moot point but your mind is made up and I think it is obvious that your staying clear of Australia would be the best thing for both you and Australia, so why waste time and energy debating it out? I have to point out, however that ubiquitous discrimination comes pretty naturally to Indians. It may not be necessarily racial, it could be religious, caste based or socio economic prejudice but it is deep rooted in our ethnicity. And yet we are content to coexist quite harmoniously. But that's a topic for another day."

She turned to her hostess, "Sorry if I was a bit blunt but the one thing everyone going overseas needs is an open and unbiased mind." She took the haughty girl in from top to toe and added, "Kids have to understand that sporting low riders doesn't qualify them as ideal overseas candidates. They need to open the windows of their mind, get a reality check. There's good and bad everywhere. Thank you Asha for a most interesting evening." Namita turned on her heels and quite elegantly stormed out.

Rukmini had stood by silently through the stormy discussion. She addressed the company with quiet dignity in her pronounced British accent, "She is right. You have to accept that any place can be as inhospitable or an inviting as you view it. You kids heading for the U.S. or U.K.? Believe me the streets most definitely are not paved with gold. Now if you'll excuse me, Asha, I need to be with Namita. Thanks for the evening."

Rukmini settled in the car with Namita and consoled her friend. "Don't let it upset you. We had such a nice evening." She gave the driver the address of Namita's guest house and turned to look at her friend. "I'll get off first and he will take you back to your hotel." Namita looked tired and troubled. Rukmini patted her on the arm. "Sure you're going to be okay?"

Namita nodded resignedly "It's probably jetlag. Yes we did have a lovely evening. I just feel troubled I got baited. I'll be fine by the morning."

Rukmini thanked the driver and pushed the car door shut. In the beam of the car's headlights she saw an outline lurking in the shrubbery. Driver Ram Singh jumped out shouting and ran to the bushes. He pulled a figure out shaking it vigorously. Rukmini hazily made out it was Kamala and assured Ram Singh that it was okay.

"What is it? Why are you hiding?"

"I wasn't hiding bibiji. I just sat down here to wait for you and when your car came I got up. I want to talk to you." She added significantly, "It's important."

"It's okay Ram Singh. I'll talk to her inside. You make sure madam gets safely to her hotel." Rukmini watched him drive away hoping that Namita wouldn't take the idiotic kids' invective to heart. She led the maid indoors. Sameer and Natasha sat reading in the living room.

Kamala pressed something into her hands for safekeeping. Rukmini was aghast to see small tight bundles of Rupee notes trussed up in bits of cloth.

"Bibiji please keep this with you."

"How much is there?"

"I can't count. I am an illiterate. Also, can you help me to get my money from the bank tomorrow? You must have found my bank book somewhere."

"Your bank book? No."

"It was in my name and your in-laws' names. I have an account there in the bank in the market."

"Really? How much money is there?"

"I don't know but I will need whatever is there. I am getting the filote tomorrow. I have to reach there with the money by noon. Please help me bibiji."

Rukmini felt a bit panicky. "Kamala, how much does the plot cost? Did they give you any papers or anything?"

The woman promptly searched all over her person and produced some papers stored in a tattered Ziploc bag.

"They gave this. You can read it."

Rukmini struggled to read the fading print in Hindi with some entries made in near illegible ink.

"Congratulations Kamala! This clearly states that you will get a plot. And it is totally free. You don't have to pay anything. Take your money back. Just show them this paper."

"But bibiji the man asked me to bring all the money I have, tomorrow. He said that there are many people who can prove that they are poorer than me so then they will get the filote. But if I give him something, he will make the papers in my name."

"How much?"

"Whatever I can give."

"Wait here." Rukmini walked up to the phone.

"Roy, this is Rukmini."

"Are you alright? Is something wrong? How's Namita?"

"She's fine. I just had a question for you."

Rukmini talked at length to Asha's husband, a lawyer with a reputation that was something of a legend. What she heard saddened her.

"Bribes even from such poor people? Roy she has nothing. Absolutely nothing. She has just brought me her life's savings," Rukmini glanced down at the paltry bundle, "there can't be more than a few thousand here."

"Rukmini if she doesn't cough up a decent amount, they'll throw her case out."

"And by "decent amount" you mean?"

"Forty fifty thousand at least."

"Roy she's a domestic. A helper. This house cost my father in law a hundred thousand…"

"I am only giving you the bare facts. Of course, should she need any help, Asha is always looking around for a worthy cause."

"Let's hope I can manage."

"Rukmini remember one thing. Do not go there! It could ruin it for her. I'll explain later."

"Yes I understand."

As she replaced the receiver Sameer emerged from the study with a large leather folder. "This must be it! I saw it in dadaji's drawer. It has some checkbooks and things."

Kamala was evidently excited by the new find. "It's in there. A blue book" she remarked as Rukmini examined the contents and pulled out a blue rexine covered pass book. Her eyes lit up as she leafed through it. "Kamala there is plenty of money here! We will go and take it out tomorrow."

Kamala looked excitedly at their glowing faces. "Okay bibiji, I will come with my older boy. He can take me straight from the bank to the government office."

Rukmini sent Kamala off and started putting away the delicate pieces of jewelry she had worn from her mother in law's collection. The heated discussion with those kids had left a bitter taste after such a lovely evening. She hoped Namita was not particularly rattled by the kids' tirade. She sighed. If there ever were youngsters in need of reigning in!

A tired Namita returned to the guesthouse down in the mouth and uneasy at the way she had handled things. If only Namish had been there! He would certainly have made things clear to those misinformed kids. Was it wrong to take up cudgels for another country? She knew how deeply saddened she had been over the spate of crime against Indian students and she knew Australians who were equally saddened.

She was severely jetlagged and sensing that the evening's events wouldn't necessarily lead her to restful slumber, she decided to email her family and in the process unburden herself of that needled feeling. A bystander would have told her she held her own well, but Namita came away discomfited and a little humiliated.

There was no way she would turn her back on her country, either country, she owed each one so much! She recalled her late father's teachings and the words "Janmabhoomi" (nation of birth) and "Karmabhoomi" (land where one earns a livelihood) rang in her ears. Disconcerting thoughts saturated her sleep deprived mind as she struggled to plug in and set up her laptop to send a short mail home. She turned on the switch and barely had the laptop flickered to life when everything went dark.

A small pilot light came on in a corner. She felt her way to the door blinking in the darkness and peered out into the hallway. There was the sound of voices and scrambling footsteps. People were chatting on their mobile phones and the guest house attendants were scrambling about with torches. From all the chatter she gathered that the power outage would last for a couple of hours. Making her way carefully to the large windows she pulled the drapes letting in faint light from the street below. She sat by the window listening to the muffled sounds of traffic moving in random patterns. There was nothing to do but wait the night out till sleep deigned to descend. As she gazed down she felt a strange disconnect. It was alien to her. She smiled at the reversal. She had spent the first few years abroad pining for India and today she was already missing her home in Australia!

She peered at the street below through the rising haze. Tiny stick figures strolled on muddy sidewalks. A couple crossed the street. The lady wore a brilliant magenta sari. Namita recalled a similar one she used to have.

Her throat and mouth were dry from the evening's oily food. She yearned for a hot drink but didn't dare step out in the pitch black hotel passage. Her eyes crinkled as she looked down at the ever changing view in the street below. Was it only a day since she bid Namish goodbye? It seemed so long ago.

SIX

Sunshine danced on the puddles in the pavement cutting miniscule rivulets in the grassy cracks. Namita waved to the car swiftly diminishing in the meandering ascent up May's Hill till it was no more than a speck. He would be in Canberra in good time. It was a lovely morning. As she walked back to her tea table in the shade, their conversation played back in her mind. The thrill of the chilly July morning sent a light shiver through her.

"Take care Mum and keep texting. I'll see you soon. Remember not to drink tap water or venture out at night."

"Thanks for the travel advisories. Just let this print off. Here," She handed him the printout, "the address of where I'll be staying."

The young man's eyes turned to the computer screen, "What's that?"

"The venue of the wedding, it's an old fort or palace or something."

He let out a whistle.

"It's a hotel now. Six stars!"

"You're kidding! I thought they only ever gave five stars!"

"See there, it says "India's first six star hotel"!" Her eyes shone, "I'm going to live it up! How I wish you guys could have made it!"

Her son couldn't take his eyes off the slide show, "Oh man! This is the life! Wish I could have joined you but India in the summer's just not my thing." He looked out of the window as a car honked politely. "Got to go mum. Take plenty of pictures of this palace and try and get away to check out the other historic forts. I believe it is simply awesome. You're going to have a great trip."

Namita smiled. It felt funny to hear her son speak of India as if it were a foreign land.

She poured herself another cup, reached for the arrowroot biscuits to dunk and propped the newspaper up against the teapot. Sweet smelling air wafted across the flower patch as she turned her attention to the violent albeit justifiable voices of dissent in Arabia. What a calamitous place the planet had become! Hurricanes, killer floods devastating landslides and impious volcanoes spitting their wrath too!

The breeze carried tinkling laughter as chattering school kids skipped alongside their mother pushing a creaky pram. Between the hedge leaves, Namita spied the familiar cobalt uniform. They would cross the street at the next junction and cut across the emerald grass of Jones Park. She knew. She had followed the same routine some years ago.

It seemed like only yesterday. A single innocuous exchange in the car while dropping Namish to school one wintry morning in Delhi had irreversibly and sneakily transformed her life forever.

"Everyone's applying for a migration to Australia, the new land of hope and opportunity. I think we should give it a shot."

"You mean to go live there forever? Australia's so far."

"Don't act so naive Nam, nothing is far anymore. It could be the best thing for Namish."

She threw her mind back to that day over and over again marveling at the speed and ease of the paperwork for permanent residence in Australia. Here they were, a few months later, in Sydney, Australia.

The first few days in an alien place can be as terrifying as exhilarating. Exploring the nearby Westfield Shopping mall was so engrossing that even shopping for basics took over two hours.

Every evening and all weekend was spent house-hunting. She learned to tell the difference between 'fibro' houses, wood clad houses and brick ones as also units, townhouses and standalone houses. They understood that rents could go twice as high for properties close to the station, a school, or a mall. Certain suburbs boasted identifiable uniqueness on the strength of their ethnic population.

"You from India?" Ehsaan asked one morning, clearing the junk from his car's backseat to make room for Namita and Namish. Ashish nodded.

"Then you may want to stay in Liverpool, Harris Park or Blacktown".

"Not necessarily" said Ashish," I think it may be better living closer to a school, a station and the motorway."

Ehsaan shrugged "Fine by me. Mostly, Indian people - they like to live in these suburbs yeah? You have the Indian shops and the Indian movie library and Indian grocery shops nearby. You like Indian movies? I like Indian movies they are very popular and the music is very good."

"Bollywood has got to be India's most absurd export!" Ashish murmured as Ehsaan reeled off names of Indian movie stars.

"And the hugest money spinner." Namita muttered.

The houses in their budget were pretty much the same with a couple of bedrooms and common areas but Namita couldn't contain her amazement at the lack of decent toilet facilities.

"What's with the clumsy planning? That's the fourth place we've seen with a toilet in the wrong place! The backyard, the kitchen and now this one is in a shack on the front porch!"

"If we wanted open air toilets why would we have left?"

Namita glared at him, "I do like the sunroom though!"

"Beat me why we need a sun room to begin with. The whole place is bathed in sunlight fourteen hours a day." Ashish mumbled.

The only house that suited their budget and was located close to the shops and a school was close to a rubbish dump. "You'll never get any smells or bugs," declared Ehsaan, "they lock up the place".

"Why? Is it valuable?" chirped Ashish. Ehsaan's laughter rang out loud and clear. A silver tongued businessman, he liked this polite family.

"Look, you take it and I'll get them to leave everything behind. Almost all of it is good furniture and it could save you buying new stuff. That's quite a packet!"

Uneasily Namita's eyes took in the threadbare carpeting and faded soiled curtains.

"Mummy let's take it. I can easily walk to school from here."

"Nam, we have to settle for something. At least this is convenient. It may only be for a short while. I'm signing the lease."

Namita cast her eyes around. She felt an intruder in someone else's home. But there was no arguing with Ashish and the family moved in right away.

She spent all day hanging up curtains and sheets on the sun drenched "Hills hoist" which, Namish enlightened her, was an ingenious Australian invention. After a good scrub, washed curtains up and brightly embroidered bed spreads, the place assumed a new identity.

Namita vowed to learn Australian English but every now and again would get stumped by an odd word or phrase. "Manchester! What a strange name for linen!"

"Maybe they originally imported it from Manchester in the early days and the name sort of stuck," joked Ashish, "they haven't the kind of creative trait to adapt. Like changing Curzon road to Kasturba Gandhi marg or Wellesley to Dr. Zakir Hussain. Then again almost everything we use today comes from China, but we can't name everything China can we? Bring me my China, not my China!" he mimicked a snooty, nasal feminine voice sending Namish into peals of laughter.

Namita smiled and sat down beside him. "How do you do it?"

"What?"

"How do you keep up the cheerful good humour and jokes?"

"Honey, one of us has to be funny and we agreed it would be me. Have you forgotten?"

Ashish walked Namish to school each morning. Then, armed with a file of his certificates and resume', he would commence his rounds of job hunting. Most people on his list of "contacts" had disappointed. The Migrant resource center and the Immigration office weren't able to fit him in anywhere but hastened to inform him that he would not be eligible for any financial support for two years.

As the job search progressed, the pile of newspaper cuttings grew and Namita struggled to stash them wishing she had a "wire", the contraption that her father always attached his electricity and water bills to. It was just a long thick wire curved at one end and attached to a wooden disc at the other. You just pierced the bill, threaded it through and hung it up on the pelmet near the radio. Almost every Indian home in the seventies had one.

With the boys out all day, Namita tackled the cleaning and cooking careful to use products and ingredients economically. She was handling the work that two maids had done for her in India and realized she was not a very enthusiastic homemaker. She pined for the sights and sounds of her beloved Delhi. She missed having "A.I.R FM radio" chime in the background. She missed hearing the sounds of children playing outside, hawkers announcing their wares, birds flitting in and out and the general busyness of over population. The silence and calm of this place scared her, the tedium of uninspiring chores bored her and the disinterest of employers in her husband made her anxious.

"You will feel better once you have made a few friends and found your way about. It can be a bit disorienting at the beginning. I know, you'll meet some nice people at the Khanna party this weekend." Ashish assured her.

The Khanna mansion was a massive double storey structure with tennis courts, swimming pools and separate snooker and cards rooms. "This is almost like a small club", thought Namita.

It was a small select group in a large sprawling mansion that sat back in plush armchairs sipping fine Australian wine and debating the destiny of "the new kids on the block", the Aryas. Dr Khanna was most upset to hear about their new address. "No, no! You have to start with the right suburb this side of Strathfield. The Indians living out west are narrow-minded, parochial, and insular. I tell you. Ashish, you will never find a job living there."

The evening proved a complete disaster except for Namish who enjoyed his time on the play station and X box. Ashish was disappointed that Khanna could not guide him in any way to find work and Namita was sick to the point of nausea listening to the ladies ramble on about designer outfits and $120 beauty treatments.

Weeks passed and Ashish was compelled to take up a part time late night job at a nearby fuel station. He returned each night exhausted and heavy-eyed.

"We regret your qualifications and teaching experience in India do not qualify you to teach at any Australian school." Namita's eyes filled with disappointment at the cold, direct rejection. She crumpled the letter in her hands and stared teary eyed up at the sky, despair and frustration overwhelming her.

The sequence of events in the past few weeks had been troubling. She had been declared unfit to teach at any of the Universities as her subject was not relevant. She decided to give teaching at school a shot, but today's letter dashed that last hope of hers.

The optimistic emails from home further depressed her. "How can a chemical engineer like my son not find employment? I knew you would surely succeed. Everything takes time in a new place! I am relieved and happy for you. Aminchandani's son was a mere B.Com and he is so prosperous, naturally, my son will do far better! God Bless you." Namita stared at the screen. What exactly had Ashish written to his father? She scrolled down to Ashish's mail. "By God's grace and your blessings, I have secured a good job and we have moved into a comfortable house."

Namita wondered how her in-laws would react if they heard that their son managed a petrol station and worked all night! The idea was, at best ludicrous. She could picture her mother in law all decked out in crepes and pearls lording over her "kitty party" friends secure in the thought that her son was raking in the moolah and the next deck of cards she offered for "rummy" would certainly be from Australia. She saw why Ashish had sent that mail. There was no way his parents would ever understand or accept that their engineer son, the apple of their eye couldn't find work.

Namita's thoughts turned to her own parents. Their daughter, a gold medalist with years of experience, not good enough to teach here! She couldn't bear to tell them that she didn't have the right qualifications!

In an absurd sort of way, she felt she had failed her parents, her husband and her son. Back home in India, she had never needed to work, not for the money anyway. Ashish's princely salary was more than adequate and all her earnings were spent on trivial things or treats and celebrations. Once more she cried inwardly. Why couldn't her husband just overlook the general dishonesty back home? Wasn't it enough that they were upright and straightforward? She knew deep down she had the answers.

One day while walking by Namish's school, she saw an elderly Australian lady mowing her lawn. She had been filled with ceaseless admiration at the way the elderly took care of themselves, their homes and gardens. As she approached the lady's house preparing to sing out 'Good morning' the old lady abruptly collapsed to the ground. The power cord of the lawn mower had entangled itself around her legs and the poor woman did a dead man's fall right before Namita's eyes. Namita rushed in, turned off the mower and helped the lady into her tiny living room. Her knee was cut and bleeding and her elbow was grazed. "How do you feel? Shall I send for an ambulance?" The woman looked faint and Namita bent over her quite helplessly.

She opened her eyes and managed a weak smile. "Make some tea, love, let's have some tea. This will heal."

"Are you sure you don't want me to dress it for you, or just bathe it in some antibiotic?" Namita asked softly.

"I'll be fine. Lucky you were there just then!" her jade green eyes twinkled and some color returned to the lovely face.

Namita brought her food each day till the woman's knee healed. She learned that the 82 year old lived alone as her daughter was an airhostess with a leading airline. She proudly held up a framed photograph of a smiling young lady.

"She's beautiful!" Namita stared at the picture carefully.

Betty admired the intricate embroidery on Namita's dupattas and brought out samples of embroidery done in her youth. They enjoyed their mornings together. The walk to and from Namish's school was a beautiful one, as beautiful as the rest of Sydney, tidy streets and parks that were neatly framed by rows of tiled houses with their shiny red roofs, flowery gardens and artistic mailboxes. The sun shone brightly, a bit too brightly out of clear blue skies.

She cringed each time she had to turn down her son's request for a comic, a game or even a chocolate. She longed to give back to him the life of abundance he had had back home where he wanted for nothing. She remembered how their fridge used to be bursting at the seams with chocolates. She cursed herself for denying her little boy the special pampering that lives only in a grandparent's heart.

Namita decided she had to secure some form of employment. She approached the counter at Woolworths awkwardly and asked for an application form. The counter girl's mascara laden eyes took her in from head to toe, "you speak English?" Namita wanted to say "At least as well as you", but instead smiled and said "Yes I do."

"No offence", the gum-chewing girl chanted out mechanically.

"None taken" Namita added smartly, walking away feeling certain she could do the job better than the wannabe sales executive.

Another week, another regret. All positions have been filled but would Ms. Arya prefer if we kept her application in the active file for three more months?

For the first time since their arrival from India, Namita wept, first softly, then bitterly. She was desperate for work, a job, any job. She longed for her old job at the girls' college, her lovely home, her maids, her driver, her weekly movies and outings. Her heart ached for her mother. She wanted to put her head in her mother's lap and weep. She cried for over two hours.

She determined to maintain a happy façade for the sake of their blameless son who hadn't asked to immigrate, who did not understand any of it. He would see only his mother's resolve and optimism.

Namish's regard for his mum reached a pinnacle one evening. They had walked down to Merrylands and picked up dinner from his favourite Chinese take away and as they strolled back that beautiful evening, they saw heaps of discarded furniture and other stuff on the pavement.

"It must be time for that council pick up" mum said as she walked through the bits and pieces that people had dumped. She stopped short and turned around. "How's this?" She ran her hands along the top and sides of an old fashioned writing table. "It has drawers and a little cupboard too."

Namish hesitated and was about to reply that it was too bulky and heavy for them to lug up the hill.

"Here take this." Mum thrust the "take away" bag at him and circled the table weighing it with her eyes. Namish stood awkwardly by, formulating a sentence to express his thoughts on the impracticality when she bent over, grasped the table with both hands and in one brisk move swung it up on top of her head. She wiggled a little to position it comfortably "Come on son," she called out as she swayed on half bent knees, crab like all the way up the hill. Namish looked around mortified and kept checking over his shoulder praying that no one would see them. No one did. It was dark and quite late.

Wretchedly he thought she reminded him of the vegetable vendors in Delhi who brought their wares to sell balancing baskets on their heads. He angrily shook away the image. She didn't stop until they reached home and then she crouched low and smoothly eased her burden off with a delighted laugh. "Lucky we found it before anyone else!"

She scrubbed it clean and set it up with his books and table lamp, her face flushed and sweaty.

The vision of her carrying the table for him remained in his mind and heart. He hated what they were reduced to. A lady who was accustomed to every luxury was practically crawling home carrying people's discarded furniture, when one phone call from her would have had attendants from Delhi's posh furniture stores scurrying to deliver custom made furniture to her doorstep.

One weekend they attended a lunch at the Joshis. Mridula had a job with a local bank and asked Namita to give it a shot. "Figures scare me," Namita confessed.

"Okay then, how about Dinesh's store? He needs someone to take care of it from nine to six and the pay is negotiable."

It gave Namita three days to get organized, cook meals for the next six days and search out the routes to Harris Park, but it was a job.

The work was exhausting, the commutes long and the pay a pittance. She spent long hours weighing out, marking and sealing spices into plastic packets which she displayed on the shelves. Her fingers bore orangish yellow stains and constantly reeked of spice. Crates and boxes dumped by the suppliers at the loading dock behind had to be hauled in and unpacked. All day she made copies of Bollywood movies for the video library and ran the store single handed. At times the sweet and heady smell of the incense mixed with the aroma of spices made her sick and she rushed into the street to get a breath of fresh air. She dealt with a range of customers, the fastidiously finicky, the ever complaining, the snobs, the successful, the struggling new comers and the friendly university students.

One day she was buttonholed by a peculiar woman wearing a loud floral skirt, ample gold jewelry and flowers in her bun. She clicked her fingers and nodded disdainfully at Namita who was busy making packets of tamarind. "Excuse me, come here please," the tone was commanding, the accent muddled. Namita dropped the tamarind, wiped her hands and rushed to her. "How much you will charge to come home and cook three days a week?"

Namita's voice caught on a small throb in her contorted throat. She could barely find the right words, "I'm not a coo... I don't go....I mean I just manage the store", she burbled. The large woman made an impatient sound and strode off with a swish of her garish skirt leaving Namita staring at her, tears of humiliation welling up in her eyes.

Another day, a middle aged man came in and asked for the "other" kind of movie, but she was at a loss and pointed to the stack of movies arranged in the store. His friend pulled him away whispering in vernacular "maybe she doesn't know". The first man retorted in a loud, drunk voice, "then why she is minding the store?" He advanced aggressively towards her shouting, "Manager. I want manager". Fortunately, his friend dragged him away just as Namita was getting ready to grab a pot to throw at him from the piles of woks behind her.

Ashish wasn't having a much better time through all this either. While the fuel station ran by itself quite smoothly, the little convenience store inside it was proving to be a challenge. It attracted a number of teenagers without cars who came in to make small purchases. Ashish noticed small things like chocolate, batteries, pens and shaving foam going missing and decided to watch that group of kids closely. They had a well-rehearsed modus operandi. They would spread out in different corners of the store and one of them would distract him to a spot in a corner, while the others picked odd items. By the time he got back to the counter, one of them would be waiting to make a legitimate purchase of a loaf of bread or some milk while the others would call out loud goodbyes and leave. Right away Ashish would find some things missing from the same area they had been standing in.

Sohrab, the shop owner was getting more and more upset about the shop lifting but rejected Ashish's suggestion to install a surveillance camera. It was up to Ashish now so every time the boys walked in, he got busy. He'd walk around the aisles keeping a hawk's eye out. If the boys asked for an item, he directed them from wherever he was standing, his eyes darting about. He could sense their frustration as they left angrily without making any purchases.

The next day he saw Sohrab chatting with a group of youngsters at the far end of the petrol station. That was the same group of kids. When Sohrab came in, Ashish told him he suspected the same guys for the shoplifting incidents. Sohrab's reaction was curious. He pointed a finger at Ashish and said "hey don't mess with them guys, they're all my mates." Ashish patiently explained that he had very nearly caught them red handed and ever since he had been watching the gang closely, the stealing had ceased. Sohrab would have none of it. Raising his hands palms out, he shook his head loudly proclaiming, "Look, you got the wrong guys. These guys are innocent."

Ashish had had it up to here with Sohrab's seriously hostile attitude and unsympathetic air but the job helped pay the bills and put food on the table.

That night Namita narrated her story of the silly fat woman and the drunken man. She whispered softly to him in bed, so Namish would not hear. Ashish pulled her closer to him as she sobbed quietly, her face buried in his chest. Her sobs brought tears to his eyes. He knew she missed home. The food on the table that night had been so frugal, it broke his heart. The servants and the driver back home ate better.

Since their arrival Namish had not once been to the movies. A few months after they arrived, they had found a small discarded T.V. on the sidewalk, cleaned it up and fixed it. Namish watched kids' shows on it. The sidewalk had yielded more stuff for their home – mattresses, a bookshelf, an armchair and even a washing machine. Sadly, he couldn't fix it and he and Namish had dragged it back to the road.

He thought of what the family had had to endure. Namita had a wan and tired look with dark circles and a nervous, hunched up gait and Namish had become serious and quiet. Each afternoon Ashish would get Namish from school and take him to the petrol station with him. They would stay there until Namita picked him up after work. Namish quite enjoyed it and even learned to pass things under the counter till they beeped. Ashish usually let himself in at night after work and slept through the morning.

He stroked his wife's hair, "It's not easy for me either Nam, but we have only been here a few months. You have to give a place at least a year before you start thinking about going back."

Namita sat up, "one more year?" She tried keeping her voice to a whisper "that's impossible Ashish, don't please don't ask me for another year; look the sooner we return, the easier it will be to get our old routine back."

"Nam, we have nearly done one year, it's just a matter of another year."

"Are you happy?"

"No of course not. Sohrab's a thug and I hate the job but now that we are here…"

"Then what? After two years, you get the citizenship of a place that you don't belong to, an alien culture. Face it Ashish, it works for some and doesn't for others. We are the others. The migration bubble has burst. There is no paradise over the next hill. We left our paradise behind, only we didn't know it back then. It will benefit no one. Namish has less than a fraction of the work they did back home and he gets it done in fifteen minutes flat."

"Whoa slow down Namita, just the other day you were thanking God for the stress free school days that Namish is blessed with. Didn't you say you were glad for the well rounded curriculum with music, sports and art?"

"In the long run, yes! It is a terrific system if he can go the distance because I know they finally get there by the H.Sc. but not if we return to the heavy load in India now. Each day lost would take a month to cover!"

Shaking his head slowly, Ashish looked at her befuddled. "Nam you're making no sense."

"I ask you, why do you think we made it through the selection process for P.R.? Because of our qualifications, because they thought we could come here, take up responsible jobs, make a meaningful contribution to the community and become integrated members of the multi racial tapestry of this wonderful country. Not because they thought we would breeze in here, exploit the system and jazz off! Do you believe you are using your education and your experience?"

Ashish was looking more annoyed now as he realized that Namita's argument made sense "Are you?" he retorted.

"Obviously not, and that is why I am willing to accept defeat and return. Don't you see, we live in an Australian house, use Australian transport, roads, medical facilities, send our son to an Australian school free of cost, and at the end of it, you want to get your hands on the trophy and walk away. Doesn't the futility of it depress you? It strikes me a tad selfish, exploitative and downright criminal."

"So why are you blaming me? Blame the system that grants you a visa but doesn't provide any means of a livelihood."

"No Ashish, let us cut our losses. We need to return and salvage whatever we can back home. I don't know about you, but it will weigh on my conscience forever. I just love the Australians, so naive, polite and decent. We really can't blame the country. Why did we place so much trust in all those "contacts" that we brought with us? Not one has bothered to help us."

"They are busy! Who has the time? You have to do it the right way. I have sent out my resume through a local Aussie placement agency, they have forwarded it to six places and I am not giving up. Going back is not an option. You hear me? It is just not an option. I still have hope."

By now they were talking in rather loud voices and Namish walked in, crying in his sleep. Namita took him back to his sofa bed in the living room and both Ashish and Namita sat staring at the little boy drawing some peace out of his quiet tranquility.

The following day Sohrab was in a terrible mood as he had discovered some expensive roller ball pens and other stationary missing. Not one for mincing his words, he accused Ashish point blank, "No offence but I don't think I can let that boy of yours stay here all evening. I don't really trust kids - always poking their noses here and there. You won't like it if I blame him when I find something missing."

An infuriated Ashish would have liked to lash out and say so much, but he realized it was pointless even trying to reason with the self opinionated, arrogant swine and nodded, "I understand, Sohrab".

Ashish told Namita that Namish would have to go somewhere else after school. He didn't want to anger her with what Sohrab had actually said so he made up a vague excuse. "I don't know exactly. Some insurance hassles."

Costs for after school care were prohibitive and Namish risked becoming a latch key child when Maggie, the Chinese lady next door offered to supervise him in the afternoons for free. Her granddaughter went to the same school a year behind Namish and spoke English haltingly. Back when she didn't have a job, Namita used to help her with her homework and little Chelsea had made much improvement. Maggie thought Namish would be a huge help with Chelsea's homework and insisted that Namish spend the afternoons at her place for no payment as she realized that it would be a mutually beneficial arrangement.

Life continued, routine and dreary but the Aryas chose to live on in hope.

One winter evening as she returned from work, she noticed a youngish bloke sauntering along aimlessly. He would walk in one direction, stop for a bit as if he'd forgotten something, and then turn around and walk in the other direction. Namita had been watching his suspicious behaviour as she walked across the vast expanse of the park in the gathering dusk. There was no one on the dimly lit street. *"That's one of the problems! It's so lonely and quiet, it's scary!"* Irrationally, she hoped he would meet up with whomever he was waiting for. She trudged along trying to shake the uneasiness she was feeling. She would have to walk past him to get home. Where were all the joggers, evening walkers, and mums with pushchairs? She reached the end of the park and stepped onto the asphalt sidewalk. A massive tree with branches touching the ground shielded the young man. She was, for a bit, in a blind spot as she fussed with the branches, trying to press past the fence. The man turned around pulled his beanie over his face and started jogging in her direction.

Would she panic? Would she scream? What would the struggle be like? He felt evil excitement as he lumbered towards her. Namita's face broke into a beautiful smile and her eyes crinkled as she let out a short, relieved laugh. The man glanced backwards. Some people had crossed the road and were walking towards her. The trio called out to her,

"What took you so long?"

"We decided to walk to the bus stop to meet you!" It was Namish, Chelsea and Mrs. Lee.

The man jogged on and entered the park. He must keep jogging. The woman probably didn't suspect a thing. She was carrying a heavy bag and was weighed down by her overcoat. He watched them cross the street and disappear. No harm in hanging around here. It was getting dark now. Good, the darker the better. Many young girls lived on that street, younger and prettier than this one. The fat one with auburn hair and a nose pin had not returned yet and the curly blonde also lived alone in the corner flat. She had been coming home with that bearded guy for some time now, but maybe she would be alone this evening. It wouldn't hurt to wait. He decided to keep jogging.

Namita thanked the little old lady and unlocked her door switching off the porch light as she pulled the door shut. Absently listening to Namish's account of his lab experiment, she pumped soap on her hands and turned on the hot water. There was something, some niggling thought that bothered her. Was it something that Mrs. Lee had said? She dried her hands on the towel, pulled out food from the fridge and popped it into the microwave. Namish had already set the table for dinner. The television was on and an advertisement came on for some new crime serial.

Namish rattled on about creating a water cycle at home and how their sir had told them about acid rain. His words were white noise as Namita's mind was inundated with a million thoughts. She stared at the glow of the heater, her eyes narrowing. That face! It was the same as the mug shot she had seen of the rapist earlier. He was attacking girls at knifepoint on lonely streets in the western suburbs. Her heart hammered against her chest gutturally and her throat felt dry. She had looked into his face for a good quarter of an hour on the folded newspaper of the man sitting opposite her on the bus. All she had seen was the mug shot upside down, and a small part of the headlines, "Police warning to females over serial rapist threat in West" The image replayed itself in her mind like a video.

She recalled the aimless strolling around, the beanie hiding his face and that awful expression in his eyes! Namita's knees trembled. She felt positive he was running at her and not past her. She realized with a gasp that their neighbors and her son had probably saved her.

"Mum you okay?" Namish looked at his mum, worried.

Namita murmured something he couldn't understand. She grabbed the phone off the hook and shakily dialed 000. "Are the windows upstairs shut? Go and check." Namish did as he was told. He knew they were shut tight and had been for the past two months. It was too cold. But he didn't argue. There was something in her tone. He heard his mum speak softly but clearly and almost conspiratorially into the telephone. She was describing someone, their clothing and stuff. Now she was telling them how to get to Jones Park outside their house. What was going on?

By the time he came downstairs Mum had placed hot food on the table and pulled all the drapes shut.

"You okay mum?" Namish sat down and started serving himself.

"Of course!" she said cheerfully, "So tell me about acid rain."

Later that night she narrated the incident to a stunned Ashish, who had also heard about the elusive prowler from customers at the petrol station. She murmured softly to him in bed not wanting Namish to hear.

"There is something about the police here. I feel I can trust them. They're dependable. They moved in swiftly and found him right where I said he would be." She turned to look up into Ashish's troubled eyes. Her husband's grasp tightened around her.

"It's okay!" She whispered pressing his arm, "A flash on the late news said the police were able to catch him on a report made by a passing motorist who caught sight of his face in the headlights of his car and thought he resembled the wanted man! Takes the blame off me completely! He will be put away for a few years."

"It's still a scary thought. It could have turned out so badly!" He glowered as he visualized the peril his wife had escaped. Banging at the quilt in silent frustration he barked in loud whispers, "One job! That's all I'm looking for. One decent job."

Namita rubbed his back trying to calm him but knew it wouldn't do to speak when he was in such a temper. She watched silently as he strode across to their makeshift work station and turned on the computer to scour for jobs. She sighed. He would be at it for hours. She turned on her side and fell asleep sending up a silent prayer of thanks for her near escape that evening.

SEVEN

As winter receded the days became longer. The Arya family had discovered a Hindu temple just behind the petrol station where Ashish worked. Namita started going there every evening with Namish. She would pack dinner and carry it to the petrol station, visit the temple, eat dinner together and then walk back with Namish. A few months went by and they were, in a manner of speaking, fairly settled in their lives. Ashish had to regularly field Sohrab's slights at the fuel station shop and Namita swallowed her pride each day as she arrived at the service entrance of "Spicy Indian! The one stop Shoppe for all your home needs". She had cringed at the pretentious and largely erroneous shop name but didn't challenge it. The fact was that it was popular and frequented by scores of customers.

One day while unpacking cartons of newly arrived sweets for the festive season she saw some chocolate that Namish used to love back in India. For one wild moment she thought of appropriating a few bars for her son and then shook herself out of it, "I'm developing a criminal mind." She decided to splurge and purchased a bar of chocolate and a box of cashew sweets that Ashish loved.

A light spray drizzled softly as she walked home. They used to consider it a good omen back then. Young and in love, they used to enjoy walking in the rain down the tree lined avenues of Delhi University. When the rain got too strong he shielded her with his body as they ran to find shelter.

The drizzle amplified into a light shower and she turned her walk into a swift trot. Another image came to her mind. She remembered taking a drenching in the monsoon rain on their terrace in Delhi with Namish. It washed over their faces, hair and clothes. Giggling helplessly Namish said it had been the "funnest" time but hated peeling off wet clothes.

Nearly home, Namita scurried up their common driveway. Just as she was about to ring Mrs. Lee's bell she noticed that the lights in her own house were on and quite suddenly Namish's chubby face popped out wearing a secretive smile. He looked like he was bursting to say something. Namita walked in and Ashish called out "Hi honey, what took you so long?"

"Ashish, what are you doing home so early?" Namita asked, offloading her things and shaking out her damp hair.

Ashish handed her a sheet of paper and Namish continued grinning from ear to ear. Namita saw it was an appointment letter from Aus-nitro, one of the large fertilizer companies.

"Thought you might like a bit of good news hmm?" said Ashish taking her in his arms.

"Is That really the salary?"

"Umm yes except for a few perks like medical insurance and a car!" Ashish added with a laugh. Dazed, Namita looked at his glowing face. It was as if ten years had been wiped off in one stroke. He had his warm smile and boyish flamboyance back.

Namita sat down, her knees weak and trembling and looked down at the letter once more hardly believing it was real. She hugged Namish and smiled through her tears at her husband. "This says you have to join in three days!"

Ashish quit his job the very next day and vowed never to buy fuel from his petrol station even though it was just around the corner. Sohrab misconstrued the resignation, "Hey is this because of what I said about your boy? Don't worry about it! Kids adapt." He protested, stretching his hand out patronizingly.

Ignoring the outstretched hand, Ashish shoved his hands in his pockets and turned away grimly, "See you around Sohrab". His parting thoughts weren't happy ones. Let those goons come and rob the bastard blind.

Ashish's new salary would be twice as much as their combined incomes and he urged Namita to leave her job and scout around for retraining options. Namita handed in a week's notice at the Indian store. "We'll still see you as customers." Mridula said. Namita doubted it. The prices were inflated, the rice and lentils bins rat infested and the freezer temperatures a touch too high.

Rummaging through their boxes she pulled out Ashish's business suits. He hadn't had much use for them that past year. She ironed them out just like the laundry man did back home carefully using a wet cotton dupatta to protect the costly fabric from scorching. She sent Ashish for a haircut and laid out a selection of ties, handkerchiefs and socks.

She decided to sign up to re-qualify as a teacher with The Department of Education. The elusive light at the end of the tunnel seemed to be brightening and life appeared to be looking up!

Soon it was their first Diwali in Australia. Namita set up the Laxmi-Ganesh idols on a table and they performed puja as a family. They sat down to a lovely meal laboriously prepared by Namita. Namish started reminiscing about the Diwalis back home. He recalled how firecrackers used to be bought weeks in advance. He recited the names of all the cousins who would gather for Diwali and secretly raid their goodies laden pantry.

Each one recalled their personal memories of Diwalis back home. Namita remembered shopping for new clothes, lights and gifts and cooking large quantities of Diwali sweets like "gujiya", "barfi" and "laddoos". She fondly recalled decorating the house with intricate "rangoli" using flower petals, mirrors and clay lamps.

A flood of memories came rushing to Ashish. Not recent ones but those of his boyhood and youth. He remembered the day a firecracker in the shape of a flowerpot burst into flames with a loud explosion when he was still lighting it. He was fortunate to escape without hurting his eyes. He recalled the fairy lights all over the roof at Diwali and the taste of sugar animals after Diwali puja.

Namita looked down at the empty dishes. How well they had eaten! She got up to fry some more puris and Namish filled their glasses with coke. Ashish saw Namita wipe her eyes. Realizing that the memories of all the grand diwalis back home made this one look shoddy, he took a crack at levity. "Hey who remembers the three hour drives on jam-packed roads during Diwali shopping, or the smoky pollution and incessant noise?"

"Whatever you say will not stop me from missing India." Namita said gruffly.

"Maybe a puri will," said Ashish stuffing an entire puri into Namita's mouth.

Namish laughed so loud to see his startled mum's mouth bulging, his eyes started watering.

Namita looked at her son. It was so long since she had seen him laugh with such carefree abandon. She sensed that they had in some way transmitted their anxieties to the child. Her husband added, "The fact is, we remember only the happy times, not the discomforts. Once you take a realistic look back you will recall it in the right perspective. This is our life now and we'll get there with baby steps!"

She knew he was right. They were slowly getting settled in to their sparse but cosy life and Namita was thankful for it.

Something troubled Namita about Namish but she couldn't quite put a finger on it. She had observed the little boy looking about nervously when he entered the school. He had started talking in his sleep and his old stutter had returned. He had been counseled for stuttering when he was five and the child psychologist had told Namita that the stutter could re surface if Namish came under stress. She had also asked them to ignore it, not correct him too often or make him feel self conscious about it.

Whenever Namita asked him about school and if he had made any friends, he would either avoid answering the questions or look away and say "Everyone is my friend." Namita knew he had no problems with the schoolwork and thought it a passing phase. She made a secret promise to herself to meet his teachers as soon as possible but became completely engrossed in her teacher training program. It meant long hours and Namish started carrying the house keys as Mrs. Lee had taken Chelsea to China for a long break.

One afternoon as Namish walked home after school, he cut across the large football field sauntering carelessly, lost in the thoughts of his new Play station games. Quite unexpectedly four or five boys jump on him from behind. Pummeling and punching, they pushed him to the ground before he could hit back. They vanished before Namish could recognise any of them. His arm was badly twisted and his face had nasty bruises. Winded and hurting agonizingly, Namish just lay there staring at the sky, unable to move, partly out of the pain and partly because he just didn't want to. He didn't care anymore.

He hated it all. "Stupid idiotic kids who can't even spell or do basic math in their heads, wicked bullies"! He missed home a lot and missed his grandparents even more. "If Dadaji (granddad) had been here he would have called the police. These guys should go to jail." He lay there tears streaming down his face till a passerby noticed the schoolboy lying in the middle of the field and alerted the school authorities.

Namita's train had just pulled in at Parramatta station when she received the call from the hospital.

The next few hours were a blur as Namita rushed to her son's side. Namish had been hit rather forcefully and had sustained some injury. The teacher was unable to elaborate on the incident but he assured her that the school was looking into the matter. Namita sat gazing at the bandaged face of her little boy looking small and helpless in the large white hospital bed.

"Brave lad," Dr. Whaite smiled kindly at Namish and explained to Namita that the wounds were superficial but they would like to observe him for a bit before sending him home.

There was another boy in the next bed with a broken leg who decided to watch the T.V. at a rather loud volume. Namita rushed to draw the curtain partitioning the beds. Namish glanced at her from under the bandage and whispered "Simpsons", with a smile.

After some time had passed, the doctors were relieved to see that he was alert and responsive and all his vitals were within normal range. "It could have been much worse," Dr. Whaite said, "Any idea, how it happened?" Namita had nothing more to add to what he had already been told by the school authorities.

"I suggest you look into it. That's an unkind blow he took. It's ok; you can take the little guy home now but bring him back if there is any vomiting or dizziness."

Clutching her bag under her arm, Namita wheeled Namish out to the taxi rank. She helped him into a taxi and got in herself. "Mays Hill please. You can make a right at Burnett Street from Great Western Highway, thanks." She snuggled up close to her son to absorb any shocks from road bumps. Namish closed his eyes and cuddled closer.

"No problem Bhabhiji (sister-in-law), I will get you home. What happened beta (son)?"

Namita looked up surprise. It was Suraj Aminchandani's, smiling at her in the rear view mirror. "Suraj, what a surprise and what a coincidence!"

"Not really, I am usually on this route in the evening. So tell me, what happened?"

Namita narrated the whole incident holding Namish close. Gazing aimlessly out of the window, she rambled on about their experiences that past year, almost as if she was speaking to a close friend.

They arrived at the house and Suraj carried Namish carefully into the house and laid him on the sofa bed. Namita made some Milo for Namish and offered Suraj tea. She placed a plate of biscuits before him.

Suraj chatted on about his life since he came to Australia ten years ago. He had initially come to study Accounting. "A product of Xavier's and the best commerce college in Delhi, I came to do a Master's in Accounting, but soon realized that without a CPA, the equivalent of what we call Chartered Accountants back home, getting that dream job was out of the question. After a few unsuccessful attempts at finding work I lost the drive to continue with my studies. It was easier to find part time work at the stores, and the whole higher studies conundrum appeared too tedious. I was a fun-loving guy and took the easy way out. But I was in a quandary about how to tell my folks back home that I had dropped out and become a taxi driver! They would never understand or accept it. Plus returning to India was not an option as all my friends had grown in their careers. It was a no win situation."

"We all thought you were a company executive. Ashish's parents told us to get in touch with you, but Ashish couldn't locate you. So where do you work now?" Namita asked, stroking Namish's hair as he drifted off to sleep, the painkillers taking effect.

"I just told you, I drive a taxi!" Suraj smiled.

Namita stared, "And that helps you make a decent living?"

"Can't complain, I am doing great. I have two properties. I live in a three bedroom place with a garage and a garden, and I have leased my unit."

"That's terrific Suraj. All this from driving a taxi!" Namita said incredulously, recalling inwardly how her chemical engineer husband ran from pillar to post job-hunting for months on end.

"What's wrong with driving a taxi?" asked Suraj, the smile never leaving his face. "I also teach driving during the week."

Namita laughed, a little embarrassed. "When will I ever stop mentally classifying people by their occupations?" She murmured.

"It will take you a long time," said Suraj, "I still haven't told my parents what I do. I know they will never understand. They think I am employed in a bank. That's why I haven't married. Every time they found a match for me, I knew I would have to tell them my real occupation." Suraj got up and made for the door. "I've taken up enough of your time. Look after Namish and say hi to Ashish for me. Here's my card, in case you ever need a cab. I live close by."

He let himself out as Namita stared into space, trying to make sense of why anyone would want to live a lie for ten long years, in a foreign land, performing an uninspiring job day after day with no family to go home to.

Absently she got dinner ready, the attack on Namish overwhelming her to a point of sickness.

What did it say about his safety at school? Why hadn't her child ever mentioned these bullies before? How could they have attacked her mild, straightforward, simple boy so mercilessly? She turned the day's events over in her mind remembering Suraj's startling revelation. She realized with a shock that she had not paid him for the taxi ride. Covering Namish with a blanket, she sat down on the floor beside the sofa cum bed and watched over her sleeping child.

Ashish was appalled at the attack on Namish and stared grimly at the little sleeping figure. "I must remember to carry my phone on the shop floor." He whispered, "I feel so bad you had to handle it all alone."

Namita remembered her meeting with Suraj and filled Ashish in. "We should pay him." Ashish nodded, "I'll go see him one of these days. I know you are surprised by his story, but it's not all that uncommon. I have heard of engineers driving taxis and bank managers selling train tickets. It makes you wonder why they don't return to the comfortable life back home."

"But they don't go back." Namita looked down at the worn carpet she was seated on and slowly shook her head, "they don't go back" she whispered.

Their meeting with the school didn't go quite as expected and they came away feeling as if a little more action on the school's part might be in order. There was this notorious gang at the school known to cause trouble often. The boys had been warned, punished and talked to.

Namita shifted awkwardly in her chair as the principal and teacher explained things to her. For the hundredth time she tried processing the discipline system but couldn't help comparing it to the one she knew so well! In India these children would have been suspended if not expelled for such behaviour." she thought.

"Namish is an excellent student and has endeared himself to all the teachers within such a short time. We feel awful about what happened. I have had a stern talk with the boys and I do assure you, I feel convinced it will not happen again."

When Betty saw poor Namish's bandaged head, she murmured. "Time was when such an incident would have brought out the cane! Things have changed! You watch your step son!"

Namita learned that the boys would harass him in class too. Once when Namish had made a presentation, one of the boys raised his hand to ask a question. The teacher allowed it and Namish stood up waiting for the question. Lolling lazily on the chair, the bully said, "Naah! I just wanted to see if you would stand up when I click my fingers." Most of the class remained silent but his mates laughed out loud. The teacher ticked the bully off but it didn't seem to deter him. Another day when Namish was telling some kids about his computer project, the gang of bullies butted in shouting, "Cook your lame ideas in a curry" "curry" being crude slang for people from India, Pakistan, Bangla Desh and Sri Lanka. Namish had just smiled tightly and walked away.

Namita was relieved to see Ashish getting involved in Namish's school issues. It was really important to restore the disturbed boy to his old cheerful self. Both parents worked hard with their son to help calm him down and start making friends. To their relief, many kids were keen to be his friend and all of them unanimously despised the gang of bullies. Namish usually had a couple of kids to walk home with and sometimes they stayed back to play with him. Namita noted with relief that her child laughed easily again and participated cheerfully in every school activity.

Just as things appeared to be looking stable, a teenage driver put his car through their fence and nearly came and hit the house. Namita and Namish ran out hearing the loud noise. She rang Ashish and the distressed driver called his father. Ashish was on his way home and assured Namita that insurance usually handled things so she needn't worry about it. Surprisingly some of their neighbours they had barely exchanged pleasantries with came across to ask Namita if she required any help. She was shaken by the incident and asked one or two of them to stay with her till Ashish came.

She looked around horrified. The fence was uprooted and broken in many places. A slender tree had broken in two and all Namita's little flowering pots were squashed.

Very soon the father of the boy arrived just as Ashish drove up and the two talked it over. The man apologized profusely and appealed to the Aryas to not contact the police as his boy was an underage driver. He beseeched them to give him a day giving his absolute assurance that he would come and fix the fence himself. He said, "This is my job! See, I am a handy man and I can make this fence good as new for you. Please give me one more day."

Ashish wasn't so sure, "This could have been very serious if my family had been in the yard. Besides, I don't know how I can explain it to the owners." The man looked pleadingly at Namita. "No need to tell anyone! I will finish the job tomorrow. Please I ask you to trust me!" He scribbled his phone number and address and handed it to them. "If I don't come, you call the police on my boy. Okay?"

Reluctantly they allowed him to get away not really convinced about his credibility. Namita waited for him the following day and the day after but nobody showed up. She dialed the number he had given but it was a digit short and she began to feel sure even the address was fake. The Aryas had to accept the smooth talker had never intended to keep his word and Ashish kicked himself for not calling the police.

Nothing remained to be done now but to get the fence fixed. That weekend Ashish stood outside assessing the damage and calling up for quotes. Seeing him some of their neighbours came out and on hearing how the culprits had got away, offered to help fix the fence. "You shouldn't have taken him on his word. Look I have some material lying in my shed and some tools too, so why don't we just put it back together?"

Ashish was game. The men succeeded in putting a decent fence up in just one weekend. When Ashish offered to pay, the man just laughed it off saying "No worries! This was my old fence, just lying there rotting!"

"Then allow us to cook you an Indian meal," Ashish offered. This was welcomed with much enthusiasm.

One day, watching Namish playing with the kids from their neighborhood Namita said to Ashish, "Fate plays tricks. We should never have trusted those guys, but then would we have made so many friends on our street?"

Not always was Namita the perfect mother. In their early days when Namish's class was to make a diorama for Geography, he came home and asked for her help. As always she nodded and said they would do it over the weekend. He was relieved to hear that. What she didn't tell him was that she would have to get down to absolute basics for this project. After dropping him off at school she rushed to the local library and took notes starting with a dictionary meaning of the word "Diorama". Never one to work with her hands, she dragged her feet over it and on the last weekend started to put together something in a shoe box. It all began with the plastic camel from his toys and progressively got built around it. A glass out of Namita's compact served as a lake in the oasis. They grabbed some soil from their yard and tried to stick it down around the mirror. The net result was pathetically amateur. Namish wished he was one of the kids who hadn't made one at all and had to give up sport one afternoon. It would have served a double purpose - save him embarrassment and get him off sport on that hot and muggy day when he could have peacefully worked indoors on his Sudoku quizzes. The class of kids was polite and quiet. They stared at it and asked weird questions but nobody outright insulted it. Sadly, it was placed right next to a diorama made in a display case crafted by hand from a fruit crate. It had a working motor to pump water to real live plants that looked like palm trees, and a tiny switch to operate the lights. The soil in Namish's diorama had collected in a corner revealing some cardboard from flattened apple juice poppers, the compact mirror had cracked and become two oasis lakes and the plastic trees were smaller than the camel. The figures posing as Arabs had been taken from his soldier collection and the white cloth headgear or painted on beards didn't quite cut it.

Namish realized that even his mum had her limitations and tackled the next term's project alone. He researched industriously and presented a brilliant composition on "The History of Time". It was superbly published with graphics and proper referencing. This time nobody sniggered. Namish scored a perfect score and got a teacher's award.

The Aryas found themselves integrating into the cosy May's Hill community quite nicely. Ashish organized weekend cricket matches with the local kids and acted as coach and umpire while Namita served up lemonade and snacks. The other parents pitched in as well and soon Sunday sports became an interesting weekly event.

Namish was not a natural sportsman. He usually remained the twelfth man but enjoyed playing non-competitively. The best part was that he never resented his dad coaching so many other kids. Maybe that was why everyone called him a good sport.

Namita made friends with some of the other mums and found them sensible, sweet and caring people, a lot like Betty. It was nice to feel that sense of belonging that had been missing from their lives since they arrived.

"We play scrabble or other board games when we meet for coffee'. She mailed her friends back home. "The hostess does very little as each lady brings a dish, and you can't imagine how they loved my potato pakoras! It's usually quite a simple affair, a far cry from the "kitty" parties back home where your designer sari is vying to outshine her diamonds!"

As the year drew to a close Namita got excited about joining the teaching work force. It would be Christmas soon and Ashish had an invitation to the office party. Now, confident in western clothes, Namita planned her outfit carefully. Although Ashish had a reasonable salary, she still couldn't afford to consider designer clothing. She found a great black cocktail dress at half price, teamed it up with antique silver jewelry and had her hair done. "You look stunning!" exclaimed Julie, one of the mothers who had dropped by to take Namish home for the evening. Namita hoped Ashish would think so too. She had taken great care to get "the look".

The evening was magical and meeting her husband's colleagues opened up a new side to her. She was particularly tickled to hear such good things about him from his mates. "I'm a lucky mama! First Namish's perfect report this morning and now yours Ashish Arya!" She giggled as he led her on to the dance floor.

"I told you I love my job!"

Namita couldn't stop smiling. "I doubt they will appreciate Mrs. Two left feet Arya too!" but really didn't care. After very long she was truly happy and determined to enjoy the evening.

He led her delicately to the romantic strains of Strauss and she glowed in the knowledge that they looked fabulous together. Her perfume and shampooed hair floated about them. Even so, he talked as if they were catching up at the end of the day.

"So what about Namish's report?"

Namita smiled. Just like a man.

"There are gaps in his Math. I picked up some workbooks. I thought you could work with him." "I'll take a look at them." The music ended. Her ankles smarted as he sat her at their table and went for a refill. Her eyes followed him. He was certainly the most charming man in the room. She reached down to rub her ankle. No more dancing in these high heels!

The party ended with small gift envelopes for each employee. It was more than generous and Namita held the cheque excitedly as they rode home in a taxi, also provided by his office. The bonus took Ashish by surprise. He had believed one needed to be a part of the organization for longer before receiving such bonus.

"Let's get you a car, a nice one!" Ashish suggested.

"Really, can we afford it?" she asked.

"I think so.

In a sense, Namita was the last of the Aryas to settle. The move had robbed her of her originality. She had spent a larger part of the previous year looking worried, old and exhausted. Ashish observed she was getting some of her spark back in the New Year. It was when her quirkiness surfaced that you could be sure Namita was back. She teased Namish and played crazy games with him. She cooked up a storm each weekend trying out new recipes and when her husband offered to get her a car, well Namita declared, she had always wanted a "Herbie"!

Namita had decided it would look cute for a school teacher to go to work in a VW Beatle and there was no changing her mind.

Ashish reasoned, "It is hot most of the time and the car has no air-conditioning. There are far more comfortable cars ..."

"A red one, preferably, but I don't mind yellow or blue either!" Namita addressed the heavens.

Luck was on her side and they managed to acquire a bright yellow Volkswagen Beetle on their budget. Ashish smiled to himself as he heard his wife on the phone blathering on about her new vehicle. He rolled his eyes and shook his head but knew that she had got exactly what she wanted. She did look cute driving it to work at the neighborhood school. He powered on his laptop to catch up on a little office work. The words that flip-flopped on his screen brought another smile to his charming face.

> "Three things ruin a man, power, money, and women.
> I never wanted power. I never had any money, and the only
> woman in my life is up at the house right now."
>
> Harry S Truman

It was a sad day when Betty decided that she could no longer live by herself. She confided in Namita, "All my friends are either dead or have moved into a home of some sort. I have a tidy sum stashed away and I think I should move out in a month or so. I am mentally ready, I just need to pick a place, pack a few things and then I'll be off. I invited you to tea with a particular purpose. I wanted to ask you something." Betty looked earnestly at the recent but dearest addition to her small circle of friends. "Would you like to buy this house? It has brought us years of joy and comfort and I don't think Tara is moving back to Sydney."

Thoughtfully, Namita strolled back to the cricket match on the grounds from where Betty had hailed her as she had been delivering lemonade to the hot cricketers.

Back home later that day, Ashish was curious at this shock announcement. "How much did she think we could pay?" He wondered, as they weighed their options.

"It's right next door to my school!"

"For just two more years," Namita murmured. She glanced around at the deteriorating state of their house, "but hers is a really nice house, spacious and very well maintained."

"How much, Namita?"

"I didn't think to ask."

"I have an idea how much loan I can get and though it will be tight, I think it is a good time to buy a house rather than go on paying rent. Why not go talk to her?"

That evening they walked hesitantly towards Betty's house. Ashish looked down at the grass as he walked deep in thought. Namita knew it would put much strain on him as she would not be made permanent for another few months.

She asked, "So, do we propose a figure?"

"She's your friend, you talk to her."

"Ashish! I don't know how to ask her! It's awkward!"

"Okay I'll think of something. Just introduce me and say that I'd like to look around the place."

They cut across the Jones Park green and approached the pretty yellow house on the same corner as Namish's school. A bunch of people stood around talking in low voices. This was strange for a street where usually there was no more activity than a couple of children on bicycles. Even Mr. Parsons, the Principal was there. On a weekend!

He walked up to them as they approached the house.

"She went quietly! Exactly the day that she was to pick her retirement home, she passed on in her sleep, peacefully!"

Namita stopped in her tracks speechless. Tear welled up in her eyes as she stared at Betty's house incredulously. An elderly lady walked up to her while Ashish propped her up. "My dear, you were her most faithful visitor I have to say!"

Most of Betty's neighbours recognised her and tried to console the sobbing Namita who was quite beside herself.

Slowly they walked home, Namita hardly able to compose herself as a deluge of memories of the happy time spent together flooded her.

It was almost a week since poor Betty had passed away yet Namita expected to see her smiling face waving to her from the little glass window on the patio as she walked up to bring Tara some food.

Tara was touched. "You are too kind!" She talked softly to her as she cleared out her mum's cupboards. Smells of potpourri and lavender were carried on waves of grief. The air was heavy with the sorrow of losing one so precious. "You were a sincere friend to her. I know. She would tell me about you every time I called."

Namita looked around the little house disconsolately, "I miss her so much! She was the first real friend I made here. We used to swap life stories! She was intrigued by our lives in India and I by hers. She told me she had worked in India and Bangladesh, even the middle east and Afghanistan."

Tara looked down at the hands in her lap and nodded. "Yes she was in Afghanistan too."

"She was an exceptional woman! You were lucky to have had her as your mum."

"True."

Namita picked up a picture from the stacks that Tara had been packing. "Is that you? Betty looks so young here! And you look…"

"…absolutely nothing like her!"

"Gosh! Do you resemble your father?"

Tara looked from the pile of pictures to Namita's face and flicked her glossy black hair back, her large, dark eyes quite blank.

"I don't know! I never knew him, or my mother."

Namita looked puzzled.

"I thought it was obvious! Mum adopted me!"

Realization dawned slowly as Namita got the answer to the question she had asked herself often. Why were there no pictures of any man in Betty's home!

Tara spoke on, "I always knew that I had been adopted. It didn't bother me. I had a perfect life, never wanting for anything - a sensible upbringing, great education. Of course there was a time I called myself a "Duft head"!

I must have been 6 or 7! It was funny!" Her sad face lit up momentarily as Tara recalled an innocent childhood incident.

"How was school honey?"

"Good. We got a new boy. He's also a duft head."

"He's a what?"

"A duft head, like when your real parents died and someone else took you."

"It's "adopted" sweetie."

The two ladies laughed through damp eyes.

Tara sniffed and wiped her eyes, "She had never told me how or where she had got me and really, it didn't matter one bit to me. I loved mum and she loved me. Kids at school used to ask if she was my nana and when Alicia's nana died I was scared that mum might too. I prayed extra hard that night. I wonder if she even noticed that I cleared the table and did the dishes that night without her asking!" Tara looked at the beautiful smiling face in the picture, "I didn't want her to die!" She sobbed a little and Namita held her close.

"But when I heard of the circumstances of my adoption, I was staggered. I remember the very day of the revelation. We had just moved into this house when I was a teenager.

The movers had left and we were emptying out the boxes. I always took time to arrange my books because I would leaf through each one before shelving it."

She looked at Namita smiling, "People inscribe books when they gift them and I liked reading that."

Namita understood exactly what she meant. She gave a little laugh, "back when books were regarded good gifts."

Tara continued her narration, "I finished with my books and lifted the box to discard it. Oops! No not yet, there was something at the bottom. I peered in. Not this again!

I reached in a pulled that old doll out. Why must the ragged old thing follow us everywhere? Limp, shapeless, wonky eyed apology of a doll! It has been the recurring motif in my life for as long as I could remember. This was one thing that had survived every spring cleaning. It always went to the back of mum's cupboard.

I always asked the same old question: "Why do we keep this old thing?" and I always received the same old answer: "I'll tell you when you're old enough!"

Years went by but her answer was just the same. Yet again, that day I carried the raggedy doll into mum's room right here and announced, "Special delivery!"

I held the doll by its leg between fore finger and thumb and was about to fling it on her bed as she sat sorting through her boxes. But she reached out for it with both hands as if it were a newborn.

I had had enough. "I know it is special and I know there's a mystery tale to go with it. I also thought families didn't keep secrets from one another?"

Flopping on the bed, I asked her, "Am I old enough?"

Mum sighed. "I do not know if you will ever be old enough, but I'll tell you if you insist."

"I insist."

"She held the raggedy doll lovingly in her hands almost as if she were cradling a frail baby and was afraid she would hurt it. She narrated the tale in her gentle voice and I just sat there stunned."

Tara looked at Namita shaking her head slowly, "This story just blew me away! I don't mind sharing it with you. This is exactly as my mum told it to me."

EIGHT

Namita settled in the vintage armchair and listened, her hand cradling her chin.

"It was at a time when medical relief was urgently required in a remote frontier village. Red Cross workers had been detailed to go and set up a relief base.

Almost every house in the village had suffered some damage. The shells would fly across the sky in a curved trajectory and pierce through concrete buildings. Their mud and thatch huts didn't stand a chance.

The little girl ran around bare feet, a wide eyed, scruffy little thing. When the relief workers arrived, people fell upon the vehicles, arms outstretched making a lunge at whatever they could grab. The men sent their women to queue up beside the first aid and water stations while they carried away blankets and prefab materials to build makeshift homes. The kids lined up for rations and clothes. Everyone got busy.

She toddled around aimlessly, barely noticing the hectic activity all around. Her eyes had tired of looking for a familiar face. Her tears had dried up. The little bedraggled dress she wore had once been pink with a bit of lace at the neck, sewed lovingly by her mother. Her father had swung her chubby little body up in the air and her sister had tied pink bows in her glossy curls, now reduced to a mangled, knotty jumble of hay.

The banging of hammers and grating of saws began as sturdy men started putting up shelters. Large trucks backed up to offload supplies and set up the mobile dispensary. Nothing distracted her. When she felt tired, she just sat down, looking but not seeing, hearing but not listening. No one tried to rouse her, feed her, talk to her. Even the stray dogs got some stuff thrown at them but everyone was oblivious to her.

There the tale of her pathetic little life would have ended but for that rosy cheeked, plump Red Cross nurse.

She walked around the camp carrying the little malnourished, emaciated bundle. "Is this your child?" She asked again and again.

Like a jack in the box, a woman popped her head out of her tent and lifted her veil "Bombs. Shelling. They all dead. Her mama, dada all dead". She disappeared behind the veil and retreated into the tent.

In that climate of hatred and uncertainty, no one could be bothered with another mouth to feed. The nurse cradled her half starved, dehydrated body, feeling her forehead, searching for a pulse. Unexpectedly, she felt a soft fist close over her finger. She looked at the tiny, wizened, mud-smeared face and was greeted with a most beautiful smile that warmed her heart and made her choke back tears. Nurse Rita had no one to call her own and felt peculiarly maternal towards her tiny charge.

Through the next few weeks Nurse and her little ward were a familiar sight around the camp. The elderly lady carried out all her duties to the background of gurgling and cooing. The toddler slowly regained her strength and a pink tinge appeared in her cheeks. She had found an abandoned little ragged doll somewhere and carried it around imitating all that the nurse did to her patients.

It was a limp, hand stitched cloth doll whose once pink face was soiled and whose button-eyes had dropped off. The stuffing had poured out of one of the arms and the dress was in shreds.

"What do you want with that ugly thing, you funny bub?" Nurse would laugh watching the little one's antics.

In time, the child was well enough to hobble around on her chubby little legs, wandering away a little too far at times and every now and then, one of the refugees would carry her back to Nurse Rita's tent.

With the camp up and running, it was time to pack up and leave. Nurse called upon all the elders in the camp to ask one family to adopt the little nameless baby. Nurse called her anything she liked and the little one always responded with a shiny smile. The child had enriched Nurse Rita's lonely life in so many ways, it was hard to say goodbye.

"She is not old enough to be a servant. She is no use. We do not want her."

"Deaf mute children, especially girls, very hard to look after."

"She's not a deaf mute!"

Shrug, "Never heard her speak."

Nurse turned away to hide her tears. It was not fair to blame them or express the exasperation she was feeling. She, who had come to their rescue when they had lost everything, could not justifiably impose an unwanted burden on them. She didn't fault any of them. She just felt a strange disquiet at their feelings of animosity towards the hapless child. What alarmed her more were the unusually strong maternal feelings she had developed towards the little mite. She looked down. The little face smiled at her in pure faith.

An aid worker passed by busily and shouted out to her. "The Medical Aid convoy leaves at dawn!"

It was the longest night.

Nurse Rita watched the sleeping child. She lay down next to her as she had done those past few months. Her heart broke into a million pieces at the thought of parting with her. She touched the glossy curls and felt the warm breath. "Nobody wants you, little one." The diminutive figure curled up in a foetal position lay sound asleep, unmindful of the turmoil she had caused in the elderly woman's life.

There was only one solution.

Tara Eva. She named her Tara for her shiny eyes and Eva meaning life. Ironically enough, their surname Gallagher meant "lover of foreigners"!"

Namita gasped. She contorted her face trying to process what she had heard. "That's amazing!" she whispered.

Tara stared distantly out of the window and swallowed. Namita squeezed her hand.

Tara continued in a shaky voice, "Mum looked up at me through tears. No words were necessary. All the missing pieces had come together. My love for my kindly mum, Nurse Elizabeth Rita Gallagher grew tenfold! I held the little rag doll, looking at it with a renewed interest."

Tara wept softly for her sweet kind mum on Namita's shoulder.

Betty was hard to forget. Namita struggled with the loss but went round to check on Tara every day. It was weeks before Tara smiled. Her swollen eyes betrayed restless, tearful nights. Munching on Namita's curry and rice she chattered on as she packed up her mum's well arranged wardrobes.

"Do you know, besides the story of my birth, the other revelation this house brought us was pretty unbelievable." She pointed to the buff kitchen floor.

"When we bought it, the kitchen had a really bright coloured Lino on it."

Namita's brow was furrowed as she looked up from Betty's collection of dainty handkerchiefs.

"You know, linoleum, that burlap and resin kind of floor covering."

"Oh yeah! I've seen it in my childhood."

"So mum and I decided to peel it off and keep the kitchen floor bare wood. We started burrowing and digging around the sides to yank it off. The lino was old and held on stubbornly. We poured some sort of a solution that the Home Depot guys said would dissolve the adhesive. We thought it would take days but we awoke the next morning to find it had come off and rolled up around the edges! It was easy to just yank it off after that and between the two of us, we carried it out.

Mum grabbed the vacuum cleaner as we returned to the kitchen. What do you think we found!"

"Bugs, mice, rats?"

Tara gave a sudden stare. She hadn't really expected an answer.

"No. Actually the floor was surprisingly clean under there." She came and sat down on the bed next to Namita, her eyes wide, face aglow, "We found, taped to the ground, five envelopes of money."

"What!"

"Five aged packets full of money! Well of course mum wanted to find the rightful owners, so we contacted the estate agents who had helped us buy the place and they said that the house had belonged to a lady who died and the rest of the family really "don't care what you done with it as it's now yours, so if you think the Tiffany lampshade is antique, just keep it!"

Namita gulped in amazement. "Oh my, how much was it?"

"This is where the story gets even more interesting. Those were old banknotes. I had never even seen them. We were using the new ones! In fact some of them were in English currency, pounds and shillings and only mum could remember using those. So we showed them to our bank manager and what do you think, he was happy to redeem the money for us as it retains its legal tender!"

"Wow!"

Tara spoke with a mouthful of potato curry and rice.

"Listen on. While we waited at the bank, the branch manager gave us yet another suggestion. He said that they could give mum face value for the notes, but there were collectors of old currency and things who might give five or ten times that!"

Namita stared open mouthed. She moved her head slowly from side to side "Such events, only in books!"

Years of narrating this tale had taught Tara to recognise that look and she understood Namita's telegraphic language.

"But it must've been great to know that your mum could live comfortably in her old age."

"Quite a relief really! Always nice to have a surprise windfall! As they say, life is full of surprises."

Namita wended her way back thinking about Betty and all her struggles. She thought back to the story of their migration. It hadn't been easy and it hadn't always been pleasant but as she took in the bright purple agapanthus below the towering trees and felt the delicate mist gathering over Jones Park, Namita hugged herself thinking solemnly. No it had not been without pain but it had been worth their while. A cool wind enveloped her and she turned to get back home with comforting thoughts of a cosy meal.

School teaching added a new dimension to Namita's talents as a pretty authentic mimic. She regaled the guys over dinner each evening with an account of her day at work. She copied the accents as a child pronounced pickles as 'pickools' and couch as "key-ouch".

Another day she narrated how she was very nearly stumped, "Can you believe it, I had to take Genetics today!?"

"What do you know about Genetics?"

"Not much except for X and Y chromosomes and the eye colour thing we did back in class eight. But I had some videos and an hour to prepare. As I walked up to the demountable fiddling with the keys, students poured out of the next class and a bunch of them came to me. They helped me get the door and one of them asked, "Miss, are you from India?"

Another goes, "what colour are your eyes?"

And a third says, "She's not Indian! Look how tall she is!"

"I seized the opportunity and used myself to introduced genetics to the class! It was such an interesting discussion and I know most of the stuff will be sorted out by their regular teacher, but I was glad to answer their question."

Aromatic vapors drifted around the bright red bowl of Thai green curry, her latest culinary endeavor. She ladled it out over steaming hot jasmine rice, the next best thing to costly Basmati rice.

"I give it 5 stars!" Ashish declared shoveling a forkful into his mouth.

Namish had bulges in each cheek and raised a "thumbs up" in appreciation.

"Not bad eh!" Namita beamed.

"I vote for once a week."

"No worries! It's easy."

She was content if a dish was a hit. She chattered on, "Yesterday I worked with the Special Education kids. Never a dull moment there but mercifully we managed a good bit of work like numbers, alphabets and sport. One of the other teachers had found some Frogspawn and brought it in a glass tank for the kids to go peer at. You know the little tadpoles?" She wiggled her fingers to indicate swimming tadpoles.

"Well, at the end of the day, when the kids were being picked up one by one, I walked into the room to see this little guy by the tadpole tank. He pulled his hands away looking a bit guilty as he backed off. I looked at his hands and one was wet. I assumed he had been trying to reach the little critters and wiped it off telling him not to worry the tadpoles.

"Just look."

"Juss look." He repeated a little unconvincingly.

Today, I see the same little fellow being hauled away, so I asked the teacher why.

"Eating tadpoles."

"What!"

"I caught him swallowing one. He's always by the fish bowl and I notice there is a lot less animals in there than three days back."

I panicked, "Is he okay? Is it safe?"

She glanced down at the scamp, "Seems fine, but I am going to let the doctors decide and I am getting rid of that thing."

Namita had to stop her narration as her husband and son collapsed into hysterics over the way she recounted everything imitating each one's voice.

Namish uploaded pictures on his Face Book page of their explorations of Sydney. There he was touching a stingray through the Plexiglas at the aquarium and crawling through a submarine in the harbour or smiling into the camera as fireworks lit the New Year's sky over the Harbour Bridge. Namita remembered that evening. When they were recent arrivals, they met some Indian families to watch the fireworks together and Namita was introduced to some people. The topic that dominated was to do with admission to a Selective High School. The other ladies enlightened her about all the extra coaching classes and tuition that people were getting for their kids, "every weekend across 2-3 years!"

"What for?" Namita asked.

"To ensure the child passes the entrance test."

"Doesn't that defeat the purpose?"

"How can you say that?"

"Those schools are meant for kids with aptitude not those who qualify after years of coaching! It certainly defeats the purpose of migrating! If this was what I wanted, he was fine back home where even kindergarten kids receive private tuition."

The ladies persisted, "If you do make it into a selective School, you are kind of set for life."

"Actually what I worry about is, what if you "make it" after all that drilling but aren't able to cope?"

Namita came home bogged down by all the dope and sat mulling over this new information the following day.

"What was Jain's wife blabbing about?" Ashish asked.

"Oh! That was so weird! She said she was so distraught after Bandana didn't qualify for any selective school that she had cut off all social contact for the last six months. It appears that if your child doesn't make it, other Indians look down at you and sort of denigrate the parents." Namita looked nervously at Ashish who burst into a roar of amused laughter.

"What's so funny?"

"I don't know what to laugh at more, your ridiculous story or the expression of total horror on your face!"

"Ashish this is serious."

"Which part? It is serious that I will be ostracized by every migrant Indian or that Namish is doomed if he doesn't pass the test? Forget it! Doesn't the rest of Australia get educated?"

"I am not going to talk to you if you're going to mock at me."

Reluctantly Ashish agreed to check out the coaching centers but not before laying it out clearly, "I strongly believe they want the kids to sit the test without preparation. That is the only way they can get the truly gifted ones. Training Namish for a year or two so he qualifies is majorly cheating the system."

Namita stormed off in a huff and even though Ashish knew she would calm down in a bit, he was annoyed by the unnecessary strain the previous evening's conversation had imposed on their family. He hated when Namita sulked and Namish buried his nose in a book, feeling scared to talk to either parent.

Ashish turned on his computer. An interesting quote flip-flopped on his screen. It seemed appropriate:

> "There are only two tragedies in life: one is not getting what one wants, and the other is getting it."
>
> — Oscar Wide

Namita came in shortly and asked if he would like some tea. That was her way of calling a truce. As she put on the kettle she smiled as she remembered something, "There was a funny bit though when she told us how they prefer to spell Bandana's name with the letter B instead of V; the teacher thought it was cute to name a child after a headscarf!"

One summer afternoon, Namita and Namish trudged back from the local library on one of Sydney's typical "scorchers". Having spent the afternoon in an air conditioned library, returning to their searing house was all the more distressing. Setting their dinner to cook, she came out to sit in the lounge. She directed the fan at her face as she sat there with her feet up enjoying the silence.

She threw her head back and closed her eyes.

It was a tiny rustling sound. She was too drained to even lift her head. She would have to go and stir the chicken in a bit but until then she was going to let the fan blow at her face. The rustling seemed louder and closer. Unmistakably something was sliding or hauling itself across the ground. Dry leaves crackled and crunched as if they were being stepped on and dragged right there, outside the glass doors next to her. She parted the curtains. There was nobody. The sun was still high in the clear blue sky and the air warm and clammy. Her eyes took in the dry grass, bare trees and carpet of brown leaves across the backyard and patio. Then she heard the same sound again and sensed a movement by the patio floor. She looked down. Her heart raced. How she stared at it, hardly breathing, as it slid around unhurriedly dragging its hulking body bit by bit across the patio. The creature didn't notice her at all as she gaped at the grotesque thing speechless. It hauled itself across the smooth tiles, stuck its snake-like neck out and opened its bright pink mouth in a yawn. A purple flat, floppy tongue rolled out and grabbed something, a snail or a bug off the floor. Unimaginable dread and creepy revulsion gripped Namita's pounding heart. Shaky knees could barely support her as she stared unblinking at the hideous creature. "Namish" she croaked out in half a whisper.

With classic gusto the pressure cooker's whistle shattered the eeriness as Namita lurched into the furniture and stumbling toward the kitchen hollered for Namish.

"It's a dinosaur with a snake's head or something. Be careful. We have to call, whom do we call? I don't know! I'll call dad."

As he walked to the glass doors, Namita stayed a safe distance away getting on her toes and peering at it. Namish had pulled up a chair and was examining it fascinated. He looked back at his mum and grinned. "It's a blue tongue lizard mum. It is harmless. It's a native of Australia like the marsupials and monotremes. Come take a look."

On shaky legs she approached the French windows and gazed out at the somewhat unattractive species of Australian reptile. Mother and son gaped and gawked at it until it disappeared into the thicket at the edge of their yard.

Namita usually remarks casually to visitors, "I am quite used to seeing it idle about and keep hoping it takes off soon, but for now it rather favors our neck of the woods!"

Lately a piece of news had bothered and troubled Namita and it miffed her further that nobody else gave a fig about it! She read in the papers about some missing rocket launchers and assumed they were some small parts that had gone missing but would eventually be located.

Ashish had befriended a former army man, Roger, in the neighborhood and he occasionally stepped in for a chat while returning from his evening walk. They usually got him to recount some exciting wartime incident and Namish hung on his every word! From his vast experience, Roger generally made clever observations on the current world scenarios and Namish, an ardent current affairs buff enjoyed talking to the senior man.

Namita could not hold her unease back. "Roger, I couldn't get my head around the news in the papers, about rocket launchers missing from the army."

Roger smiled and shook his head, "Can't imagine how that is ever possible!"

"Do you think somebody's hiding them and they will just turn up?"

Roger gave off an uproarious guffaw through his bushy moustache.

"How big do you think they are?"

"My spatial ability is not too good but about this big?" She held out her hands about a foot apart.

"Let's just say, one of them is about as big as your coffee table."

"Nine of them, each this big?"

"How heavy?" Ashish asked.

"Oh about sixty kilos."

"So no one could have walked away with them."

Goodness no! Probably loaded them on a lorry and drove out!"

Namita looked truly frightened. "And we are ok with it?"

"I guess so, until we find them!"

Ashish said he read about a "Sergeant from some school of Artillery who had stashed away some stuff."

"Yes but did you hear how much he stole? Shoulder-mounted rocket launchers, hand grenades, guns, caterpillar tracks, periscopes, ammo and some medals as well! In fact, one of the reports in the papers said there was enough to fill six freight containers."

"Six freight containers!" Ashish threw a sidelong glance towards his wife. He thought Namita might pop a blood vessel.

Roger nodded gravely but there was no real hint of panic.

And that was what infuriated Namita. The shrug of the shoulder, the tilt of a head and the condescending nod that she got each time she asked anyone what they felt about the rocket launchers.

Time heals all wounds but hers had not had so much time before a governmental authority made a statement to the media stating that "every so often the odd weapon does go missing" and that there was just so much anyone could do about it.

Whether Namita lay awake nights awaiting a rocket launch attack or not will never be know because very soon she had to field another bombshell, this time from Namish's school.

She walked through the deserted school one afternoon looking for her son's class teacher. He had sounded serious on the phone and had agreed to wait after school to see her. He sat somberly at his desk, hands clasped before him.

"Mrs. Arya," he hesitated, "I know I have spoken about Namish's Mathematical ability earlier."

Namita cried out fervently, "Yes, Mr. Taylor I think he takes after me, but you should know, my husband's an engineer. I will ask him to take Namish's Math."

Mr. Taylor looked at the nervous lady springing to her son's defence and raised his hands reassuringly, "I don't think you quite understood. I am sorry I don't mean to alarm you. That is not it at all. What I am saying is that Namish has been surprising us here at school with his Math. He far surpasses the class average and that of all higher classes at this school. We even set him some work from a high school workbook and he has managed a near perfect score!" He took a deep breath, paused and looked up at her over his glasses. His beady blue eyes bore into her.

"What are you saying?" Namita searched his face, her eyes darting about uneasily as the man's words sank in slowly.

"That we think he may be a Math prodigy, a genius, even a savant but would like to ask you to consider seeing a specialist."

"Are you certain it wasn't just the schoolwork he's been doing every day? I...I brought him some practice books and sat him down to do them! Could they..."

His eyes didn't leave her face. He shook his head. "Thirty years in the profession, I have never encountered such a sharp mathematical mind!" He handed her a print out about some chap called Orlando Serrell and added, "It's not impossible you know!"

He stood up and patted her on the back adding gently, "It's a lot to process, I know, and we have been there," he pointed to Namish's books on his table, "for weeks! But we didn't want to call you till there was absolutely no doubt. He's certainly gifted! I can't for the life of me imagine," his kindly blue-grey eyes held her, "why or how I could have said that Namish was not quite as good at Math. I do apologize."

Namita stared at nowhere in particular shaking her head slowly from side to side. "He wasn't!" She whispered almost to herself, "he was always weak with numbers, always."

"It's not rare to see a child pick up in a subject once he feel settled and begins to apply himself, and now with the bullying issue quite sorted, I thought he had found a love for Math but what Namish is displaying is an exceptionally unusual ability." He removed his glasses and rubbed his eyes. "He should have every possible help and support, that," he looked about the room, "we may not be able to provide here. Would you like to speak to his father and perhaps meet us later in the week?" He handed her a card, "This is the number of a very good Psychologist who might..."

"Psychologist?" Namita almost yelled out. "Why? What for? He's well settled here, I...I don't want to disrupt his studies at this school. He loves it."

"He is a gifted student and we are privileged to have him here! Look, Mrs. Arya, why don't you take some time and think it over? We could speak again. It's a great deal to handle I do understand!"

Till the day he moved on to high school, Namish continued at his beloved primary school raking in many of the top awards at the year end. He excelled at High School too and went on to pursue actuarial studies. He joined the government as an advisor but his first love still remains History. He has a photographic memory, isn't very good at games, isn't too social, loves to read and has an adoring girlfriend who makes up for all those deficiencies being an excellent sportswoman and a popular, sociable girl. After all, they are childhood friends, he and Chelsea.

Roused by the soft purr of the Postie's bike Namita rose to collect her mail blinking in the piercing glare. That is the worst of a receding winter, the sun warms too fast. She squinted at the mail as she rubbed her stinging exposed arms. The stiff cardboard of a bulky wedding card in ochre and gold dwarfed the flimsy Telstra and Integral Energy bills. This was going to be some wedding! The school bell for morning tea chimed in the distance as Namita cleared her tea things and carried the tray indoors.

Not such a long time ago the school across the fields had churned out a "genius, a prodigy, a savant"! The jury of doctors and teachers was still out on that but for the mum, he was her little boy who used to write his sevens facing the wrong way and who now was nicknamed a human computer! She didn't care that in Khanna's view they still lived on the "wrong" side of town.

Back in the guest house Namita shook herself out of her reverie and slumped on to the bed with the fervent hope that power would be restored soon. There was nothing she needed more than sound sleep.

The aircraft cabin metamorphosed from a cadaverous tomb into a buzzing, energetic, social scene. People lined up in the aisle awaiting vacant washrooms. Unsurprisingly, Jane struck up a spontaneous conversation with the bunch of strangers. Soon they were chatting and laughing easily. Arti stirred and awoke to the lively discussion rubbing her eyes as she stretched in the cramped space. She looked up befuddled to see their quiet corner turned into a social hub and Jane chattering on with random strangers as if she'd known them all her life.

Jane turned to her, "Oh Hi! G'morning! Feeling rested?" She proceeded to introduce her new found friends and Arti nodded, managing a weak smile.

"Are they all waiting to use the washrooms?" she asked Jane softly.

"No! The washrooms are free. Go ahead. We're just chatting!"

An auburn haired girl pressed herself against the bulkhead to let Arti pass and turned to Jane, "So tell me, did you two just make friends?"

Jane's instant reply was full of promise. "You're never going to believe it! We two are..."

As Arti slid the cubicle door shut she had a pretty good idea what Jane's account of their "lost and found" story would sound like. Jane had that rare blend of warmth and joie de vivre that made her immensely likeable.

Arti washed her hands and looked in the mirror. She smiled thinking that despite the polarities of Jane and her personalities they had kept up an intriguing conversation through their protracted journey. She splashed water on her face and replaced her glasses. The aircraft gave a rough jostle and she lurched against the door hurriedly grabbing the rail. She returned to her seat stumbling as the plane swayed precariously. The turbulence had dispersed Jane's newly formed coterie. Jane firmly held a cup for Arti and handed it to her. The warm coffee was as welcome as Jane's update that they had just a couple of hours to go!

"So you held your audience captive with the story of your life! And mine I suspect." Arti grinned.

Jane tilted her head and laughed, "We're pretty interesting people you know! Besides, I love getting to know people, what they do, where they're headed, you know, their life stories. I think about them long after. It's better than reading fiction. I love making that connection." Her hands moved back and forth. It's a kind of social evolution!"

Arti sipped the warm coffee and looked skeptical, "What?"

"If we care to listen, share, empathize and connect it leads to newer bonds being formed! I feel we should talk to everybody. Cutting ourselves off will have the reverse effect. We become narrow minded, insular and uncharitable."

There was nothing Arti could add to that having lived a fairly reserved life herself. Much as she might have liked to be gregarious like her friend she firmly believed nothing would change her personality at this stage.

Draining the last dregs of her drink she turned to Jane, "Oh yeah, you were telling me about this charity…?"

"Yes before you fell asleep." Jane sat up enthusiastically, "I am not the type to go around preaching, but I share with people I care about. I am going across to Maharashtra to check out this place that has taken my fancy."

"Where do you hear about such places? And more importantly, how do you know they are not a part of some scam?"

Jane nodded her curly head vigorously, "That is a sure shot risk especially in India. That's why I have to visit it and see everything for myself.

So coming to this new one, I read about it in a NRI magazine. Now, this lady's daughter, my friend wrote a piece on her mother's extraordinary life and how she came to being involved with the place that I am headed for."

Jane fished out a few chocolates from the seat pocket and handed Arti one, "Do you feel up to reading something?"

Arti waved the candy away, "Sure! I usually read on a plane. What is it?"

"The story I was talking about, you know, the charity lady? I have it on my ipad."

Arti polished her reading glasses and watched Jane rifle through a Burberry tote that Arti knew cost over a thousand dollars. Jane pulled out a neon green spectacle case studded with multicolored rhinestones.

Arti looked at it head cocked to one side and laughed softly.

Jane polished her glasses busily. She looked at Arti abruptly, "You know the word "Bling"?"

"As in, shiny accessories such as ..?" She gestured with her eyes towards the case.

"Yup, I invented the word."

"Get out!"

"Honest! I did!" The curly head bobbed spiritedly, "At school! Remember during the war, we had to bring in food tins and stuff for the Prime Minister's relief fund? One of the nuns at school suggested we put up shows in our neighborhood and I had organized a variety entertainment in our balcony. I raised a bumper 11 bucks though 15 kids came. Two were siblings and three said they'd pay later. We weren't too clear with our charter of credit rules back then. We had a magic show, some gypsy dancing and a play based on my story "Weevil from Wee Ville."

"You gave them their money's worth alright!"

Jane nodded, "Sure we did." She sighed wistfully. "Eleven lousy bucks and we practiced for weeks!"

"Wrote the play yourself?"

Jane nodded, "It was quite a faithful adaptation of the town mouse-country mouse tale but in my story the rustic weevil decided to get some "bling" to feel right in the big city. That was the word I used when it wasn't even popular."

She chewed on a strand of the blanket's edging and murmured almost to herself, "Should I stake a claim, I wonder?" She looked down absently at the ipad in her hands.

Arti giggled, "Idiot. Give it to me. So this is about the place, the organization?"

"Nope. It's about this woman's life. She didn't start it, she helps run it. Read it and you will understand. Her daughter's a journalist and this is her oeuvre. It featured in the annual souvenir edition that was a part of a felicitation event honoring charitable NRIs. The entire family volunteers for it and Mini, the daughter told me that they had just appointed a new manager, some really capable NRI who has recently returned for good. Says he wants to raise his kids in India. She says he was very keen on an honest charity and this suits him well."

Arti raised her eyebrows skeptically and Jane nodded, "I was a bit surprised myself, I mean, going from a lavish western lifestyle to a pretty basic kind of life in the interior of Maharashtra, the very centre of the country sounds a bit harsh, especially if you have kids to educate but then, they say he is a bit idealistic. I'll be meeting him too."

"Okay, "Arti said cautiously, "I'll read it but how does it connect up with the charity in Maha..."

"Just read it and I shall nap."

"Nap now? Everyone's awake and the place is abuzz!"

"I couldn't sleep earlier. I have this gizmo." She slid on some designer eye shades, slumped down in her seat and reclined her head pulling the blanket up to her chin. Almost instantly Arti saw Jane's head fall limp and she appeared to be a picture of calm repose. She smiled. Thinking back on all they had talked of she felt a rare admiration for the friend of her youth. It had not been easy for her and yet all she wanted was to seek new ways to help others.

Arti turned off the small screen displaying a tiny section of the yet unachieved flight path. She couldn't fathom how Jane could sleep with so much commotion and bustle but decided to attribute it to exhaustion from talking so much. She smiled at the resting flibbertigibbet and turned on the ipad.

NINE

Shivaneri 1935

She was the Zamindar's (landowner) eldest daughter. Her mother, Bai Saheb, resplendent in the gold jewels and rich saris, was a vision. A compassionate and charitable heart beat in that aloof, royal reserve. She had the kindest green eyes that would well up with tears at the sight of a sick child in a farmer's arms. She was the original social worker, like her large hearted husband. When the river was in flood, the "Zamindar", would plunge in and rescue two men at a time. Good, kind people they were. Lila had everything; good food, rich clothes, love and care.

It was late afternoon and the sun cast long shadows on the broad stone veranda shaded by a massive peepal tree. Lila set out her tiny brass and silver toys and her cloth dolls. She was going to cook with the neighbor's little girl Vimal. Then they would take the "food", bits of jaggery and roasted gram in tiny dishes and serve it to their mothers. Lila looked longingly at the tiny snacks. Vimal is late. She scanned the muddy trails for the familiar figure of her friend clutching her mother's hand skipping along, usually humming. Vimal always hummed. Lila's eyes gazed out to the endless fields as far as her tiny green eyes would see. She would ask her mother, "There, at the end of all our fields, is that the end of the world?"

"No!" her mother would laugh hugging her playfully. "The world is very big Lila, enormous!"

They came in a dusty black cloud. First it was small, faint and distant, like a speck. It moved rapidly and fleshed out as it approached. Men from the fields ran around with sticks in a wild, bewildered scramble. In the distance on a broad stone verandah a diminutive figure watched in horror, clutching her cloth doll, as the black cloud hovered over the plantation and descended in a pall flitting just on top of the vegetation. The hoard of dragonfly like insects buzzed agitatedly abutting each other. The farm hands screamed frenetically for her father, Rao Saheb. Lila squinted as her young eyes took in the terrifying sight. Her tiny feet scorching on the flagstones, she watched her father dart across to the fields kicking up a cloud of dust and then she lost him in the horde of men. The strange dark cloud rose, hovered over the field for a while and moved away, diminishing as it went, now just a speck. Petrified, Lila stood rooted to the spot and then turned and ran inside shouting "Ai laukar yay" (Mother, come quickly).

The locust invasion threw the village into a gloom. The thundercloud of buzzing insects reduced fields of mature, ripe wheat to bare stubble in a matter of minutes.

A contingent of farmers came that evening to meet Rao Saheb. They carried their wives' jewellery in small cloth bundles to offer in lieu of the 'lagan' or tax. Six year old Lila knew something was amiss and watched from an inner room as her mother called her father in. A whispered conversation followed.

Rao Saheb returned to the verandah and sent them all home. "I can't accept your wives' gold. Take it away and come back tomorrow. I will open the granaries. No one will go hungry in our village."

Yes they were good kind folk, simple, naive and trusting; in fact just the kind of people that others took advantage of.

By the time Lila turned twelve; more siblings had been added to the family. The rains had not come in three years. Most of the farmland had been sold and their head of cattle was reduced to a single pair of bullocks. There was only one thing to do. Lila knew her worried parents were in preparation for something and heard her father's soft, persuasive voice struggling to calm her sobbing mother. It was quite late at night when Chandu Kaka arrived.

"We leave at dawn, vahini (sister in law)," he told her.

Her mother tearfully put together Lila's things in a small tin trunk.

"Where are we going Ai?" Lila asked again and again following her around.

Ai cried a lot that night. She brought little Lila close and spoke to her earnestly. "They are making me send you away little one. You are going to the big city, to the big house in the city. There you will get a good education."

"But will I never see you Ai?" Lila's lower lip quivered but she wanted to be brave.

"When you become a great big educated lady, come and take me with you." Ai was inconsolable. Lila and her sister were packed away with just a few things the very next morning. Hungry and scared, the two little girls reached the big city after a bullock cart ride and a long train journey.

It was a palatial house with stained glass windows, oak paneling and crystal chandeliers. The sitting room that was opened only for special guests had a leopard skin stretched across the wall, a piano and velvet covered settees. There were other uncles with their wives and children living in that mansion. It felt strange to meet so many cousins. Lila missed her mother terribly and cried herself to bed every night. Their grandmother loved her a lot and kept her close. She made ambiguous promises to bring the parents there soon. Little minds have little memories. Lila felt reassured and started joining in the games with the cousins.

The sisters were measured out for new clothes by a bucktoothed tailor who sat down right there in the veranda and stitched puff sleeved dresses with bows and frills made out of yards of taffeta bought from the sly Chinaman's bundle of silks and brocades. He came every six months with pretty fabric and all the girls would sit around gawking at his wares. Each one got two new frocks.

Before they could enter school the girls had to be brought up to scratch and a tutor was employed. Lila didn't much care for him. "He has hair growing out of his ears." She complained. Math was a mystery; the printed word was unfamiliar and writing on paper with a pencil a novelty. The village school had had no books and they had just chanted rhymes, played with smooth stone counters and written on a slate with chalk.

In contrast the massive school in the city seemed to dwarf her and the multiple classrooms and teachers were intimidating at first but she adapted fast. Lila loved the chatter and camaraderie. She felt happy in the company of other little girls and didn't bother much with her books. Nothing made sense anyway and most days she just doodled or drew things in her books, happy to have notebooks and pencils all to herself.

A taunt at school changed cheery Lila's frivolity. "Your grandfather is the judge and rides around in a big car; you live in the biggest house; your family is the most superior in all of Nagpur and you can't even get pass marks in any subject!"

Malati Damle did Lila a big favour that day. Her cheeks burned at the girl's sniggering and her eyes overflowed with hot angry tears. She was older than her peers and after hearing these barbs, she began to feel awkward amongst her younger classmates. That afternoon she sat in her room by herself still smarting from the other girl's jibes. She picked up her books and started flicking through them. The teacher's lessons returned to her mind hazily. How hard could it be? Everyone else seemed to do it.

She settled with her back against the headboard, stretched her legs and started reading. This was pretty interesting. She ignored her cousins' shouts to come play. She vowed she would make Malati eat her words. Lila picked up the math homework and her brow furrowed. What had the master been talking about? She needed to concentrate a bit more when the teachers spoke in class. Before long Lila began to devote every waking moment to her studies.

She recalled how, back in the village, when she had no other books to read, she used to sit on the platform outside the temple every evening and read The Ramayana to the villagers. She had actually started reciting excerpts from it without reading as she could memorize pages effortlessly. She applied this unusual gift to her studies and surprised most teachers within a few weeks.

"Who would have imagined Lila could actually hand in such immaculate work! Her homework is perfect!" Mrs. Mohite wasn't a teacher easily pleased but the new student's work had impressed her. Lila began to feel a special thrill in tackling challenging assignments and loved being the one with an answer in class. She got support from an unusual source. Jeroo Patanwala loaned her books and even taught her to write good answers during lunch. She was a clever girl, and she had regular tuitions at home. Her father, Dr. Patanwala, a kindly and good-natured man was their family doctor.

Four years later, Lila stood proudly as the principal pinned on a gold medal for top marks in the entire state. Aji (granny) was so thrilled she had sweets distributed to every house in the neighborhood. Her grandfather presented her with a gold watch and her younger cousins reveled in her feat, but none of her uncles and aunts spoke to her for a week. Most of them had barely passed school and some of her aunts had struggled to get past class 4. Their sulks and anger were to be expected and Lila was unfazed. The gold medal was just the first step.

It was an electrifying time and before long Lila had been accepted at the prestigious Medical College in the capital. She read the telegram over and over bursting with a mixture of pride and trepidation. She thought of her dear, ailing mother and wondered if anyone would send a telegram to her parents. She wrote long detailed letters to her mother with cheerful news careful to leave out anything that would worry her. She frequently enquired after her health but never got any replies.

Her thoughts kept drifting off to more practical matters like the huge fees or the crucial issue of the elders consenting to sending her to New Delhi at all.

Five days remained before the first installment of fees and the consent form had to be dispatched to Delhi. She walked by her grandfather's writing table several times that day stealing a glance at the paperwork for her higher education. It lay right on top of his papers, unsigned.

On edge, Lila went about her duties around the house. Most of her uncles and aunts weren't speaking to her and others just barely acknowledged her. She brought tea on a large tray and handed it out in abject silence. The cups rattled in their saucers as she offered them to each of her elders. Lila picked up the empty tray and stood hesitantly for a bit as if about to say something. Then she walked away quietly, followed by nasty glares.

Sensing their antagonism her grandfather decided to give them a hearing. A court held in the circular living room deliberated over her future. Each one put forward more or less the same argument. She had to be married one day and hence, spending so much on her education made little sense. Also, the man she married may not even allow her to pursue a career.

Lila could not sleep that night. She tossed and turned waiting for the elders to cast their votes. She paced up and down in her tiny bedroom, adjacent to her grandparents' room. Everyone had insisted for the room to be given to a young boy, just in case they needed anything at night. Her grandfather had brushed away all protests on the assertion that "she is as good as any of your sons". Throughout her stay at the mansion, they had showered her with favors for which she found no good reason. At times she even felt irked by her grandmother's noticeable partiality towards her. Lila knew this favoritism rankled her aunts immensely.

Today, the same people were taking a decision about her future. Dinu kaka had actually brought a proposal of marriage from a 28-year-old head clerk. Manu Kaka carried news clippings of the unrest in Delhi as a prelude to the imminent Independence of the nation from British rule. Each one came ready with a well-rehearsed argument designed to bring to an end the drama of Lila's audacious aspiration.

She sensed her Aji was also up in the next room. The chattering of voices below died down. She heard the lights along the long corridor downstairs being turned off one by one followed by the creak of the wooden stairs under Ajoba's portly figure. The conference over, the chairperson was retiring to his resting quarters.

Aji met him at the top of the stairs in the veranda. Lila strained to decipher the whispers and muffled conversation. All she could hear was the indecipherable drone of her grandfather's deep voice interspersed with Aji's sweet, slightly nasal one.

She had to know. She came to the connecting door and put her ear to it but that wasn't much help either. She gently pushed the heavy door crack open and listened. The patriarch related to his wife everyone's reservations at this one girl receiving higher education at such a great cost. Her grandfather appeared to be in agreement with them. Lila's heart thudded as she eavesdropped barely breathing. He also added that one of her uncles had serious doubts Lila would be able to pass the tough examinations at the Medical College, which would be a colossal shame. Her grandmother softly asked, "Do you think she will not pass?"

"I would bet my last penny on this girl surpassing even her matriculation result."

"Then why is it such a hard decision?" Aji asked in her soft voice.

"It is a huge expense and none of these men in our house would be willing to pitch in if I ever need a supplement or if something happened to me"

"Nothing will happen to you."

"It is still a big amount of money."

Silence ensued. The old couple weighed their options and nobody spoke for some time. Her grandmother cleared her throat. She usually did that before speaking. Then Lila heard the words she would never forget.

The old lady's voice quavered, "If that is the only snag, take all my gold! Use it for Lila's medical college expenses. Whatever you do, don't deny this girl an education", she urged her wise husband.

Lila stood rooted to the ground scarcely believing the old lady's passionate assertion. The near sacred connection between an Indian woman and her gold was legendary and for no reason would she ever part with it.

Moved by the extraordinary gesture, Ajoba looked intently at his wife and taking her hands in his, he whispered, "Anasuya, you know I would never take your gold. I have my answer. Lila will be a doctor."

Lila's wobbly legs could hardly carry her. She flopped on the soft bed and dissolved in tears, overwhelmed by a mixed flood of gratitude, relief and nervousness.

****

Enjoying the distinction of being the only women's medical college in the world, the imperious structure dominated central Delhi as a classic landmark famous for its redoubtable academic standards and exclusivity in admitting top achievers.

One summer afternoon Lila hopped delicately off from the Tonga and stared timidly through the giant wrought iron gates as the clip-clop of the horses hooves faded away. The porter carried her bags to her room after leading her to the stern warden's office. She felt as if in a trance as she followed the servant boy across a flower bordered courtyard through long, shaded corridors. It was a Spartan room with two each of beds, writing tables, table lamps and wardrobes. A large window with gaily printed curtains overlooked the open courtyard. A woman sat with her back to the door, writing at the table. Without looking back she pointed to the right side of the room. "Thank you" Lila muttered and tucking in her sari pallu hurried to her trunk neatly marked with her name in white paint. Lila bit her lip as a twinge of homesickness touched her. All her little cousins had got together to help her with her packing. She already missed the white noise of chatter and laughter in that big house. The household had been swept up in a stir of excitement as each one was assigned a task related to Lila's going away to study Medicine. The deafening silence of these sterile surrounds unsettled her for a while. She started unpacking her things on the bed and carried a pile of clothes towards a cupboard.

"Not this one. That's your almirah." The Voice in a head of dark glossy curls informed her.

Lila tiptoed around as she unloaded the simple white cotton saris and other plain but durable garments her grandmother had put together. She slowly walked to the empty desk and put her books and stationery in place. She studied the sheaf of papers the warden had given to her to fill out and uncapping her fountain pen, pulled out the chair. It screeched against the cool floor. The other student turned impatiently. It was a charming, dainty face with a longish hook nose and beady eyes. She indicated with her eyes at the papers, "Complete that and return it to Mrs. Baker immediately."

Lila nodded obediently and said, "Thank you." For the next few minutes the only sound on that summer afternoon besides the whirring of the ceiling fan and chirruping of birds outside was the scratching of pen on paper. Lila finished it with a signature and studied it as her ink dried.

"Take it to the warden's office" the other girl told her. "Tag," She handed her a piece of string with metal ends. "Mrs. Baker won't accept it otherwise."

Lila's head nodded in a servile compliance, "Thank you."

"Do you know any other words?"

As she tied the papers together Lila glanced up. "Yes." She said shyly.

The girl indicated with her eyes towards the door.

When she returned her roommate was sitting on the chair wagging her feet propped up on the bed. She wore a loose white salwar and a fitted chikan work kameez.

Lila entered hesitantly.

The girl stuck her hand out, "Roshan Master."

Lila took her hand and shook it just as she had seen her grandfather do with the English judges. "Lila Apte."

"I know." She pointed to the door behind the wardrobe. "Have a bath and get dressed. I'll take you to the common room before dinner."

Lila nodded in assent. She had hoped for a Marathi speaking roommate and was terrified at Roshan's fluency in English. It was a little overwhelming to see how smart and self assured the petite girl was.

They strolled about the sprawling college campus, Roshan rattling off a running commentary. She spoke the King's English to perfection.

"Lecture theatres, common room and swimming pool; you swim?"

"A little."

Roshan continued with her guided tour accompanied by cryptic comments that the wide eyed Lila absorbed nervously.

"I don't want to startle you but don't wander about these grounds at night alone."

"Alright." Lila swallowed, her eyes looking enquiringly.

"Snakes."

"S-snakes?" Lila turned alarmed eyes towards Roshan.

"Also Leopards and the occasional cheetahs and hyenas." Lila saw a twinkle in her eyes and relaxed.

She smiled as she answered, becoming a little more comfortable, "I am not scared. Our place in the village has plenty of snakes."

Roshan led her into a pretty common room with high cathedral ceilings, elegant draperies and rich carpets. Lila looked about the room feeling a touch out of place in her white cotton sari, stiffly starched and firmly pinned back. Her grandmother had decided that all students of medicine must wear spotless white. Lila realised what a huge cliché that was when she took in the bunch of stylish young women in chiffon saris sporting strings of pearls and floating on clouds of French perfume.

She immediately faced the more tricky issues of the British accents and high-flown language of the English professors employing those complicated medical terms. Each evening her classmates would change from their dowdy, white cotton saris into elegant dresses, and assemble in the common room. Lila recognized that she needed a serious makeover on both fronts and had to manage on her modest allowance. She enjoyed her evenings in the company of those cheery bright girls. Immensely likeable and cheerful, Lila usually made friends easily. She swapped life stories with girls from different parts of the nation intrigued to hear about their families and homes.

Roshan, her roommate opened up a yet undiscovered world of literature for Lila. At first she was amazed how a third year student could find the time for recreational reading.

"The study of medicine alone can be stifling. I prefer to read something as unrelated as possible at bedtime. It is relaxing." Roshan handed her a pile of books, "Here try reading something different!"

Intimidated by the huge stack, Lila shook her head, "No thanks. I have to keep studying. My grandparents are banking upon me to get a good result."

"And you will! Nobody studies as much as you." Roshan ran a finger down the pile in her hand and pulled one out. This is an absolute must, a classic. Read a page a day. Surely you have the time for that much!"

Decades later, Lila still had the book, a bit worn for the wear in her bookshelf. There were some days she still liked to read it at bedtime, Jane Austen's "Pride and Prejudice". Roshan's hobby, like a contagion affixed itself to her. Those five years marked in her, the evolution of not just a medical professional, but also a voracious reader.

It was during this time that the Imperials decided to grant the nation her independence. On an unimaginable day, the students of her college were invited to a glittering "High Tea" at the Viceregal House as England bade farewell to the jewel of the Raj. Each lady dressed in her very best. Hoping to fit in, Lila spent an entire month's allowance on a gorgeous Banaras sari and some gold ear rings. She needn't have worried. With her clear complexion and gorgeous green eyes she was by far the prettiest in their cohort.

Not one of those girls would ever forget the magical evening at the palatial Viceregal Mansion. Khitmatgaars (bearers) in white waistcoats served a most lavish fare on an elaborately decorated banquet table. Exotic flower buds in crystal vases adorned each place amidst exquisite tableware and ornate silver cutlery. With trembling hands the ladies unwrapped damask napkins into their laps and engaged in pleasant conversation with an immensely likeable and unexpectedly informal English couple. Lila walked on clouds for days. How her life had transformed in just a few days! Most of the girls didn't sleep a wink that night recollecting the wondrous evening.

Sadly, the smiles were swiftly wiped off the young students' faces. Cleaved in two mismatched twins, the nation plunged into a veritable bloodbath. Sporadic rioting gave way to widespread unrest. A curfew was clamped on the city. The large wrought iron gates of the medical college were shut. With each passing day offerings from the hostel kitchen became frugal, even paltry but the students, their appetites faded, barely noticed. The horrendous cases that were wheeled, carried or dragged in were enough to put the girls off their food for a long time. Inhumanly maimed or limbless bodies, victims of rapists' lust, mutilated and blinded cases cut an indelible scar of repulsion and disgust on the hearts of those young medicos. Not one of them would ever forget toiling in the unbearable August heat for days on end on bare minimum victuals.

The red sand stone building assumed an identity for Lila, of a haven, a sanctuary. The walls enveloped her as she wept over the telegram bearing news of her parents' death, first her mother followed a few months later by her father. She drew comfort from the solid rocklike structure the day a cousin's postcard casually mentioned that her sister could not be traced from the orphanage she was "accidentally" dumped in after her parents' passing. Imposing as it was, the structure brought to her something more than comfort and solace. It made her even more resolute.

****

Many years later, Dr Dev drove herself up to work for yet another day in the pathology lab of the busy bustling hospital she knew so well. All her colleagues, students and subordinates held her in high esteem. Most of her students considered her the best dressed and most attractive doctor at the college and many wondered what the pretty, green eyed lady found intriguing in waste and pus samples. She was as tough as she was kind and wouldn't stand for stragglers or shirkers. The doctor's landmark publications and presentations at periodic conferences and seminars were usually the outcome of groundbreaking research. She ran the lab efficiently, delivered well prepared lectures and researched tirelessly. She seemed to thrive on that hectic schedule of hers day after day never showing signs of exhaustion. This particular October day was no different.

Dr. Dev walked briskly to her room to find Dr Ganguly waiting for her.

"Good morning Doctor, am I late?" asked Lila reaching for her lab coat.

"No I came in a little early…" The senior doctor started to speak hesitantly.

"What's up Boss you look paler than an anemic WBC!" she chuckled.

"No I'm fine."

"So what's the matter? You depressed about India getting a woman P.M. again you MCP? I like Indira Gandhi."

Dr. Ganguly managed to raise a weak smile, and then taking a deep breath, said, "The results of the professor's interviews are out"

Lila slipped on her coat and looked at him in anticipation.

"I'm sorry Dr Dev; I am so sorry."

Disappointment clouded Lila's pretty face as she stared wordlessly at her senior in complete disbelief, "I suppose it is Tomar?" She searched his face hanging on a tiny hope that someone more capable was being brought in. She did not see the answer she wanted. Dr. Ganguly appeared discomfited as his eyes barely met her gaze.

Lila slumped into her chair and looked hard at Ganguly "is this a joke?"

"Do I look like I'm joking?" A stunned Lila shook her head, completely at a loss for words, barely managing a whisper, "You were there on the selection board. Where did I go wrong?" she asked in a defeated tone.

Ganguly held out both his hands palms up and shrugged "Nowhere! You were perfect. I tried to reason with them but they were in a majority."

Lila composed herself and fixed an intent stare at the table, not really looking at anything. "Tomar, Seriously, this Tomar?" she asked jabbing a thumb out of her fist in the direction of the door. "He's just a kid and anyway doesn't know the first thing about Pathology!"

"I was going to say "the first thing about Medicine", but let us give the devil his due."

Lila couldn't even raise a smile.

"What dues are we talking about Dr Ganguly? This devil hasn't paid his dues. We owe him nothing. Have you forgotten that I stayed up night after night to rewrite this guy's entire thesis so it would get accepted, or that this candidate failed twice in his MD exams and only qualified because he had no more attempts at appearing for the exams remaining?"

A rueful Ganguly sat spinning a glass paperweight on the table "I agree with all of it and believe me, I tried as hard as I could to reason, even plead with the board but…"

"But you were in a minority and no one listened to you."

Dr Ganguly winced at the word "minority", and squirmed awkwardly. The new arm twisting laws had left the board with no choice but to appoint a person from one of the recognised lower classes even if it had to be one as inferior as Tomar. Dr. Ganguly was aware that Lila wasn't questioning anyone's rights, just the merit.

"Tomar H.O.D. Wow, we evidently live in a functioning democracy! So, while I organize a memorable farewell for a much loved professor I have held in the highest regard, he is himself going to walk away leaving me at the mercy of an idiot not fit to be a lab technician let alone a Professor." Dr. Dev mumbled to herself quite oblivious to Professor Ganguly's growing unease. Tears welled up in her eyes and her cheeks flamed a fiery red.

"I will leave you alone now Doctor." Dr Ganguly made a getaway from the hurtful shock and dismay his news had brought.

Working under Dr. Tomar, Head of department grew harder day-by-day until it was more than Lila could bear. The young doctor's personality metamorphosed overnight from the beseeching and bumbling unsure doctor from a pathetic rural medical college to "the boss".

Sadly, all the lower staff rejoiced at Tomar's appointment as a kind of victory and Dr. Dev found herself losing interest in her job, her research, her paper presentations and even the lectures she used to delight in.

Her children were too young to understand any of it. Lila faced humiliation regularly at the hands of the ineffective incumbent. With Bharat, her husband and soul mate overseas pursuing a post graduation, Lila found herself trying to cope single-handedly with the distressing situation.

It was the most unpleasant time of Dr. Dev's career. Tomar was a cocky, self-confident boss but let things slip in administration and the Pathology Department was reduced to a disorderly, grubby place. The floors and toilets looked unclean and neglected while the lab barely got a perfunctory mop up. Each time Dr. Dev tried to get the sweepers to attend to their duties, she'd find them squatting huddled in a circle smoking and chatting. Their standard response would be "you carry on Doctor Saab, we'll be there soon." but they never came. Their blasé attitude frustrated her to no end. In desperation Lila confronted Tomar in his office. "The laboratories are filthy. We have to maintain high standards of hygiene. These fellows don't listen to me. Can you tell them?"

"Sir!"

"What?"

"You have to call the head of department Sir!"

Lila looked scornfully at his despicable face. "Yes Sir! I am requesting you to do something about hygiene or it will be impossible to work here." She uttered through gritted teeth.

He shrugged, almost as if to say "Be my guest. Stay, leave, who cares." She saw that her frustration seemed to please him.

Looking at him aghast, Lila asked, "So? Are you going to do something about it?" She was aware that her voice was raised and she was about to lose her temper. "Look at them Tomar, they don't care! I'm sorry but if you don't get them working I…I'm going to have to report…"

"Report to?" He eyed her cockily, "You have reported. Now get back to your work."

Lila stormed back to her desk. This was it. She couldn't bear it any more. The filth in the lab would lead to endemic infections at the hospital and she wasn't about to take the blame. In a rage she pulled out her writing pad and pen and started writing a resignation based on adverse working conditions. She stared at the page. Salty tears dropped in big blobs on the pale blue Bond paper. She dropped her pen and clenched her hands helplessly. She couldn't leave. There was just a month's salary in the bank. Her need, Tomar knew was greater. He was banking on her not taking any drastic measures till Bharat's return. Ludicrous as the situation was, she had to work under the smug rascal. Her love and veneration for the institution and for her profession compelled her to carry on, even if it meant personally tipping Nathu the watchman to come and clean the labs and toilets.

She sat up night after night by the bedside of her sleeping children, agonizing over the sad turn of events that had changed everything. Painfully aware that she had no choice but to continue until Bharat's return, she dragged herself to work unenthusiastically day after day.

One dreary grey December evening just as Dr. Dev was leaving for the day she heard sounds of chatter from Tomar's room. She had thought she was the last to leave and wondered if Tomar was actually working. She peeped in unseen from behind a water fountain. A rather merry Tomar and four others sat with their feet up, drinking and playing cards.

Dr. Dev froze. The sight of their committing such audacious sacrilege in the room of the Head of Department sent a wave of rage through her. She was tempted to storm in there and give him a sound ticking off, but held back conscious of her vulnerability. She took in the hideous sight with unbelieving eyes. The head of Pathology was actually gambling with the riff raff in his office in a government building. She felt nauseous as she slowly slipped away.

The chilly evening mist swirled around her as she made her way across the car park. Nathu the watchman rose from his little bonfire and ran across to help her with her things. He put her files and papers carefully in the back seat and with a silent "salaam", watched her drive away.

Angry tears flooded her eyes as images of Tomar and his cronies drinking and gambling in the Head's office kept flashing across her mind. She just couldn't bear to think of those villains sullying her beloved institution, her house of worship.

She drove into her garage and was jolted back to reality when she caught sight of Shanti her maid at the window carrying their younger one wrapped in a shawl, anxiously scanning the dark street. Dr. Dev wiped her eyes and hurried in to a chorus of "Mummy's home".

"Memsahib, baby was feeling very cold but her forehead is hot. Maybe she has a fever."

She took one look at little Manjiri's flushed face and blood shot eyes and said, "Yes she has a temperature. I will get the medicine started."

"Shall I warm your dinner madam? The children have eaten."

"No thanks, Shanti, you have dinner and go to sleep. I am not hungry."

Shanti worried about her "Memsahib". This was becoming a habit. The lady would usually eat no dinner. She had started looking wan and tired, and was always worrying about something. Shanti believed it was time her "Saheb" returned from America where he had gone to get a higher degree. The simple soul had no clue what was bothering Dr. Dev and recalled the promise she had made to her master when he left. "You go Saheb; I am here for Memsahib and the kids. You go become a big engineer and don't worry about a thing." She had struggled to convince him of her devotion to his wife and kids. Little did she know that Bharat had absolute faith in the trustworthiness and loyalty of the simple woman.

He had considered his options when he received the plum offer, essentially concerned for Lila and the children and for their finances. Not having any parental support they lived solely on their salaries and had nothing to fall back on.

Whenever he needed to be with his thoughts he would take a long walk. He ran things in his mind. The children were still young attending the best schools in the city. Lila was a front runner for the professor's position and that would augment their income a bit. He looked about him as he walked through their guarded government colony. They were fortunate to have likeminded and caring neighbours all of whom had assured him of their support for Lila and the children in his absence. He felt reassured and by the end of his walk had made his mind up to avail of the opportunity extended to him by his government. There were many to prop his family up in case of any emergency. He valued, above all the trustworthiness and constancy of Shanti who was devoted to his little family.

Shanti knew her anxiety for her mistress was not baseless. She understood little else but was certain that making contact with Saheb would bring her mistress solace. She hurried to her mistress's desk and brought out a writing pad and pen. She carried it in to the children's bedroom. Both children were asleep bathed in the glow of the blue night lamp. Lila sat observing little Manjiri's breathing. Shanti brought the stationery to her, "Write to Sahib and ask him how long before he can come back. He must have completed his studies by now. You need him here."

Sitting by the children's bedside in the glow of the blue bed light, Lila narrated the events of the past few months to Bhaskar. When he had asked about the professor's selection, she had said there had been delays, but today, disillusioned and dejected, she poured it all out.

Mini's fever didn't come down the next morning and Lila called in sick.

It turned out to be a tranquil and relaxing day though one of the gloomiest of that harsh winter. The children stayed in their cotswool pajamas playing scrabble, delighted to have their mother to themselves. It began to rain and they sat at the window seat and looked out. Mini, feeling decidedly better, asked for soup and noodles. The house was warmed by the heater's radiant orange glow and Lila thanked God for her safe and happy little family.

Shanti brought in a tray of food and Lila sat on the bed, feeding Mini. The children gulped it down amidst giggles. Mini rubbed her tummy and said, "No more. It's very fulling."

Akshay countered, "Not "fulling" silly, it's "filling"."

"No" Mini was determined; "I meant fulfilling. The food is fulfilling and I am not silly." She said smacking her brother with the back of her spoon. He flung himself on his sister like a little puppy and there was much squealing and shouting. Lila believed Mini was on the mend.

The shrill ringing of the telephone cut through this happy scene. It was the Dean of the medical college. "Dr Dev, You are to report for duty at once."

"But my child is unwell" protested Lila.

"I am sorry about that, but Doctor, why didn't you report three liters of methylated spirit missing from your store? Banwari, the sweeper has died of spirit poisoning and you are to report without delay to my office for investigations."

In the dean's office it was clear that suspicion lay heavily on Dr. Dev primarily because all the witnesses who were Tomar's cronies declared that she had openly resented Tomar's appointment. They alleged that she privately supplied spirit out of the locker to bootleggers and had by mistake left one bottle out the previous night. Murari, another sweeper claimed to have seen madam leave with bottles of spirit in her hands. The allegation was so ludicrous that Lila had to laugh through her amazement.

"When did you see me leave Murari?"

"Last evening" Murari glared reproachfully at her.

"Really, last evening, when all of you were sitting gambling and drinking in Dr Tomar's office?"

Murari glanced at Dr. Tomar and looked down at the floor. Tomar leeringly took her in from top to toe, eyebrows raised, a sickening smirk on his nasty face. Lila stood rooted to the ground, a stunning awareness overpowering her. The rogue had covered all his tracks.

"This is a very grave accusation Dr. Lila"

"I beg your pardon Dr. Stanley; it's no more serious than the charge made upon me. For your information, I handed over the keys of the hazardous substances locker when Dr. Tomar took over. I have never operated it since. These are not my signatures. Someone has faked them"

"But your bunch of keys has a duplicate." Tomar drawled glancing away and grinning.

"Dr Stanley, you can't accuse me without proof." Lila spluttered.

"There will have to be a detailed enquiry Doctor. Please make yourself available when called upon."

Doctor Stanley's tone was harsh and accusing. Lila felt her entire world collapse around her.

She barely ate or slept for the next few weeks. The newspapers were full of the scandal. The press placed poignant pictures on the front page and every tabloid screamed for justice for the "downtrodden". Suddenly Lila's Brahmin origins were brought in question.

One foggy night Banwari's wailing widow and kids landed up on her doorstep seeking compensation. Lila's children were deeply troubled as the woman's wailing rend through the stillness of that frosty night. Shanti deftly handled the woman and press reporters, capably shielding the family she adored.

By the time the enquiry began, Bharat was on his way back. Lila was placed under house arrest as her children had no one to stay with and two policemen watched her door day and night.

Dr. Ganguly heard about the scandal in Calcutta and placed a trunk call through to speak to the lady he so greatly respected, not just as a doctor but also as a terrific human being. "I can't come there but will certainly have a word with Dr. Stanley right away."

"That would be a help I'm sure," whispered Lila, "they are calling upon almost anyone who has worked with me, running a kind of character check and are examining all my confidential reports."

"Most of them made by me," observed Dr. Ganguly grimly. "Dr Stanley can search all she wants. There isn't one negative comment there."

Her request for an "In Camera" trail was declined. The courthouse swarmed with muckrakers and newshounds. Lila believed she was condemned before the trial. The lawyer recommended by Dr. Ganguly had an imposing public persona but Lila saw that he too doubted he could get her off.

It entered case law books as the fastest trial in the history of Delhi courts. One by one all those she had worked with, paraded into the judges' chambers as Lila sat stunned, barely listening, her eyes lowered, painting a consummate picture of guilt. Her co workers could scarcely recognise her. They gawked at the uneasy figure, colorless and pale, a glaring contrast to the stunning woman they had admired. Every person declared the same thing, Dr Dev was the most honest, trustworthy and loyal doctor they knew at the institution. They also swore that they were not there on the evening of the incident. Several "Harijan" (lower caste) workers came forth to place on record that they would gladly put their lives in her hands any day.

There were no witnesses to prove her innocence but four who adamantly claimed she regularly filched spirit and other hospital supplies. It was up to the judges now.

TEN

Newspaper headlines screamed, "Humble gardener restores falsely accused doctor's dignity! Dr Dev absolved, reinstated."

Nathu the gardener's statement saved the day. He clearly remembered placing just a few files and papers in Doctor Saab's car, but was happy to produce the spirit bottles from his own home where he'd taken them to sell to the "kabadiwala" (rag picker).

"Where did you get them from?" the public prosecutor demanded from the simpleton.

"From under Professor Tomar's table. That is where I always took bottles home from sir," stated the simpleton.

"Are you saying that there were spirit and liquor bottles in Dr. Tomar's room before this incident?"

"Yes Sir, almost every day. They used to be there till late evening and then it was my duty to clean the room and lock up. I still have all the bottles in my house. I collect them for selling. It is good money, 15 paisa per bottle," he admitted with disarming honesty.

The courtroom rang out with laughter for the first time during the tense trial.

Lila did not read on about the forensic reports or fingerprint evidence. She had struggled to keep all the newspapers away from the children's prying eyes and placing this last reminder of the month-long nightmare in a folder with all the other cuttings, pushed it far into the dark recesses of her wardrobe.

Dr Tomar was arrested and replaced by a doctor from Bombay. Bharat was shocked to find his lovely wife reduced to a ghost. Wordlessly he heard the saga of her ordeal, incensed that his gentle wife had had to contend with such a sordid nightmare in his absence.

Dr Stanley invited Dr Dev to meet her. In respectful silence Lila watched the senior lady spell out why it had been mandatory for her to act upon the rule of law.

154

"Thank Goodness that is all out of the way now and we can have you back!" Lila had other plans.

"I was waiting to clear my name before resigning. We leave for California next month." was her curt reply to Dr. Stanley's proposal.

The elderly lady remembered Lila from her student days and appreciated that the self respecting Doctor would never have been able to live down the media hype. As she watched the upright, dignified figure walk down the long corridor, she knew that she would never earn her former pupil's respect, and wondered if she had been too harsh in conducting the enquiry. What a loss for a nation that badly needed such exceptional doctors. The retreating figure rounded the corner. The clicking of her heels faded away, leaving Dr. Stanley strangely discomfited. The elderly lady sighed turning to her pending files. She had a hospital and medical college to run.

****

The airport had transformed noticeably both in size and décor. Lila gazed at the magnificence of silk brocade and multihued tapestry as her feet sank into plush carpeting. Just one of those gates would have made up the entire airport when she last bade farewell. Thinking back at a time three decades ago when an ugly chapter could have ended her career, Lila stepped out to the crowded, noisy foyer of Delhi's international airport. A throng jostled in the horse-shoe shaped arena outside the airport exit. A warm, clammy blast mingled with sweatiness and strong fumes invaded her nostrils. She had been instructed to look for a person with a placard; she had not been prepared for an ocean of them. Her eyes strained to find her own name on a placard. Exhaust fumes hung like chiffon curtains in the dank warm night air as she scanned the sea of gawking faces feeling a tad disoriented. Confronted with strident voices that chorused invitations to hotels, taxis and "Farmhouse bed and breakfast" that she could hardly decipher, she turned away to return to the reception area and await her hosts. Turning the wheels on her stubborn trolley she headed purposefully to the exit but a uniformed policeman barred her way. Lila struggled to explain her predicament but the policeman loftily asserted, "No entry. Egg-jit only".

Maneuvering the obdurate baggage trolley, she decided to wait in a corner but the policeman would have none of it and practically shooed her off into the noisy bedlam. Two excited voices hailed her over the throng, "Madam!"

"Dr. Dev!"

Relieved, Lila waved to the youngsters brandishing a placard with her name and was, shortly out of the throng, ensconced in the safety of a luxurious air conditioned car.

Her young rescuers updated her with their well laid plans and suggested she 'take rest' till their flight the next day.

The car drove through smooth wide roads and sailed across overpass after overpass. She learned they called them flyovers. She barely recognised Dhaula Kuan and peered out to gaze at the neatly laid out cantonment houses.

"Ask the driver if we can drive past Andrews Ganj please?"

The young man turned around, "Do you want to "call on" someone? It is the middle of night…"

"I just want to drive past it. I think it's near South Extension? They were very old houses. I don't know if they are still there."

The young lady sitting next to her answered, "They are. There is a flyover in front of them and a big shopping mall. It's quite a busy place."

Gaurav told the driver to make the detour.

He detailed out their itinerary, "We will pick you up after breakfast Dr. Dev and catch the noon flight. It's not a long flight. Then we have to drive to Shivaneri." The driver muttered something and Gaurav gazed out, "This, I think, yes, this is Andrews Ganj Ma'am."

Lila gaped in amazement as the houses slipped past. Silhouetted against the midnight skies they stood mute and dark. Never would she have imagined their sleepy street as a busy, brightly lit boulevard flanked by colossal mega malls. Memories both blissful and frightful thudded in her head. Heavy eyed and drained, Lila looked forward to a comfortable hotel bed. This was going to be some trip.

"All the plans are ready to begin refurbishment of the Haveli (mansion) in Maharashtra. You might need to send up a few photographers to capture the scenic beauty and use it in the ad campaign for Bygone Abodes Heritage condominium. Don't forget to highlight that "Chaudhary Constructions" will be overseeing the restoration."

Gaurav rattled off instructions as they prepared to undertake the last lap to their destination. Lila had been quite taken aback to see smart, efficient air hostesses in their domestic flight. Even though their flight touched down ten minutes early, the air conditioned car awaited their arrival.

Gautam carried on an animated discussion on his mobile phone. "This will be a prototype of the kind of restoration work we shall be undertaking all over India. But we can't start right away."

Lila assumed the person at the other end asked "why not?"

"I am escorting the sole surviving owner, Dr, Dev to the "Haveli" now. She can stake a claim on all that she wants. After that we will begin our work. So you should issue this release sometime next week."

The car sped across the countryside and Lila captured the briskly moving landscape on film. Narrow twisting lanes led to farms and they saw immeasurable weed covered plains dotted with cows. They passed flowing canals and verdant fields. She clicked an old village signpost that had once boasted of bright lettering looking faded and grimy. They flew past large farmhouses with flowery hedges and imposing iron gates and they passed simple sparse huts symbolic of the ever widening gap in the nation's wealthy and poor.

She put away her camera and sat back staring out at the forgotten and largely transformed landscape as it whizzed past.

"Madam, don't mind, but you don't look as if you have lived abroad for so many years. The Indian clothes, the bindi and mangalsutra, it's all so traditional. I am reminded of my mother and she has never stepped out of India. It's just your accent that is American."

"I never felt the need to change. They accepted us for what we were not what we looked like." Lila laughed.

"How long has it been since you visited India?"

"It is more than twenty years since we left India but a lifetime since I saw my home in Shivaneri."

The car hurtled past dense green woodland on both sides of the bumpy road. It was a clear and bright day with golden sunshine raining upon vast expanses of farmland. Lila's eyes took in the repetitive scenery occasionally spotting a farmer's hut or barn. It had been ages since she had seen bullock carts or children playing around a haystack. The farming community seemed full of activity with their harvesting. She stared fascinated at women in colourful saris balancing gleaming brass vessels chattering away as they walked along in single file.

The car arrived Shivaneri in very good time but they had no clue how to get to the house, "Shiva Niwas" (Abode of Lord Shiva). They asked shopkeepers and passersby but nobody could direct them from just the name of the house. They drew a blank everywhere.

"This is most unusual. I have never met anyone in India not prepared to give directions!" Gaurav murmured.

Lila looked around at the bustling town trying to find any evidence that this once had been the sleepy little village of her birth. They had stopped yet again to enquire at a dairy. Under a massive metal canopy, bulky cattle chewed lazily, shooing away flies with long tails. Milk maids moved between the animals clattering their pails and prattling spiritedly over the rustle and clank.

Gaurav got involved in a heated dialogue with a large flat faced man who informed him that there were no names to houses, just street numbers. Beginning to get quite worked up, Gaurav peered in to his passenger in the back seat, "Ma'am, did the street have a name?"

"There was no street. It was just a house in the middle of nowhere with no other houses nearby."

Lila gazed around in bewilderment and disbelief. Could this be the same hamlet of her childhood? It boasted a "Seventh wonder of the world restaurant", a "Mona Lisa hair salon", "Venus Barber" and "Trendy Boutique". Banners advertised the best prices in P.Cs, printers and state of the art home theatre systems. A "Musique Shoppe" stridently belted out popular Bollywood numbers making it hard to hear anything else.

The din didn't seem to affect anybody as they went about their routine calmly.

The men had started a prolonged discussion about the likely whereabouts of "Shiva Niwas". The dairy owner, suspecting the house wasn't even there, started asking clever questions. "Which Zila?" Lila recalled "Zila" to mean district. "What was the house number?" "Which other houses were near it?"

How could she say to him that it was the only large mansion of its time and needed no address?

Typically, a crowd formed within minutes and every person had an individual take on how best to locate a house without an address.

In exasperation Gaurav hopped back into the car and pointed to the one largish road, "Take this one" he instructed the driver.

Lila looked at the little store across the road. A bevy of giggling college girls were shopping for knick knacks and trying on costume jewellery. She looked beyond them at the shade under a massive banyan tree with a stone platform all around. It was some sort of communal gathering place. Here and there children played with homemade contraptions while some elderly people sat chatting and smoking through clay hookahs. Women in colorful bisected saris sat on cots busily stringing beans and cleaning vegetables, feeding the discards to a couple of goats tied nearby. Everyone chattered like magpies.

Her driver stopped two sociable boys on bicycles more eager to take a peek inside the Toyota than hear him out. One pulled out a comb from his pocket and fixed his hair in the wing mirror while the other pushed his sunglasses up and narrowing his eyes shrewdly asked the driver for a PIN code. It was obvious they were as clueless as the rest.

The banyan tree stirred something inside her. Lila called out to them in pure vernacular,

"Do you know where the ancient Shiva Mandir is?"

Immediately she got the desired reaction. The youngsters spoke up pointing in completely opposite directions. They knew the old Shiva Mandir and they now understood which house they were looking for! "Bhooth Bangla!" (Haunted house) they told each other excitedly. One of them offered to hop in and direct them, but Gaurav said that he just needed directions. Mr. Sunglasses continued with his interrogation, "Who wants to know?" Gaurav explained edgily that the real owner of the mansion and heir of Rao Sahib Apte had come from California. Lila felt four eyes bore into her with a blend of curiosity and awe. "California is in Hollywood, I know." stated Mr. gelled hair. Tearing out a sheet of paper from their note book, the boys smartly drew him a map.

They followed the surprisingly accurate directions and very soon the car pulled up in front of the stately family home.

****

In the massive stone courtyard, a giant tree towering above the tiny temple showered its leaves on the stone stage that used to be the venue for travelling shows and religious celebrations. Two circular paths converged at the centre of a wide verandah. The imposing, heavy wooden doors with brass handles were ajar. She walked as if in a trance. Her ears rang with the music of 'bhajans' (hymns), communal chanting and the clanging of bells.

It was just as she remembered it but it had lost its lustre. It stood proudly though the paint peeling off its walls evidenced a need of repair. She stepped into the cool, dark interior and instinctively moved towards the broad bank of an imposing staircase bending upwards in a gradual curve. She ran up the stairs to the wide stone landing just outside the door to her parents' room. Her eyes searched for the precise location. She glanced backwards and took a few steps as if to measure the distance. She came to a corner and knelt. Bending over a corner wall tile, she jiggled with the little wedges that formed the ornamental skirting. They were tiny geometric pieces of marble and coloured stone combining to form an intricate pattern.

Years of dirt and dust had glued the loose tile back but Lila was sure this was the one. She prised it open using a key and finally felt it come loose under her fingers. Very carefully, Lila slid the ceramic oblong out and placed it on the floor. She bent low to peer into the now exposed cavity exactly where the wall met the floor. It was just a tiny hollow but it held something precious that meant everything to her. She gingerly inserted her thumb and forefinger into the tiny space that once used to engulf her entire little fist. She wiggled her fingers about. It had got to be there. No one knew about her hidey hole and no one would ever have thought to look there. Her finger felt it and tried to get a grasp of it but it just moved further with every jab. It turned and she felt a bit of hanging metal. She hooked her finger through it and gently pulled it out. With trembling fingers she held the small, intricately carved silver box not quite as blackened as she had expected. Perhaps the stone had protected it. She tried to steady her quivering fingers as she lifted the latch and opened it to reveal a pair of gold earrings nestling patiently on the royal blue velvet interior. A diamond suddenly gave off a cheeky sparkle as if to say, "Well you certainly took your time". This was the only piece of jewellery remaining from her mother's vast collection.

She recalled the summer day that her mother had given them to her during one of their trips home from the city.

She must have been in her early teens and used to wear the 'parkar polka' (long skirt blouse), a black dot on her forehead and her hair was always in neat, oiled braids. Her mother took her up to her room and brought out a cloth wrapped box from her wooden cupboard. She handed her first born the earrings, three diamonds in a floral setting with a gold leaf on either side. "I didn't let them take these away. I hid them. My mother had them made for you when you were born to give to you when you came of age."

Lila looked at them and then up at her mother's face.

"Where are all your ornaments Ai? Why don't you wear them anymore?

"I have kept them away for you and your sisters. I don't need them anymore; they'll just look dull and old if I keep using them."

Lila peered into the sparse cupboard, "Where are they? Show me."

"Not now." Her mother hurriedly shut the cupboard but not before Lila took in the bare shelves. "Here, let me put these on for you." Her mother urged.

"I can do it Ai" said Lila pushing away her mother's hand.

Her father called out to her mother from downstairs his booming voice echoing through the house. Her mother hurried off and Lila stared after her, stunned at how old and tired she had started to look. She had grown thin and weak in the years that they had been away. Even though she cooked them special meals each day and looked genuinely happy to have all her children with her for the summer, Lila noted that there was something different in her eyes. The sparkle was gone. The sparkle was gone from pretty much everything else at "Shiva Niwas". Her young mind struggled to comprehend and accept the misfortune that had fallen upon their lives. Were there robbers and thieves in their village? Her eyes fell upon her little treasure and she clenched her small fist tightly. She thought of the safest possible place and rushed to stash away the earrings in her little silver treasure box. Just as her small fingers closed up the hidey-hole behind the skirting, her mother called out to them. The "Tonga" (carriage) to take them to their uncle, Eknath Kaka's had arrived.

"Ai, I'll stay with you. I don't want to go." Lila begged her mother.

"No! Go all of you. He wants to meet you."

"I'll only go because you are tired."

Lila felt it was all her incessant chatter that made her mother tired and vowed to keep quiet like her other siblings as she watched the lone figure waving at them till she looked very small.

The hot and dusty ride to the next village was very long. Eknath Kaka lived in a large house, not as big as "Shiva Niwas" but newer.

When they finally arrived the girls were helped by a housemaid to wash up and led to the large and cool dining room where their plates had been set neatly along the walls with straw mats to sit on. Pretty patterns of rangoli adorned their plates.

Eknath Kaka came in and sat down chatting with them and making her younger sister collapse into helpless giggles at his monkey imitations. The maids started serving the food and Kalpana Kaku dressed in bright orange came and sat down beside Eknath Kaka. She looked beautiful in a garish sort of way. Lila didn't like to think it, but she looked a bit like their maids when they dressed up to go to the village fairs.

Lila stared. There was something not right. Lila couldn't put her finger to it, but there was something that made her uneasy and a bit excited.

"Lila, eat something. Don't you like it?" asked Kalpana Kaku.

Lila bent her head and ate some more rice. Her sisters kept laughing at her uncle's jokes. She examined her plate thoughtfully. The maids brought in some more food but Lila put her hands out, "No thanks no more," she said.

"Come on this is your Kaka's place, don't feel shy." Kalpana Kaku coaxed her in a syrupy sweet voice.

"No thanks, I am full." Lila looked up at the lady and her gaze stopped at the woman's neck. That ruby and gold necklace was Lila's mothers! She remembered that from her childhood as she used to finger the large red stones that made up the petals on the necklace. How she stared at her aunt. Those bangles and even the gold pendent on the bunch of keys hooked on her aunt's waist belonged to her mother. There was no mistake; those were all her mother's ornaments. Why was this woman wearing them when her mother just wore some black beads on a string? Her mind struggled to comprehend issues far beyond her years. She had very faint recollection of a bygone time, when the rains had not come. She remembered her mother handing over a red cloth bundle in which she had tied up her ornaments to her father. Eknath kaka had been sitting downstairs.

Lila felt sick to the stomach.

It may have been the bumpy ride in intense heat, the rather sour "panna" (raw mango juice) served to them on arrival, or this brand new discovery. Lila felt all the food gush up to her mouth with a rumble and could not control it. Instantly all that she'd eaten shot right out onto her plate and on the floor all around. The retching over, she was helped by one of the maids to wash up and clean out her dress. She remembered Kalpana Kaku covering her mouth with her sari pallu and briskly running out of the room.

When she got back the mess had been cleared up and Eknath Kaka was there with her sisters to ask how she was feeling. She could barely meet his gaze and just nodded dumbly. She wanted to go home to her mother at once she said. They were all bundled off in the Tonga and sent back.

Lila hotly confronted her mother "that woman was wearing all your jewellery. That's why you aren't wearing any. Did you know that Eknath Kaka stole from us?"

"He didn't exactly steal little one. We had to pawn it to him as your father was heavily in debt and now I don't think we'll ever recover it. I wanted you girls to have it." She looked at her daughter's young but wise face and passed her hand over the child's brow hugging her close, "When you are a big famous doctor, come and get it all back. Your father and I are tired now." Lila remembered making a solemn vow then and there to bring every joy and every comfort to her mother when she grew up.

"Dr. Dev! You okay up there?" Gaurav, the architect from Chaudhary enterprises walked in from the huge wooden doors downstairs. She could see him from where she sat at the head of the staircase but it was too dark upstairs for him to see anything clearly. His eyes squinted trying to accommodate in the darkness. "Dr. Dev!"

"I am up here!" Lila called out cheerily looking down from the little overhanging balcony.

"Just checking, you have been in there quite a while."

"It's been over 50 years, you know, I may be a long time!"

"Of course, of course, I am sorry! We have coffee and sandwiches, if you like."

"Thanks maybe I'll come down in a couple of minutes."

"Sure Dr. Dev, take your time."

Lila walked from room to room turning on the fabulous crystal chandelier lights saddened that the workmen had put in only a few light bulbs in each. "Tomorrow I'll get them to put in all the light bulbs." She thought, opening a wooden cupboard. It was stuffed with bundles tied in bits of cloth torn out of old saris and bed sheets. They were all covered in a thick coat of dust. Lila cast her eyes around the room. Yellowing plaster flaked off the high walls covered with diaphanous webs. That crib was still there like a large wooden jail with sharp brass latches.

In the middle on the cool delicately patterned floor sat three little girls playing that silly game that involved throwing up small pebbles, a lot of clapping and chanting some odd ditty. A sweet-faced woman holding a baby sat in a rocking chair. The lady smiled at Lila and turned her eyes to the playing girls. It grew dark outside and the sun disappeared behind grey clouds. The playing children stopped their game and ran to look out. Their mother turned to light a candle by the bed stand.

A lady's voice echoed through the house, "Ma'am do you need a torch?" Another member from Chaudhary's team clambered up the wooden stairs, "I think we just lost power and it looks like rain."

"Oh? What about your people?" Lila looked from the window to the girl's face.

"We are moving all our things into the big lobby at the entrance. It is sheltered. Shalini Shukla" she said extending her hand.

Lila shook her hand, "Lila Dev. Pleased to meet you. Shalini! That's a very pretty name. It was…" she threw a backward glance at the bare room, "It was my mother's name."

"Really ma'am? What a coincidence! We were all talking about you downstairs," she said pointing with a finger downwards, "Actually we were all wondering how a person born here," she pointed to the floor, "could have gone and settled in California!" She jerked her thumb out from her body. "Did you live many years of your life here?"

Lila shook her head sadly. "No not very long."

"Which years?"

"Oh a very long time ago!' Lila said with a laugh. "It's amazing I still remember it as if it was yesterday. The parents' room, the Puja room, our room." Lila talked absently as she walked in and out of the large rooms in wide eyed wonder.

She turned abruptly, "Did someone mention coffee?"

"Yes of course ma'am, would you like to come downstairs?"

As the two of them started walking down the broad, curved expanse of stairs Shalini noticed the silver box in Lila's hands. "Did you find that here?"

Lila looked down at the box in her hands and nodded, "I retrieved it from where I had hidden it."

"No! Really? That's awesome! You aren't joking! You actually found it after so many years!" Shalini gazed in fascinated disbelief.

"Um huh!" Lila shrugged and smiled, "believe it or not!"

They came downstairs and joined a cosy party from Chaudhary Builders around a marble topped table. The front doors were open and the rain was pelting down heavily. Lila looked out at the huge square with the little Shiva temple centered under the shade of the large peepal tree. The entire village used to congregate in their courtyard around the temple for festivals. She remembered that "Shivratri" when her father sang and played on his harmonium. The celebrations had gone on all night. Everyone had been so happy. Simple folk with simple pleasures they had been.

"Dr Dev, are you disappointed to find the house in such a state?"

Lila turned, eyes narrowing. She considered his question as she inclined her face to one side, "No, Gaurav, not really! In fact I'd expected to find it worse! If you have to look at it," she swept her arm across, "it is structurally sound, I mean look at the floors and walls; they are just fine. Of course it's a bit musty, though I must acknowledge, you guys have done a fantastic clean up and I can see your team worked very hard," she paused a bit and slowly shook her head, "No I can't say I am disappointed with the house. It's more as if I have disappointed the house, if you get my meaning." She moved her eyes from the ceilings and massive staircase to face the group.

"Yes" Shalini looked at the doctor's face.

Lila pointed to a large wooden sideboard, "That glass is beveled Belgian. You rarely get to see such fine hand cut setting anymore!"

"True. I mean we've only seen it in our books." Gaurav pointed out.

Lila nodded, "that was my grandfather's doing! He had visited the continent and loved Italy. That horse head is from Murano in Venice." She pointed to a sculpted crystal horse head affixed high above them. "We had plenty of crystal doorknobs," she cast her eyes about, "I don't see them now," she pointed to the doors, "but each of these doors had one. I learned about the finer things from my grandfather well before I moved overseas. Now I too have imported some Italian pieces for my house in California."

"They're here," said Gaurav moving to the large teak cabinet and pulling out a bag from a drawer. "We had the workmen remove them while polishing." He approached her with the bag.

Dr Dev reached for the crystal doorknobs, her eyes shining, "Yes," she whispered pulling each one out and examining them with a girlish glee. She laid them out lifting each one delicately. They reflected the candlelight casting circular rainbow patterns.

"This is no ordinary glass my boy. You need to use a special kind of cleansing mix. We used 'reetha' a kind of a nut that grew on the trees at the back. But I'm sure you have many modern methods.

The young man smiled at the outmoded advice, "Yes Ma'am, we use the best. The restoration will be flawless. It will recreate the old world charm using modern technique. We also plan to fix the great chandelier in the lounge and replicate the velvet curtains and valances so we actually plan to make a minimum number of changes."

"The grand chandelier, is it still up? I haven't been in the rooms here,"

Shalini placed a mug of coffee before her, "No. You just ran straight up."

Lila rose. "It used to have candles and oil lamps and the servants used a pulley to lower and raise it." She said as she moved towards the sitting room. "Then they got the place wired and we had to bring in light bulbs from the bigger cities! They only lit the chandelier on special occasions." Lila strolled slowly to the enormous archway that led to the living and dining area.

She explored the massive kitchen, storeroom and pantry with its gas powered refrigerator and returned to the living room. She pulled away dustsheets from the ornate but faded velvet sofas and her eyes fell on the pullout desk in the corner. It opened out to reveal the tiny drawers and shelves with their stationery still stacked cozily, a dried and crusty inkpot and pen rested by the side of yellowing paper. A packet of letters and postcards lay in another corner of the desk; the ink on them faded in parts and completely wiped out in others. A bunch of sepia photographs of long gone ancestors slid out of a brown paper wrapped packet tied with cracking string.

Lila imagined Kalpana Kaku playing hostess in their tasteful sitting room, but couldn't conjure up a picture. The woman was low caste, uneducated and not half as cultured as her mother.

This room had seen festivities year on year. Lila remembered the "Haldi kumkum" her mother hosted seasonally. The room was dressed up with dolls dating back to her grandmother's girlhood. It was a way of paying obeisance to the Goddess. Intricately carved votive utensils that had been cleaned and polished all week by the servants sat on silk covered tables holding sweets and rose water. Plenty of rangoli decorated the floor and garlands of flowers hung from doorways. The heady fragrance of camphor, incense and flowers spilled into the lugubrious afternoon air as the ladies arrived sporting gorgeous saris in jewel shades.

Lila sighed. Ghosts walked about her. She looked out of the open window. The clouds had parted to let the sunlight stream through. Buffaloes soaked lazily in a pond and chickens and goats moved aimlessly about. A woman balancing a bundle of grasses on her head wend her way home silhouetted across the fluorescent pink and orange sky. The stark purity of ordinariness and naturalness sent a shiver down her spine.

She looked down at the papers in her hand. There were some old letters written on post cards that bore different people's signatures in faded, discoloured ink.

She felt a strange discomfort in the room. There was something there in the air, something uneasy. What was it? Lila could not make it out, like an old forgotten tale or some past occurrence that she sensed she needed to know more about. Lila strained her memory. Was there something that she needed to attend to? She began to feel stifled and suffocated. She needed to get outdoors. The team of workers had dispersed after the rain stopped. She walked carefully lifting the pleats of her sari as she avoided the little puddles and rivulets; her Marc Jacobs sling backs making a crunching sound in the dank, grainy red soil.

She sat down at a newly installed wrought iron garden bench and inhaled deeply. The air was fresh with the fragrance that follows a shower. She examined the packet of yellowing old letters that almost shredded in her hands like crumbly pastry. Fading ink and the convoluted script that she had learned and forgotten to read made it hard to decipher the long forgotten messages. Oddly enough, as she pried it open Lila realised that the letter had never actually been opened or read in over 40 years!

"Madam, it is getting dark…" Gaurav had this habit of materializing out of thin air.

"Can you get me a magnifying lens?"

"I'm sorry?"

"Magnifying glass," she gestured with her hand, "a magnifying lens, you know something to enlarge things?"

"Yes I know what it is," he glanced at the papers in her hands. A wave of realization shot across his face, "Yes of course! I've got one with my plans!"

Shalini the young architect settled herself down next to Lila, "Madam, your brothers and sisters, how long is it since you met them?"

"Too long. Far too long." Lila sat mumbling to herself, oblivious to anything around.

"Two of them passed away in childhood. With my parents terminally ill, my uncle had put my sister up for adoption and before our grandparents could reach the village, she was gone. There was no way to find her."

Lila remembered her grandmother's anguish as each attempt to hunt for her sister terminated in a dead end. The aged lady suffered with heart rending helplessness coupled with dreadful despair for months on end. At the tiniest strand of information she would rush one of the uncles to investigate. After several agonising months her grandfather called a halt and nobody was allowed to mention the issue anymore.

A shadow of pain and sadness clouded the pretty face and her blue-grey eyes overflowed behind her glasses. Obviously she needed some space. She didn't even look up as Shalini slowly walked away. Lila's thoughts were far, very far.

That day at Ratlam station returning from medical college for the summer, she stared out of her first class "Ladies Only" coach window at the crowds looking at no one in particular. Amongst the throng she sensed someone watching her. She looked back at the face in the crowd straight into a pair of green eyes studying her. Uncanny! It was like looking in a mirror. That young girl looked at her with a considered recollection. Could it be? She would be all grown up by now. It most certainly resembled Sandhya. The portly guard walked past, his shrill whistle piercing her ears.

The train started to pull out. Lila looked back. The eyes still followed her, a slight hint of panic in them. The pretty face looked a little troubled, uncertain. The lips parted as if to call out. The train picked up speed and just like that, it was over. Lila struggled to recall. Was she alone? Who was she standing with? Did she appear well looked after? She weighed the chances that the girl she saw wasn't Sandhya, but there wasn't a bit of doubt in her mind.

For a few agonising minutes she sat thinking. Was destiny trying to bring them together again after so many years? Whom should she tell? What could anyone do?

Her grandfather was dead and her seriously ill grandmother was not expected to survive much longer. Most of the family had moved on and servants tended to the old lady. Even at the age of twenty two, Lila had more practical wisdom than many older people. She smoothed down her peach coloured French chiffon sari, accepted the tea on a tray served by the waiter in spotless white and returned to her novel, one of the recent arrivals at the bookstores, The Citadel, by A. J. Cronin.

Lila strolled through the grounds. Evening shades cast protracted shadows across the dark exterior as distorted silhouettes clung to the white washed walls as if questioning Lila, demanding answers. A sudden draught swirled around her, whispering with the rustle of the leaves. Lila trembled a little. Feeling chilly she rubbed her upper arms. She lurched a little as the heels of her sandals burrowed in the wet soil. She turned around. Footsteps crunched on the gravelly red sand.

"Ma'am, you look exhausted. Would you like to go rest at the hotel? You can return to look through these things tomorrow." Shalini proposed soothingly, handing her a magnifying lens.

Yawning wearily Lila looked appreciatively into Shalini's face. "Right, I was just about to call it a night. I will be able to make overseas calls from the hotel won't I?"

"Sure. From anywhere really! Your family must be waiting to hear from you." Shalini walked her to the car.

Lila glanced at her wrist watch, "Yes they should be waking up now. I should catch them before they get going."

****

Clutching at her newly found treasure and the letters; Lila arrived at the accommodation downtown. She had stopped marveling at the transformation of their little hamlet. Nothing, she decided, would surprise her now, but was bowled over when she was politely informed that the entire hotel was Wi-Fi enabled.

The family had to know absolutely everything.

"Hey mom, did you find the window at the top of the house where you could see the river from?"

"The river has changed its course and really, it's barely a stream now."

"What about the fields?"

"Non existent, the place is all factories and row houses."

She chatted with her family as she leafed through the tattered papers marveling that the ink hadn't disappeared altogether like the printouts today.

Lila answered the question absently, straining to read the dusty old parchment in her hands.

Bharat finally got his turn, "Tell me more about the house! Did you remember it exactly as it was? How do they propose to transform it into a hotel? It must be quite a solid structure. Are the chandeliers still intact? They would fetch a king's ransom today wouldn't they?"

"Mom are you okay?"

Lila couldn't find words to express her sentiments but answered their questions mechanically.

"I'm fine, just very tired. Let us talk tomorrow. Look after yourselves. Love you!"

She sat down and began looking through the papers. She yawned, exhausted. This would have to be tackled in the morning. She decided to indulge in a calming bath and an early night. Preparing to retire for the night, she flipped back the bedcovers and was about to open a book when the phone on the bedside rang.

"Dr Dev you have some visitors here in the lobby."

"Visitors for me? Who are they?"

"Doctor saab, could you come down?" The voice sounded uncomfortable.

"But I don't know…no one knows I am here unless, is it someone from Chaudhary constructions?"

"No madam, can you come down please?"

Lila came down the stairs surprised to find their road-side guide Mr. Hollywood with a very old man. He was wearing the traditional dhoti kurta and jacket and his shoes were polished. He had on a Gandhi cap. The plain brown face was wrinkled and covered with white stubble. Thick glasses, the kind that cataract patients have to wear, rested on a large misshapen nose.

She was taken aback and also a little annoyed.

"What is it? What do you want?" She wondered if Gaurav was supposed to tip the youngster.

"Good havening Madam." Hollywood was most polite. "I am Sachin. I am showing you the way in afternoon."

"Yes." Lila switched to Hindi and asked him what he wanted.

Sachin pointed to the old man. He continued proudly in English "this is Kailash Kaka. My mother uncle. He want to see you because he was 'mali' (gardener) in your father house."

Lila looked at the old man. He stood with folded hands and a smile as he peered through the thick glasses. He spoke in a dialect that she could not recall. Obviously she had absolutely no recollection of him, but asked them to sit down on the futons in the lobby. It made a droll picture, the three of them quite unequal, conversing in the smart hotel lobby. Lila struggled to keep her eyes open.

The young man told her that her arrival had caused quite a stir in the village as no one had expected any of the family to return.

The old man spoke to his nephew almost inaudibly, his eyes welling up with tears.

Sachin, acting as an interpreter said, "He is asking if you are the one who became a doctor. He says you used to recite from the holy books."

Lila's throat choked up. She said gently, "Yes, I am the one. Ask him if he knows anything about the rest of the family."

He peered at her smiling a toothy grin, his face full of pure joy at having met someone from his beloved master's family. He replied haltingly in a sing song lilt, never taking his eyes off Lila.

Sachin told her that the old man thought her parents were godly people. They had given him, an orphan, shelter and he felt shattered when their own children had to be given away. Lila's eyes filled up. She nodded sympathetically at the old man.

Lila asked him about her parents' last days and the man filled her in with Sachin acting as their interpreter. She heard about her father's paralysis. He told her that he had been with her father to the end but left the job when Kalpana Bai had taken custody of the house.

The old man softly told Sachin something which considerably agitated the young man. Sachin fired a barrage of questions at him as Lila struggled to comprehend the vernacular. Lila saw that the old man was holding back on something, causing much torment to the younger fellow. Frustrated, Sachin told her, "He says you must take back your mother ornaments from pawn shop."

"What pawn shop?" Lila whispered.

A bunch of people entered the hotel lobby. It was the team of architects returning after dinner. They stopped when they saw Lila sitting with the two men. Gaurav came hurriedly towards them, "Ma'am, are they bothering you? Let me handle it." He positioned himself on the settee between the two men and her as if they were about to carry her off.

"Wait Gaurav let me talk to him." Lila tried to make him get up. "He says he's our old gardener!"

Gaurav sighed, "Ma'am this is going to happen every day. Now that the village knows you are here, there will be gardeners, old cooks and maids surfacing on a regular basis asking for "inaam" (reward). They just want to exploit your naïveté. Let me get rid of them for you." He turned to Sachin and in a loud voice addressed him, "How did you find out where madam is staying? What is this new trick eh?"

The old man cringed at the word "inaam" and cast his eyes down. He held Sachin's arm and cowered as if he thought Gaurav was going to attack him.

Lila stood up, "Gaurav, nobody is exploiting me. I am perfectly capable of handling this. Could you please let me talk to them? Now please leave them be and don't frighten the poor man! You're welcome to stay if you like!"

Sadly the unwelcome commotion agitated the old man who clammed up and refused to say a word. He gestured to Sachin that he wanted to leave. Lila was confused. She asked Sachin, "What's the matter? Isn't he going to talk to me anymore?"

"He's angry that man calls him liar and thief." Sachin glared at Gaurav and rose to leave.

Lila followed them, "wait please don't go! There's so much I want to know from him."

The old man walked on muttering to himself and Sachin helplessly followed but made a parting promise, "I will try tomorrow bringing him meeting you."

Gaurav glared at their retreating figures, "Dr Dev, this is to be expected. They're all con artists. No one who knows anything about your family is alive. Believe me, I have tried. That is why we had to contact you! He comes up with some obscure information today and sends you on a wild goose chase, another will surface tomorrow." He sighed, "Ma'am please understand, this kind of interference is only going to delay our project. Lila glanced uncertainly from his face to the two men slowly walking away in the dimly lit street and back again.

Gaurav implored her, "Please, let me handle such guys henceforth."

Too tired to argue, Lila allowed herself to be led back to her suite where she fell into a deep sleep instantly.

Shadowy visions came and went. She saw herself running in cotton fields, chomping on sugarcane and stealing a joy ride on bullock carts laded with gargantuan bundles of the cotton crop.

She glanced back and saw the two men from the lobby chasing her. They can't get to her. She hears muffled shouts as they chase her cart. She looks at them bewildered and a bit scared. They are calling out to her and the urgency in their voices makes her want to stop the cart. She looks at them again and hesitates.

The cart is moving very fast. She loses a foothold and starts sliding off the huge bales of cotton wool. The ground is very far below and the cart is moving rapidly. She starts falling faster and faster. Frantically clutching to the burlap she digs her nails into the suppliant cotton wool that breaks off in clumps.

The chasers are left far behind. Her feet are dangling and her hands sliding downwards. Terrified Lila shuts her eyes waiting to plunge to the ground below. Her breath caught in her throat, choked her with paralysing fear.

She awoke with a cry. It was dark in the room. She reached across the bed but Bharat wasn't there. She tried to sit up taking in the unfamiliar contours of the room. Awareness seeped in and she fell back. She turned over and over in her mind the surreal events of the previous day and swearing to herself that she would see the old gardener again, fell sound asleep.

The next morning the memory of the previous night's encounter was dim. She dressed and asked for the "Indian breakfast", delighted to have a taste of "bhaji puri" and lemon pickle again.

As she ate in the hotel balcony watching the village slowly awaken to a new day, Lila took another shot at trying to decipher the letter she had found. It was easier in daylight under a magnifying lens. Startled to see that it had been addressed to her, she flipped it and saw her father's name at the back. Her father never wrote her long letters. He just added a line on the post cards that her mother used to send. Shaking with a mix of excitement and curiosity she spread it out on the table and smoothed the creases delicately.

My Dear Lila,

I don't know if anyone will post this letter. I have little faith in those around me at present.

Your mother's and my blessings and prayers for your safety and your success go with this letter. I was so proud and happy to hear that you are off to medical college. I understand the British have built magnificent premises and they have excellent staff.

You were always a brilliant girl. I feel sorry that I had to send you away from home at so young an age. It broke your mother's heart. You were her treasure. Today she is too ill to write to you.

I also know that living in that house must have been hard on many fronts but was always secure in my faith that you would be looked after and protected. Now you are leaving that circle of security. New Delhi is a very big city and unlike

173

Nagpur, you know nobody there. Remember you are the light of the Apte dynasty and that name stands for dignity, self honour and pride.

You have chosen a hard field. You have the intelligence to handle it, but if you have the softness of the Apte hearts, you will find it hard to cope. A doctor needs immense mental and emotional control. Our blessings are always with you, for that is all we have remaining.

The shine is gone from everything. As you remember the past, try to bear in mind the days when laughter filled Shiva Niwas. Above all, have no regrets. Go through life with your head held high and a pure and clean heart. Be true to yourself and the rest will follow.

You have many gifts. People here remember you for your compassion, your generosity, common sense and honesty.

Never forget the poor. Even when you attain extraordinary success, which I know you will, remember that you are never too big to help the needy. Pursue your career and perhaps one day, our daughter will find a cure for cancer, the scourge that is eating us both.

Our life was dedicated to the upliftment of our little village and even though we were cheated by our own, I feel pleased that this village is on the path of prosperity. There is no one to carry on the good work.

Always bear in mind the Apte motto. Be in the service of the deprived and needy of our nation. As a doctor you will not have to look far. When the British leave, India's problems begin.

Try to carry on our unfinished work in any way you choose. May God always be with you. Never forget how proud we are of you.

With blessings from us both,

Yours,

Baba

This latest reminder was the final stroke in that tempestuous emotional upheaval. Lila dissolved in tears and cried as she had never done in her life. She cried for the tragedy of her parents, for her siblings, for the helplessness of their lot and for the futility of this current exercise of hers. She lamented the hollowness of her own life of comfort, for not being the true daughter of her altruistic parents. Her heart wept in the memory of the phenomenal service of her parents in caring for their village through years of drought and disease. Didn't she, as the eldest daughter also bear such a sense of duty? Lila reflected on it for a long time, the faded and tattered missive in her trembling hands.

That evening, having scoured through all the rooms, Lila spoke to Gaurav, "I won't be too long. There is very little that I want, just the framed pictures off the walls and the bric-a-brac from the display cases.

I would, however, like to make a trip to Nagpur and take a look at the place I was raised in. Also, there is an old friend who may still remember me."

"Madam, I could make enquiries for you."

Lila looked nostalgic, "Her name used to be Jeroo Patanwala. She is also a doctor, but that's all I have. It has been very long. I could give you the address. And oh yes, her father was a well known doctor, but that was a long time back."

"If she is still in Nagpur we will find her." The ever willing Gaurav promised.

****

It was an unforgettable meeting. Jeroo had married a wealthy lawyer and though she was Mrs. Billimoria now, she practiced as Dr. Patanwala in the same clinic as her father. Lila called her family in the US from her childhood friend's house

"She's still the same caring, quiet person. Married into affluence, she says she has everything she needs and has turned to social service. Do you know her family volunteers with a section of truly disadvantaged people? It's somewhere on the outskirts of town. We are visiting it tomorrow. Bharat it sounds a lot like what we've been thinking about."

For the first time in days Bharat noted the moroseness from delving into long forgotten regrets was absent from Lila's talk. Her characteristic cheeriness was back. He was happy to encourage her but couldn't help remembering how many ponzi schemes had been unearthed lately. She sounded happy and he wanted that above all else. She would doubtless consult with him before committing to anything.

Anyone could have told the two friends that to swap life stories in a few hours was unattainable, but that certainly didn't prevent them from trying. They sat in their nightgowns chatting late into the night. Lila relived the past two days as she recounted them incident per incident to her dear friend. Jeroo saw a gamut of emotions flash across Lila's face as she recalled each momentous encounter with the past. Every discovery, small or big and every revelation had thrown her deeper into the abyss of her forgotten past.

Jeroo nodded sadly. She reached out and patted her friend's hand. There wasn't anything more to say. She could see the blow every incident like this dealt on her friend. She could have told her to consider herself lucky to be dealing with a reasonably straightforward organization that made the effort to contact her and arranged for her visit. She could well have listed out numerous cases of illegal acquisition of neglected property but she saw little meaning in any of it.

Lila took in her friend's unlined face, the pink cheeks, untamed curls and bright eyes. Life had been kind to dear Jeroo. She took in the unpretentious but comfortable home quite reflecting the owner's personality.

"Why are reunions so enchanting?

"Because they take us back to our childhood, a simpler time!"

Lila looked thoughtful, "Or because a common thread run through these memories of innocence and ambition and struggle. Those days we wove dreams without a clue what the morrow promised and today we can look back with contentment at how those little pieces have come together to form interesting pictures."

Jeroo looked at her dear friend's face. She looked weary. "Go to bed now, you're drooping!"

They called it a night and decided to visit the ashram after breakfast.

Suppressing a yawn, Jeroo mumbled, "Lilu you're going to love it. I just know it in my heart."

They picked up their chatter the next morning as Jeroo's shiny car negotiated busy streets and slid on to the wide highway. Urbanized landscape had replaced sprawling expanses of farmland.

Jeroo pointed to a copse of trees. "We're approaching the orchards. Not very long now."

The car turned into fenced in premises with carefully tended grounds and immaculate gardens. They entered a low white building with a red sloping roof. Everywhere you looked there were people busy at work. Some moved slowly, hunched over or limping.

The spotlessness of the place was striking. Even in such hot weather they were treated to a stroll on lush green lawns framed by flower gardens in full bloom. "All tended by the inmates" Jeroo informed her.

As they walked around, Lila was impressed by the meticulous vegetable gardens and orchards. "The focus is on self sufficiency", Jeroo said, leading her past the handicraft department. Spotlessly clad workers in an assembly line were busily printing handmade paper, weaving baskets or crafting durable footwear.

Lila surveyed the emerald expanse with pure admiration. The gardens delighted her senses. Every conceivable bird, plant and flower seemed to thrive in the little oasis despite the sun scorched heat. They strolled across to the kitchen wing. Through the cracks of zigzag rocky pavements wild flowers poked their tiny heads.

Lila took a peek at the dining area. Straw and rag rugs were laid out on cool concrete floors as cooking smells wafted from shiny pots. "Duties are allotted by rotation." Jeroo explained. "This is a model communal cooperative."

She was obviously well loved by everyone. A man tending to some rose bushes clipped two large red roses in full bloom and brought them to Jeroo hurriedly wrapping some paper around the thorny stems. Delighted, she chatted with the man for a while, asking after his family. She appeared to know them all by their first name. Lila soaked up the harmony and accord that lent the ashram blissful serenity.

Jeroo spoke softly as they moved around, "These people were rejected by the community, even by their own families. They can cohabitate here and live with dignity and a sense of belonging."

Lila sighed, "Our society has stigmatized this disease for centuries."

She remembered their teachers asked them to use the term Hansen's disease instead of leprosy as the latter seemed to have a derogatory connotation. She brought to mind the picture of her elderly professor gently taking the patient's hands into her own without trepidation.

The doctor had narrated tales of how lepers were stoned and ostracized. "We as doctors have the imperative responsibility to treat not just the physiological disease, but also the psychological one. It is not for everyone but if you find it in yourself to be able to commit to such a cause, do it. You may not get awards or your name in the Lancet, but the commitment is reward enough." She smiled and reminded them of the motto of their Alma Mater, "To the stars through difficulties".

Lila spent an idyllic two days in the company of her friend reminiscing and visualizing alternate lives that she may have lived. She was mesmerized by the ashram. "All the way here I had been thinking about my father's letter and agonising over how best to find any such charity. I think I have found it. It's as if he led me here! The country has changed so much, it is hard to trust anyone, especially if there is money involved. You have opened a meaningful window of opportunity Jeroo."

"What would your husband have to say? I wouldn't want you making such a big commitment without consulting him."

"I won't. It's long since we both have been on the lookout for any honest charity to attach ourselves to but did not find a single one convincing enough."

She made a promise to herself while taking leave. She was going to uphold her father's dying advice to her.

Bharat had his reservations. "You are full of the idea now. Why not let it sink in a bit? Also consider what hardship you will be facing. Ask yourself if you would be able to forswear the luxurious lifestyle, a lifestyle that we have worked very hard to build. It sounds brilliant but, to my mind, a tad idealistic."

Lila was adamant. "Do you remember how we had decided it would be worth our whiles to return and serve if we could find a just cause? Well here is a genuine selfless charity! I am overwhelmed and terribly moved by the selfless service of the founder. This place needs more such brilliant philanthropists who dare to chase a near impossible dream.

"No harm in giving it a thought, but don't jump into making any commitments."

"Bharat I am not moving in tomorrow, but if I can spend some time of my life in their service, or make periodic visits and perhaps rake up some sizeable donations for the ashram, I would feel worthwhile as a doctor and a human being."

Bharat agreed, "There are numerous possibilities."

ELEVEN

Arti shutdown the laptop and gazed out into the star speckled inky blackness her thoughts still in the grip of Lila's absorbing life story. She thought she had just watched a movie. Who would have imagined that a girl child born in an unenlightened archaic Indian village would wind up saving American lives! She thought it might be fruitful to volunteer with any one of Jane's various charities.

She turned off the ipad and slid it into Jane's bag. Her thoughts turned to her home in Delhi. The next few days would be busy with the wedding but thereafter she needed to get involved in some constructive work.

On Mamta's plush ranch-like farmhouse near Delhi, preparations for the pre wedding party were on in full swing. The entire place was to be covered in tiny drops of multi coloured lights. The performers for the sangeet were setting up their stage and mikes at one end of the lawns while at the other end a team of chattering women laid out arrays of colourful glass bangles along with the tools and gear for applying henna not just for the bride's hands but also for as many women guests as could be managed in a day. Floral garlands adorned bamboo archways all the way from the entrance giving a heady fragrant ambience to the festive mood. Behind the gay canopies, teams of chefs labored over gargantuan pots of luscious delicacies.

At home, rummaging through her mother in law's wardrobe, Rukmini scrutinized her options in dress and accessories not wishing to be a disappointment at the "wedding of the year". She held up jewelry to different saris attempting to visualize the final result.

Natasha walked in with her phone. "Asha aunty."

Asha was urgent and commanding, "Rukmini, can I pick you a little early? We have to collect the other girls on our way to the Mehendi and it's a good way out from here."

Rukmini was apologetic, "I might not be able to get away early Asha. Something urgent has come up."

"Rukmini!" Asha chided, smelling a threat to her meticulously drafted schedule. Hauling several families unharmed to the event was no mean task and she had devoted much thought in drawing up her plan.

Her friend stuttered to fill her in regarding Kamala's vital cash withdrawal from the bank but Asha was running out of patience.

"Rukmini!"

"Asha I hate messing you around like this but I've got to do this for Kamala. Can't you come for us last of all? Please, if that's possible?"

"Okay but I'm not waiting if you are out with Kamala."

"Super! We'll be right here!"

Sameer watched his mother in all her finery pace up and down the front lawn gazing up the street and glancing at her watch now and then. They were to leave soon for the pre-wedding party and he could sense the swelling urgency in his mother. He appreciated the worth of the "filote" and looked searchingly out of the gate at passersby hoping to catch sight of Kamala. Rukmini was clearly ill equipped for the heat and humidity of a Delhi August. Perspiration dripped down her face in large droplets. She deposited herself in a verandah chair dragging it to a less sunny spot. Sameer looked worriedly at his wilting mother wiping her reddened face as she squinted anxiously into the dry dusty street. A sudden wind churned up mud and dry leaves in circles and Rukmini promptly extracted a pair of sunglasses to shield her eyes.

"She should have been here by now. Wonder what's keeping her."

Sameer longed to escape to the cool dark interior but decided to brave the clammy heat a little longer. Their eyes searchingly scanned the crammed street. Delhi's multitude chugged past on the scorching tar road that sunny afternoon. Two wheeled vehicles zigzagged through traffic quite mindless about right of way or any traffic rules, cows ambled along languidly and large vehicles tore through haphazardly, their harsh musical horns blaring deafeningly.

"Do you know where she lives?"

His mother shook her head as she wiped her sweaty face agitatedly, "I never asked her. She said she would come early. The bank shuts in half an hour."

"Can you get the cash and keep it ready?" Sameer anxiously suggested.

His mom shook her head, "she is the only surviving account holder who can…" her eyes grew big. She leapt to the gate, "Where's Kamala? She has to hurry!"

A lean boy stood by the gate balancing his bicycle on one arm. Dressed in crushed clothes and grimy slippers, the disheveled boy looked anxiously at Rukmini as she scuttled to the gate.

He addressed her politely, "Ma can't come today. She is hurt. There was a lot of fighting and a riot broke out at the land license office. The police shut everything down. My mother got hit on the head. They took her to hospital and she sent me to tell you that she won't come, but my sister will do the work." He shoved a young girl before Rukmini and swung the bicycle around, "I will come by and pick her up at night."

"Wait, where's Kamala now? Which hospital? I want to see her. And you can take her back." She pointed to the girl, "It is okay, I'll manage."

"Who will do all the work?"

Sameer butted in, "Don't worry about it, just take care of Kamala didi."

The youngster looked at Sameer and took in their formal attire. "You must be going somewhere… I"

Rukmini ignored his query and spoke urgently, "Just tell me the name of the hospital and I will go and see her."

"Also, do you know when they will give out the "filote"?" Sameer butted in taking the initiative.

"Filote"? They will issue a notice for plots later." He pronounced it correctly and stared at them oddly. He pulled out a small scratch pad and pen and wrote in clear English the hospital name and ward number. "It is the zanana ward, for ladies." He glanced at Sameer from lowered eyes, "they will let you in madam. I think we may bring her home tomorrow. The doctors said it is not serious."

"Wait a bit." Rukmini halted him, "Sameer, pass me my bag quick." She turned to the boy, "it must be quite costly, let me give you some money. It is Kamala's money - her savings."

"No need madam, she is in a government hospital. It is totally free for us."

She pressed some money into his hands, "take this, you might need…"

The youngster turned away and called to the neatly dressed young girl to hop on. "Thank you madam, we are okay. Please wait for a day. I will come back tomorrow and tell you everything." He swung the cycle pedal with his foot, glanced back at the little girl and sailed off.

Sameer and Rukmini looked dismally at each other. Natasha stepped out gingerly from the cool room to announce that Asha would be there shortly. Reluctantly Rukmini murmured, "We should go I suppose." She went to freshen up dreading the prospect of spending such a sultry day in the open air expanse of a farmhouse dressed in commodious silk garb. As the family sat apprehensively speculating about the gravity of poor Kamala's injuries Asha's car honked urgently in their driveway. There was nothing left to do but carry on to the celebrations. Amid Asha's incessant chatter and running commentary on the expansion outside Delhi as she pointed out the new malls and townships, Rukmini didn't get a moment to mull over Kamala's issues.

Mamta and her husband stood in sartorial elegance cordially welcoming their guests at an elaborately festooned archway entrance to their farmhouse. Stretching behind them was a vibrantly bedecked expanse elegantly decorated with bowers of brightly coloured flowers.

Rukmini gasped in pure delight. It was undoubtedly the prettiest venue she had seen. The cynosure of all eyes, the bride sat with arms outstretched as two girls worked intricate henna patterns on her hands and arms. Bangle sellers slipped tinkling glass bangles on to young girls' slender wrists while stewards bearing trays with delectable snacks waited courteously at tables. Live performers dressed in traditional garments, strummed musical instruments and strolled about singing tuneful wedding melodies.

Asha pulled out her invitation card and a young man counted all the guest accompanying her, nodded and let them enter. As they walked up the carpeted walkway Asha murmured to her, "Each person at the party is worth a million bucks. So worth kidnapping! Every guest requires a special pass to enter or someone has to vouch for them. Mamta's husband has organized private security. You can spot the bodyguards. They are in black suits and wear earpieces."

"Many men here are in a black suit and wearing an earpiece." Rukmini gazed at the sea of stylishly primped up wedding guests as Asha steered her to a beautifully decorated table with remotely familiar faces.

Asha greeted the bunch of ladies fondly. She introduced Rukmini to old friends and acquaintances whom Rukmini could scarcely place. She sat down with a drink and looked around the table trying to recognize the ladies while Namita held court, narrating her early experiences as a new migrant in Australia.

"Yes I must confess, the taxation really threw us to begin with, but then you receive so much in return! Good medical care, fabulous education and really good public facilities. Everything is absolutely free. You should see the schools! I doubt if any of these pretentious, so called exclusive schools for the affluent here can match them. They have well stocked libraries and computer labs and everything is provided for the kids including the notebooks and stationery! Namish has received top quality education at no cost and has involved himself in any number of community based activities, again absolutely free!" She leapt up, "Let me get a refill, I'll be right back!" She breezed off unaware of the reaction of her naïve chatter.

An overdressed, large woman turned her painted mouth disapprovingly, "Seriously, how excited can anyone get about such things? She has used the word "free" like a hundred times today!"

Another lady that Rukmini vaguely recalled added, "I know! What's with that? I just don't get it. I mean we have free schools here too. Our servant's kids go to them. What has happened to Nam?"

Rukmini wanted to interject that their comprehension of Namita's comments was a touch lopsided, but decided to keep quiet mainly because she still wasn't quite sure who was who.

A pleasant faced lady said softly, "I think she's just sharing."

"Okay, but must she make it out to be some sort of paradise?"

"But isn't that what migrating has always been about? Seeking pastures greener?" the pleasant faced lady queried.

The large woman snapped, "These are the green pastures now. Tell me why every multinational is coming to India?" She reached out for a plate of snacks and started munching noisily. She had an exaggerated speaking style punctuated with guttural vocal fry tones that made Rukmini's hair stand on end. She strained to remember if she was from their school or college but drew a blank. She accepted a drink from the steward and shifted self consciously in her chair.

The large woman declared in her falsetto twang, "People should be begging for an Indian visa!" She turned to another smartly dressed woman and congratulated her on losing five kilos. "I can't do it baba! The thought of the gym makes me sick. I don't want to pretend to look half my age. I am what I am. It is our hormones (pronounced "harmones") you know. 'Afterrall' we all put on a little, but have to know how to carry it."

Immediately the conversation became a free for all with each woman advancing her own theory on weight loss and hormones as Rukmini suffered in abject silence. Listening to that large woman's pretentious nails on a chalkboard voice was worse than a root canal.

Before long the discussion focused on jewelry. Rukmini felt out dated in the ancient gold jewels she had abstracted from her mother in law's locker. She felt she had fallen through the looking glass as she sat listening, acutely awkward in the awareness that she had little to contribute.

She couldn't recall many details about the ladies at her table except for one certainty; they were all the heirs of really wealthy families and had evidently married into their own kind. She gazed in awe at the lavishly dressed set of friends with whom she felt she shared little else than the name of their alma mater.

Looking away from the table at the gaily bedecked venue, she gawked at the fabulous jewels and beautiful saris everywhere and thought about what Sameer had summarized about India. "Right from primitive days everyone wanted to come to India, some to plunder and others to let down roots. That is why we are all the products of a double dyed gene pool." She was impressed by how much he had absorbed from his grandfather's books and a little remorseful she hadn't educated him at all about the country.

Namita carried back her glass to the table clueless that she had been the butt of their unfriendly gibes. Some of her friends were encouraging her to tell them more about Australia. Rukmini was tempted to pull her back but got drawn into Namita's arresting account.

"Obviously I had expected it to be totally different from here and then out of the blue, reminders of home just crop up. Driving up a criss cross of roads I was blown away to find myself parked on a road called Delhi Street!"

"How weird! Even we don't have a Delhi street in Delhi!"

Namita continued, "Would you believe it if I told you it was the junction in Sydney where Delhi Street and Bombay Street cross Simla Street!"

There was a ripple across the table.

"Amazing!"

"How did that happen?"

Namita nodded and spoke with her mouth full. "My guess would be some British officers were transferred from India to Australia and just got involved in naming those roads!

"Namita, is it just street names or is anything else remotely Indian there?"

"Well we have Bollywood dance classes! And the Indian shops stock almost all our provisions, cleaner and better! Even the coriander is so clean and free of mud or soil." Namita spoke with her mouthful, "That's because it's grown hydroponically."

The ladies looked at her.

"On water!" She elaborated, "You add the nutrients, shine some sulphur lamps on them and the plants grow beautifully. It's cleaner and easier. This is the new practice all over!"

"Wow! Why can't we do that here? I wash my coriander thoroughly and yet there are times I feel the grit in my mouth."

"Start up costs are huge. Oh! Oh!" she placed her plate down and wiped her mouth hastily "This reminds me of a crazy incident back at school. You've got to listen to this one. There was this elderly teacher who had that experiment going in class where each kid plants some dried beans in a jam jar and water it every day."

"Yeah and it sprouts and grows."

"Photosynthesis, yes I remember that!"

"Does every story have to be about this school of yours?" The same richly dressed bulky woman who Rukmini felt certain couldn't have been from their school asked slyly.

The other ladies hushed her.

"Let her be!"

"Don't be so nasty!"

Rukmini's fingers itched to upturn the bowl of Kulfi on her ridiculous bouffant.

"Go on Nam, so it's this sprouting thing, and…"

"And this one little kid had missed out as he was home with a sprained knee. By the time he got back to school, most of the other kids' saplings were a few centimeters high and he felt left out! This teacher, very kindly told him that they would sow his beans that day and then added encouragingly that his shoots would last longer than the other plants. That calmed him down.

As luck would have, the school organized a fire drill that afternoon and the kids went straight home after that. When she was packing up, the teacher realized she had not planted the little guy's beans and decided to do it first thing in the morning.

Now, the next day this boy arrived at school carrying a small seedling tied in a bit of plastic. Quite aware of the ribbing he had had from the other kids showing off their plants, the teacher looked at it and asked him, "Did you find a little plant at home?"

"He nodded."

"Did you want to plant that one?"

He nodded eagerly and she thought no more of it. She brought out the jam jar and said that he could go and collect some dirt from the field. She hurried to borrow a small shovel from the class next door.

Now a word about her colleague in the next class. He is the world's most expressionless person. Nothing ever shows on his face. No joy, misery, anger, anxiety, nothing. So anyway, he was walking about the class giving a spelling test when he turned around to see the teacher from next door holding the little green plant.

"Mr. Carmody, could we borrow your little spade please?" she sang out.

Carmody's face changed many shades of crimson and his eyebrows shot way above his glasses settling somewhere near his receding hairline. He strode towards her rapidly and dragged her away from the doorway.

"Where did you get this?"

"Oh this little fellow in my class brought it. He wants to use it in place of the beans but I am going to plant them both…"

"Don't you know what this is?"

"What? The plant?"

"It's marijuana!"

"I think he would have added "you idiotic twit" if she hadn't been that old."

Her listeners were stunned. "Gosh! Where did he get it?"

"At home, in his mum's bedroom." Namita told her rapt audience, "I'll cut a long story short."

"Too late for that!" The fat woman drawled tactlessly but the rest of Namita's loyal friends shot her down.

"Let her speak!"

"Don't interrupt!"

Rukmini began to rethink the Kulfi idea.

Namita glanced sideways with huge eyes and bent forward. "They were growing weed!"

"Why weeds?"

"Not weeds, "weed". Drugs!"

"Gosh!"

Namita nodded slowly, "Hydroponically, using nutrients and solar lamps. I'm not in the know but that's what I've heard."

"Don't they get caught?"

"Bet this child's father did!" another friend leaned in, "So Namita, what became of that kid?"

"Not sure, but I believe one of the girls said she saw the dad yelling at him at "home time" and he was crying."

Her listeners laughed. "Poor kid!"

Rukmini who had been standing behind Namita's chair sat herself down while the ladies processed Namita's intriguing tale. "Imagine how they could mint money with it here!"

"The power cuts would wreck it!!" Everyone burst out laughing.

The topic changed with the arrival of a tray of sizzling snacks.

"Anybody for the salad buffet?" one of the ladies asked.

Namita jumped up excitedly, "I have been waiting to check it out! What a treat!"

"Treat" was understating just a bit the lavish swoop of banquet tables stretched across the vast lawns with chefs under little canopies, standing by to cook and serve promptly whatever the guest wished. Exotic fruit displayed amidst ice sculptures and creamy sauces graced the salad trolley that counterbalanced an equally laden dessert display.

Rukmini saw that Asha had left the table and was walking briskly towards the henna stalls. She hurriedly caught up with her and broke into chatter, "Asha, who are these people? It's unreal. I mean each one is a snooty fashion plate and all their chatter centers around their obscene wealth in one way or another! The fat lady talked about the upholstery in her pricey car and having her maid's room wall papered and that other one had to acquire an additional vault for her expensive jewelry." She mimicked the pretentious nasal drawl "My drawers are brimming over and I sometimes forget how many jewelry sets I have!" Asha giggled at the imitation. Rukmini became serious, "tell me, did we really attend such an elitist school?'

"Not really. I mean our school was classy with plenty of broke bureaucrat kids like us, but Mamta has maintained contact with just those who are rolling in the stuff, who, you know, married equally loaded guys."

A young girl called out to Asha from across the gathering and Asha waved to her. "Look I need to rush up to the house. I'll see you in a bit."

Before Rukmini could say anything Asha broke into a nimble sprint.

Not wanting to return to the table of patronizing, affluent snoots Rukmini decided to walk off some of the rich nibbles she had been wolfing down. She strolled about admiring the tastefully arranged soiree but couldn't help wonder how much it must have cost to put together.

Loud Bollywood numbers rang out across the plush, magnificently bedecked farmhouse. Exquisitely dressed socialites mingled as stewards carried drink trays offering the middle aged Indian's staple scotch and soda and the youngsters' latest fad, vodka shots. Rukmini steered herself towards the farmhouse in search of the restrooms and was buttonholed by a uniformed security guard.

"Bathroom?"

He motioned away from the building to some portable toilets set apart in a field with doubtful undergrowth.

"Can I go inside?"

The man shook his head and pointed yet again to the prefab restrooms.

Rukmini turned reluctantly lifting her delicate silk sari high.

"Where are you going Rukmini?" Mamta leaned out of an open window and called out in her clear voice.

Mamta motioned to the guard to let her in, "Don't go there. Come in here!"

The inside was lavish as expected. Enormous Bohemian crystal chandeliers hung off ornate ceiling roses intricately worked in gold and ivory. Ornamental pillars stood on sparkling granite floors and elaborate gilt framed paintings hung off walls. As Rukmini walked with Mamta, she was enthralled by the expensive silk carpets and embroidered curtains cascading from high pelmets. She gulped as she took in the sheer opulence.

As Mamta waved her towards the washrooms she explained impassively "that guy is posted outside because my husband's buying guns."

"Oh!" Rukmini smiled understandingly and then stopped in her tracks, "G-guns! Did you say guns?" she repeatedly rather stupidly, "why?"

Mamta giggled and shook her head, "Rukmini, seriously sometimes you behave as if you've come from a village! Everyone owns guns these days. India has changed honey!" Mamta rushed off and Namita escorted Rukmini to the tennis court sized toilets complete with gold plated fittings and a miniature swimming pool for a bathtub.

"Five star hotels would pale in comparison to these plush trimmings." Rukmini thought to herself.

Namita offered the bewildered Rukmini lilac coloured, linen hand towels from a silver basket.

"Just chuck it into that bin," she added helpfully.

Rukmini dried her hands vigorously as she turned things around in her mind. She cocked her head to one side and murmured to Namita, "I didn't understand what…"

"I know. Let's get out of here. There's some weird stuff going on."

Namita steered her out of the farmhouse in the direction of the richly decorated seating.

Rukmini looked baffled. "Namita did you hear Mamta mention something about buying guns?

I didn't quite get it."

"Neither did I but then there are so many things I don't understand I feel it's best to shut up and listen. Some explanation always follows, you know, because everyone talks so much."

"Did you hear what she said? He's buying guns at his daughter's wedding."

Namita settled down on a brocade covered lounge chair and pulled one closer for Rukmini. "Though technically this is just a party, you know, to celebrate the Mehendi and have a sing along. The wedding isn't for a week. So let him buy guns if that is how he wishes to use his time." Namita philosophized rather irrationally.

"But guns, I mean who buys guns at any time?"

"So why not at your daughter's Mehendi party? Now shut up, enjoy the fanfare and eat something" she added motioning to the bearer of a delectable snack tray.

Rukmini declined. The thought of any more food was revolting.

"What's up? You look a little frazzled" Asha took in her friends.

Rukmini couldn't hold herself back, "Mamta's husband, what does he do?"

"He's a contractor, a builder. They have many of Delhi's finest skyscrapers and hotels to their credit. The groom's family is also in the same line of business. Why?"

Rukmini looked uncomfortable.

"I don't suppose builders now days are packing heat?" Namita asked collapsing into giggles.

Getting more flustered by the minute, Rukmini snapped, "Namita, gun play is no laughing matter."

Asha sat her portly figure down, elegantly holding the pleats of her striking sari and regarded her two friends grimly.

"Please tell me what's wrong. I am accompanying her husband with the jewelry cases later."

"Good! He'll cover you." Namita smiled encouragingly.

Rukmini glared at her. Namita was beginning to annoy her with her drollness.

"I can almost guarantee your safety," Namita added with a smirk.

Asha's eyes took bore into them. "A joke's a joke but I don't like it when I can't understand it."

"She saw him buying guns in there, in a rec room; you know the one with a pool table" Namita declared biting into a multilayered barfi.

Asha nodded gravely and grimaced, "Terrible isn't it? This is what our country has come to. Everyone needs a gun for self protection and until it's made legal, the black market flourishes. Actually, he is one of the crusaders of the movement to assure every Indian the right to bear arms, US style! I believe there are some twenty million illegal guns in Indian cities today! Can't see why the idea so appalls you."

"It would be abhorrent to anybody who knows India from her early days. This is shocking really, in the land of Mahatma Gandhi!"

"Rukmini, shut up. That was decades back. It's out of control now. With so many irresponsible brats toting guns, our girls are not safe, our homes are not safe and this government has allowed it to proliferate so now it comes down to each one for himself!"

"Basically there is nothing you can't get if you have the cash."

"Not in India, no. Of course you need some connections too. But really, money is all that you need here. If you need a good doctor, which we all do from time to time, you can have the best for a price, get your traffic offences pardoned with some loose change, get your kid into a good school or college for a few lakhs…" she put out her palms and shrugged indifferently, "That's the truth unfortunately, but don't look so surprised! It's not as if you never lived here!"

"I did, but remember I was raised by a fanatically honest government employee and married into another such family. I knew there was corruption and bribery but never thought I would see gun violence here! For that matter, the local police in England don't bear arms!"

"Why do you think we moved?" Namita joined the chat. "It was becoming increasingly difficult to remain on the fringe and we knew we would have to accept all this or face a daily battle. I saw students with average marks securing admission in prestigious institutions where high achievers failed to get a seat. People spoke of "fixing" and "managing" things with cash. It's our mentality. Even in Australia when Namish secured admission into a Selective School, I had total strangers call me to ask how I had "managed" to get him in, all Indians of course!"

"Not in the U.K. thank God!"

Namita giggled, "I think it's a Pavlov's dog kind of conditioning with us. If you obtain something, you must have bribed someone." Rukmini looked pained at the anomalous linkage but Namita just laughed at her own joke.

"That is what I was trying to explain to those kids last night about the class of recent migrants to Australia but I am not sure I succeeded. Just because everything is up for sale here, it doesn't mean that you go trying to mess with the systems in other countries where it's all completely above board. I couldn't let those insolent kids get away with making cheap shots at Australia."

Asha addressed her regretfully, "I'm so sorry Namita about last night. Kids these days get charged by anything projected in the media. Tomorrow, if the news channels start promoting Australia as a clean and fair nation…"

"Which it certainly is," Namita added,

Asha nodded in agreement, "… the whole lot will promptly pledge to move there. But their parents were very displeased with them for confronting you like that. I feel so bad that you had to leave suddenly!"

"No worries. The only real regret was that I wasn't able to get through to them. That's the power of biased propaganda! Thank goodness Namish wasn't with me! He would have taken them on! What I wasn't able to get across with all their snide remarks was that everyone settles down pretty well ultimately."

Asha spoke soothingly, "It's a passing phase. There was a time some decades back that people here couldn't stop asking every Indian in America about the "dot-busters" and some people even called the NRIs in the US greedy for risking their lives to live there! It will subside like all other fads. Don't let those puffed up loudmouths get you down. I don't think they were at all prepared for your reasoned justification."

A boisterous dance ensemble took the stage and they were treated to some energetic performances in which the bride's mother and father, sans gun, participated gaily. Each of the ladies was invited to shake a leg and a troubled Rukmini sat watching pot bellied men gyrate unselfconsciously with women in low slung saris bobbing rolls of gelatinous fat. Uneasily she took in the obscene display of pelf muttering to herself, "Does everything have to be enjoyed in profusion, food, drink, revelry, home shopping for weapons?"

Evening gave way to twilight and Rukmini strolled about restlessly. She couldn't bring herself to indulge in any more meaningless yarns. Her thoughts were dominated by Kamala's plight. She had seriously intended to do all that was in her capacity to help the poor woman and this latest setback had thrown a spanner in the works.

Rukmini frowned as she settled down in a sheltered corner deep in her own thoughts. A worried Asha looked at her from a distance. She studied her friend's face looking beyond the subtle make up and elegant sari. She had had some experience in interpreting Rukmini's feelings but today she was at a loss. She walked slowly towards her. It was hard to decipher what worries were occupying Rukmini's mind. She reached out and touched her on the arm with a clatter of bracelets, "You alright?" Rukmini jerked her head and looked up into her dear friend's concerned face giving a small smile. "Of course, why wouldn't I be?"

"Come on", Asha, steered her back to their table. "What's the matter with you? It's a wedding not a funeral."

Thinking better of saying anything about a mere maid servant at such a gathering, Rukmini said the first thing that popped into her mind, "I am worried about Lekha."

Asha shook her head in disbelief, "Rukmini leave her be! She hasn't had many privileges and not as many opportunities, if this is the way she likes to live her life we just have to support it! Lekha's a bit of a maverick but she's harmless."

"Isn't she here?" Rukmini looked about searchingly.

Asha shook her head firmly, "She's sent regrets but you will see her at the wedding." In a low voice she added, "I suspect Avatar may have come on a flying visit."

"So does he expect her to just drop everything for him?"

"Not everything, just superfluities."

"What does she do with her time when Avatar's away, like ten or eleven months of the year?"

"She is a programmer. Makes cartooning visuals for a top U.S. company. Another cog in the outsourcing machinery! It keeps her occupied and is well paying though she does keep unusual hours. By the way, Avatar visits India every three months."

"How such a lovely woman can squander her life away for a hopeless relationship beats me!" Rukmini murmured as she allowed herself to be led back to the table of the haughty heiresses.

Little did she know that in distant California even Avatar wondered about exactly the same thing. Mental pictures of Lekha dogged his days and nights. Her unwavering attachment and loyalty was as much a mystery to him as to Rukmini. Nothing could explain why such a gorgeous, smart and talented woman would while away her life waiting for him. What was this unshakeable faith she had in him?

His mind flashed back to the day he had arrived on an eleventh hour business trip and paid her a surprise visit. He alighted from the taxi early one morning and as he was paying the cab driver, he saw the object of his love approaching from across the street. Even in the early morning with casual attire and unkempt hair she was a vision! Unbeknownst to her he watched in silent enchantment as she elegantly crossed the narrow lane dodging morning traffic, strands of hair flying across her gorgeous face. He watched her, a soft admiring smile playing at his lips, as he stood there hands akimbo waiting to be noticed. She crossed hurriedly and drew closer to her apartment building. Barely had she caught sight of him and like beads from a necklace, the shopping bags fell from her clasp spilling vegetables on to the dusty street. Oh what a mess! They laughed and they cried as they dusted and gathered the bruised vegetables. He looked at her suppressing the urge to wrap protective arms around her fragile and almost ethereal beauty.

Three idyllic days she worshipped him with a love so rare, so pure. There were many, far too many who would condemn them but she shrugged it off saying she had no use for the approval of others.

He affected Lekha in a way that she could not define. She thought of him constantly in the days that followed each visit and it filled her with a profoundly rich ease. She lived in a self enclosed sweetness causing her to spurn the company of teeming eager, young courters. It might have appeared that she spent a lot of time cloistered in her room, but therein she created a make belief world of untainted love where no fingers were pointed at her, reliving the melody of their togetherness and drenching herself in fond reminiscences.

Asha looked at Rukmini in quiet exasperation. "I really don't think she is bothered by gossip anymore. She's taken that stance and all I say is that if this is what she wants, so be it. With her mother gone she's all alone in the world and I for one don't intend to abandon her just because of her questionable romantic choices."

Lekha was past caring. She had been shunned long enough to care a whit for peoples' opinions. She thrived on a random assemblage of sweet reminiscences of a distant but not forgotten past. Memories of riding pillion for miles on his trusty scooter, sharing a Kulfi falooda in the corner of a dark café with warm yellow hanging lights, strolling through misty streets in Delhi's chilly winters lived inside her.

Rukmini looked heavenwards gloomily, "Oh Lekha! Lekha!" She sighed, "Why couldn't she have married some dull sod, had a few kids and got over this fellow?"

Asha's expressive eyes moved away from Rukmini's face, "Oh look! Here comes our friend who married a dull sod and had a few kids!" Then she added in a hurried whisper, "He is actually a big shot in the government!"

Rukmini turned around to look at an approaching couple.

Grotesquely out of place in a dated Tanchoi sari with her hair neatly fixed in an oily bun and some old gold jewelry, carrying a large green handbag Lata strolled in with a distinctly superior air. Rukmini thought she looked older than her years. The face still had some sweetness but the eyes looked tired. There was a weariness hanging about her.

She collared Asha's husband and whispered to him indicating anxiously towards the bar her husband had sidled up to.

"She's asking him to keep an eye on her husband's drinking" Asha murmured, "Honestly it's like a moth to a flame! Is drunkenness mandatory for this guy?"

Rukmini bent her head, "Shh. They can hear you."

As Roy walked up to him, Lata's husband held his glass high and called out "Hey, marvelous party!"

Rukmini looked at a smiling Lata, "How have you been?"

"Fine! So many years! How are you?" She settled herself at the table and smiled up at Rukmini, "So you are based in London?"

"Yes!"

That was it. There didn't seem to be anything else to say. It was as if time had come to a standstill.

They seated themselves near Lata at a table creaking under lashings of delicacies.

Asha looked across at Lata, "Nice necklace."

"Thanks. My wedding set and the sari also! Nothing happens to these old things! I don't really like the new designer stuff these days with that gaudy embroidery and patchwork. Anyway, it's all so ridiculously overpriced!" She glanced contemptuously around the table but everyone was engrossed in conversation.

Lata accepted a drink and filled her serviette with a good number of snacks. She scanned the huge gathering taking in the grandiose displays of ostentation. "This must cost a fortune!"

Rukmini agreed, "It is most certainly the most extravagant party I have seen."

"Wait till the wedding. Now days they are so intent on outdoing each other's shindig, nobody gives the bride and groom a second look."

Rukmini nodded. "It's alien to me. Honestly it's almost as if I am a foreigner here! It has been such a long time! You didn't come to Mamta's place the day she invited us to view the trousseau. I was quite bowled over by the pink diamond necklace!" She recalled listening quietly as Mamta traced the lineage of each jewel or narrated how the outfits had been meticulously designed and created by fine craftsmen from various parts of the country. She also heard one of the ladies ask if "real crystals" had been sewn on to the wedding dress making her wonder what "fake crystals" would be like. It was like she had never belonged to this world. She mulled over it a little and realized that she never had! The world she was raised in had been was totally different from this one.

Lata took a break from stuffing her mouth with snacks, "Trousseau my foot. Call it what it is, dowry. These business families don't marry their kids they merge their empires. This is the new breed of Indian oligarchs."

A number of ladies walked over to say polite hellos to Lata almost as if they were paying obeisance and Lata treated each one with a withering glance. After exchanging a few obligatory pleasantries, the posse' retreated. Lata glanced at Rukmini in an amused but cynical sort of way. "Did you see how that woman looked at my sari?"

"No. But hers must have cost a bomb with all those semi precious stones and silk embroidery!"

Lata murmured sneeringly, "Thousands. It's peanuts for the wives of those shady crooks."

Rukmini looked aghast and gave a small, awkward laugh.

"I am not joking!" Lata dangerously waved a chutney loaded snack precariously as she spoke, "We have to scrimp and save just to arrange tuitions for our kids. My husband is the guy making all the tax laws to generate some funds for the state and these scoundrels devote their energy to devising ways to evade them."

"Surely some must be honest businessmen." Rukmini needn't have said anything, Lata wasn't listening. Moving her chair closer to Rukmini's, she raged on. "Rubbish. They are all unscrupulous crooks. I hold my head high and live on my husband's honestly-earned salary and these women feel they have the right to stand in judgment over me!" It seemed to Rukmini as if she swore between her teeth. "How dare they? All of them are useless parasites and nincompoops. Do you know, at their New Year party they served some bloga Caviar and you should have seen all those fakes trying to eat that stuff on dry biscuits."

"Bloga? Beluga caviar is really expensive!" Rukmini whispered, coming to realize Mamta's husband's significant monetary value. "I didn't think Indians even liked caviar!"

"They don't. Most of them don't even understand what it is but if they've read about it or know it to be elitist, they'll lap it up. It's a hollow, decadent society and unbelievably idiotic. These fools open champagne on their kids' birthdays and," She flung her arm out, "look around you today scotch flows freely."

"I wonder if Scotland even brews as much "Scotch"!"

Asha joined the two of them shepherding a steward bearing a tray-load of appetizers. Rukmini passed up on them muttering "I won't be able to eat any dinner." But Lata helped herself lavishly. There was a burst of loud laughter and cheering from the stage.

Asha looked wistfully toward the bridal couple. "Doesn't she look fabulous?"

Rukmini nodded and was about to speak when Lata, having polished off a few more snacks, decided to plod on, "Anybody would look nice in such pricey clothes. Take a walk around! You'll see those silly girls showing off Armani and YSL baubles even though you can get equally nice things made locally at a fraction of the price. Blow up the Pop's money without a care. The black economy in India is larger than some countries' annual budget." In a loud conspiratorial whisper she said, "Do you remember Mamta? What was she at college anyway? She was a pass course student who had a compartment in H.Sc. She hasn't worked for any of that money."

Rukmini smiled. "Accident of birth! She has a rich father so she got a rich husband!"

Lata was still fuming, "Look at her, idle lazy thing. If she comes here lording her wealth over us I'll throw something at her."

Much as Rukmini would have loved to watch such a diversion she did the right thing, "Even so it is her daughter's wedding!"

Lata's eyes bored into the victim of her onslaught. She spat out fiercely, "Frauds, all of them. Especially that husband of hers nothing but a scheming swindler with skeletons in his closet!"

Asha suddenly acquired a philosophical touch, "India is an odd place today. It's really a matter of who you are, for some it's an earthly paradise, but a dystopian nightmare for others."

Lata touched Rukmini lightly on her arm and spoke quite earnestly, "Corruption has taken hold of this place like a termite infestation, Rukmini. You are very lucky to be so far away. Don't come back."

Rukmini could hold herself back no longer. In a low voice she leaned over and asked Lata, "No offense but Lata what exactly are you doing at this party? You despise each one of them so passionately!"

"She invited us, we have to be here!" Lata spat out. "Even when we don't gel with their class, they have to accept that I am married to a powerful man. I think they use him as a status symbol. Just to show all their cronies that they are close with him probably means a lot. I just come along to see this vulgar display. I am satisfied, Rukmini, in the belief that my husband is incorruptible."

Asha gave a little sardonic laugh. "So you see, all those women came to kiss the ring." She burst into loud laughter at Rukmini's bemused mystification.

TWELVE

As the evening gave way to dusk, strings of tiny multicolored lights came on all over the place. The farmhouse glittered as the setting sun cast long shadows.

"Come let us get something to eat." Lata ushered Rukmini to the buffet table Rukmini walked gingerly, skirting the rose petal strewn path and stepped daintily on the sides. Her face belied her dismay at the colossal waste. Didn't anybody see the prolific decadence? Crushing fresh flowers underfoot to celebrate a wedding! She raised her eyebrows but held back from commenting.

Lata turned around and called out, "Are you okay?"

"Coming," Rukmini called out muttering to herself, "honestly what an appalling waste!"

Jane bounced up just behind her and hugged her fondly. "Love that English accent! Honestly Rukmini, all you need is a hat with red roses and a carpet bag and you could be our very own Miss Marple! I just expect you to say "Rawther! Instead of 'yes' any minute!"

Rukmini turned around to see a demurely dressed Arti with Jane in an outlandish off shoulder outfit that turned quite a few heads. Rukmini shrieked in pure joy, genuinely thrilled and immensely relieved to meet friends from the past with whom she had a connection.

"You're one to talk! With this pronounced American accent!"

Jane frowned, "The rose petals bother you? Me too. I was furious to see they are real!"

She smiled at Rukmini. "Are you headed to the buffet? Watch out for some more display of waste. Those tubs have discarded plates and some of them are full of food."

Rukmini grimaced and nodded.

"It's a loathsome way to fritter away your wealth I feel."

"Why bother! Just enjoy it for an evening. You don't have to see them ever again."

"I suppose you're right." Rukmini answered uneasily.

Rukmini turned to check on her children who had made friends with a bunch of youngsters and appeared to be enjoying the feast. She was amused to see them stroll around in a group balancing laden plates and conversing as if with old friends. The Irony struck her! She marveled at their capacity to befriend total strangers while she fumbled for words in the company of those she had known almost her entire life.

Lata's husband tottered unsteadily towards them. Asha, always politically correct, mumbled something about how good it was that they could make it.

"Wouldn't miss it for anything!" he slurred in an unnecessarily loud voice. He looked about uncertainly and sighting a drink-laden table lurched unsteadily towards it. Lata looked beseechingly at Asha.

Asha sent a steward after him with a warning, "no more drinks for saab."

Back at the table Rukmini nibbled on bits of salad, a little nauseous at the sight of all the uneaten food dumped in the waste baskets.

The same pleasant faced woman asked conversationally, "So where is your house Rukmini?"

"Greater Kailash II."

"Pretty far! How Delhi has spread!" the unpleasant fat woman exclaimed.

"Right! It just isn't the same sleepy place of our childhood. I remember when Delhi was a neat, pretty city with its flowery roundabouts, vintage street lights and much less traffic." Asha said wistfully.

The large woman's strident voice sneeringly growled, "And so crowded! It's all this mass housing that attracts unwanted migrants from here and there." She added derisively, "cheap housing. My husband gets disgusted at the mention of DDA flats. I can't imagine how they live in those houses all crammed in. They make me feel claustrophobic."

Namita retorted in an even tone, "We lived in those before leaving for Australia and Arti still lives in one."

"I'm sorry! I didn't mean to totally condemn…" The fat lady's faux apologetic stance fooled nobody.

Arti turned to look at the lady and replied smoothly, "Sweetie, You know where I live. You have been to my place several times. Your little one attended my nursery school for a few weeks!"

The large woman shook her head rattling the jewelry in her ears and hair, "Must have been years ago! I can't imagine what has happened to me I just forget things these days."

Arti's face wore an odd expression and she was about to ask, "Didn't you also live in DDA flats then?" but stopped short, thinking she might be mistaken.

Rukmini looked around for a brick if not a Kulfi. She realised that everyone was well acquainted with the woman Arti had addressed as "Sweetie". Feeling certain it was less an endearment and more likely her real name, she strained to recall any Sweetie in her faded memory and looked hard at the woman but nothing came to mind.

She heard Asha chatting excitedly with Jane. No kidding! You didn't really! You're making it all up!"

Jane responded fervently, "Nope it's true. We met on the flight and we sat together all the way here. Ask us anything about each other! Anything about any of you too" Jane added with a twinkle, waving her index fingers about.

"So how did you get seats together?"

"Long story" Jane scooped up a handful of cashews and summoned a steward with a mildly shrill whistle.

"Jane!" Arti looked astounded.

"Relax. This is my friend's party and nobody even heard me. They thought it was those squeaking mikes." She requested for a stiff scotch and looked around. "This is divine!"

Rukmini sighed with pure elation as she looked around the table at friends of her childhood and youth. Lata greeted Arti warmly and Jane a little stiffly. She treated Jane with the same superior look she had employed to wilt the sycophants earlier.

Arti came and sat close to Rukmini and asked after her family warmly. "I can't believe we are meeting after so long! I was at your wedding! And oh yeah! I just heard from Jane about Anil's prestigious award! But then, it was a foregone conclusion what with his extraordinary brains! He's paving the way to a Nobel Prize I'm sure!" Rukmini smiled as she thanked Arti for the simple, sincere praise.

Jane addressed the company, "First of all, hearty congratulations!" she declared with much ceremony holding up a glass of strong stuff, "on Dr. Anil's amazing accomplishment! Which, I am sure is richly deserved and well earned!"

Rukmini's eyes shone. Trust Jane to have noticed the announcement. "Thanks Jane!" She said graciously. Jane mock curtsied and turned to fill the blanks for all the curious queries that her flamboyant toast generated.

Suddenly Rukmini was showered with compliments and a few questions. Even Lata deigned to congratulate her. Jane smiled contentedly at the flurry she had churned up. She turned to Rukmini, "So now can we safely say the bit about there being a greater woman behind every great man is true?"

Rukmini would have none of it and vehemently shook her head laughing, "Not in this case! Anil gets all the credit."

She asked Jane, "So, when did you move to the States?"

Jane covered her full mouth and rolled her eyes about, "Hmm, let's see, Reagan was in the White House The First Gulf War was on, Madonna and Flash dance were popular," she touched her shoulders, "shoulder pads and leg warmers were in vogue!" she summarized with a laugh.

Arti sat down close to Rukmini. "How do you like it in the U.K.?"

Rukmini smiled, "Can't complain! We've had our share of challenges but then who hasn't? The world is shrinking and it doesn't matter so much anymore where you live.

"True." Namita joined the conversation, passing around a tray of delicacies. "Hey I love your kids, Rukmini. I met them inside. They were in the pool room and some old "Friends" re-run was on. It's the first one I think, with Rachael trying to explain to her father that she does not love that guy she dumped at the altar."

"See! There you are! They have it pat out West!" Jane chomped on a searing hot samosa her legs stretched across another chair, the picture of comfort. Her gown fell away from the long side slit exposing a substantial view of her shapely leg. Lata clicked her tongue disapprovingly. Jane ignored her and addressed the bunch lazily, "You don't get married without being in love!"

She glanced around to see if she had everyone's attention and continued, "I think arranged marriages in our country were all about legitimizing sex."

"What!" shocked voices shrieked at her. Some ladies cast hurried glances over their shoulders. Jane's was not a soft voice.

Jane examined the snack trays a touch too carefully and picked one delicately placing a blob of chutney on it. Then she addressed her agitated audience in an unperturbed drawl "Overseas you do not marry unless you are in love. The love element is totally misplaced here. Love for money on the groom's side, love for status or security on the girl's side and passion, yes much passion, going by the way these newlyweds are proliferating. I attended a wedding last year and yesterday, I encountered that bride pushing a pram!"

"Jane, don't be ridiculous."

Jane checked off on her fingers, "I mean come on, think about it, you check pedigree, you give and take cash and gold, sometimes more, a bungalow or factory or something, like this you know," She pointed with both hands at the general fanfare, "some dowry deal; you throw a few bashes, each feeding a few hundred people, even those you hardly know but they live in the neighborhood or are the relatives of relatives, and that's a wedding. They sing emotional songs of romance and I can see many getting all wrapped up in it but in my opinion, it is pure schmaltz. The bride and groom know nothing about each other! What would you call it?"

Asha retorted good humouredly, "Your analysis is a bit arbitrary, and is certainly better than those women in your parts walking up the aisle in their third trimester or even getting married after having a few kids with different men."

Jane acquiesced "That I will grant, but tell me, would you describe the feelings in our arranged marriages as love? It's about status and a bit about education in some cases, but mostly about the moolah! Hence, a girl from a middle class home has to lose every bit of self esteem and bow to the demands of the husband's family for the rest of her days!"

Someone else joined in, "Hey that is what she has been at her folks place anyway. Instead of serving the father and brother, she serves the husband."

"But give it ten years and that guy starts feeling devalued too."

"And he goes out and has an affair!"

Jane called out, "Way...way ...wait we are meandering. I was talking about the rottenness of arranged marriages!"

"This is the fallout!"

What we need to do with arranged marriages is to switch the paradigm to a more liberal method.

"Forget it. What's going to happen to checking family status, horoscopes or caste?"

"That's the liberalism I refer to. Otherwise Indian women will continue to be squeezed by the same torturesome yoke." Jane banged her hand on the table making the glasses rattle. "She has to break free! This country has taken enough from its women."

Lata raised her voice at Jane, "Hey don't waltz in here as if you are "made in U.S.A." and start listing out things wrong with the country that gave you your first twenty one years."

Sensing a rapid erosion of three decades of friendship, Asha stepped in to ease the heated situation, "Everyone just calm down take one deep breath! Also, Lata I think you should know that Jane is here every three months overseeing her charity work and they are really good causes."

"And that gives her the right to look down at us?" Lata looked unimpressed.

Jane abstracted another drink off the tray and wagged a finger at Lata, "I was not listing but analyzing. I do not look down my nose at anybody and I never claimed to be made in the United States though I could make out an argument that I was reborn there." She smiled a little, looked up at Lata and continued gravely, "and it was 23 not 21."

"What?" Lata enquired haughtily

"I left here when I was 23. I am older than you. I was a sickly child. Polio. I wasn't exactly healthy in college either as you doubtless recall. I was a deformed cockeyed floppy girl who shuffled about. I am the girl you, no doubt, secretly made fun of all through college. I was the pet whipping boy that anyone could laugh and point at. I'm surprised you don't remember. I have copped a million mocking humiliations and survived them all. Nothing you say can make a dent in this thick hide."

Lata looked mildly uncomfortable but continued to regard Jane's multi coloured halter neck gown with scorn, "This is a wedding, not a fashion show."

Jane replied in a flash, "Sure, but no one mentioned it was a retrospective on the eighties!"

A few ladies giggled while Lata turned scarlet.

Namita smiled, "It's not what you wear but how you look and I have to come out and say Jane you look stunning!"

"It is Indian silk and I just love the colours. I had it tailored here too. I just love shopping here."

"Thank God you can see something positive here." Lata interjected.

Jane barely glanced at her, "Oh I see more potential here than most of you, then again, the uglier side of it all just gets my goat. Didn't a bunch of people get together and hold a protest rally against corruption?" She took a sip from her cocktail.

One of the ladies spoke vaguely, "All it did was cause massive traffic jams."

"Where does all the rallying get you? All they're pressing for is a bill or some sort of a law banning corruption, as if it were ever legal. We have a law against dowry too! It's certainly a step in the right direction but the question is will they follow it through to the end? I bought a place lately and I'm not wild about paying a bribe so when they told me it would take six months to get a power connection, I decided I would wait six months. Anyway I was going to be away from India for that long. When I returned nine months later I was told I would have to wait another 8 months for a meter. Finally, I had to pay out a hefty bribe! I swear, no jokes, I literally threw the money at him most discourteously but the guy just picked it up with a hideous grin and I got the meter within the hour. I wanted to pull his guts out and strangle him with them but ..." She shrugged.

The ladies looked at each other unfazed.

Lata remarked, "You will never manage to live here if such small things bother you. And don't tell us these stories as if we don't know all this."

Almost as a well timed distraction, Roy, Asha's husband escorted two elderly ladies to their table. Asha sprang up and dashed over to help them to their table. Playing hostess was second nature to her. The trio approached their table as Asha warbled on, "Mind your step, Roy get some more chairs and ask the man for some virgin Marys."

As the guys pulled out chairs for them Rukmini's eyes narrowed. Asha laughed, "Don't tell me you've forgotten my mother and mother in law?"

Rukmini was blown away! "Oh my God, this is wonderful! How lovely to see you after this long! You look so beautiful!" she breathlessly took in their glowing faces.

Asha's mum laughed. "Thank you. Maybe we have reached a point where we can't age anymore!"

"Of course not, you're aging gracefully!" Namita lifted the food platters and offered them to the elders."

Rukmini sat near the two ladies catching them up with her life in London. It made her feel like a little girl again after so many years. She considered this the best part of her evening. "I don't think I've ever seen you two apart. She asked, "Weren't you two neighbors?"

"We still are! Going on 50 years I think!"

Mrs. Roy smiled, "We had elevenses together every day! Not a day goes by that we don't see each other."

Rukmini's eyes shone as she recalled, "You did many things together! The ladies clubs, the morning walks and even some cooking."

Mrs. Roy nodded, "Exactly! You remember a lot! Asha's mother sewed and I used to love knitting!"

Asha inserted her share of memories, "That's why I always wore hand stitched nighties and even party clothes stitched and embroidered by my mother or woolens knitted by Roy's mother, sweaters, gloves and caps back when Delhi had proper winters."

Asha addressed the guests at their table, "Can you believe it, my mother still churns her own butter and makes ghee at home? Then it is delivered across to my place."

Rukmini added, "It was delivered to Anil's place too! Jams and pickles as well!"

"Don't tell me they were friends as well?" Arti asked.

Rukmini nodded, "My mother in law and these ladies were dear friends, but this friendship" she pointed to the two old ladies, "is special!"

Some friends of the Roys came to say hello.

Namita sat down near Rukmini, "I had heard that Asha's mother and mother in law were best friends but I had never met them."

Rukmini smiled warmly, "It was a beautiful friendship and do you know why? No ego!"

"Or maybe each one is a really nice person?"

"Agreed, but something needs to sustain a friendship for this long! I feel it was because each one got a well meaning, therapist with whom she could share everything!"

Namita smiled at the ladies and said, "I'm not surprised you got your kids married!"

Mrs. Roy nodded, "We had always wanted it but thought we would let the children fall in love. Thankfully they did!" Roy's mother chuckled, her cheeks turning pink.

Everyone laughed with her. Her endearing manner and simplicity warmed Rukmini's heart.

She remembered something and addressed Asha's mother, "Saraswati aunty I think you might be able to help me. Something's been bothering me. I was going through the bank locker where Anil's mother kept her jewelry and I unearthed something unusual that I have never seen before. It's a small slab, like a small brick but it's quite heavy and looks as if it may be gold plated or something. It's got a beautiful golden sheen."

The smile left the old lady's lined face. She looked at Rukmini blinking thoughtfully. A flicker of recollection seemed to flash across her face. Everyone waited politely. Rukmini squirmed uneasily kicking herself for bringing up something that had such an unsettling effect. The elderly woman cleared her throat and stared ahead thoughtfully. She murmured, "So she had it all along!"

Rukmini strained her ears and leaned in. The woman seemed to be grappling with her thoughts. Looking up at her solemnly through aged eyes, she spoke gently, "It is gold. I can't believe it is in your locker."

"A gold brick?" Rukmini looked perplexed. A whole gamut of thoughts raced through her mind. Where did it come from? Was it real? Was it stolen? No! Her in laws were upright, honest people. Did it belong to someone who had left it for safekeeping? If it was their own legitimate possession why wasn't it in the form of ornaments? Why would her in laws have lived a middle class existence if they had that much gold?

Her face belied her bewilderment and she looked up shaking her head. "I don't understand."

The elderly woman spoke haltingly. "It was a long time ago when she lived in Mumbai! Her mother loved having gold ornaments made for her daughters and her father used to tell her mother that gold didn't drop from the skies, but one day it actually did!"

The woman cleared her throat and took a sip from her glass. Her voice was so soft that it was a strain to catch what she was saying, over the uproarious celebrations. Rukmini leaned in to listen.

"This was during World War Two. We were young girls. The family had gone out of Bombay to attend a wedding taking their servants with them and only returned after the explosion. Their taxi driver informed her father that there had been a Pearl Harbour style bombing in the port and a ship carrying bullion had been hit. There was panic everywhere. Anyway, he brought them safely home. While the family was unpacking and taking their baths her father tuned in to the news on the radio. We didn't have TVs back then." She smiled sweetly at Rukmini.

"So tell her what you know Ma!" Asha was impatient as only a daughter can be with her mother. The old lady turned her eyes towards Rukmini and continued, "It was when her mother went out to the balcony to hang her towel

206

that she found a gold ingot. Kanta, your mother in law, told us this tale many years back but I really didn't think they had kept any of it." Saraswati aunty sighed, and shifted in her seat pulling her sari around her slim shoulders. She spoke somewhat guardedly, "We asked her many times if her father returned it to the British government, as we knew it was being impounded, or if he had secreted it away, but she said she didn't know!" Mrs. Sen fixed dark, watchful eyes on Rukmini as if looking to cast the shroud of guilt on her.

Rukmini stared at her, incredulity writ large across her face. This bit of information was a staggering shock! She toyed with the gold ornaments at her neck wondering if they had come from the ingot. Her friends at the table, who had fallen silent at the startling revelation, turned their eyes to the hullabaloo on stage attempting to avoid the awkwardness.

Asha softly enquired of Rukmini, "How big is it? Do you think it is the same thing?"

"How many gold bars can be floating about Asha?" Her mother snapped.

Rukmini looked at the old lady in agreement, "Actually...it's not very big," and holding out her fingers measured a six inch length, "but it is quite heavy!"

Asha smiled and added in a reassuring manner, "Well don't look so stricken Rukmini! It's not stolen goods," her mother clucked and hissed as the daughter continued, "you didn't even know about it. This was over sixty years back!"

A sudden tiredness overcame Rukmini. This trip to India had drained her. What with the complexities of selling their house and dealing with Kamala's problems, an alarming revelation such as this was quite simply the last straw! The strain of it all had taken its toll on her. She yearned for the mundaneness of her simple, predictable life where the height of excitement had been the award for her husband's medical research. It had hit the newspapers and the newscasts for a day or two and faded away. Anil was the last person to make a big deal of that passing hype. In his view, much remained to be done.

Sensing Rukmini's discomfiture, Asha promptly created a diversion, "I have heard another fascinating tale of the second world war from my grandfather. This was towards the end of the war. Some of the Indian army, then the British Indian army were stationed in Rangoon to protect the locals who presented them with small gifts as a gesture of gratitude, usually bamboo umbrellas or brass vases. While they were freeing Burma, this young Major said had "found" a chamois leather bag full of Rangoon rubies and emeralds!"

A gasp went round the table, "A bagful of precious stones?"

Asha laughed, "Not a big bagful, but one of those pouches that you keep jewelry in, you know, the kind with a drawstring?" Cupping her hands, she indicated a something small. "Ok, so this elated officer returned dead tired to his tent, hung up his tunic and slept off leaving the stones in his pocket. He woke the next morning and called for his orderly but there was no response. Other orderlies reported seeing him go into the jungle at night but had not bothered about it. They didn't think anyone could consider deserting in that region since no one could make it very far without transportation and anyway the war was nearly over. People expected him to show up eventually.

When the Major joined the others for breakfast, he narrated the story of his extraordinary good fortune the previous evening. Naturally, everybody was curious to take a peek at the stones so they accompanied him back to his tent. When he reached into the pocket of the night's tunic he realised he had been burgled!"

Everyone gasped. "What! No rubies and diamonds?" Namita wailed.

"It was rubies and emeralds honey, and no, all gone." Asha wagged her index finger and added rather dramatically, "All but one! It would appear the bag wasn't tied very securely so when he shook out the pocket, a single red stone fell out. He held up the solitary ruby against the light imagining what a fortune he had lost."

Ignoring the sighing and groaning Asha finished up her fascinating little tale, "That Major went on to become my grandfather and the ruby," she reached for her mother's bony hand and pointed to a shiny red stone, "is on my mother's finger!"

Everyone peered to get a look at the big Rangoon ruby. The old lady's fussing ceased and she drew in her fingers fixing her daughter with a fierce glare.

Asha looked wounded and feared some repercussions later on, but was content to have closed the subject that made Rukmini squirm.

As the evening drew to a close, little footlights blinked here and there on the massive sweep of land. Strings of coloured lights flickered in the soft breeze and it was as if a painter's brush had swept across the bright evening landscape coloring everything in shades of the night. Party guests started filtering out. The ladies strolled across the sprawling emerald lawns to the massive gates as chauffeured cars swept up to pick the Sahibs and memsahibs.

Almost everybody had left when the ladies made their way to the exits, having bid farewell to Mamta.

"What do they grow here?" Namita asked Asha who gave her a blank look.

"It's a farmhouse so what do they farm?"

Asha burst into peals of laughter. "They are not farmers Namita! They don't grow anything, you know, for commercial purposes. This is just a weekend home."

"So the term farmhouse is ...?"

"Bit of a misnomer if you have to take everything literally." Rukmini quipped.

Asha was about to say something when she heard yelling and shouting as a few men came dashing in "Saab! Saab ko bulao!" (Call the master)

A few policemen walked briskly behind them. Namita looked terrified and Rukmini looked as if she was about to cry. Asha stopped one of the men and asked in Hindi,

"What happened?"

"Mamaji's car crashed! Sonu Bhaiyya was driving it."

"Which Sonu bhaiyya? That young boy who was dancing here?"

"Mamaji has only one son. I have to tell Saab!"

THIRTEEN

Rukmini put down the day's papers astonished. She had been following the case closely. This was the closest she had come to such a horrific police case. With a mixture of anger and dread, she read as the police investigation unraveled the "mystery" of a straightforward hit and run case. Within days of the incident the investigating officer disappeared. A few days later they declared there had been no eye witnesses. Rukmini fumed. Half the guests at Mamta's party must have witnessed the accident! Relegated to small columns, the reports slowly moved away from the front page. At the end it appeared that the case might be dismissed, as the police had just one eye witness who clearly remembered it was a big truck and not a car that collided with the victim's car. The newspaper rustled in her trembling hands. She sat seething, not just at the manner in which the case had been manipulated, but more so at the stark realization of that infinite power that holds innocent citizens to ransom each day. What she read nauseated her. It sickened her even more that the woman who was planning her daughter's wedding road show did not give a hoot about the immoral criminality in her family.

That afternoon while Kamala was upstairs washing out the terrace, a young girl, the same girl who had come to substitute for Kamala earlier, came to the door hesitantly asked for the maid. Rukmini sent her upstairs and returned to her reading. Captivated by the pretty face, expressive black eyes and long glossy hair, she watched over her glasses as the young girl carefully walked up the stairs. She was a natural beauty. She wondered if she was any relation, though seriously doubted it. Poor Kamala was no beauty. Her pock marked face and tired eyes added to the plainness, but it was evident that she couldn't have ever been beautiful.

Kamala rushed down wiping her hands on her sari and asked to leave urgently. She hurriedly added that she would ask Mrs. Chopra's maid to substitute, if she couldn't come the following day.

210

A puzzled Rukmini walked behind her as she put away the brooms and found her slippers, "What happened Kamala?"

Tearfully Kamala said, "Again they have taken my husband into custody." "Why?"

"I'll explain later Bibiji, I have to rush now."

Before Rukmini could ask her anymore, Kamala hurried down the road clutching the young girl's hand. Staring after their retreating figures, Rukmini thought regretfully she should have given her some money.

Kamala arrived the next day having pawned her gold bangles for the bail money. Rukmini was appalled and perplexed as she hadn't quite understood what kind of trouble her husband had been embroiled in. Kamala moved around crab like, mopping the floor and nattering on. Her voice was like white noise that Rukmini was only vaguely aware of. She was tackling an invasion of a bunch of prospective buyers for their house.

She and the children weren't accustomed to having inquisitive strangers traipse through the house scrutinizing every detail. A bunch of them were talking in loud voices at the top of the stairs, while others had settled down in the living room. Disconcerting as it was, Rukmini knew, with scarcely a month for them to return to England, it needed to be done. She sat in a corner waiting for the agents to see everyone out.

She realised Kamala was still talking. "Madan, my husband had a good government job, but he lost it as he used to be sick all the time. They say he has blood pressure."

"What government job did he have?"

"He was a gardener in those big government buildings up at Boat Club."

"Really? How lovely! Can he still garden?"

Kamala replied earnestly, "Yes, yes bibiji he is very good. Even I know gardening. We are from a farming community. He would dress up the office tables with flowers and his bosses appreciated his hard work. But after his operation he used to faint easily and tallied up too many sick days so they sacked him."

"But is he better now?"

"Yes now he is well but they won't give him his job back."

Rukmini was looking out at the shabby disrepair their front garden had fallen into. Dry leaves swirled in the dust and dirt that had blown in from the street. All the flowers had died and the grass was overgrown and untidy. It had never been so neglected before. She cringed each time she passed it but there hadn't been any time to deal with it.

"Do one thing. Let him come and tend to this garden of ours and I will see if some other people want to employ him up our street."

With a delighted shriek Kamala jumped up from the floor, "I will bring him with me tomorrow! She looked out at the uncared for patch and turned to her mistress, her eyes shining. "You watch. He will make it so beautiful, passersby will stand and stare!" She stood before Rukmini with folded hands, "You are just as kind as your in laws. God bless your family." She gushed.

For the rest of her days Rukmini would not forgot the glow of gratitude on Kamala's face.

Mr. Singh, the property agent, called out to her and she rose to meet yet another lot of would-be buyers.

The following morning was cool and breezy a rare departure from Delhi's blazing summer. Natasha and Sameer set up their chessboard on the patio while Rukmini sat indoors studying the offers that had come in for their property. A delicious smell floated out of the kitchen as Kamala prepared breakfast.

"Mum who's that man in the garden smiling at us?" Natasha called from the verandah.

Rukmini stuck her head out and smiled, "don't worry, it's Madan, Kamala's husband. He's going to garden for us. You kids can keep playing. I'll have Kamala bring the breakfast out in a bit."

The game of chess had arrived at a tense do or die moment and Natasha searched desperately for options to save her queen. She deliberated before slowly and thoughtfully making a move. She glanced around the board warily as she surreptitiously moved her rook, then she slammed her hand to her chest with a gasp of relief.

"Buying time? Your death at my hands is imminent sis!" Sameer drawled portentously.

"Even if you win this one, we'll be even." Natasha chewed her nails and stared hard at the board. Rukmini came out with a laden tray and noted how much the girl resembled her father when she sat thinking like that.

Chess forgotten, the kids turned their attention to the delectable spread. Rukmini poured herself some tea and moved her chair out of the sun. "Should be moving in soon," she said looking up at the sunny skies.

"So what about this new gardener?" Natasha helped herself to Kamala's tasty offerings, glancing at Madan unloading flowery plants from a cart.

Rukmini explained to her children why she had employed the man.

"Is he not well?"

"Not very well. He has just one kidney."

"Why? What happened?"

"He was duped into donating his "Gurda"." Rukmini spoke absently.

"What?" a puzzled Sameer asked chomping hungrily.

His mum gave a short laugh, "I am talking like Kamala aren't I?"

"Yes you are and I don't like it." Natasha flicked her hair off her face and mumbled through a mouthful of egg paratha.

"Kidney. It means Kidneys. These two got caught up in a racket." She shrugged and tilted her head, "Maybe it was greed, maybe ignorance but they fell victim to a scam. This guy's cousin conned him into it and they didn't even get paid the promised amount. I am guessing there were post surgery complications and he ended up losing his job."

The children's reaction was righteous indignation.

"Good God!"

"How awful! Don't they have any laws here?"

Rukmini shrugged, "Apparently not! Nobody bothers with such people. They are certainly naive and perhaps a bit dense but look the poor things are paying for it!" She sighed and looked at the thin man slaving away at the overgrown hedges.

The children fell silent not knowing what else to say. Sameer murmured, "So they live on Kamala didi's income? Is he sick or something?"

"You can live a fairly normal life on one kidney can't you?" Natasha asked.

"Yes you can but I think he took long to recover, so his employers sacked him. Thank God he survived. The surgery was most likely performed by some quack. So he began selling vegetables on a hand cart but some local goons roughed him up. There was a scuffle and he got arrested two nights back. The police expect to be bribed just to allow him to peddle his wares on a specific corner! Kamala pawned her gold bangles to have him released," Rukmini threw up her hands exasperated, "Oh I don't know, it's a horrible mess you wouldn't understand, and I know your father wants to keep you two away from such things but I feel…"

"Mum please don't get involved in all this." Natasha interjected.

Sameer looked at his sister "Can't you see she's trying to help?" he turned to his mother, "What's going to happen to them after we sell the house and go?"

Rukmini murmured grimly, "Don't think that doesn't worry me."

Her mind flashed back to Kamala's earnest face, "We trusted them. They promised us so much money. Whatever it may be, I had told Madan it's not correct." She sniffed and tossed her head,

"It is not right to sell our body parts. We want to die with all our organs intact. In the next birth you may be born with something missing."

While Rukmini had regarded the premise grossly illogical, she was nonetheless intrigued by Kamala's most troubling account. She had conducted some online research and, learned, with a combination of sadness and alarm, of the flourishing black market run by doctors who harvested poor but healthy people's kidneys for affluent overseas buyers. Sadly, the ignorant donor usually received a pittance.

Kamala brought a dish of cut mangoes the children eagerly helped themselves.

"Good morning!" They turned to see Asha walk in at the gates.

"Hi Asha aunty!"

"What a surprise! Come join us Asha." Rukmini invited.

"Isn't it hot?"

"Now it's getting a bit warm but it was lovely all morning, maybe because the lawn was been watered.

Asha looked at the gardener with curiosity. She raised querying eyebrows, "What's up? Who's that? Aren't you planning to sell the place?"

Rukmini hesitated. She didn't like getting into an argument with her friend in the presence of the children. "I'm just helping out. He's the maid's husband."

"But you are selling?" Asha probed, "Singh will be here soon. He has a few good offers." She checked her watch and looked towards the gates, "Why can't these people ever be punctual?"

"He'll be along I suppose. Have some fruit."

"Yeah, I guess he will show up ultimately." Asha murmured.

"Spend some time with me!" Rukmini looked her friend up and down, "you look lovely, as always!"

Asha smiled, "Thanks. It's too hot. Let's go in."

Kamala cleared up the breakfast plates and the children carried the chessboard delicately between them.

"Have you looked at the buyers' details? Just ask Anil about the black – white break up and the POA."

They walked in to the nearly cleared living room. Asha stared in disbelief. "Who would have thought the place was this big!"

Rukmini agreed, "It's really a very roomy house. All it needs is a lick of paint and some renovated furniture and it would look beautiful." She glanced suspiciously at Asha, "Black, white? POA? What's that?"

Asha strolled about taking in the tall ceilings and wide teak doors. She answered casually, "Cash payment. Normally you would be paid about half or more of the deal in cash and the rest by cheque which is the "white" payment. It saves on estate duty or something and anyway, who would have that much white amount?"

"Cash? You mean bundles of notes of Indian Rupees?"

"Rukmini! Surely you don't think anyone is going to pay you a couple of crores straight into your bank!"

"Why not?"

"It's just not done."

"What does the law have to say about it?"

Asha clucked impatiently. "You, girl, have a lot to learn about how this thing works. This Singh is an experienced guy, trust me. He will take care of everything but you need to get off your high horse about the modes of payment. This is the norm."

Rukmini was having a hard time following her friend's offer, not because she didn't understand what she was saying, but because she couldn't believe her friend would ever inflict such conditions on her.

She replied stiffly, "I do understand but I just don't need such complications! I really don't give a hoot about what the norm is."

The property dealer arrived at a clearly explosive moment and sat down unsurely in front of the two ladies.

Rukmini continued, "There must be one honest buyer!"

"On paper it will appear completely legal!" Asha assured her fervently.

Rukmini sighed gloomily, thinking to herself, "Not on paper this nation needs to abolish corruption in its heart and mind." She was long gone past the frustration of how impervious all the people she knew and respected had grown to these daily irritants.

Asha briskly explained to Singh and, shrugging her shoulders, added, "You alone can make her understand."

Singh looked taken aback and glanced from Rukmini to Asha, "Madam, that will be very difficult, almost impossible and also it will bring the price down drastically! Please ask Doctor Sahib to reconsider."

"This", Rukmini replied, "is my decision. Doctor Suri is too busy."

Singh sputtered listing out some precedence in his defence but Rukmini unequivocally brushed away all his arguments. "At least make an effort! Somebody has to take the initiative in doing the right thing."

Singh mumbled somewhat apologetically, "Madam it's the estate duty you see, it will be too high. No one can pay that amount." He rose to leave.

Rukmini looked brightly at Singh, "So we'll pay for half the stamp duty! I'll even lower the price a bit but I will not accept any black money. If the house remains unsold, so be it. I will wait for your answer." She dismissed him curtly.

Asha glared at her, "You're never going to make a sale with that attitude!"

"Honesty you mean? Asha, I find the business of "Black Money" quite intimidating."

"No one will ever know!"

"How can you be so sure? Actually I'm sure everyone will know as soon as I make the sale. And anyway that's hardly the point! I will know."

Asha sighed, "Rukmini! Don't take the moral high ground with me..."

"Excuse me? And anyway what would I do with so much of Indian currency in cash?"

"Change it!"

"Change it?"

"Change it. Buy British Pounds and carry them back. You can, each of you, legally carry a specific sum and leave the rest here until your next visit. In fact, why wait? Mamta's husband would probably exchange the whole lot for you in one go!"

"You mean, I should accept a few guns in lieu of the house?"

"Don't be silly Rukmini, he'd arrange to have cash delivered to you in Southall, or Coventry, I mean wherever you live."

"Hampstead, that's preposterous! I can't even bring it up with Anil! He'd think I was off my rocker!"

"So what are you going to do?"

"Let us persevere and hope good sense prevails. We just need one honest buyer."

Rukmini had not been exactly cooperative that morning and Asha was getting edgy with her. She clenched her fists and spoke in measured tones, "You mean one honest millionaire. Do what you like. I have introduced the best guy in the business to you."

"Well, I have set him a challenge."

Asha made an exasperated sound and changed the topic fearing their argument would turn nasty.

"I came to ask if you want to go sari shopping for the wedding. Maybe Natasha can come along and pick something. We have very little time."

Rukmini's answer stunned Asha. She sat staring as if she'd been hit by a thunderbolt.

"This is ridiculous Rukmini. What does the accident have to do with the wedding? Our friend's daughter is getting married and you have to attend. That's all. You are to accompany us in our car and we will all stand by Mamta as she gives her daughter away in the fabulous Rajput palace. Let the police look after the other business. Why allow it to spoil the fun?"

Rukmini glowered as she replied agitatedly, "Obviously you haven't seen the news. That kid is going scot free, the investigating officer has been taken off the case and every witness has disappeared!" She flung her hands up in the air, "Disappeared! The case is closed! He will be there Asha! This killer will come and dance at the party barely a week after running down an innocent family! Doesn't matter what your thoughts on my moral judgment are, this is unacceptable." Her voice quavered as she gulped down tears of indignation and anger.

The slight didn't escape Asha, who looked gravely at her obviously disturbed friend as she continued her incensed tirade, "Look, here I know I am a "Nobody" and can't bring justice to the wronged family but I sure as hell know I am not going to join in the merriment with a murderer and his deceitful, unfeeling family!" Rukmini's agitated voice rang through the house and her children peeped in anxiously.

Sending the worried children away, Asha regarded her friend apprehensively. She had underestimated her friend's indignation. She saw it as the last straw in a series of cumulative, disquieting events that Rukmini had been hit by ever since she arrived. Asha patted her on the shoulders as she prepared to leave.

Rukmini calmed down and looked at her friend, who had moved to the large French windows. "You left the house to go buy saris and I bombarded you with all my problems. Sorry! You should go shopping!"

Asha tapped her foot impatiently as she stood uncertainly staring out of the window. She answered absently, "I don't need saris. I suppose the painting, that was meant to be done while you were away at the wedding is also scrapped."

"Of course not. Singh is right. The house would look more presentable once it gets a lick of paint. I would love to go paint shopping. I mean, if you have the time?"

Asha was watching Madan at work outside. She replied curtly, "Whatever you like. We could go this evening. Rukmini this guy is good! How much are you paying him? I could do with a new gardener and so could my mother next door."

"Don't judge him too soon. It's his first day. I am only hiring him to help them along…"

"Shh." Asha motioned with her eyes. Rukmini walked to the French windows and gasped. The garden was transformed. There was a row of colourful flowers by a trimmed hedge and the grass was neatly mowed. Madan was carrying away bundles of dried shrubs to a hand cart outside the big gates.

"It would be great if he could get some more jobs. He does need the work. Let me talk to him."

"Better warn him. My mother's very particular, almost nitpicky!"

Rukmini chuckled, "Does she still have topiary hedges and borders?"

"Of course, and the cacti and roses!"

They were walking to the gate, Rukmini relieved they were able to converse easily. "I think I will ask him to trim our hedges like that too."

"You're not going to see results in two months!" Asha smiled tightly, "get back in. It's too hot!"

Rukmini waved her goodbye and turned to have a chat to Madan, decidedly pleased in the hope that he would be gainfully employed before she left.

Asha left in a bit of a huff. While she could see just cause in Rukmini's resentment she couldn't forgive her for giving the wedding a miss.

Rukmini went indoors to write out addresses for Madan giving him verbal directions to Asha's house. She briefed him about Asha's mother's fixation for her garden and warned him about punctuality.

Just as Madan left, Kamala walked in, delicately holding an armful of expensive saris. "Bibiji shall I have them ironed for the wedding?" Rukmini gave her a blank look. Something struck her. "Kamala listen, do you remember what my in laws paid for your children's education?" Kamala looked confused and stretched her arms out as if to say, "Let me get this job at hand done first."

"Put those saris away. I'm not attending any wedding. Now tell me how much they paid for your kids' fees, uniforms, shoes and books?"

The simple woman placed the garments on a chair and sat down on her haunches staring into space, "God give them peace. They were such kind people! If they had lived, my older boy would have fulfilled his dream of becoming a soldier. The middle one," she sniffed, "would have completed his education. and the little one would have joined ITI for stitching classes."

Rukmini was aghast. "Have they all just stopped their studies?" She asked Kamala incredulously. "Why didn't you at least bother to check with me first?"

"Don't be angry bibiji, I didn't think about it. With your in laws, I never hesitated…"

"Okay listen, I want them to get back to school. Take the money from me for readmission. Better still, I'll go with you if the school makes any trouble. Everything goes back to as it was before. I will find a way to organize the funding."

Kamala burst into shrill laughter, "They will be so happy! The boys still read their last year's books and keep practicing writing some things."

"Tell them Anil sahib and I will keep supporting them provided they keep passing their courses." Rukmini felt a pleasant excitement. She had a plan. For the first time since her arrival she felt worthwhile. She walked busily to the phone. As she lifted the receiver, Rukmini recalled seeing the little girl with Kamala's son. She called out to her.

"Why did you say you have only boys? I saw your daughter the other day. She came here."

Kamala cleared her throat and spoke simply. "That's not really my daughter. She's an orphan girl. She was born a day before her mother died. They got the father remarried and he went away leaving the girl here. I used to watch her sitting outside my door, neglected, unwashed, picking things off the ground. She started crawling into our house and my boys would feed her, even wash and dress her in my younger one's shirts. She started looking nice and chubby and we really loved her. But she belonged to them."

Kamala looked down at her feet, "Then one day my husband saw the uncle behaving improperly with her. This was a man who didn't usually live there. It made us very worried for her future. That very night Madan went across and asked the grandparents if they would let us adopt her. Of course we had to pay them, but at least now we have the satisfaction that nobody can harm her. Your mother in law, God give her peace, knew about our daughter. She always sent clothes and gifts for her."

Kamala sat brooding over it for a while then gave a short laugh, "My son, the younger one, used to keep asking me to go the hospital and get a baby girl. How could I tell him I had had the operation? Now the boys have a sister and God gave us a daughter."

Rukmini sat motionless, too moved to speak. The thought of Kamala and her husband's willingness to burden their family of four when they barely had enough, touched her deeply. She also gained valuable insight into the magnanimity of her parents in law and realised with much relief that she had probably salvaged the situation in the nick of time.

"All I want is to be able to let her finish her tailoring course. You should see her embroidery, bibiji. All those things in the shops pale in comparison."

"Really? Bring something to show me. What does she do now that she stopped her classes?"

"That lady in the market gives her sari falls to sew and a good amount of embroidery pieces. She makes a tidy bit and also takes care of the house when I am here. May God give everyone such a good daughter." Kamala lifted herself off the floor busily murmuring to herself that it was time to make fresh lime juice for the children.

Rukmini, having just discovered the true meaning of charity as her in laws had intended it, determined to put in place a financial arrangement that would help Kamala's children attain their goals.

She picked the phone and called Asha who snickered into the phone, "I knew you would come around! So pick you up next week as agreed?"

"Nothing doing. I need to speak to Roy, consult him. Please get me an appointment with him, urgently."

"He's right here. You want to sue the Seth family?" Asha cackled at her own somewhat misplaced humour.

"Just let me have a word with him please."

She believed that Roy could be relied on to put in place a legally viable fund for Kamala's family. The elder Suris' philanthropy would live on in the burgeoning careers of those underprivileged kids. Roy's crisp voice came on sounding business like and a tad preoccupied. He heard Rukmini through and understood what she was looking for. He fired quick queries and rapidly took down some details. He promised he would work on it.

FOURTEEN

That evening, Rukmini sat chatting in Asha's pretty drawing room before leaving for paint shopping.

"It doesn't make any sense for you to live there while it is being painted. Move into our place while we are away in Rajasthan." Asha glanced at Rukmini's determined chin and asked hesitantly, "Still firm on giving the wedding a miss?"

"Nothing will change my mind."

"I know you were terribly disturbed but..."

"Please Asha I have made up my mind. This project will keep me creatively occupied. I want to paint each room in a different shade. The house was new when I got married and I want it to shine again."

She sighed thoughtfully, "Old age is such a terrible thing! Anil's parents were house proud. I remember his father telling us over the phone once, that he was scared to bring labour into the house. It was around the time when the local police had issued warnings of stabbings and robberies involving elderly people who lived alone. I think he had wanted to paint the place but towards the end, he let things slip."

She looked at her friend, "I want it to look nice again, even if we don't have it for very long. This is the least I can do for that very special couple. I have acquainted myself with their lives and it's as if I never knew them! I mean not just the bridge parties and their popularity, but most importantly, the charitable streak!"

Asha poured from the silver teakettle wheeled in on a dainty tea trolley by Bina, her efficient and almost invisible maid. "Why didn't you visit them like all other NRI families that inundate the city every summer?"

Rukmini hesitated, "Anil barely got any time off."

"Hollow excuses. You mean he didn't take any leave? What about vacations and holidays?"

"Well normally the children went off on summer camps or I would plan a short getaway somewhere in the U.K. itself. Remember both he and I had full time jobs. Poor Anil was a broken man when he heard about his mother's passing away. It was an agonising time, I remember. You can never understand his frustration and angst. He knew he could have given her better medical care and extended her life. I do not think he would have left her here had he any idea she was going to take seriously ill. How can I explain to you the agony of losing a parent while overseas? It's a torturesome mixture of regret, helpless frustration and of course the pain of the loss that takes over your entire being! Anil was beside himself! You know how he adored his mother."

Asha nodded somberly, "She was rather adorable."

"Also, he had developed this distaste for, umm, life in India after living overseas for so long."

"I see." Asha pursed her lips.

"No, don't get him wrong. He had been overseas for most of his life. You sort of get used to the lifestyle. So when he visited his parents back in India he would get quite impatient by the power cuts, water shortages and the general inefficiency. I remember him recounting the day he couldn't get through to the airlines office number for over three hours to change his flight. It was when his mother had suffered a heart attack. Even the level of care his mother was getting had upset him terribly. A retired government employee, his father was firm about having her treated only at a government hospital. You can't imagine Anil's disgust when he saw how long it took just to get his mother a private room. And the lackadaisical attitude of the attending nurses simply infuriated him. He did hold the doctors in high esteem though, their sincerity and dedication!"

"We should be grateful!" Asha said archly.

Rukmini stopped and looked away.

"I'm sorry. That was rude of me, Rukmini. Please ..."

"It's ok. It doesn't look very good from where you're sitting I know. Look, Anil hates poverty and well, he has a theory that India need not be saddled with such a huge rich poor divide. It's, it's very hard to explain but in a nutshell, it frustrates him that any government can be as callous as this towards the issues of poor citizens."

Asha's face betrayed a "well what you can do?" look. "Didn't he miss his parents?"

"Of course he did, most awfully and very frequently. That was why he procured permanent visas for them and we upgraded from our terrace house to a much larger place, so they would have their privacy, but then they flatly refused to come and live with us! They said they felt out of place and didn't know how to occupy themselves after the first few days."

"But natural, don't you think?"

"Of course, now that I have met with their friends and am beginning to form a picture of their busy lives, I can see why they wouldn't have wanted to move there permanently, but they didn't even visit us. They just told us to come when we could and Anil almost never takes leave from work.

Honestly, I was blown away by the support the children and I got those early days when we came here! I had forgotten the warmth that is India! Each day a lovely, home cooked meal would arrive at lunch and dinner!"

"But that's customary. Wouldn't you do the same for your friends?"

Rukmini shook her head, "Not really. Perhaps for a day and that too amongst close friends, but by and large no! You can see why I found it so overwhelming!"

"I don't think it is just the social circle. I think it is the existence taken in its entirety. There's a special bond in the personal contact one forges with the household staff, even the milkman. Then there is the daily dose of cable programs, the visit to the temple, picking choice fruit from the vendor's cart right at your doorstep, or picking bouquets from the flower seller down the road, each exchange laced with simple banter! It may appear humdrum to you, but it's an essential element of our lives."

Rukmini nodded slowly, "There is comfort in routine!"

"Once they were certain Anil wasn't coming back, they probably decided to build up a social circle just to keep busy." Asha sighed loudly, "Really, I can't see how anyone can forget his roots."

She put down her teacup, glanced quickly at her watch and rose without waiting for a reply. "I'll go make myself presentable and be out in a bit. I cleared out the garden shed, just in case the new gardener needs it!" She brushed her lightly soiled clothes and moved away.

Rukmini was tempted to call out after the retreating figure, "Don't interpret Anil's absence for indifference," but recognizing the futility, held back.

She stirred her tea, reflecting on her husband. Poor misjudged Anil! She thought of the brilliant doctor he was, dedicating his life to vital adjuvant research for crucial medical advancement. She wanted to tell her friend that she herself and their children had made sacrifices along Anil's extraordinary journey, peppered as much with failure as with success.

She recalled the day he came home disappointed, having spent hours at the lab. She watched helplessly as he expressed his aggravation, "A step forward and two steps back!" He voiced his frustration. "I know the answers are out there somewhere." She had soothed him with what she knew he considered inane platitudes. Over the years he grew reclusive and distant from the family as he came closer to a phenomenal breakthrough in his research.

She wished she could wipe her friend's mind of the bias against him, but she knew that she could not blame her for wholly misreading him. People called it like they saw it and in Asha's eyes, Anil was the prosperous son of simple parents who disappeared overseas to a life of abundance and comfort, and never looked back.

Even she, Rukmini, had not, to begin with really understood the obsessive perfectionist that Anil was, but over the years had come to believe in him, appreciating his complexities and accepting his quirks. She found herself reassessing his tetchiness and mood swings that had offended her early in their marriage.

She had initially found Anil an extremely complex person to live with. His expectations of her were high and sometimes unreasonable. No matter what time at night he worked until, he expected her to be waiting with hot food when he returned. Before marriage, he had lived a structured, ordered life, organising his wardrobe with as much meticulous detail as he would his patient care. Rukmini had been rendered speechless at first sight of the well appointed, little kitchen, everything marked and dated neatly. "You don't want to keep any spices longer than three months," he had explained.

After reading through his published papers and research on various facets of Clinical Oncology, she came to realize slowly that he was as modest as he was brilliant. The respect and almost deferential admiration he commanded from peers and even his superiors was emblematic of his standing.

It was enough for her to know, in her heart, that her husband had always wished the very best for his parents, but could not find words to explain the awkwardness that had crept into the father-son relationship after the mother's passing.

Rukmini drained her cup thinking back to her first few days in England as a new bride, not quite cognizant that she was married to a genius. Everything was quite new and strange. She had to learn to use The Tube, shop on a budget and manage all the housework alone. She had heard that every Indian bride going overseas got overwhelmed at some point with the huge workload, having had maids back home, but Rukmini remained composed as she worked through her initiation to the English way of life. She made a few friends and settled in fairly quickly.

The biggest challenge was trying to understand her husband's mind. He worked relentlessly at his painstaking research and never seemed more alive and driven than when he talked of it. His eyes lit up and his face glowed with a rare passion when immersed in deep discussion with his colleagues. Rukmini felt barren and empty that she could never inspire a similar spark in their mundane and brief conversations. The real Anil emerged in the lab where, shielded from the outside world, he wrestled fanatically with his findings. Rukmini learned to cope with loneliness and deal with his moods. It called for deep personal investment on her part.

Anil obsessively persisted with sedulous determination knowing he was on track to a major medical breakthrough in cancer therapy. Sensing she was wasting her time idly leafing through magazines, he began calling upon her to proof read his publications or presentations. As she glanced through the compendium of his research manuals and scribbled notes, she not only understood how his brilliant mind worked, but also came face to face with an astounding truth about her genius husband.

He had fears, fears that he usually faced alone. Anil was apprehensive of facing defeat. Having made it this close to that pivotal point, he feared having to face that all those days and nights of tireless hard work had gone to waste.

Ever since he could remember, Anil had won every award and every competition. He had never returned empty handed from math's Olympiads or Junior Mensa quizzes. At medical college, he might as well have not left the dais when they handed out medals for highest scores in each discipline.

Today, to face defeat at the hands of a pertinacious foe was not merely frustrating; it was overwhelming to the point of being emasculating.

She accepted that all she could do was to support him, take away all his worries on the home front and try not to distract him. Rukmini had found her role as a wife. She had to be there to prop him up, not allow him to lose hope, but encourage him to keep up the fight. She reminded him that even one life saved brought the world closer to defeating this menacing scourge. Anil welcomed the strength and power his wife inspired in him, little realizing that it was all she could do to muster the strength in herself. She waited up nights for him, often falling asleep at the dining table. She dedicated herself to ensuring he ate right, all along painfully aware that nurturing his body was not half as challenging as fortifying that brilliant mind.

He had exhibited a rare elation to hear they were expecting a baby, but quite soon got buried in his work. Little wonder then, that she had kept him out of the loop with her morning sickness, sonograms or visits to the doctors. She had had a quick labour and it was only when she knew the baby would be there very soon, that she asked them to call him from the lab.

At the maternity ward, after spending a few minutes with mother and baby, he started pacing about restlessly, quite oblivious to the surrounds. Seeing that he was at a loose end, she packed him off to his beloved lab. "I'll see you later Anil."

It was, of course, an amazing time in the couple's life, but Rukmini accepted that the "baby" her husband was about to deliver, which could bring solace and hope to thousands, would always take precedence in his life. She never minded that his patients dominated his thoughts, continually propping his spirits up as his quest for crucial breakthroughs continued interminably.

She had to hurriedly shed the arbitrary housewife roles that she had grown up with and adopt a more expanded approach. She secretly hated the Indian housewives who lived for coffee sessions while the ayahs took charge of raising their babies and running their households.

Natasha's arrival in their lives involved much more work and a greater strain on their budget. At the same time, her presence made things easier and Rukmini began enjoying London. She walked her baby's pram, tied with vivid colored balloons, through leafy Hyde Park sitting by the Romanesque fountains, delighting in the little one's fascination with the spirited parakeets and waterfowl. Passing under the park's tree lined avenues she would stroll on the famed Oxford Street, mostly window shopping in the elite fashion district.

Anil became devotedly attached to their adorable daughter and, much to Rukmini's amazement, started making serious efforts to be home early to play with Natasha delighting in her baby antics. Rukmini adored being a mother and albeit Anil's mercurial moods, life had meaning.

A mynah sat on Asha's flowery balcony squawking throatily. It fluffed its feathers and bobbed its head as it examined a large flower pot, cawing raucously. Rukmini looked out. The sun had begun its descent. She glanced at her wrist watch. How much longer would Asha take to dress for a visit to the paint store? India housewives had too much time on their hands, she decided. She had hoped to finish off the paint shopping much earlier and was consoled that Kamala was with the children till the evening. She needed to call Anil and update him on her revised plans too.

She smiled to herself remembering her lovable albeit quirky husband. Natasha and Sameer were bright but not brilliant students and Rukmini had watched Anil scanning through their school report cards. Quite amused, she observed, "Don't take after the genius parent do they?"

Anil put the reports down looking pleased. "Did you know that less than 5 % of "genius" kids maintain their early potential or fulfill any ambitions? Hence I prefer to reject the title." He was glad for well rounded, courteous children, content that they enjoyed sporting activities and music, areas in which he had scant success. But he loved beating them at his favourite game of chess.

He cured Natasha's acne even before anyone thought he had seen his daughter's face. One day at breakfast he scribbled a prescription and shoved it at his wife, "Get this from the chemist's and ask Natasha to start applying it on that dermatosis, just a three hourly dab." Rukmini stared. He had come home after midnight and hadn't even met the kids. Rukmini asked, "How did you know?"

"I popped in to see her when she was asleep."

Rukmini smiled tenderly, "And you diagnosed the acne?"

Anil cut his egg and toast meticulously into six equal pieces, "It's obviously not acne. Just get her this gel."

Later that day he was tickled by the gratitude lavished upon him by his ever grateful daughter, who proclaimed he was "The world's best doctor!"

Rukmini looked at them from the kitchen and smiled. Their daughter might have unwittingly stated a truth that the world would soon acknowledge.

She watched them walk out and settle on the patio swing chatting comfortably. The father who couldn't bear to see a blemish on his daughter's face, a face he thought was perfection itself and the daughter, who accepted her abstracted father's compelling need to dedicate every waking moment to saving mankind, were soon absorbed in rare chatter. He learned she wanted to be a botanist, like her mother and made a prompt mental note to change that shortly, while she learned that he was a step closer to discovering a panacea.

In his own way, he was an appreciative husband and brought her presents and flowers not necessarily on the right days. "It's the thought that counts," Rukmini smiled to herself as she arranged the brilliant lavender hydrangeas her husband had sprung on her that evening and watched the rare spectacle of her husband while away his time with their children. Nothing Asha or anyone said would ever shake her respect, admiration and adoration of him.

Rukmini looked up as Asha breezed about firing instructions to her "staff" noting how smartly turned out she was for a trip to the hardware store. She remembered Lata's observation "Fashions in Delhi change so frequently that we are always passé!" Asha was wearing a silk tunic and scarf made out of coordinated material. She had even matched her accessories. Rukmini gave thanks secretly that she was, for a change equally well turned out having paid a trip to Asha's regular boutique. She wondered if Anil would notice the makeover she had acquired. She felt sure he would.

They were driven to a most inspiring sanitary ware store. They had put up designer rooms with matching décor, even coordinating hand towels and bathroom tiles. "It looks like a page out of those magazines about beautiful homes! I shall be spoilt for choice with all the variety." Rukmini smiled at Asha,

"What I like the best is how everything is home delivered!" It was easy to place the order for supplies as Rukmini had brought the room measurement along.

They drove through crowded streets with unruly traffic and Rukmini flinched as the driver sped through the throng, swerving dangerously to avoid a cyclist. She was grateful for the air conditioning vents blasting icy cold air at them. "Very disagreeable weather we have had all through our stay." She frowned as she looked at the messy chaos on the road.

Asha looked at her in disbelief. "You have forgotten everything haven't you? This is how things always were, chaotic and messy!"

"I haven't forgotten" Rukmini sighed, "I just can't understand how it works." She peered out at the large shanty towns and slums. "How many people per square mile live here?"

"Hundreds, perhaps thousands but that is not as dangerous as what lurks beneath."

"What do you mean?"

"I mean crime, drug mules, prostitution, child labour and even espionage and other underworld stuff! Nobody is what he seems. Each of those guys has just one aim, to make as much money as possible and as fast as he can."

Rukmini looked out at the gigantic slum, as dwellers carried about their daily activities. A grubby little girl in a tattered frock watched a bunch of kids playing with colourful paper windmills. She stood there laughing just looking at the colorful bits of paper twirling in the urchins' hands. It was laughter from the bottom of her heart, spontaneous, uncontrolled laughter. Rukmini stared, her heart warming to the small chuckling child. "I bet she has nothing, hasn't had a full meal in a long time or ever slept in a clean, soft bed but look how she is laughing. Isn't she adorable? She is able to take pleasure in some other child's toys! Oh do look Asha at this beautiful little baby!"

Rukmini found her eyes filling up. Asha followed her eyes and smiled pityingly. "Another few years and she will be accompanying her mother to someone's house to do the washing. Let her laugh today."

Rukmini looked at her in dismay. "That's their future?"

"That is where Indian housewives get their cleaning women. It's a dog eat dog world. Avarice and greed dominate each one's life." She pointed out with a manicured, gold encrusted hand, "Her parents probably built that mall. All this gentrification! With nowhere to go, they will start filling the parks!"

She spoke in a whisper almost as if to herself, "Sometimes I wonder we live in such close proximity, us and them, what prevents them from, one day marching into our homes and ousting us? What would we do?"

Rukmini shook her head sadly, "That's a scary thought! How do you live with such ideas in your head?"

"Oh they come and go. I push them out. If you have to live your life waiting out the odds, I don't think we would ever step out of our homes or let any servants in!"

Before Rukmini could think of a reply, a deafening boom reverberated through the air, churning up dust and smoke.

Asha glanced out, "Good God! Diwali is months away and firecrackers are already blasting our ear drums! Who says this is a poor country?" Her eyes searched for the source of the bang. They felt a deliberate nudge as their car got abruptly jostled from the rear by a behemoth SUV, attempting to sneak by through a precariously narrow space.

Rukmini looked out anxiously, "You got nicked I think."

The driver muttered under his breath and said aloud, "Sahib will be angry."

Rukmini looked about at the disorderly clutter of vehicles clamoring to edge past each other with little regard for lanes. "It's a wonder more cars don't get pounded,"

"Traffic is slow." Asha explained.

Rukmini's reply was drowned in yet another loud blast accompanied by a flash. Their car lifted briefly and landed back with a violent thud, throwing everything in disarray. Rukmini bumped her head against a sharp edge on the roof and Asha felt as if something had pushed her backwards. She held her neck writhing in pain from whiplash.

A furlong ahead of them was a messy gridlock of traffic and pedestrians, all in a mad frenzy. There was shouting and yelling as people clamoured to get closer. Their driver lowered his window and craned his neck to look over the crowds, the thickening haze stinging his eyes. Asha asked him what was going on.

She murmured to Rukmini as she peered out of her window, "Must be some religious procession or wedding. See, we think they have no money, but it's these people who celebrate in style."

Oblivious to her words, a petrified Rukmini shook Asha's arm and pointed out of the front glass. Ahead of the crowds, masses of thick black smoke billowed out around tongues of fire. Some people climbed onto vehicles trying to capture the scene on their mobile phones, while others just yelled into them.

It was as if day turned to night in minutes. The ladies searchingly peered out through smarting, watery eyes. They were enveloped in voluminous smoke as it snuck into the tightly shut cab. Bleary eyed Rukmini stared at the bedlam ahead. Some people left their cars and rushed to the scene, where injured and stunned victims were limping to the road side. The two bewildered friends took in the hysterical commotion. Amid the dusty chaos and flames they saw shattered glass and water from a burst pipe flooding the street.

Ram Singh stepped out calling to the other drivers.

"What's happening?" Rukmini held Asha's arm tightly in panic and fear.

A grim Asha tried to calm her, but her voice quivered timorously. "Relax Rukmini, it is ok, we are safe."

Ram Singh returned in a flash and purposefully revved up the car. He reversed slightly and made an irregular U turn into pedestrians and cyclists. Holding her sore neck with both hands Asha shouted frantically at him. "What are you doing?"

Ram Singh murmured incoherently, propelling the vehicle through on-coming traffic. Vehicles were slowing down as they approached the troubled spot and Ram Singh called out to as many drivers as he could that there had been a bomb blast. Rukmini clutched Asha's hands. Ram Singh swerved to avoid a bus. He drove the car on to the edge of the road, looking for a break into any neighborhood by lane.

Asha screamed shrilly as a speeding station wagon came hurtling towards them, the driver looking straight ahead at the smoke and flames of fire. They missed each other by a whisker. Ram Singh nearly put their car in a ditch. He veered sharply, straightening out just in time. He turned into a side lane and wove his way deftly through narrow alleys taking sharp, brisk turns.

Asha fired a volley of questions at him but only got any answers once they were on to a relatively calm street. He told them what he had gathered from the other drivers. A couple of bombs had been set off, they believed from a bus. Expecting the crowds to increase in a crazy scramble and fearing being cordoned off to make way for police cars and ambulances, he thought it best to get out promptly.

He fiddled with the car radio, hoping to get a news update. Rukmini shivered like a frightened rabbit. She stared from Asha's face to Ram Singh as they discussed the shocking event.

Asha made a stab at some light conversation, "This market is just too congested. Someone leaves a brief case full of explosives; no one's going to know. I guess we will get more news soon or else we'll watch it on T.V."

She looked at Rukmini and was alarmed at her petrified expression. "Are you alright? Rukmini! You're shaking like a leaf!"

"How long before we get back to the children?" Rukmini swallowed, and asked in a shaky voice, "Can I use your phone?"

"Of course, here let me dial for you." Asha stared at her phone jabbing at its buttons. "I think this phone of mine is dead."

The car radio blared out some jingles and returned to the news. The newscaster announced just what they already knew, the place and time of the blast. Asha asked Ram Singh for his mobile phone and handed it to a shaking Rukmini.

"Relax! You left them home, safe."

Rukmini got Kamala at home. She asked her how the children were and Kamala assured her that Sameer was doing fine. "He is reading a book on the terrace and watching all those kites in the sky. I am just taking him a snack."

"What is Natasha doing?"

"She went out with Chopra bibiji's granddaughter."

"Where?" Rukmini shrieked.

"Some mall. I don't know where."

"Can you please stay until my return? I will be back as soon as possible."

Rukmini hung up and swallowed deeply, "Natasha is out, gone to some mall with the Chopra kid." Her voice was a fearful whisper.

Asha's eyes grew big and she stared at Rukmini. "Which mall?"

"Kamala doesn't know."

Asha pointed to the radio, "There were five blasts across the city, one outside a mall." She put an arm around a stupefied Rukmini and softly instructed her as if she would a small child, "Call the Chopras and ask them where the girls have gone."

Rukmini shook her head and whispered in a daze, "I don't know their number."

Asha hesitated, "Then call..." she grabbed the phone and called Kamala again.

She calmly asked Kamala to get Sameer on the phone and dictated to him the driver's phone number. Then she barked orders to Kamala to deliver that number to the Chopras and have them call back urgently.

She handed the phone to Rukmini adding, "We should be back before all this happens, but let's get in touch with the girls anyway."

In one of Delhi's many posh suburbs, Natasha and Rhea strolled through a glittering mall, Natasha quite taken with the alluring store-windows and Delhi's "smart" crowd. "They have absolutely every international brand label here! It's incredible! My mum doesn't even know about this place!"

She held up her shopping bags gleefully, "Wait till I show her this terrific shopping! Sameer will go crazy when he sees this unique chessboard, so ornate and beautifully sculpted! It looks like it is ancient, like an antique or something. He loves such things, rich in history."

"Are you tired?"

"No not quite. I've had so much fun!"

"Me too! Sure you don't want me to loan you some cash? Your mom could pay my dadi."

"No thanks. I'll come back with her again. There's a month before we leave."

Rhea turned an excited face to her, "You're gonna love the food court. It's got the most amazing choices!"

They entered the lift to get to the food court at the top. Rhea told her that this was the only place she was allowed to visit by herself in Delhi as it was "safe and decent". Her phone chimed out as soon as they stepped out of the lift. While Rhea answered the call, Natasha strolled around admiring the dressed up shop fronts and making a mental note to hit the mall as soon as her mum could get away. She looked pleased at the bargains she had picked up. She ran through her mind all the things she wanted to buy when they came back. Cooking smells wafted across from the massive food court. She saw a man in a chef's cap flipping tikkis at one counter while the next one was selling Indian style noodles. Natasha was ready to pig out. She looked toward Rhea, blathering spiritedly into the phone, her voice loud and edgy. She turned off the phone and rushed towards Natasha, her face flushed, "We have to get out of here now!"

FIFTEEN

On Delhi's outskirts Avatar and Lekha's car swerved to avert the deluge of unrestrained traffic spilling onto the national highway with utter disregard for the changing lights on traffic signals. Their driver swore under his breath. Avatar asked if there was a cricket match nearby and the man answered evenly "Must be the bomb blast at Munirka. This road meets that one."

"What bomb blast?" Lekha wasn't sure she had heard correctly. The driver, not one to show emotion, rattled off what he had heard over the air. "The radio has been on. I thought you were listening."

Avatar and Lekha looked at each other cautiously. He squeezed her hand, "No, we weren't really paying attention." He added unnecessarily, "This has started happening quite frequently!"

"This nation has no dearth of enemies Saab, if it isn't from one side they sneak in from the other side. This Kashmir issue will never get solved. All we will have is years and years of hostility."

"Did they say who was responsible?" Avatar asked sharply.

"They don't need to. Everyone knows."

"How can you be so sure?"

"Why would anyone set fire to his own home, Saab?" he pointed to the shiny concrete structures of Delhi's satellite city and added sagely, "They can't stomach our country's progress. We keep advancing, while their country is falling apart at the seams. They know, they are losing on all fronts and this is the only way they can express their anger. You are right, it's becoming routine now. Tomorrow some minister will make a few strong statements, announce some cash compensation for the injured, order an enquiry and a few days later it will all be forgotten."

Lekha joined the conversation, "It is unbelievable that they can sneak in to the country and nobody notices!"

"Our country is porous memsahib. First Punjab, then Kashmir now the North East. They slip in easily through those dense forests. They're hardy chaps, so only they can survive in the jungles."

Avatar glanced at the stack of newspapers lying beside the driver, both English and Hindi.

"You are educated?"

"B.A. pass."

"And you work as a driver?"

The man laughed cynically, "There are more graduates floating about on our streets than stray dogs. You can't get a job without references and contacts." He sighed, "You know the practice Saab nothing is concealed from anyone. I wanted to study in the vocational college when I was young, but my father thought that with a B.A. degree, I would get a good job and become an officer. It's not so easy."

"What did you want to be?"

"Car mechanic, I don't have the diploma but I can fix any car, imported or Indian. I picked up while helping out at my friend's car garage. But this job is ok. Everyone wants to be a driver and when I take foreigners to Agra, I get really good tips." He smiled into the rear view mirror, "A friend of mine is trying to take me to the Gulf. He says all the drivers there are from India. I have got my passport made and I think I should get a call soon."

"Hope it works out for you." Avatar murmured encouragingly and settled back close to Lekha.

They had been furniture shopping at the city's classiest stores but nothing had appealed to her. As they drove back empty handed, he murmured "Another day on floor cushions" reigniting the passion of the previous night.

She blushed, tossed her head and shrugged, "It was too cliché, all brocade and velvet! I want something different."

He gave a small laugh, "this city hasn't enough shops!" he murmured teasingly.

Lekha's thoughts went to the chic apartment she had just purchased. She had waited a long time for it and wanted to dress it up distinctively. The car sped down the wide open highway sending curly ringlets flying across her face. She unconsciously fixed the bloom in her hair that had come loose and Avatar reached over to shut the window. She turned to smile tenderly at him and he held her hand, gently stroking it. How precious were these stolen moments for them! She wondered if he knew how she lived from meeting to meeting, clutching on to moments from their ephemeral trysts. She looked out again. Something caught her eye and she shrieked excitedly for the driver to stop.

Scrambling out, she rushed toward the roadside displays of coarsely crafted, handmade furniture. As she glided from this vendor to that Avatar stood some distance away in his characteristic pose with feet apart and hands akimbo. He had been through the same drill all day and expected a frustrated Lekha to return to the car any minute. Lekha, a striking picture of dignified grace and flawless beauty made heads turn wherever she went. She was soon immersed in discussion with one of the craftsmen. The man waved her towards some workers at the back and continued buffing an antique looking standard lamp. Lekha lifted her sari pleats and elegantly made her way to the back.

Avatar's eyes followed her as she nattered on animatedly trying to describe what she was looking for. He glanced at his watch more out of habit. There was only one thing on his three day agenda, Lekha.

In the past he had wrestled with himself over the tangled mess he had created for her and for himself, but for the present he had stopped agonizing over an issue that did not warrant deliberation. At least not for three whole days. His heart warmed as he looked toward the only woman he would ever love and realised with a start that she had quite disappeared behind the stalls.

He walked up to take a closer look. The ethnic wooden pieces and arty furniture were really quite good. He cringed to see how inexpensively priced they were. In an overseas market some of the gorgeously worked-on mirrors and tallboys would fetch a king's ransom. He leaned over to look at where Lekha was standing amongst larger furniture pieces. She waved to him delightedly, removing huge sunglasses from her face to examine something closely. Avatar grunted and made his way to her slowly. She jubilantly pointed to her selection of a set of exquisitely crafted living room furniture.

"It was worth the wait!"

He watched uncomplainingly as she placed an order for the dining table, to be made using an ornate cart wheel as the table top.

The rustic craftsman examined the design she sketched for him. He nodded, then looked up and stated simply, "You will have to get the glass cut. We don't do that. Here, we only work with wood."

Lekha turned to Avatar, a look of anticipation on her earnest face and he nodded, an amused smile playing at his lips.

Later in the cosy comfort of the floor-seating in her bare apartment she rattled off excitedly, how she would place the furniture.

Sighing contentedly she sank further into his arms, "My very own house! It feels like a dream!" Listing out her plans for decorating the apartment, she pointed to the covered balcony, "I already have my herb garden, coriander, mint, fennel, basil and in those big pots I grow jasmine and green tea!" A light fragrance of the aromatic tea leaves wafted in. Avatar tightened his embrace. He thought he had not seen her look more beautiful.

He looked up into a painting she had done once, on an impulse, when they were driving across a barren countryside. Like a photographer peering through his lens, she wielded her brushes capturing the landscape unerringly. She smothered the canvas with the dynamism of desert shades, executing a faithful impression of long shadows on a sighing hillside at dusk. It was his all time favourite. "I could gaze at it forever."

"I know." She agreed, snuggling closer.

It intrigued him how she filled her loneliness with an assortment of pursuits to divert from the gnawing pain of their separation.

He stared at it intently, "Never part with that one. It's the only one left."

She giggled, turning to look up at his face. She knew he alluded to the showing he had staged for her paintings. It had been an incredible night. Stupefied by her resounding success she surveyed the empty hall wide eyed. There was not one canvas to ferry back.

He smiled deeply, "They all got snapped up that night!"

"This one got left behind by mistake!"

"It would have been picked up right away." You should do some more." He goaded her gently.

"That was quite amazing wasn't it?" With typical level headedness, she corrected herself, "It is easy when you display in a gallery that loaded, influential people frequent I suppose!"

"Modest as always!" He kissed the tip of her nose.

She cuddled up to him, "To think that my work will adorn the walls of homes around the world is very humbling."

She turned to look up at his face, "Did you feel hideously left out that day?"

Posing as just another visitor, he had strolled on the gleaming floors of the gallery. He shook his head and looked tenderly into her eyes, "It was your day and I loved watching you transform into a celebrity."

"Flash in the pan."

"Not at all. This, my dear is awesome work."

"You, my dear have this effect on me."

Lekha had never thought that a hobby, initiated to distract from her loneliness, could have turned into a runaway success. All she had been trying to do by dabbling in painting was to erase thoughts of Avatar from her mind.

She did carry in her heart the fear that he may eventually stay on in California and she would have to fend for herself, but for now she had chosen to adopt the path of least resistance and simply submit to her destiny. She stoically accepted the certainty that his wife, Jharna would never accede to his demands, never set him free, if he ever decided to ask for a separation.

The anguish of forbidden love could have destroyed her but, having been tempered through a life of deprivation, she had been drilled in lowered expectations. One brief email sent with love lit up her day putting the bounce in her step and the pink in her cheeks.

She looked up, smiling. The glow of pure happiness on her lovely face reminded Avatar of the glaring extremes in his life. It took so little to delight Lekha! Just some daily emails, fleeting visits and furniture from a roadside vendor!

He frowned. Jharna, in all probability, would fault every item he had bought. Though he had amassed bagsful of trendy offerings from the malls and boutiques, he foresaw profuse criticism. She usually rejected most items on the grounds they made her look fat or old which she undeniably was. He was accustomed to the disgusted slights at his common taste. It usually ended in a fiery argument that drove his wife into a three day migraine.

Naturally, it was unfathomable for him how Lekha never voiced her grievance at the injustice of their little understanding. On the contrary, when they were together, she displayed a euphoric joie de vivre so contagious it erased from his mind every part of the life he had reluctantly forged in California.

Little did he realize that he was that rare person who brought to Lekha's life the sense of dignity and acceptance she had never received. So habituated was she to being ignored or treated with unkindness that she had welcomed with open arms the attention of an ardent admirer, readmitting him to her lonely life even after his imprudent marriage to Jharna. His marriage had crushed her, leaving her feeling as if her father had walked out on them all over again. She never cared to revisit those past days, nor did she want to look to the future with much hope, for she hated disappointments. She had had too many. To reinvent their relationship from the vestiges of a shattered dream could have taken a heavy toll, but Lekha had grabbed at an opportunity to rebuild herself from the silences after the storm. She drowned herself in the exuberance of the moment clinging on tightly, wishing it to last forever.

She heard a click and knew he took her picture with pinkish gold sunlight illuminating her face. She smiled to herself as she imagined him pulling out his drawer to glance lovingly at her adoring smile. She shook her head and told herself he didn't need a picture. The memory of their time together could never fade in him.

She giggled as she pointed to the farcical sky, a sunny glow at one end, and big blobs of rain at the other. Lying in his delicious embrace and watching the rain pelt the window panes she wanted to capture time there and then.

It is usually on such idyllic sunshine that dampening rain chooses to drop unannounced.

"I have to leave early tomorrow." He murmured into her soft curls.

Her arms tightened around him, "I know. I have packed your things." Her voice shook a little.

"Will you be alright?"

She nodded. "Remember I'm off to Rajasthan?"

He frowned, remembering they had been arguing over it. "I'm not happy about you going by yourself to this wedding."

"I'll be fine. I do it all the time when I go off on my health retreats."

"Why can't you go along with the rest of them on the bus?"

"I don't like all of them and they don't all like me." Sulkily, she twirled her hair in her fingers not looking at him.

"But you will see them at the wedding."

She nodded, "Hmm. Asha and Roy will be there besides a few hundred people."

"Sure?"

"Of course! Don't worry! I'm going to be very busy the next few days! I have to go gift shopping, pick out something to wear…"

He gave a start, "Oh!" He looked down into adoring eyes staring up at him and delicately moved her off his lap. In a flash he rushed to the large pile of shopping dumped near the front door. He had completely forgotten his gift for her!

Rifling through the bags, he knelt by her side pulling out cardboard boxes tied with red cord. "I have something for you!" He held the box out to her like an excited schoolboy bringing his mother flowers. "Is this what you girls call "designer" saris? Pick one."

Just then, his phone rang out and he walked towards the window to answer it.

She opened the boxes eagerly, laughter in her eyes, then stopped. "And the other?" She looked towards him, eyes wary.

He hesitated and covered the phone with his palm, "Just, just pick one."

She sat glaring at him as he attended to the call. He put away the Blackberry and turned around, expecting an effusion of appreciation. The store girls had guaranteed him this was the very latest look in saris. Lekha fixed him with a stony look.

"Who is the other one for Avatar?" The steely calm in her voice scared him. Then all hell broke loose.

"Didi? Isn't it for her?" It was comically ironic that they both had called Jharna 'didi' or elder sister before he married her. But this situation was far from comic. Lekha's eyes burned with angry tears. The bulwark capsized and the pain of years of abandonment, betrayal and lonely nights tore through in a torrential rush.

Avatar defended himself as best as he could, fumbling for apt words that usually abandoned him during a crisis.

"Come on, you seriously think I don't buy her saris?"

Lekha slumped on the mattress mumbling softly, as if to herself, "I try not to think of all that you do with her. I shut it out. I live my reality. You could have been more discreet about it though."

The multicolored length of silk caught her attention. She lifted her flaming face at him.

"And you bring it here and rub my face in it?" She cried hysterically, "Which one? Which one?"

In a jiffy she had unfurled both saris and began twirling them around. A swoosh of resplendent silk flapped in his face, as he backed away astounded.

"How could you! How … I never asked you for anything I have never taken anything from you. Why Avatar why?"

She flung the saris away anguish writ across her face like someone peeling a scab. She spoke bitterly, "But you had gone to the store anyway, so two birds," she flung one sari at him, "one stone!" and she hurled the other one. She looked around for something else to throw, all along her verbal harangue ramming into him as he dodged her missiles, shell shocked. Never before had he seen this side to Lekha. All he wanted was to bring her a nice present!

He didn't actually see it her way, but making up to her on the silky five yards with passionate hunger awakened in him a new realization, a perception of the imperativeness of his role in her world. He glimpsed into her solitary existence, seeing for the first time how his presence dominated that emptiness.

Later that night when he thought Lekha was asleep, he mulled over a drink on the lofty balcony forcing himself to rip the chimera and face reality.

Lekha lay on her side, miserable. She was angry at herself. She had vowed never to show him her resentment, her insecurity. She had been loath to share it with him, shackled by a nameless fear. Never did she want to hurt him or remind him of the pathetic mess of his sorry marriage. Today she had done just that. Silently she propped herself up and looked out through the darkness at the solitary figure in the dim starlight.

She thought of their fight as some bitter sweet medication, acidic and sour but one they had needed to get past. She remembered the taste from her childhood when her mum crushed a bitter tablet into honey and fed her. The sweet viscosity did little to disguise the harsh bitterness.

The precariousness of their elongated liaison had left her feeling like an expectant Mother who would never give birth. Many lonely evenings she craved his company remembering small details like his habit of glancing sideways briefly and smiling as he talked even though he rarely made eye contact. She recalled the way he walked, one hand in his pocket or how he enjoyed the taste of her cooking, eating with his hands and licking each finger clean. She wistfully recalled their nights of long conversation in their world of make belief. When she felt lonely or the ache in her heart grew unbearable, she reached into her trove of beautiful memories and amused herself, till it was time to check her inbox for a mail from him. Lekha looked outside. She wondered if Avatar would ever have any perception of what it meant to walk in her shoes. Perhaps not. Then again, it had all along been her individual choice in the absence of any promise or commitment. She considered joining him out on the balcony but decided to leave him be.

Oblivious to her scrutiny Avatar chewed over the day's events, his thoughts on his beloved. Lekha did not know how she filled Avatar. Her every word remained with him and echoed within him day and night. Nothing not his success, his riches or his eminence, could eclipse the aching hunger and vast yearning that consumed him. Far below, traffic criss-crossed in silvery lines on dark, drenched streets. An uneasy disquiet swathed him as he pictured her daily struggle against prying eyes and reproachful looks. In an insular society it would go beyond just covert glances, but he never heard of it from her. He shook his head at the injustice. Why should she have to face the battle of the all or nothing choice alone? He wondered yet again for the thousandth time if she ever felt resentful or insecure. Why wouldn't she choose a life of comfort with one of her ardent suitors? His regard for her was at an all time high when she had replied honestly, "I can't make anyone else happy. Why deceive someone into a loveless life?"

He was weary of being tied down to a self centered woman, bereft of refinement of spirit. He was married to Jharna only on paper. There was the total absence of love, passion or even respect and today he was beyond caring. He was sick of his lonely frustrated life, divided between two unequal contenders. She, Lekha was his body and soul, easy to be with, endearing, while the mere presence of Jharna rankled him. Her hollow spuriousness was a sharp contrast to Lekha's genuine devotion.

No longer could he stand for their connection being viewed as a sullied, illicit one. He recalled how, after their hastily arranged nuptials years ago, Jharna strutted about the office, brandishing their marriage certificate like some sort of trophy. Avatar felt speculative about her reaction to a plea for divorce. He smirked at the irony. What a trivial thing is authentication!

He remembered that Lekha had tendered her resignation the day following his marriage. On his first visit to India, his mother's funeral, he had paid her mother a visit, primarily to thank her for taking care of his dying mother in her last days. Lekha returned from work as his mother was serving him tea. He barely glanced at the person, who walked in, till her mother said, "Don't you remember Lekha?" His heart missed a beat as he took her in, astounded at the complete metamorphosis. She stood awkwardly, clutching her handbag and then quietly slouched away. Was this gaunt, worn out person the same sparkling girl he had known? What illness could have so totally stripped her of her radiance he asked her mother. Her answer sickened him to the core. The teacup trembled in his hands as he struggled to understand the old lady's quavering tone "It's not as if you were engaged or anything but your mother and I had always hoped. This hope is a terrible thing when it gets crushed." He had selfishly been regarding himself the helpless pawn in Sarkar and his daughter's little travesty, but today that was history.

Today, he stood staring at the ghost of his past life, a sacrificial lamb he had unwittingly squashed on his way up the ladder of avaricious triumph. Certain that she must have grasped the first suitor's fervently outstretched hand and settled down to blissful matrimony, he hadn't expected to see her at all. The scales fell from Avatar's eyes, as her frail mother spoke of the disenchantment of heartbreak and the toll it had taken on her poor child.

Sitting under an indigo canopy of stars Avatar watched sections of their life playing out in stark contrast. As he moved from strength to strength attaining unimaginable success in Silicon Valley's magical universe, she struggled to keep alive. Lekha believed it was a good thing she had never learned to be dependent on anybody. She vowed to make a success of her life. The costs of keeping abreast with the advancements in I.T. technology were prohibitive so she worked various jobs day and night from tutoring to programming and data punching. Both had begun their careers together but a small leg up saw Avatar touching the stars, while Lekha's salary barely covered her household expenses.

Avatar's marriage strengthened Lekha's resolve to never depend on another but to muster courage and build her own life. With the mushrooming of a plethora of computer institutes, Lekha was spoilt for choice with job offers. Following years of struggle, she was finally able to taste the triumph of ambition realised. Along with it came respectability. It was a luxury to not have to wear something stitched by your own hands. It was a comfort to pay upfront at the local grocer's instead of running into months of debt. Even the neighborhood found it in their hearts to overlook the stigma attached to her family and show some respect for the industrious girl.

She was surprised at first, but quickly got used to meeting smiles from a previously hostile and awkwardly silent bunch of neighbors. Life had meaning. She walked tall on the very streets she had skulked in all her life, not comprehending why people had averted their gaze whenever she approached.

The slur her father had smeared across their family name adorned each one of them like Hawthorne's Scarlet Letter. Back then, elders exercised more discretion. While no scandal was openly exposed, the story of her father's outrageous crime had reached every household in the neighborhood in hushed whispers.

To Avatar it had mattered little what her father had done or so he projected in his considerate and non judgmental treatment of her. He scarce knew it that he remained her inspiration. It was as if her personality evolved from his teachings. Never had he let her bemoan a lost childhood "what will you gain by looking back? You can't bring it back can you?"

His casual remarks attached themselves to her psyche and rang in her ears. "All we have is our ability and the potential for working hard. Others have the backing of rich influential parents. We don't, so we have to push a little harder that's all! Why focus on the negatives?"

He had laughingly added, "Least of all someone like you, with the label of an elitist school and those breathtaking good looks!"

He hated her misplaced compassion. He would get angry if she uttered "poor thing" when she saw a beggar and never let her slip them some coins.

"Don't pity them. That weakens them and they are vulnerable enough as it is. Each one needs to get out of the rut and do something."

High among his dislikes were those clad in Episcopal saffron, shamming as priests and duping gullible victims. The one time she saw him really angry was when she stuck her hand out to one such scam artist on the sidewalk. He dragged her away fuming, "If he could tell you your future and", he glanced at the coloured rings and beads, "offer a cure, how come he is sitting on the roadside, not applying those cures to his own sorry lot?"

She lapped up his philosophy, a practical guidebook to living without regret, anger or retaliation. He was her savior she, his humble devotee. What more could she want to fill her empty existence?

She reinvented herself under his care. Sporting the bright red hibiscus in her hair, she strolled confidently in her black bordered, white Tangail sari turning heads. Onlookers gawked at the sensual walk, the long plait caressing her bare back, the passion in her full, slightly parted lips and the bashful liquid gaze of kohl-lined eyes.

SIXTEEN

It was a lazy autumnal afternoon in Delhi. Hot and sultry mirages danced on tar roads and everything was swathed in the hazy veil that the city dons so becomingly. The girls gathered for a farewell meeting at Rukmini's freshly renovated house. Stepping in from the blinding sunshine Asha peered into the cool dark interior. She instructed her maid to carry the food containers to the kitchen and remained in the doorway, unnoticed by the ladies chatting comfortably in the Suri's newly decorated drawing room. She looked appreciatively at the peach coloured walls, taupe silk drapes and revamped sofas gleaming with brocade covers. The room looked enormous with all the extraneous stuff moved out. Asha prided herself in decorating, but had to acknowledge Rukmini's aesthetic taste in pulling off such a triumph. The decoration was unpretentiously chic, not self consciously "ethnic", overtly rustic or Mughalesque. No high paid designer could have conjured up a more pleasing vision for the neglected house. She glanced across the room at a becoming cluster of old sepia photographs in wooden frames. She recognized some of the vintage lamps from the old couple's collection and appreciated how Rukmini had put it all together so effectively. The result was magical.

Rukmini quietly came and stood beside her, "Quite a transformation eh!"

Asha nodded, "Fantastic! And to think you pulled it off in such a short time! Handling labour is usually quite an exasperating challenge."

"They worked round the clock and I paid them double." Rukmini laughed. "I am so glad I decided against selling it. Kamala and her family will be quite comfortable in the garage and outhouse, much better than where she is now. I have told her to contact you if she has to convey anything to me."

Asha handed her a parcel. "Here's a small gift for your new living room!"

Rukmini accepted it with shining eyes, "Thanks Asha! Let me get you something to drink."

"Relax, I'll help myself." She walked over to join the rest of their old friends who had formed small pockets of conversation around the room.

Kamala and Asha's maids circulated food laden trays and Rukmini handed out delicately embroidered napkins.

The chatter mainly focused on the ostentatious wedding, and Asha inexplicably addressed Rukmini, "Seriously, how does one pass up an opportunity to be pampered for three days in a lavish Rajput palace? And that means sleeping on silk sheets, cool boat rides and picture perfect scenery! The food was just awesome! Can you believe there were eleven desserts?"

Lata piped in, "Fresh flowers everywhere, and it's a desert"

Jane gave her a look that said, "What a moron!"

Rukmini turned to Asha with a shrug, "I will find it in myself to overcome the agonizing regret of missing the wedding of the century. Asha, it's over and done with, why bring it up? Let us just say I don't enjoy partying with a killer!"

"It isn't as if the hosts were murderers and anyway can you vouch for every person at any party you go to?"

"Excuse me? What's that supposed to mean? I do assure you, I am pretty sure..." Rukmini took a hold of herself and decided not to be baited. "I am a bit uncomfortable with violence and I feel humiliated to think that those wealthy people think they can click their fingers and I'll run salivating. Eleven desserts indeed!"

Jane waved her hands in the air, "Honestly, it was so crowded! Even to get within a few feet of the bridal couple was impossible!"

Namita added, "That is what you get when you invite Bollywood stars to come perform!"

Lata interjected, "Not invite, hire."

Asha was determined to paint the perfect picture for Rukmini, "Everything was just right! Fabulous forts and palaces and multi colored houses, much like the tie and dye fabric we bought."

"So they organized shopping sprees too?"

"Yeah, we got mojaris, durries, bedspreads and heaps of jewelry."

"Well I got exactly the same stuff from Agra!"

Asha looked amazed. "Really? You didn't leave the painters alone in this house?"

"Oh absolutely. They lived here and Kamala and Madan kept watch. You don't suppose I was going to live here in the grime and dust? The kids and I just took off. We also got a taste of the palatial rooms with silk sheets and we too shopped for cushion covers and silver jewelry. It was incredible nice and I didn't mingle with criminals!" she added triumphantly.

Most ladies giggled at the logical veracity of Rukmini's argument but Asha was quite adamant. "You think you might be blaming the wrong guys? Besides, what does it say to an old friend when you abandon her at her daughter's special day?"

Rukmini tore away the gift wrap. "Asha, this is just beautiful! And I have the right spot for it right there!" She pointed to a bare wall between the windows and walked up to it holding the canvas. She spoke as she sized up the painting in her outstretched hands.

"No use trying to give me the guilt trip and I seriously wonder if Mamta even noticed I wasn't there. Quite simply, it's about doing the right thing. I mean looking at the kid's age he could have been let off with a shorter sentence but pretending he hadn't committed a crime is just wrong."

There were murmurs around the room and a degree of certain discomfort crept in.

As if on cue, Namita walked in giggling, "Rukmini, your kids are unbelievable. I just love the way they have adapted to staying here for almost two months without protest."

Rukmini laughed, "They even watched that new Bollywood movie with me!"

"Yeah I know they were telling me. They particularly liked the part with the Eurovision in Prague."

Asha asked Rukmini, "Did you like it?"

Rukmini tilted her head a little and considered, her eyes fixed on the picture, "Movies have come a long way in many ways. But I was blown away by the hero. He is so talented!"

"It's in his blood. Look at the lineage -parents and grandfather."

Rukmini smiled, "True but then you have some pretty mediocre star kids. This boy is special. There is sincerity in his rendering."

Namita said, "I was a little surprised at what Sameer is reading."

Rukmini smiled, "He wants to absorb as much as he can of India."

"What is he reading?" Arti asked.

Rukmini smiled across the room to her flamboyantly dressed friend, "It was a gift from Jane."

Jane looked up, "Lapierre and Collins. He is so curious about India, I thought that a perfect book for him. I loved your boy's comments though. He thought it a pity that the saga of a country with such a rich history should have been written by two foreigners!"

The room fell silent momentarily.

Rukmini took a step back and gently reached out to correct the tilt.

Asha nodded sagely, "So true. It's a great book. I think that was the first book I bought when I joined college."

Jane said thoughtfully, "I think Sameer's sensitive critique is what blew me away! By the way I've invited them to California and they have accepted."

Rukmini looked up in mock horror, "No "I'll have to ask my mum" or anything?"

Jane shook her head, "Nope. They said they would email me with the dates of their next break."

Rukmini, satisfied with the positioning of the canvass, called out, her eyes affixed to the painting, "Asha, there's something about this painting. It's got a mesmeric quality. I can't take my eyes off it. Thanks awfully!"

Asha stared deeply at the picture and drained her glass of juice, "You know the artiste."

Rukmini shook her head puzzled, "No, not really. Who is it?"

"Lekha! She's done some truly exquisite oils. I purchased this amazing piece at her showing last year."

"I thought she was a programmer!"

Chomping on a mouthful Asha mumbled, "Yeah that's her job but honestly, I don't think I know another person with as many hobbies as her! That girl's got talent and surprisingly little arrogance."

It had taken much for Rukmini to reconcile herself to Lekha's chosen lifestyle but she'd come round to accepting it after much deliberation. "That's truly creditable. She had accepted my invitation for today but cancelled this morning. She said something had come up at the last minute."

"She keeps unusual hours."

Arti declared, "She was by far the most gorgeous woman at the wedding."

Namita added, "I can't help noticing how well maintained she is!"

Lata turned her podgy self on the settee and nodded vigorously, jiggling her double chin comically, "Yeah why not? She hasn't pushed two kids out of her body or had to run a household of six on a sarkari salary!"

Asha interjected hurriedly, "Do I sense a twinge of jealousy for our poor "left on the shelf" friend? She may have had other things to cope with, how do we know? She glanced sidelong at Jane. "I feel we must acknowledge that bit, Lata, Lekha's a real beauty."

Lata was not conceding her stand. "Oh please! She's having a ball! No responsibilities no in laws nothing, just fun!"

Namita declared, "Come on guys don't strip her completely of her mystique! Fact is she is a stunning, intoxicating woman considering she's our age. I mean let's face it, we do not turn as many heads as we did but Lekha, she's something else."

She looking penetratingly at Jane, "You're keeping very quiet, in absolute contradiction to your usual self."

"It's the Halo effect." Jane drawled, chomping a mouthful. She described circles around her head with her fingers, "She has an appealing exterior and that sort of glosses over all her other flaws. It's called the halo effect. It's like most male interview panels would be partial to a female candidate."

Arti looked fixedly at Jane, "I don't know what actually the halo effect is. Everyone talks about it but really, is it all about how good looking you are? I mean I would understand if that was the case in industries such as media, television and the arts."

Jane interjected, "It is believed that taller or better looking persons get more credence."

Rukmini joined the discussion, "But if that were so, all we had to do was to bring our kids up to be good looking or well turned out! What marks do you attach to other qualities like qualification, hard work, and sincerity?"

Jane started to say something but held back as Namita exclaimed "I say this is gorgeous crockery!"

Rukmini smiled, "Thanks! It's ancient. My mother in law's Royal Wessex tea set probably bought in the fifties when they travelled to England."

Arti held up the cup "You should take good care of it! It must be priceless."

"So I have been told. But I just feel, how long can a thing be kept away for fear it might break? When can we use it and enjoy its beauty by holding it?" She pointed to a corner, "There it was stacked, in a low side-board with foggy glass doors never used or even admired, practically out of sight for ages! I shall use it and display it prominently." She pointed to the well illuminated china cabinet with little plate ledges and cup hooks.

"Just the pride of place a Royal Wessex deserves!" Namita agreed, "I saw the pictures of your in laws on the wall. Very nice!"

"I had them framed right here in the market." Rukmini said, "They had picture frames in every conceivable variety!"

Jane nodded, "They do, and the craftsmanship is superb. Isn't it amazing? I bring a lot of my pictures here for mounting and framing. I don't mind paying a little extra freight because I get the result I want."

"How nice you bring us business!" Lata looked scornfully at Jane, "Didn't think there were any aspects of India you cared for."

Unmoved, Jane addressed the rest of the company earnestly, "Look, I love my country of birth as much as any of you but I have to say I am not so excited about the pseudo version of itself that it has become. I didn't mean to sound pompous and I'm sorry if that was how I came out. Some things are very frustrating! The last thing I ever want to be is a prodigal NRI" She sat back and took a sip of the hot tea giving the impression that she wouldn't say any more.

Namita jumped in, "You aren't. You really aren't. You are a genuine person with hang ups like the rest of us."

Arti added soberly, "I agree. Given all the challenges and the rotten luck with those health issues, you're quite a triumph Jane. And I admire your generosity of spirit."

Jane munched thoughtfully, "The thing is, I have never regarded myself as anything but fortunate. I grabbed opportunities because they were there! I seriously do not want to put the nation down. I'm just lamenting the way innocent citizens are being victimized. Was it Thompson who said" Jane tilted her head to one side and moved her fingers in air as if playing the piano. "Yes I think it was, and I quote but maybe not very accurately, "All of the convergent influences of the world—Hindu, Muslim, Christian, secular, Stalinist, Maoist, Gandhian—run through India," She swallowed and took a deep breath as if she were performing at elocution, "There is not a thought that is being thought in the West or East that is not active in some Indian mind". She looked around proudly at the applause. Jane turned to Lata and shrugged, "Just another one of my charming eccentricities, Lata, get used to it!"

Determined to have the last word Lata spat out, "It's the damn politicians!"

Jane grimly put her cup and saucer down, looked harshly at Lata and pointed out of the window, "Over a billion people out there and counting.

If that huge a populace can allow itself to be held hostage by a bunch of politicians well then that's what you deserve!"

A host of loud voices mostly in protest filled the air as Jane pretended to dodge being bombarded by projectiles.

She drained her cup of tea and placed the cup on the table, "I am telling it like it is. No integrity! Just opportunism. From the police to the guy who won't give me an electric meter, not a jot of honesty." She banged her fist on the coffee table, rattling the crockery!"

Asha called out in mock horror, "Rukmini, watch out for your heirlooms!"

"Jane, your occidental mindset is a little too hasty at noting just the horrible parts. It's not as if where you live is Utopia."

Jane sighed a little apologetically, "Far from it. I never claimed…"

Lata barged in, "Let me educate you a little. India in her day was known as Paradise on earth."

"So enjoy your paradise, allow corruption and crime to proliferate," Jane retorted hotly.

Namita stared at a spot on the carpet. "I must say Jane, you have a refreshingly poor opinion of the Indian work force on the whole, but can't you appreciate the small but perceptible progress?"

Jane nodded "I totally agree," then taking Namita's chin in her hand and turning to Arti, asked brightly, "Hey, doesn't she look a lot like Reese Witherspoon?" Namita giggled.

Arti shook her head vigorously, "Stop it Jane." She looked around the room, "Yesterday my neighbor reminded her of Meryl Streep and there's that lady from California who resembles Helen Mirren. Why can't people look like themselves?"

Jane let go Namita's chin, "Yeah, Nam, I agree I have been listing just the guys who aren't exactly the shiniest example from our country of birth."

Arti remembered something, "Jane, while I was holidaying with my daughter in the States I was amazed to see these advertisements on TV urging elderly people to set aside money for their own funerals because they cost so much."

Yeah they have commercials like that during oldies' shows. What were you watching?"

"I love Lucy." Arti replied instantly.

Everyone burst out laughing. Arti looked surprised, "Why? I do love Lucy. It's better than those contrived joint family sagas you girls lap up on cable TV here!"

Jane gave off a huge laugh. "Actually I enjoyed watching Lucy too. I'll send you the DVD collection. But yeah, it's true, funeral expenses sometimes take up all the deceased's savings or even more and the survivors have to fork out huge sums of money."

Arti looked amazed, "It's practically free in India."

Asha looked at her, "Not exactly, but the costs are negligible. Nobody would require starting a saving plan at fifty just so ensure a decent burial!"

Jane looked momentarily thoughtful, "That's just a one off expense but what I am totally blown away by, is the healthcare system this country provides. When you think of the GDA and India's huge population liability, I think the national health care system is laudable. The other thing is pension for government employees, another fantastic scheme!"

Lata piped up, "Exactly, and nobody gets free medical care in the U.S. unless they are criminals or illegal immigrants."

Jane gave her a piercing look. "Don't make random statements without thinking." She turned to face the rest, "That's right. Health care dominates political discussions in the US. But that's just the point I am so desperately trying to make." She tapped on the table with her long fingernails. "This nation is not just the world's greatest democracy it is also the world best per capita provider in healthcare and education! Do you remember what we paid for our Bachelor's anyone?" She glanced around.

"I think something like Rs. 30 or 40 per month?"

"Exactly, and the bus pass was about the same. Many American kids had to quash their dreams of higher studies solely due to the prohibitive fees that kids from overseas could cough up!"

"The bride for instance," Rukmini pointed out.

"Man you really have your knife in that family, don't you?"

"No I just remembered it out of the blue." Rukmini nibbled at a mango slice.

Jane smiled and continued, "There is ongoing progress in absolutely every area in India."

Lata snapped, "Look, if we just keep saying to ourselves that we are no good until we become a Manhattan, we can never make any advancement. For a developing nation we have achieved a lot. Look at the world class metro, good eco friendly buses, flyovers, and malls. We know not everything is perfect but we can see there is scope for progress…" Jane looked at her as if seeing something unusual, "You know, sometimes you make sense!"

She clenched both fists and hit them on the arms of her chair, "And that, actually brings me back to how mad I get to see corrupt officials wrecking this great nation! And no one cares!" She spread her arms out, "The one unifier is the indifferent outlook. In my opinion, there is only one punishment for those corrupt losers." She ran a finger across her neck, "Hang them!" Breathlessly she rolled her wide eyes from side to side without moving her head.

All the ladies started challenging Jane's extreme stance in unison. Jane giggled to herself and, catching sight of Kamala entering the room with a laden tray, rushed across the large room to help her. Asha walked up to Jane and ushered her out. "Stop heckling Lata! It's unpleasant."

Jane looked at her in mock horror, "Moi?"

Asha explained, "It's not easy being in her shoes. She had dreams like all of us. She married the wrong guy! There was a time she had hoped to be his soul mate, inspiration, support…"

"Yeah I get it."

"But she ended up with an ambitious, aloof, ruthlessly self-centered man." Asha looked uncomfortably around, "It's an open secret he has a clandestine relationship going with a colleague or a junior, but expects Lata to slave over running his household, keeping his parents happy..."

Jane looked a little concerned at that, "Look I'm sorry for her, and terribly inconvenient that all her dreams didn't pan out exactly as she visualized but …."

"I know what you are going to say, "That doesn't mean you give up"!"

"Jane cursorily said, "Not at all. That is not what I was going to say. If anything, quite the opposite. That doesn't mean you become so bitter you can't bear to see the happy lives of all those that did realize theirs!" She ended in a mumble as Lata exited, looking for the washroom. They slipped back in to the living room and Jane continued, "Every once in a while she gets off her rear and announces "I want to do something meaningful" and expects something to fall in her lap.

I tell you, Asha, she wouldn't have survived a day as an NRI. Try working a full time job, running a household, raising kids, dealing with bullying, and there are no free days, mind you. Saturday routine for most NRI households is washing vacuuming, dusting, cooking for a week, ironing gardening. It can be quite overwhelming!" She pointed in the direction of Lata, "She wouldn't last a week without her devoted staff toiling away. Not to celebrate the truth of her sorry existence, I just don't care for her embittered, caustic and clearly envious remarks." Asha looked helpless. Jane reached out for the tray she had deposited on the table when Asha pulled her out and added, "I'll try to be nicer but not making any promises."

The room took on the tenor of a classroom whose teacher had left them for a bit. Everyone was chatting in small clusters. Outside the bay windows, partly veiled by lace curtains, a few leaves were blowing around in the yard, as nearly bare trees stood alongside the proud gulmohar and hardy bougainvillea. Dusty winds were being whipped up in swirls while grey clouds darkened the skies.

Rukmini pulled out some old photo albums and the girls crowded at the dining table, poring over their pictures excitedly. Looking from across the room at the happy scene, Asha thought how bare and deserted it would be the following week. She glanced outside at the fruit of Madan's hard work and accepted Rukmini's claim that Kamala would maintain the house well. Asha knew she would be expected to take a peek and check on it now and again. She loved Rukmini too much to let her labors go to waste.

There was a loud squeal as Namita pulled out a small black and white picture and called out to her, "Asha you look so tiny!" She got up to join them.

At the airport, a cheerful Avatar swings the valise in his hand like a carefree schoolboy. Drained of almost all material assets, he feels inconceivably wealthy and free, as though a mammoth weight had been lifted off of his shoulders. He had fantasized about this journey over and over for years. He can hardly believe he has slammed the door shut on his dysfunctional dystopia.

The young stewardess poises herself at the entrance, hands folded, smile frozen on an unchanging face, greeting and mentally classifying the passengers as they step in, "Student, will knock back coke by the gallons, honeymooners, should be too engrossed in each other, beer bellied middle aged guy, no more than 2 drinks for you buddy, cute kids, get activity packs and candy ready, fashion plate mother will raid the shopping trolley."

Shortly she is assisting business class fliers, her unceasing mental commentary running in top gear. "What a dignified lady! Love the quiet elegance! Let me rush to help her, Oho my lucky day, a decent traveler helps out. A true gentleman! Why can't other passengers be like them?

Avatar sits back contentedly ensconced in the window seat. He sips his drink serenely. It hadn't been so hard after all. Why did it take him this long to arrive at the one clear decision? It was a no brainer. Plucking up the strength to make a choice once and for all to shun the glitzy, glamorous world and return to the soft bosom of a love, pure and steadfast, wasn't as hard as it had appeared. His face softens as visions of the ravishing Lekha come and go from his mind's canvas. Today, he thinks, he would begin living again. He smiles to himself recalling the last conversation he had had with Lekha.

"We would not have much till I think of something to do."

"And yet we would be richer than most."

He laughed into the phone speaking softly, "Just one day."

"I can't wait!" Lekha strolled on to her herbaceous balcony running her hands over the bright blue forget-me-nots. A bulbul nodded at her from its perch on the railing and a nearby branch of magenta bougainvillea bowed under a prancing sparrow. She smiled contentedly gazing out at the vast vista of skyscrapers gleaming in the scorching sunlight. Her eyes smiled as tears washed down her cheeks. She turned to return to her world of animated apparitions. The wait was going to be over.

Back at Rukmini's place, Jane went round the room offering hot samosas and chutney. She began with Namita who was admiring a creatively detailed cushion cover. "This is the kind of stuff the women at Jane's ashram make," Asha was explaining to her. They are mostly battered or abandoned women but once they learn to work with their hands, they become self sufficient. It's a fantastic little charity and look how beautiful it is."

Namita nodded, "Absolutely gorgeous!"

Jane smiled as she carried her tray towards Arti who was saying to Lata, "…an efficiently run centre for ostracized lepers. She's pretty old, must be in her seventies. She's coming in from California, sometime soon, I believe."

Jane seated herself near them on the settee and joined in, "Tomorrow, actually. I just got a message on my phone. I will be accompanying her to Maharashtra."

Arti added "I am also visiting it next week. I am really keen to see this place."

Lata looked Jane up and down, "You aren't an easy to please type. How can you be sure you will like it?"

Jane kneeled down next to Lata's chair and examined her through squinting eyes, "I will never really understand you, will I? How do you say I am hard to please?"

"Wouldn't you say you have strong likes and dislikes? Like the Indian work ethics, corruption, politicians."

Jane fixed a blank stare at her, "And you love them?"

Lata scoffed, "Of course not! I am just saying you are choosy."

"That I am and no, I'm not making any commitments, but my research on the place is making me feel a bit partial to it. Let's see if it lives up to my expectations."

Asha spoke pensively, "What a fantastic project! I was interested the moment Arti told me about it. In a land replete with divides and discrimination, who would think to help lepers?" She looked at Jane and nodded, "Yeah I do acknowledge we are a biased lot! When I look around all I see are petty prejudices based on hollow snobbery. Rich and poor, educated and illiterate, Brahmin and non Brahmin, we are judged even by the neighborhood you live in! Remember that woman at the sangeet so openly looking down her nose at DDA flats?"

Rukmini nodded, "Irritating to the extreme. What a snob. And that voice, gosh I wanted to scream. It's this new rasping, back of the throat style of talking. Vocal fry, I think Natasha tells me that's what it's called. Pop divas use it for their numbers. Did we know her? I was considering emptying a plate of Kulfi on her elaborate hairdo."

Namita and Arti exclaimed in shock.

Rukmini turned to them grinning, "What?"

Namita shrugged, "To imagine the refined Rukmini doing something like that is unthinkable, Jane maybe!"

Everyone laughed and looked at Jane who was sitting on a floor seating by the bay window, her head thrown back watching the trees. She suddenly said, "Bina."

"Bina who? Not our batch?" Rukmini was even more intrigued that Jane remembered her.

"I won't ever forget her. After my mum got paralyzed, my dad was a mess and had taken to drinking. They met him in a drunken state at the club and Bina never stopped telling everyone in college about it." Jane straightened up and looked around indifferently.

"How nasty! What did that have to do with you?"

It seemed trivial but back then it had devastated Jane, whose fragility had taken a further beating. "I for one will never fail to spot her in a crowd, even if she gains another 100 kilos."

Namita said, "I hear she's loaded!"

Arti, who appeared to know her, added, "They weren't always that rich. Her husband worked his way up but now I hear he owns a multiplex." She addressed Jane, "She might cut you a cheque for the women's shelter."

Jane shook her head, "I'm okay on funds. Can I ask her to give up two hours from her packed "mani pedi" schedules for a good cause?"

Asha giggled, "Not unless it involves cutting a satin ribbon with silver scissors!"

Jane sighed, "So the biggest problem with her life is an abundance of leisure." She wiped her sticky hands on a pretty embroidered serviette and called out to Rukmini, "I have never eaten so many Indian sweets in one sitting!"

Lata lashed out with an angry snort, "You're saying 'Indian sweets' as if it is something alien."

Before Jane could answer, a window burst open unexpectedly, sending the curtains sweeping across a floral decoration.

Rukmini cried out, "Oh gosh a dust storm!"

Kamala scurried about busily shutting the windows and setting right the spilt water and flowers. The sky grew ominously dark as strong dusty winds rattled the doors and windows and a smell of muddy dankness permeated the room. A banging from the terrace sent Kamala nimbly racing up.

Rukmini peered out "it will settle down when it starts to rain."

The room grew dark and Asha walked about turning on lights that cast long shadows on the walls. Suspended dust lit up in the lamplight. With a deafening crack of thunder and a streaky lightening dance, the sky slapped splotches of rain against the dusty window panes.

Another lady called out from across the room, "Hey Jane, how is the "Occupy Wall Street" movement going to end? Is the job situation that grave? I heard there are people committing suicide and stuff!"

Jane looked grimly at Asha's friend, "Yeah it's bad! Speculation has its dark spots. We can't trivialize the humongous impact it had and it is a fact many Americans have lived beyond their means, depending largely on their stocks reaping rich rewards for them. It was the outcome," she paused and looked heavenwards as if searching for the right words, "of a combination of Behavioral Psych and Economics. Let me explain," She dunked a biscuit into her lukewarm tea and stuffed it in her mouth, "When a person begins to lose money, instead of pulling out of the gambit, he has the urge to keep playing. That is the psychology part, and Arti will bear me out I'm sure, because humans are optimistic by nature. So even though it was a losing battle, many people turned into outright gamblers and desperately added more to investments till that fateful day in July 2008!" She looked into the faces of a captive audience, something she was accustomed to. When Jane held court, people listened. "And it's no laughing matter that for some desperate people, suicide was the last resort. So the "Occupy Wall Street" protests started gaining traction as jobs were lost and the big banks announced huge bonuses for their top management. Then again, some people try to squirm out with the "If I go down I take you down with me" attitude and that can mean turning to illegal means. In fact I know of one such case quite closely!"

"Really? Illegal, how?" Namita asked.

The thunderstorm dropped rain in sheets against the French windows and Rukmini's garden got the fresh, just washed look. The ladies, a bit languid and heavy eyed, slumped in the softness of the plush settees.

Jane sat with both legs flung over the side of an overstuffed armchair, "Nasty business overall, a shock for many families though most NRIs were fairly comfortable, perhaps because we never really learned to live without stashing away in a safety net. But there was this one family that just disappeared!"

She had the attention of each person. She gazed out at the downpour washing the little, square window panes. She spoke meditatively, "Funny thing is that the same guy had applied to us for a position and I had rejected him. I can't explain why! Sometimes when you line up a bevy of near identical candidates, you have to rely on gut instinct and something about this guy didn't ring true with me. I was suspicious about his job experience. He was smart and presentable, even good looking if you will though he had an extremely peculiar style of dressing his facial hair…"

Arti giggled, "By facial hair, you mean beard and moustache?"

"Not really, it was the sideburns, you know the kind that were quite popular back in the 70s" she pointed to the sides of her face" Mutton chop style I think they're called."

"Like Elvis!" Namita asked.

"Yeah or Wolverine. But I believe he had a prominent and ugly scar that he wanted to hide."

"So why not a full face beard?"

"He was proud of the cleft in his chin."

"Shut up!" Arti smothered a guffaw. "Stop making stuff up, we're not idiots."

Jane turned and looked into her friend's face, "Think about it. Why would I make such ridiculous stuff up! This is what my investigation on the guy revealed. So here he was a well built, red faced guy with strange sideburns and a pompous, supercilious manner and, stop giggling. He's the kind of character you don't forget in a hurry."

"And you rejected him." Rukmini interjected, "What was wrong with his "halo"?"

The room rang out with laughter and Arti punched Jane playfully.

"Jane looked at Rukmini, giving her a "high five" sign. She nodded smiling, "Touché! What they say is true! You live with smart people and start getting smart yourself!"

Lata said playfully, "Rukmini was always smart you dodo."

"Hey who you calling a dodo?" Jane addressed Rukmini again, using her fingers to make her point, "I didn't say I made a selection based on the halo effect, I said others did. Coming back to this guy, maybe we just got off to a bad start, I can't say but I remember his patronizing attitude bugged me."

"Such guys feel a bit threatened by type "A" women?" Namita asked.

Jane nodded while talking, "Maybe it was just because I was a woman, but what I think rankled him was that I was asking some damn good questions."

"Honestly it's like a Pavlovian conditioning with Indian guys. They can't stand a smart woman. "Is woman, must be dumb"." Namita spoke with her mouth full.

Asha thumped Namita on the back teasingly, "You apply Pavlov quite liberally don't you? Arti, teach her the correct application."

Speaking over the enthusiastic reaction in the room, Arti laughed, "Ah! That's a topic for a whole other afternoon!"

"For now, Jane's saga of the GFC." Rukmini sat up and started collecting the empty trays, "But first I think some tea is in order. I'll just put the water on and come back." She rose and pulled the curtains aside peeking out at the torrential downpour. "No one can leave yet."

"Has the maid gone?"

"Yeah but don't panic I can do it. I manage my kitchen single-handed! Of course back home I use tea bags, but I'll use tea leaves to make my special ginger cardamom tea!"

"We're all ears Jane." Namita said, creating a cushiony corner on the sit down and stretching out over it. "Mm. This is nice! Rainy afternoon, hot tea, snacks and old friends."

Asha looked at her sleepily, "Couldn't have put it better myself but I think I have OD'ed on the snacks." She sighed happily, "Can't ever have enough of friends!"

Jane swung her legs out and landed them on a pouf. She wiggled her toes admiring her latest acquisition, silver toe rings. "Hmm, yeah let us call this story, for want of a better name, "Avatar!"

"Avatar … hey isn't that the name of Lekha's guy?"

"Guy?"

"Paramour, lover whatever. I really don't know what's going on with her."

"Yeah. Whatever."

"Hey Jane, you live in California! You might have run into him!"

Jane rolled her eyes and took a deep breath, "I wouldn't want to mix with the likes of..."

Asha cleared her throat deliberately. Jane glanced up at her and shifted in her chair, "Let's say that Lekha is number one on my list of 'Things I should not be wasting my time with' that's all."

Namita looked suspiciously at Jane then at Asha, "Hey! I've noticed this before. What's your beef with Lekha?"

"Nothing!"

"Come on. It's so obvious, you get all uptight whenever Lekha's around. And now at the mere mention of her name you are getting evasive."

Jane avoided making eye contact and gazed up at the ceiling, "I just don't know her well. Doesn't it ever happen to you that you don't like someone but you can't say why?

A shocked Asha gushed, "Jane! Never imagined, you of all people could nurse a grudge... all this time!"

Jane murmured angrily "Shut up," then called out loudly, "how long for the tea? I'm about to start narrating a story here!"

Rukmini emerged, "It takes a while for the water to boil, hold your horses!"

Namita wouldn't give up. "Meanwhile, tell us why Lekha bugs you so much."

Jane shook her head her eyes fixed on Asha, "Nope."

Almost immediately she was fighting off a cavalcade of voices in protest. "There is something. You have to share it with us."

Arti spoke softly, "Yeah we're not going to let it pass. And I get the feeling it isn't about her and Avatar." Jane looked up in surprise, an ambiguous mixture of seriousness and displeasure on her face.

"You got that right. You're the shrink eh, analyzing people's body language? You really want to know, don't you?"

"Yes, we do want to know. She's good company and great looking, I want one good reason why I shouldn't be her friend, besides the Avatar thing of course." Arti said softly.

Jane's voice hardened, "Okay, maybe I'll tell you."

Asha gasped and her fingers flew to her face, "Jane!"

Everyone's eyes moved from Jane to Asha to Jane again. Jane ignored her and looked up squarely out of the window, her eyes taking in the pelting rain. In a low voice she declared, "Back in the seventies Lekha's father was a low level official in the Ministry Of Defence, who," she cleared her throat, "sold military secrets to the" she moved her eyes down and fixed them on the carpet, "Pakis."

A shocked silence fell like a shroud upon the exuberant lot, each processing as best possible this stunning bit of information. This was the most unimaginably scandalous thing they ever expected to hear and they hardly knew what to make of it. The ladies squirmed uneasily. Someone shifted and coughed politely.

Asha broke the silence in a low, angry voice, "I can't believe anyone can expect the daughter to pay for her father's sins! She has had quite a struggle you know. I'm not saying..."

Jane answered, "I get what you are saying. That she is the consummate underdog. She's the works, a criminal father, dead mother, shunned by society, a victim of mean bullies. There, I summed it up, happy?" She tossed her head and stared out of the window.

"Obviously I am not condoning the act. It was treason, period. All I'm saying is that she has paid all her life for a crime not of her doing. Gosh she was probably eight or ten at the time!"

"It is the act that I remember when I see her, I can't help it. In fact I don't hate Pakistanis at all. Some of our closest friends are from there and they are fantastic people. I totally subscribe to the saying "Individuals are not nations", but I find it hard…"

Lata loudly proclaimed, "Oh great so you're willing to make excuses for our enemies, but hate the kid whose dad…"

Asha interrupted Lata, "That's not what she's saying Lata and you know it. Jane is very patriotic towards India. Many NRIs have friends from across the border, it's not uncommon. Regarding Lekha, I guess each of us in entitled to her own standpoint. From where I sit, I feel at least her friends should stick by her. And I'm totally fine if you're not on board. It would have been nice if she had found happiness through marriage. But," She shrugged, "as I see it with Avatar back in her life, she seems happy."

Jane snorted, "Another pathetic loser."

The girls called out in protest, "I hear he is very successful!"

"People say he is a good chap."

Jane smirked, "Well if there ever walked a bigger opportunist on this earth! First he milked Jharna's resources dry here, then piggybacked to the US with her and struck it rich. He may be a big gun, who cares. And now, suddenly he discovers the girl he dumped for Ms. Moneybags still holds a candle for him so, lo and behold, he rocks up and wheedles his way back into her heart."

Asha calmly stated, "That is your version of it. Who's to know what really transpired? Honestly Jane, I always thought of you as an accepting, tolerant sort."

Jane glowered, "How he got two women chasing him, I'll never know."

The ladies looked astounded.

"That's just mean!" Lata declared.

Rukmini got up to get the tea.

"You just couldn't care less for Lekha's happiness. It means nothing to you." Lata almost spat at her.

Jane fixed her with a harsh gaze and waved her hand out, "There are children being initiated into suicide bombing, nations armed to the teeth with nukes not looking very happily at the rest of the world and you wish to draw me into this mindless fixation you girls have with Lekha's passion ridden life? I strongly urge you to take a step back and place it in some rational perspective."

Arti made a valiant attempt at diverting everyone's attention and gripped Namita's hand, "Very pretty ring! What an enormous stone. Is it an Opal?"

Namita nodded, "Anniversary present."

Lata flicked her head and drawled, "They say opals are bad luck."

Namita smiled as she held out her hand and admired the stone, "In Australia they say the only bad luck about the opal is not owning one! Did you know it is very popular in Japan particularly for engagement rings?" She touched the ring and held her hand out to admire the stone set in a circle of coruscating diamonds. "Ashish got it for me." Her smile broadened at the memory of when Ashish had given it to her. She looked up into Lata's malicious sneer and her smile faded instantly.

To everyone's immense relief Rukmini wheeled in the tea with a noisy rattle of cups and saucers. Arti jumped up to help her with the carved wooden tea cart. "That's a very pretty tea trolley Rukmini!" She exclaimed.

Rukmini smiled, "Isn't it? I simply love it! It's Kashmiri walnut wood and I estimate about as old as Anil!"

"It looks antique!"

"The treasures I have unearthed in this place, it's incredible!"

She poured the tea its aroma wafting across the room, and Arti handed out the dainty tea cups.

Rukmini looked around, "Everyone fine? Okay go ahead Jane."

Asha looked up from her tea cup and declared, "It's called 'Avatar'."

Rukmini looked questioningly, "That's that fellow's name, isn't it- Lekha's friend? How come?"

Everyone looked accusingly at Jane and chorused, "She won't tell us."

Jane rolled her eyes, threw up her hands impatiently and regarded her listeners with mock disdain, "Seriously! I do not know if there ever was a more fidgety audience, with the attention span of a flea..."

Asha called the room to order, "Right. Everyone settle down."

Jane settled back on the cushions moving the spoon in her teacup with slim fingers as she gazed at the carpet on the floor and began to relate in a soft voice the harrowing experiences of some victims of the unexpected economic crash.

SEVENTEEN

Ma Durga's jewel encrusted face and large expressive eyes stared at Avatar through the clouds of incense smoke.

"Bless me, mother, give me strength". Avatar reached out with both hands to the glowing lamp..

He looked around at the congregation of richly dressed devotees confabulating animatedly over the cacophony of loud music and warbling kids. The air was heavy with cooking vapours and the heady aroma of rich "mishti" (sweets). His wife had steered him through the throng, all along singing out fleetingly "what a gorgeous sari" or "lovely bracelet" to women he had never met, as they navigated through this faithful reinvention of the Puja venues back home.

Leaning against a pillar, legs crossed, hands stuffed in his pockets he looked resignedly about him. He had lost Jharna again.

He recalled, a few decades ago a marquee not unlike this one, albeit without the glitz, where devotees had congregated. A little boy strained to peer through a gap in the garish tent fabric. He shinned up the pole and hoisted himself onto an empty paint drum, his muddy, bare feet balancing shakily. The small intent eyes took in the huge, shiny trays of mouth watering sweets. They looked tempting. He hesitated.

"Avatar let's go in. No one can stop us it's a community Puja. Come on they have lovely big laddoos." Raju and the other slum kids urged him. He looked down into gawking eyes in unwashed grubby faces and a strange awkwardness overcame him.

"No thanks. You go. I have to get the wheat ground before the mill closes."

"Come on Avatar, come with us. You should not feel ashamed; you go to the English school."

"No thanks guys. You go. Leave me alone."

"But it is Durga Puja!"

For his age, Avatar had a serious face. He replied grimly, "So? It is Durga Puja every year. Then there will be Dussera and Diwali. What does it matter? Nothing changes for us. You go enjoy yourselves. I have already said what I wanted to, to Ma Durga."

"Avatar," The gold and diamond bangles jangled as her hand shook his elbow, "Where are you lost dada?" Rudrani, his wife's friend stood before him resplendent like a jewellery store mannequin.

"Congratulations Dada!"

"Thanks."

"Such a great jump in your 'carrier'! Now, you must try and get Ranjit in haan I'll fax you his resume. Okay, enjoy!" She sashayed off with a rustle of silk leaving Avatar struggling to place Ranjit. Was he a husband, brother, son?

Jharna sailed up, "what happened?"

"That woman can talk without breathing."

His wife laughed. "Everyone is so envious of me." She declared with a smug contentedness. "I can hardly believe Sumitra was wearing exactly the same sari last year!"

"What does it matter? Can we leave?"

"So early?"

"Stay if you like, let me go, please."

He turned on his heels and made a brisk exit ignoring the obvious displeasure on her face. He had become impervious to his wife's disapproval of his reluctance to integrate in her social circle. Relieved, he drove away with a slight twinge of regret. How would she get home? He knew she would give him a call, unless she could hop a ride with someone. He didn't mind driving the long distance to fetch her, but to spend another minute amid those superficial snobs was intolerable.

Ensconced securely in his cosy study surrounded by his books and computer he found bliss. Usually unable to make small talk, he had quietly succumbed to the dubious title of "a man of few words". He was soon lost in a pile of pending office work content and quite pleased at the peace and quiet. There at the Puja he had felt like a caged animal, yearning to break free and run.

"Run Avatar run!"

The shantytown kids' favourite pastime was playing "kho kho" and Avatar loved his time with them, "Kho Raju" Avatar pushed his crouching friend and slid into his place. Dark clouds were looming above the playground. Avatar felt a blob of rain on his head and another and another. "Kho Avatar", Avatar sprang up and ran. "Rain!" He shouted. Faster and faster he sprinted, far from his playmates he ran heading home, his thoughts on his school uniform hanging on the line. He darted rapidly across the field and jumped over the fence, weaving through cars, auto rickshaws, assorted livestock, cyclists and handcarts. The skies opened up generously. Leaping straight over the wrecked cars, a permanent fixture in his neighborhood and grabbing the khaki shorts and shirt in one clean swoop he dashed into the modest dwelling they called home. He carefully folded the slightly wet shirt and shorts and placed them flat below the mattress, so as to "press" them well for the next day.

The storm was picking up. Rain fell heavily from sinister clouds, casting pitch blackness on their modest little neighborhood. He hurried to place pots and pans under the leaking roof, and hoped that his mother had carried an umbrella. Moving the stove to a dry spot he began pumping it to start dinner. Through the sheets of pelting rain his eyes scanned the rapidly flooding lanes, certain his mother would have ducked under some shelter. He scanned the network of congested little streets. There she was, her sari flapping in the wind, the umbrella offering meager cover. She treaded gingerly, wading through the brown muddy river, sari pleats held in one hand, her umbrella in the other. He hurried to fetch their large towel from the old wooden wardrobe.

The window banged as a crash of thunder followed lightening. Glass shattered somewhere.

Avatar rose, hurried to the ornate bay window and drawing aside the heavy brocade curtain, pulled the shutters secure. He looked down helplessly at the smashed Ming vase on Jharna's choice silk rug.

Cars came to a screeching halt in their massive driveway as doors banged shut over cheery chatter. He rushed to the nearest exit to avoid being collared by Jharna's odious friends but was too late. The jolly lot barged in and Avatar found himself fumbling with perfunctory pleasantries. Jharna hurried to get towels for everybody as they excitedly recounted to Avatar their getaway from the rain-soaked Puja marquee. He smiled and nodded politely, edging towards the garden door, when Jharna's ear-splitting shriek ripped through the mansion sending her guests rushing to her side by the smashed vase. Avatar turned the knob and made a smooth getaway. He walked out into a receding drizzle preferring a sprinkling to the uproarious company.

The passing rainstorm gave way to an obdurately pervasive Californian sun. Glad to escape the suffocation of stifling pseudo conversation that so delighted Jharna, he sauntered aimlessly on swashes of moss green lawn gleaming underfoot, as the setting sun sprinkled a fading pink hue. The azure in the sky above was plastered by an etiolated ashen grayness. Avatar walked about taking in the fresh moist air and shimmering twilight sky.

He had always loved lying under the starry skies sprawled on their humble cot on the terrace, his body smeared with the popular bug repellant, "Odomos", chatting with his mother till they fell asleep. Images of his mother nursing him through the brutal Malaria flashed before his eyes. Swathed in ice-cold bandages, shaking with a fever, he remembered staring bleary eyed at his poor weeping mother's face, unable to reach out and wipe her eyes. They had carried him to the hospital between three men. The dreaded "Delhi Bandh" had paralyzed all public transport. His mother never left his side for those crucial 48 hours, while the doctors struggled to breathe life into his sinking frame.

Avatar strolled about noticing the lawns of their mansion for the first time since he bought it a few months ago.

****

Lisa, Avatar's office assistant walked away from his desk just as a cup of coffee floated on to his table. Ashok looked at Avatar's face, then at Lisa's retreating figure and then back at Avatar. "They are either too fat or too thin. When they are thin, they are flat. Personally, I like a little more meat."

"Good thing I don't use such yardsticks to choose my co-workers. Thanks for the coffee."

"And that would be my cue to go away, but," Ashok placed himself gingerly on the edge of the table, "I came in late this morning. Don't you want to know where I was?"

"None of my business, this flexi timing thing is those people's problem,' Avatar jabbed his thumb towards an office at the back and turned to squint at the screen.

Ashok's voice was acrid. "I was helping Sukhbir and his family to pack."

Avatar took off his glasses and looked up into Ashok's podgy pinkish face. "Is he going to be alright? I heard about it from Jharna. He should have at least spoken to me! In fact they didn't attend our housewarming party either.

"My God man, are you human? This thing has devastated the entire family and you wonder why the hell he didn't attend the grand celebrations at your new place!"

"Look Ashok, this meltdown has far reaching effects. Hundreds of Sukhbirs are returning to India every day. It is the biggest crash since 1929. We should thank our lucky stars we are still holding jobs. Sukhbir fell victim to the 'last in first out' theory. Why are you looking at me like that?"

Ashok fixed him with a steely, reproachful stare, "You brought him here."

"And I" Avatar enunciated, "didn't ask him to leave! Did I sign up to look out for him forever? It was simple business dealing. My agent selected him, I arranged for him to come to the U.S. After that if he chose to quit the job and take off on his own, how could I be accountable?" Avatar looked at him seriously, "I brought in hundreds of IT professionals, including, may I add, you, Mr. Ashok Sharma". He pointed a finger directly at the sullen man.

"Which brings me to why I am here," Ashok tapped the table, "seeing that I too am a protégé of yours, I sure as hell wouldn't like to wake up to the same real life nightmare as Sukhbir's family did. So, I am here to ask you, if you do come across any "confidential" information," he made little air quotes with his fingers, "then, could your highness be kind enough to warn me?"

Ashok's supercilious attitude usually irritated Avatar, but today his presence was seriously exasperating. "If I get to know before you do, I most certainly will, but chances are that…"

Ashok cut him off curtly, "If you hear of anything, I would be obliged," and walked off.

In the existing fiscally crippled climate Avatar had little time to mull over past mistakes. He immersed himself totally in the rapidly shifting work environment. Every day brought a new challenge or financial dispute demanding a fresh and positive maneuver.

One such evening he and Leslie Shamus, his boss, were in an action packed head to head session with the company's board of directors. Every now and then Shamus would leave the conference room and walk uneasily in the hallway. He found himself fumbling to justify his budget before an insular board that only demanded upwardly curving balance sheets. He feared his dithering would be seen as a sign of weakness. Avatar served as a shock absorber and shielded his boss as best as he could.

Ashok walked to the photocopier with a sheaf of papers in his hands. Lately, every time a high level meeting took place, a few heads rolled. He had come to view such meetings as a sign of impending job cuts. The cafeteria had been abuzz with office gossip that certain "external experts" were being consulted and the secretaries loosely translated that to mean "all temp positions and recent appointees would get the axe".

He started making copies keeping the door of the conference room in sight. He could look into Leslie's open office as Leslie and Howard the finance director pored over some paperwork. Ashok breathed heavily. Something major was being planned out. The two men walked to the conference room and almost immediately, Lisa came out followed by the other secretaries.

This was not a good sign. It could only mean they were making some classified decisions that even the secretaries could not be privy to. He gathered the sheaf of photocopying and walked up to the partly ajar door. Moving rapidly, he quite deliberately dropped the papers outside the conference room. As he knelt to pick each one up, fussily arranging them in order, his ears tuned in to the discussion. He strained to listen as Avatar's smooth voice came through, "It is political travesty of the lowest degree. Why would Vissytec soil their hands?"

Leslie's piercing voice boomed loud and clear, "This is the U.S. election scene and the name of the game is wealth and power, that's what it is. You may not appreciate the gravity, Avatar. This is no third world election propaganda… sorry no offence."

"Don't worry about it, though, you would be truly surprised at the mammoth figures featuring in the so called "third world" elections and also, I am told the politically correct term is "Emerging Economies" but that is not what we are discussing, is it?"

"No." Leslie's bellowing voice reached the crouching Ashok's ears. He heard loud and clear exactly what he had been dreading all week.

"Gentlemen, here's a short list of the guys to go. Top of the list, I'm sorry Avatar, is Ashok Sharma. I am powerless. The company is hemorrhaging money, stocks have fallen and profit margins are nose-diving."

"Now wait a minute..." Ashok heard Avatar's voice but he wasn't listening anymore.

His heart beat with the intensity of a thousand hammers. His throat went dry, and his hands shook as he gathered up the papers, barely hearing Avatar's calm voice raised in protest. He walked unsteadily to his table, dumped the papers and crashed into his chair puffing and wheezing. It was as if someone had socked it to him. Any minute now Avatar would come out and maybe by the evening Ashok would be diabolically laid off. He visualized being escorted out the building by security as he had heard was the practice with people handling critical information.

Sitting there, staring vacantly, he was experiencing firsthand what Sukhbir meant by a "living nightmare".

As the meeting ended, the men walked away. No one approached him. He looked grimly at Avatar's table. Would he come across and ask Ashok to walk with him? Avatar made his way to his own cabin nodding sociably to everyone he passed. Would he pick up the phone and ring the knell on Ashok's employment at Vissytec? Nothing happened. Avatar was absorbed in work.

Lisa, Avatar's office assistant slid the glass partition shut as she sifted through confidential documentation destined for the shredder. She chatted genially with her boss as she worked. The girl was born to talk. Avatar indulged her, a sincere worker, as politely as possible. Encouraged, she nattered on about things that made little difference to him. He barely listened as she enlightened him about collaborative divorce and her struggles to gain custody of her son, Danny from his alcoholic father.

Then she switched to talking about India. Usually a curious person, her current interest was about life in India and her impending visit there. He kept at his work, absently answering her questions. He smiled at her naïveté. She had no idea what it was to live below the poverty line or in a house with no electricity or regular water supply.

She stopped just a little short of the model "Elephants and tigers in your backyard" questions that some blockheads had asked him. He struggled to paint as honest a picture as achievable.

"Gosh! That is mind-boggling! You have had such a phenomenal life! It belongs in a book, really!" She turned to Avatar's laughing face!

"In a book!" He repeated with a chuckle, his eyebrows rising.

"Of course! The world needs to know how you rose to such levels, made a breakout from the poverty and deprivation!"

"Lisa, there would probably be hundreds of such tales of Indians who washed up on American shores with nothing more than determination and a dream!"

"And who now own multi-million dollar mansions in up market L.A.?"

"Hmm maybe not, but are successful in their own way." Avatar mused.

She delivered some pictures taken at the office party. She scrutinized each one. "Oh! Mrs. Mathur's sari and those jewels! She looks like royalty!" She gushed admiringly. "So whatever made you fall in love with her?"

"Uh it was an arranged marriage."

"Excuse me?"

"We have "arranged marriages" in India. Normally they're arranged formally by the couple's parents bearing in mind breeding, education and such things."

"It sounds just like picking the right pedigree for a pet!"

"Not quite. I think that in a way ensures a certain degree of compatibility between the families."

"So you think it worked out well for you?"

"Well our case was a bit different. Jharna's father was my guru, my mentor and benefactor! I owe him hugely. Nobody would have bothered with a guy like me but he practically adopted me! In fact he was the one who taught me all that I really know about computers, not those institutes!"

"And that's him?" Lisa lifted the framed photograph of a smiling face.

"That's him."

"Does that mean you have never been in love, fallen in love?"

"Oh yes I have! I have been deeply and passionately in love, but it didn't work out."

Lisa's curiosity reflected in her shining eyes and open-mouthed amazement.

"No. Lisa I'm not very comfortable talking about the lady, who," Avatar handed her a tray of documents and with a wave of his hand in the direction of her table, added, "shall remain unnamed!"

Lisa stood up as she seized the tray, and sat down promptly.

"So tell me how you ended up marrying Mrs. Mathur."

"Well it's really not something Jharna would like me to discuss with a complete..." he hesitated, "I mean," His characteristic awkwardness surfaced as Avatar fumbled for words.

"I understand." Lisa mumbled as she exited hurriedly.

It was a frustrating wait. Ashok watched the shadowy figures through the frosted glass of his boss' cabin. He had been hearing laughter in Lisa's voice. Avatar was in good spirits, enjoying light banter with the vacuous Lisa.

Ashok felt sick. He scratched his hirsute cheeks circumspectly. The bastard. He was going to leave it till the very last.

He had never regarded Avatar as inconsiderate before this. Thoroughly professional perhaps, even doggedly principled but not insensitive. Well why not? He felt no remorse for Sukhbir either. Desperate urgency seized Ashok and his hands trembled as he shifted papers around. Should he go over and confront him or allow him to play the game his own way? He covered his face with his hands and let out a soft groan. No one even noticed. He looked around the office. Each one desperately hanging on to his job and speculating on who would go next. Like Russian roulette.

He craned to search Avatar's expression in the neon glow of the computer screen. The man looked engrossed, his impassive eyes scanning the computer screen. Ashok tried reading the look on his face but Avatar was completely wrapped up in the work at hand. Ashok could stand it no more. The guy knows, but won't let on. He won't even give me a fighting chance. Ashok rose impulsively and stormed into Avatar's cabin. "Anything you want to tell me?" he asked.

Avatar's eyes didn't leave the screen. "No".

"Are you sure you aren't forgetting something your boss asked you to tell me?"

Avatar turned around in his swivel chair and fixed Ashok with a hard look. "Ashok, if you have something on your mind, come out with it. All I can say is, I have nothing to tell you, so just relax."

Ashok retorted furiously, "And all I can say is, cut out the warm and fuzzy talk Avatar, break the suspense, level with me."

"Ashok, stop getting paranoid." Avatar took off his reading glasses and rubbed his eyes. He looked at Ashok and patiently started, "If anyone's been saying things to you..."

"No one's said anything to me. I want to hear from you what was decided at the meeting today."

"That would be a betrayal of confidence. Ashok, trust me there is no cause for panic. Leave it with me and stay above rumors."

Ashok could get no more out of Avatar who sent him off with a patronizing speech.

Ashok strode back to his desk frustrated and angry. He had clearly heard his own name at the top of the list! Irrationally an old saying came to him, "people who listen at keyholes never hear anything good about themselves". Ashok felt nauseous. He couldn't get his mind around doing any serious work. His thoughts kept going to the words he had heard.

Many people came to his desk that afternoon. Roger came to borrow a stapler and Abigail came looking for a missing file. Candy the young office assistant came round making a collection for the retiring janitor's farewell and sat chitchatting for a bit.

Avatar did not come.

Avatar's impassive face stared at the computer screen as he carried on routine work, exchanging pleasantries with anyone he saw, answering phone calls warmly and fixing himself his usual five pm coffee.

Sipping his coffee, he killed a yawn and gave his computer screen the once over. Seeing that there was nothing that required an urgent response in his three hundred strong mail box, he shut the computer down. He decided he would tackle the ticklish matters peacefully over the weekend. The meeting with the perverse board members had exhausted him. Through the glass partition Avatar looked at Lisa. He knew he had wounded her feelings. He despised awkwardness in the work environment. Why couldn't people respect others' privacy! He decided to call it a day. Gathering up his things he walked slowly to the elevator. An astonished Ashok stared after him as the doors slid shut and Avatar disappeared.

In the subterranean parking Avatar dumped his things in the boot and slammed it shut. He caught sight of a beam of sunlight piercing a small crack in the vents. It formed a prismatic pattern in the dark space. He heard muffled voices of playing children outside on the green. He decided to get some fresh air. There was no pressing hurry to get home on this glorious summer day. His wife would be out for coffee with friends or absorbed in some TV soaps at home.

He sat on a park bench chomping a hot dog with uncharacteristic relish. He really needed to get out more, he thought. He sat watching courting couples, children with puppies and young mothers with prams, all enjoying the balmy Friday evening. He felt a bit envious and not particularly cheered. The contagiousness of happiness, he thought, was a bit overstated.

Tentacles of unfulfilled dreams and a lost love stung him like nettles. Recalling the banter with Lisa, he shuddered to think how close he had come to revealing the circumstances of his and Jharna's marriage. It pained him to recall his mentor, Sarkar sahib's helplessness that fateful night decades ago.

"It was my daughter's foolishness." The old man mumbled through his sobs. "I never trusted that swine Raja and should have turned him out a long time ago." Avatar sat staring into space as he watched the imposing, dignified Mr. Sarkar reduced to a miserable wreck. "The doctors are not willing to allow her to abort and there is no sign of Raja. Time is running out." The man he idolized stood before him with folded hands and implored him piteously to accept his daughter's hand in marriage. Avatar stared ahead, shell shocked, unable to speak, but a decision had to be taken soon. He made his way home, his mind in turmoil.

His mother's anguished pleading hurt him beyond limits. That must have been the only time that he had conflicted with his mother. "How can you even think of marrying her? She's your employer's daughter! Besides, she's so much older and there was this other chap. It just makes no sense Avatar I can't let you ruin your life like this! How can you accept another man's child as your own?" She sat next to him, tears streaming down her eyes and placed an arm around his shoulders. "Tell me," she asked, "are you doing this just because you owe so much to Sarkar sahib?"

He had shrugged her away. Wordlessly he had turned her out of his room. He needed to think this through by himself.

He mulled over it all night. The woman he had respected like an older sister was to become his wife. It was unthinkable. But to leave father and daughter in such a predicament was not the decent option either. Sarkar sahib was not just his employer he was his redeemer in every possible way. He owed the man everything!

Never before or after in his life had he found himself in the throes of such a dilemma. "Help the neediest", his mother had always taught him, "the weakest or the most helpless, not the ones you like."

Avatar stared blankly into the inky sky, Sarkar and his mother's voices like demons stinging his ears. Time stood still as he sat weighing the options, fraught with the burden of the man's beseeching, his mother's tearful pleas and the painful knowledge that by morning he would have to deeply disappoint one of the two most revered beings in his life. The sky changed from purple to mauve and then a muted, glowing pink and downstairs outside his window, Avatar saw the milkman scurrying alongside his bicycle, clanging the milk drums, ringing his bell, as if jostling everyone into waking. Avatar rose stiffly out of his armchair and came to his mother. Her appearance confirmed she too had not slept a wink. Her eyes looked straight at him, searching for answers she dared not ask. He could barely meet her gaze. There was only one thing to do.

His mother had declined the invitation to their wedding and her opinion about Jharna remained unchanged, "She's a spoilt idiot." He stood alone beside a woman he hardly knew, accepting greetings from strangers in a hurriedly organized reception. He looked around the magnificent hall with glittering chandeliers and fluffy carpets that well shod feet sank into, mindful of how out of place he must look. Jharna lapped up all the compliments and played the coy, much in love bride to a T acutely insensible to his palpable awkwardness.

It was months before his mother agreed to speak to him and that too mainly orchestrated by the herculean efforts of Sarkar Sahib. It was hard for the snooty Jharna to look respectfully upon the woman who had once been on her father's payroll. She never learned to adapt to the tiny flat or his mother's frugal ways and after she fell off his scooter and miscarried the baby, the young couple moved into her father's lavish home.

He visited his mother everyday but could never shake the burden of guilt. To have wronged the woman who had combated immeasurable hardship to raise him became the cross he bore for a very long time.

At the office, Ashok's eyes narrowed. He clicked open his personal files and ran his eyes down the humongous debts he owed. He opened his bank statement. There was barely enough to cover the family's airfare to India. Numerous schemes swept through his devious mind. Ashok Sharma was notorious in his inner circle as a person who wouldn't accept a trouncing without putting up a fight. Today he sensed acutely the necessity for self preservation and in his mind that translated to getting a move on. "Let me stick it to them before they can stick it to me", he decided. He had to put an escape route in place but he had very little time. His head was pounding as much with ideas as with rage.

He kept his head lowered but his eyes took in the movements of every person in the office. He opened the quarterly budget review and minimized the screen bringing up his personal finances. Each time someone came close enough, he brought up the budget review and made believe that he was deeply absorbed in it.

He was certain he would receive his marching orders on Monday. As his colleagues started leaving the office one by one, each called out goodbye to Ashok and soon he found himself quite alone. He got up and took a walk down one side of the office and then turned around to visit the gent's loo on the other side taking in each table and cabin just in case someone was working late. "Not likely on a Friday, but better safe than sorry" Ashok thought to himself. He turned the corner and bumped into Roger outside the toilets. "Oops, you gave me a start!" Roger remarked.

"I am working late today for next week's review meetings!" Ashok said.

"I don't know why we even bother," Roger gave a nervous laugh. "Our days are numbered!"

Ashok glanced at him. "Do you know something I don't?"

"Of course not! So will you lock up? The cleaners don't work Fridays. I'm leaving now, meeting the family for dinner!"

"Sure will do." Ashok proceeded to the men's room.

All alone and free to roam anywhere within Vissytec's accounts, Ashok Sharma gave vent to the fury within. If they thought they could send him packing, they could think again! He had shown absolute loyalty and dedication through his tenure and he did not believe he could be got rid of with a handshake.

Ashok recalled the fiery debate at a friend's party about NRIs being forced to return to India. He had been a silent bystander to the near shouting matches. He had the knack of feeling superior to others in any scenario. Such things, he believed, happened to others. Someone had brought along a printout of the appalling outcome of the financial meltdown. "This guy, who once made more than $1.2 million, was found dead along with six members of his family! Authorities believe he killed his family and himself after seeing his finances wiped out by the stock market collapse."

The man had barely finished reading, when a lively conversation broke out.

The party heard first hand of the appalling plight of Sridhar, an equity trader at an esteemed trading and brokerage firm and how he fell victim to subprime. He related the poignant scenario of walking into an office to find his distressed colleagues wheeling away their belongings.

That was potentially Sridhar's last week in the U.S. If he couldn't find work he would have to leave America. Many guests tried to change the subject and attempted to engage the newcomers, Ashok and his wife Rekha in light conversation. But every so often the party would return to the same disconcerting subject.

A legal expert served it up in black and white. "This perpetual state of flux is hard to take especially for Indians who come from a firmly ritualized culture that lays emphasis on fiscal security. The NRI comes here with certain expectations of riches and comfort. An Indian views a layoff not as a recessionary byproduct, but more like a personal failure accompanied by social stigma."

"Yes this fear of "what will people say" is typical of our people!" their hostess added.

"Under immigration law H1" the man continued, "laid off employees are out of status as their companies are their sponsors. They have an unwritten thirty day grace I think and they can apply for a change of status to a business, tourist or student visa."

"What if they do not have the resources for either option?" Ashok's wife had asked nervously.

"You are advised to get out!"

An elderly man sitting back nursing a Vermouth cut in. "Unlike previous generations of NRIs who made the one brave move and permanently settled in homes and communities abroad, we see ourselves as part of a new Indian nomadic class. If the next opportunity is in the U.K. Europe or South America we will go! In that regard, you can say we are mercenaries."

His wife objected, "I can't accept that term, but I certainly agree that I would happily pursue a good break and not moan over losing American residency."

Her husband continued, "People have always moved to places of opportunity, so while the U.S. will remains a beacon of opportunity, other countries have started competing with it. For us, moving back to India is also an option. So you see, my dear," he patted Rekha on her back, "you need to keep an open mind! The world is a big place and yet, it is really quite small!"

His eyes twinkled and he smiled warmly as he rose to a tall, almost majestic frame. "An open mind!" He smiled all around and excused himself.

Rekha had frequently repeated the events of that evening wondering if making the move was such a good idea in the current climate. Ashok had always assured her he was secure in his job having been assigned a critical responsibility.

Seething in his fury Ashok sat staring into space vacantly. He recalled how upset his wife had been about Sukhbir's sacking and had repeatedly asked him how things were at his workplace. "Don't hide anything from me Ashok. We're neck-deep in debt and we have responsibilities." Ashok had laughed at her serious face, "You know my salary can cover it! We'll pay it all off. And the kids don't need college fees for years. Stop worrying."

How would he tell her now to pack up, to leave in a few weeks?

He thought to himself, if they had to go anyway, why wait until Monday? Why not get the hell out sooner? He could take a flight over the weekend, but not before he had provided for his family.

He tapped his fingers on the table, thinking. How much is enough, 50,000, 100,000, half a million? Ashok paused, tilted his head to one side and grimaced. Why not go the whole hog? A couple of million dollars should suffice, after all the kids are still young. Yes, it would assure them a luxurious life back home. At such times one requires a friend, a buddy, an accomplice, someone who can be trusted absolutely. He put a call through to his close friend in India.

Rajan was already at work on a Saturday at his underpaid job as the branch manager of an Indian bank. The shrewd merchant banker, he understood exactly what Ashok was proposing. He recognized the injustice that was being done to his childhood friend and saw a six figure potential in it for them both.

"Hope I am not holding you back. Is there somewhere you need to be?" Ashok's feverish voice crackled through the phone lines.

"For you, I'd be willing to stay here all night. Don't worry pal, I am with you through this one. The only good thing coming out of this ugly situation is that we will soon have you back in Delhi!" The warmth in his voice was the reassurance Ashok badly needed.

"Now listen carefully. Such a big sum will have to be distributed in many accounts so as to not arouse suspicion. Tell me the names of each one in the family with correct spellings. I will immediately open multiple accounts. Some may have to be back dated, but you just leave it to me. I should be done in an hour and I'll email the account numbers to you."

"No don't email anything to me. I am deleting all personal data as they will take everything away and I will have to surrender the laptop."

Rajan muttered a few boorish expletives.

"I will call you back in an hour and you dictate them to me in Hindi, okay?"

"Sure thing and then you can make the remittances. Also, make sure each transfer of funds is lower than 100,000, INR otherwise we have to inform the tax people."

"One hour."

Ashok Sharma felt no remorse or guilt. He felt nothing but serene contentment. He firmly believed that he had been used and exploited by Vissytec who now, in a time of crisis, would casually discard him.

He worked in a feverish rush. If there ever was a more 'time critical venture' this was it! He smiled at his own joke. Everything was usually "time critical" in this organization.

All he needed was to skim off a sum that probably wouldn't get noticed at all but certainly not until the next audit.

Damn, he was being denied access to so many areas. Vissytec was secure. Good! He liked a challenge. He felt as if he was in one of his son's games. It was like the spy vs. spy scenarios from his childhood comic strips. The only thing to do was to persevere and find some loophole, some place that would accept one of his passwords. The office building fell dark and quiet as he pored over the screen. Suddenly a high pitched electronic version of Beethoven's fifth shattered the silence.

"Hello?" He bellowed.

"What's up? Aren't you coming home?" Rekha, his wife demanded.

"I called at the house and left you a message. Didn't you receive it? I am working late, you guys have dinner and go to sleep."

"Ashok, is everything alright? You sound a little charged."

"Tell you everything later, okay? How are the kids?"

"Fine, we just finished shopping for Gauri's birthday and we sent out the invites this afternoon. The kids made them. I hope we have more colour cartridges for the printer…we ran out!" she laughed, "Oh and we just booked the clown and jumping castle. I am being a little extravagant but it's so much fun!" He could never resist his pretty wife's laughter and loved to spoil her. He had once made a promise to her father to treat her like a queen. He had sheltered her from every bit of his struggle and had never stopped to think before falling deep into the debt trap.

She would be devastated by the events at work, unless he had something to cushion the blow. He looked down at the scribbled notes and realized he had to hurry. Rajan was putting it all together within an hour.

"Yeah it all sounds good. I'll see you later; now go home it's getting late."

Three hours and several phone calls later the money was on its way into the new accounts. Rajan would send carefully coded messages to him on his wife's cell phone to confirm the deposits. He had a tough time getting hold of a moving company after hours on a Friday but finally managed. The guy, a small timer, offered a good deal and agreed to pack over the weekend for a marginally higher charge.

As Ashok packed up to leave, he picked up the framed family photographs leaving the rest as it was. For the last time, Ashok shut down and switched off his computer at Vissytec and slowly but surely walked out of the building meticulously setting the alarms and pulling the doors shut.

He entered the house stealthily. Rekha and the kids were asleep. He stepped into a family lounge strewn with shopping. Loosening his tie he dropped into a settee his eyes staring blankly before him. Some stuff fell out of a shopping bag as Ashok's eyes took in all the trappings of the lavish lifestyle they had acquired in just a couple of years. Now to transport it all back home! He walked softly into the bedroom and picked Rekha's phone off their bedside table. Not wanting to wake anybody, he walked down to the basement to call Rajan.

"Ashok is that you?" Rekha was such a light sleeper! "Yes, I am here. Just go back to sleep; I have to make some calls to India." Rekha was used to his late night calls and fell asleep instantly.

Ashok set up an office in the basement and turned his computer on just as Rekha's phone chimed out an SMS signal. Rajan confirmed receiving the delivery of ten kilos of Basmati rice. Ashok rubbed his hands. "Good. The money had started coming in!" He noticed the quotation by Franklin on his mouse pad, "Time is money" and chuckled. As he awaited Rajan's subsequent confirmations, he worked out his next strategy. They would have to pack and leave almost straightaway. Avatar would probably break it to him on Monday, by when the packers would have done their job and a sea container would be on its way to India. He had finalized the deal with the movers. He was now going to book their flights online.

"What's going on?" Startled Ashok looked back over his shoulder at Rekha. "Hey! You still awake?"

"How come you're still working? Didn't you finish up at the office?"

She looked at her husband's pasty face and did not like what she saw.

"Is everything okay Ashok?"

"Yeah yeah all well. Wait until I get things sorted out and then I'll tell you."

"Tell me what? Something's up and I want to know. Even Avatar said something that made no sense."

"Avatar? What about him?" Ashok shouted out breathlessly, "What did he say? Did he call?"

"Ashok, calm down. We met them at the mall. He said something like 'don't let Ashok scare you' but didn't elaborate."

"And then?"

"Nothing happened! We just showed them the stuff we got for the birthday party and then we came home. What the hell is it Ashok, I'm frightened."

"Don't be scared. I will not let anything ever happen to you or the kids. You are my whole life." Ashok took Rekha in his arms but she shrank from his touch.

"Stop it! Ashok you have to tell me what's going on."

"Okay listen, first promise me you won't freak out." Ashok placed his hands on his wife's shoulders and looked hard at her, his face flushed redder than usual.

"What the hell's going on Ashok?" Rekha screamed hysterically. "Is it what I think it is? Are they firing you just like Sukhbir? Tell me Ashok, tell me now." Rekha was shrieking and her lip trembled. It looked as if she was going to have a choking fit. Breathing rapidly she started gasping for breath. Ashok rushed upstairs for her asthma puffer and dashed back taking two steps at a time. Any stress aggravated her asthma.

Once he calmed her down, they both sat on the couch. Rekha drew in raspy breaths, choking back sobs and staring nervously about her. Ashok watched her as her breathing gradually normalized.

"It's okay honey. We are not on the streets."

"Of course not!" Rekha looked contemptuously at her husband. "We're okay! Have you forgotten the huge debt we owe? Where is all that going to come from? It may be months before you find another job." She sat up, panic in her eyes, "Ashok, oh my God what about your visa?"

Ashok sighed. He put his arms around his wife as she wept inconsolably.

"Look, I have a solution. You have to get a hold on yourself and hear me out without crying or screaming, okay?" She nodded red eyed and wheezy.

Then, holding her close, Ashok rattled off the entire plan to his wife, neither looking at the other's face. He was too ashamed to face her as she stared into space, barely hearing him. Deep down Ashok was painfully aware that what he was attempting was risky, unethical and largely inexcusable. Just as he finished, her mobile phone chimed out the arrival of yet another text message. He rose and clicked the chic phone open. Yes! The last of the installments had arrived. They were set for life. "It's going to be just fine," he whispered into his wife's ear.

She looked at him and at the cell phone in utter disbelief. She stared ashen faced slowly shaking her head from side to side as if trying to clear from her mind what she had just heard.

"Say something Rekha," Ashok shook her. "I need you to understand whatever I did was for you and the kids and for us!"

In the darkness of their basement two pairs of wary eyes watched as the computer generated a message from the movers. Ashok read it and impassively turned the screen towards Rekha. The container to pack and move their stuff would be at their door first thing in the morning."

At 0800 on Monday morning Avatar walked briskly out of the elevator with long strides and entered Leslie's office without a knock.

"Have you seen my messages?"

"All nine of them." Leslie regarded his colleague over his glasses, "What was so urgent that couldn't wait?"

"You can't sack Ashok Sharma. You just cannot. It will be impossible for me to carry on bringing in skilled computer professionals if you keep firing them with such regularity."

"I can't afford to keep him. He's too costly."

"It means the end of the road for him. He has a family. Besides, he will not go easily. He may call in a lawyer."

"Like I said…we are paying him too much. Okay maybe if…. Can you…" Leslie paused weighing his options, "I know, make him take a pay cut."

"What? That's absurd." Avatar held Leslie with a stern reprehensive eye. "You can't do this to a family man!" His voice was calm. He knew when his boss was involved in a pig headed argument; someone had to keep their cool. He was prepared to lay his own job on the line. Not that Ashok deserved it, but Avatar liked his happy family and knew with a certainty that Ashok wasn't likely to find as good a job anytime soon. Maybe this favour would give him, Avatar leverage on a later occasion. "Look I have worked on this proposal. We can make it work without sacking him." He opened a spreadsheet and looked at Leslie, "If you will hear me out with an open mind."

Avatar walked out of the boss's office weary but victorious. He would deliver the good news himself. He walked slowly toward Ashok's desk but there was no sign of activity.

"Have you seen Ashok?"

"I don't think he's in yet." Lisa replied.

Avatar put through a call to Ashok's cell phone but got a busy signal. He called at the house calculating mentally where Rekha would be at that time of the morning. Probably dropping off the kids. He got a cute voice mail done by one of the kids. "Hi this is the Sharma residence. We're away or busy, but please leave your name and number and we will get back to you as soon as possible." It ended with a smothered giggle.

Avatar spoke urgently, "Ashok, this is Avatar here. I have discussed everything out with Leslie. I tried your cell number too. Please call me."

It was a while before anyone realised Jane had stopped speaking.

"And?" A somnolent Arti stared fixedly ahead, too weary to turn her head. "Go on!"

"There is no more." Jane murmured.

Arti pulled herself out of the slumped slouch and looked squarely into Jane's pensive face, "So did he get away with it? Just like that?"

"Just like that!" Jane whispered unblinking. She got up stretched her lithe figure languidly as she craned out of the window to look up at the sky.

Namita commented… "They let them get away so easily? No wonder they're in such a mess!"

Jane shrugged her shoulders and smiled acrimoniously. "That's debatable, but if people change identities and vanish, is it really worth the manpower, time and effort…"

"Come on Jane, for a nation that is a few trillion in debt!"

"Exactly, so chasing after a guy who stole a million doesn't cut it." Jane turned her back to the room and stared out at the soggy evening. The company fell silent, each reflecting wordlessly on Jane's absorbing tale. The storm clouds had given way to a balmy evening, nearing dusk. Cool breeze gently lifted Rukmini's lace curtains flapping them in Jane's contemplative face.

Finally Arti spoke, "How do they sleep at night?"

Jane turned from the window, "Soundly. Judging by Mr. Whiskers' blasé attitude, I'd say the guy is on to bigger and bolder scams."

"No conscience?"

"None whatsoever."

Nobody had wanted the day to end.

Slowly, Rukmini bade each of her friends good bye at the gates. She turned around and looked at the Suri residence. The fragrant climbing bush was trained neatly to climb along a criss-cross bamboo pergola, its tiny white flowers trembling in the light breeze. The house appeared to be holding itself tall. She walked along the velvety lawn edged with proud hollyhocks and marigolds.

Through the flapping curtains she caught glimpses of the dressed up walls and sepia photographs glowing in the golden lamplight. Her mind flashed to the day they were hanging up the pictures. One of them just wouldn't hang straight whatever they did.

"Maybe it's unconventional and wants to be askew." Natasha laughed,

"Or maybe the frame is slightly heavy on one side than the other" Sameer added analytically.

"Let it be. It still looks lovely in the cluster of old photographs." Rukmini had said studying the artistic assemblage. She smiled as she approached the patio. A part of her hated the idea of leaving. The children, she felt, would soon get absorbed in their routines and she would return to her job at the lab. But she knew something inside them had changed.

Her eyes fell on the verandah. The old red wicker chair had got a good washing in the afternoon's showers. She checked herself, a little taken aback. The chair rocked gently to and fro.

EPILOGUE

As the Boeing 777 dips its nose to begin their final descent in to Indira Gandhi International Airport, Avatar rouses himself and stretches his stiff back. He smiles inwardly thinking he should be shouting out loud in ecstasy. Instead, a quiet calm has descended upon him. The touchdown is not sensational.

As always passengers paying no heed to the air hostesses request to "please remain seated while the aircraft is taxiing" start pulling out bags from the overhead lockers. He usually abhors such a practice but today, even that doesn't bother him. Finally the "fasten seat belt" signs are switched off. He rises and unlatches the overhead storage. The elderly lady on the seat in front stands up and her beautiful grey eyes go searchingly to the bag above.

"Which one?" Avatar asks politely.

Her face breaks into a gentle smile, "Oh the black one, thanks very much!"

Avatar's arms reach out and stop. There are two nearly identical cabin bags. The lady goes up on her toes, "Oh I'm sorry," she points, "It's the one on the right, with my name tag."

"Not a problem." Avatar swings her bag down and pulls out the handle "Here you go Dr. Dev!"

Lila smiles, thanking him with her eyes.

The airport is a weird and wonderful place. Not merely the junction of flights and connections, it becomes the receptacle of varied emotions. People leave behind tears of farewell and vague promises to the customary question, "when will we see you again?" Some carry hope and ambition in their heart as they set off to conquer a new world. Others stride impatiently across reading off their neon ipad screens without noticing even the colour of the carpets. A young mother prays for temporary deafness for all her co passengers as she shepherds her screaming baby through immigration. In such crowds there lurks a face that wishes to be noticed but not detected.

A face that is vain enough to spend meticulous hours trimming facial hair and secure enough in his belief that no one would ever catch him.

Amongst the crowds waiting under sheltered canopies outside the airport building, two distinctly noticeable women stand at two ends watching the electronic boards and TV monitors. One of them attracts a second look for her outlandishly bizarre dress and pinkish hair while the other habitually makes heads turn, not at all conscious of her unusual beauty.